ROBERT WILSON

A Small Death
in Lisbon

HarperCollins*Publishers*

HarperCollins*Publishers*
77–85 Fulham Palace Road, London W6 8JB

The HarperCollins website address is
www.fireandwater.com

This paperback edition 2000
7 9 10 8 6

First published in Great Britain by
HarperCollins*Publishers* 1999

Copyright © Robert Wilson 1999

Robert Wilson asserts the moral right to
be identified as the author of this work

A catalogue record for this book
is available from the British Library

ISBN 0 00 651202 X

Typeset in Meridien by
Palimpsest Book Production Limited,
Polmont, Stirlingshire

Printed and bound in Great Britain by
Bookmarque Ltd, Croydon, Surrey

For Jane
and
my mother

ACKNOWLEDGEMENTS

I'd like to thank Michael Biberstein for correcting my German and Ana Nobre de Gusmão for checking all things Portuguese. Any errors that remain are of my own making.

Over the years a lot of people have talked to me, and contributed with information, insight and books. I'd like particularly to thank the following: Mizette Nielsen, Paul Mollet, Alexandra Monteiro, Natalie Reynolds, Elwin Taylor and Nick Ricketts.

This book took some research and the staff of The Bodleian in Oxford, A Biblioteca/Museu 'República e Resistência', A Biblioteca de Estudos Olisiponenses and A Biblioteca Nacional in Lisbon, were always helpful.

I also visited the Beira and the following were particularly friendly and helpful: R. A. Naique, Director Geral of Beralt Tin & Wolfram, Fernando Pãolouro of the Journal do Fundão, José Lopes Nunes and Councillor Francisco Abreu of Penamacor. In addition I would like to thank the people of Fundão, Penamacor, Sabugeiro, Sortelha, and Barco for their help and memories. I would also like to thank Manuel Quintas and the staff of the Hotel Palácio in Estoril.

Finally, although this book is dedicated to her, that does not do justice to my wife's contribution to the work. She was tireless in discussing with me the form of the book, she put in days of research in Oxford and Lisbon, she gave me total support and encouragement through the long months of writing and she was a dedicated and intelligent editor. This would have been a doubly hard task without you. Thank you.

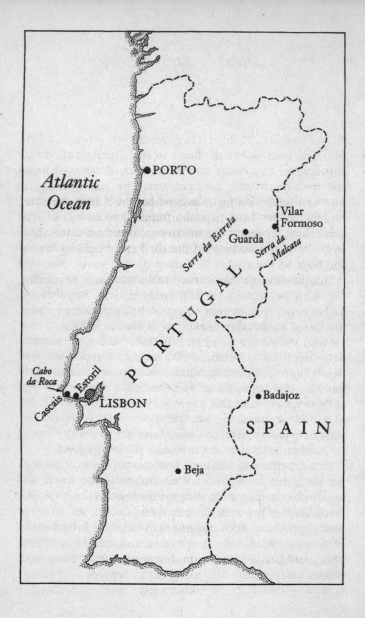

She was lying on a crust of pine needles, looking at the sun through the branches, beyond the splayed cones, through the nodding fronds. Yes, yes, yes. She was thinking of another time, another place when she'd had the smell of pine in her head, the sharpness of resin in her nostrils. There'd been sand underfoot and the sea somewhere over there, not far beyond the shell she'd held to her ear listening to the roar and thump of the waves. She was doing something she'd learned to do years ago. Forgetting. Wiping clean. Rewriting little paragraphs of personal history. Painting a different picture of the last half-hour, from the moment she'd turned and smiled to the question: 'Can you tell me how . . . ?' It wasn't easy, this forgetting business. No sooner had she forgotten one thing, rewritten it in her own hand, than along came something else that needed reworking. All this leading to the one thing that she didn't like roaming loose around her head, that she was forgetting who she was. But this time, as soon as she'd thought the ugly thought, she knew that it was better for her to live in the present moment, to only move forward from the present in millimetre moments. 'The pine needles are fossilizing in the backs of my thighs,' was as far as she got in present moments. A light breeze reminded her that she'd lost her pants. Her breast hurt where it was trapped under her bra. A thought tugged at her. 'He'll come back. He's seen it in my face. He's seen it in my face that I know him.' And she did know him but she couldn't place him, couldn't name him. She rolled on to her side and smiled at what sounded like breakfast cereal receiving milk. She knelt and gripped the rough bark of the pine tree with the blunt ends of her fingers, the nails bitten to the quick, one with a thin line of drying blood. She brushed the pine needles out of her straight blonde hair and heard the steps, the heavy steps. Boots on frosted grass? No. Move yourself. She couldn't get the panic to move herself. She'd never been able to get the panic to move herself. A flash as fast as a yard of celluloid ripped through her head and she saw a little blonde girl sitting on the stairs, crying and peeing her pants because he'd chased her and she couldn't stand to be chased. The rush. The gust of terrible energy. The wind up the stairs, whistling under the door. The forces winding up to deliver. Doors banging far off in the house. The thud. The thud of a watermelon dropped on tiles. Split skin. Pink flesh. Her blonde hair reddened. The cranial crack opened up. The bark bit a corner of her forehead. Her big blue eye saw into the black canyon.

Part One

Chapter I

15th February 1941, SS Barracks, Unter den Eichen, Berlin-Lichterfelde.

Even for this time of year night had come prematurely. The snow clouds, low and heavy as Zeppelins, had brought the orderlies into the mess early to put up the blackout. Not that it was needed. Just procedure. No bombers would come out in this weather. Nobody had been out since last Christmas.

An SS mess waiter in a white monkey jacket and black trousers put a tea tray down in front of the civilian, who didn't look up from the newspaper he wasn't reading. The waiter hung for a moment and then left with the orderlies. Outside the snowfall muffled the suburb to silence, its accumulating weight filled craters, mortared ruins, rendered roofs, smoothed muddied ruts and chalked in the black streets to a routine uniform whiteness.

The civilian poured himself a cup of tea, took a silver case out of his pocket and removed a white cigarette with black Turkish tobacco. He tapped the unfiltered end on the lid of the case, gothically engraved with the letters 'KF', and stuck the dry paper to his lower lip. He lit it with a silver lighter, engraved 'EB', a small and temporary theft. He raised the cup.

Tea, he thought. What had happened to strong black coffee?

The tight-packed cigarette crackled as he drew on it, needing to feel the blood prickling in his veins. He brushed two white specks of ash off his new black suit. The weight

5

of the material and the precision of the Jewish tailoring reminded him just why he wasn't enjoying himself so much any more. At thirty-two years old he was a successful businessman making more money than he'd ever imagined. Now something had come along to ensure that he would stop making money. The SS.

These were people he could not brush off. These people were the reason he was busy, the reason his factory – Neukölln Kupplungs Unternehmen, manufacturer of railcar couplings – was working to full capacity, and the reason why he'd had an architect draw up expansion plans. He was a *Förderndes Mitglied*, a sponsoring member of the SS, which meant he had the pleasure of taking men in dark uniforms for nights out on the town and they made sure he got work. None of this was in the same league as being a *Freunde der Reichsführer-SS*, but it had its business advantages and, as he was now seeing, its responsibilities as well.

He'd been living with the institutional smells of boiled cabbage and polish in the Lichterfelde barracks for two days, snarled up in their military world of Oberführers, Brigadeführers, and Gruppenführers. Who were all these people in their Death's Head uniforms, with their endless questions? What did they do all day when they weren't scrutinizing his grandparents and great-grandparents? We're at war with the whole world and all they need is your family tree.

He wasn't the only candidate. There were other businessmen, one he recognized. They all worked with metal. He had hoped they were being sized up for a tender, but the questions had been strictly non-technical, all character assessment, which meant they wanted him for a job.

An assistant, or adjutant or whatever these people called themselves came in. The man closed the door behind him with librarian care. The precise click and satisfied nod started the irritation winding up inside him.

'Herr Felsen,' said the adjutant sitting down in front

of the wide, hunched shoulders of the dark-haired civilian.

Klaus Felsen shook his stiff foot and raised his hefty Swabian head and gave the man a slow blink of his blue-grey eyes from under the ridged bluff of his forehead.

'It's snowing,' said Felsen.

The adjutant, who found it difficult to believe that the SS had been reduced to considering this . . . this . . . some ruthless peasant with an unaccountable flair for languages, as a serious candidate for the job, ignored him.

'It's going well for you, Herr Felsen,' he said, cleaning his glasses.

'Oh, you've had some news from my factory?'

'Not exactly. Of course, you're concerned . . .'

'Everything's going well for *you*, you mean, *I'm* losing money.'

A nervous look from the adjutant fluttered over Felsen's head like a virgin's petticoat.

'Do you play cards, Herr Felsen?' he asked.

'My answer's the same as the last time – everything except bridge.'

'There'll be a card game here in the mess tonight with some high-ranking SS officers.'

'I get to play poker with Himmler? Interesting.'

'SS-Gruppenführer Lehrer in fact.'

Felsen shrugged; he didn't know the name.

'Is that it? Lehrer and me?'

'And SS-Brigadeführers Hanke, Fischer and Wolff who you've already met, and another candidate. It's just an opportunity for you . . . for them to get to know you in a more relaxed way.'

'Poker's not considered degenerate yet?'

'SS-Gruppenführer Lehrer is an accomplished player. I think it . . .'

'I don't want to hear this.'

'I think it would be advisable for you to . . . ah . . . lose.'

7

'Ah . . . more money?'

'You'll get it back.'

'I'm on expenses?'

'Not quite . . . but you will get it back in another way.'

'Poker,' said Felsen, wondering how relaxed this game would be.

'It's a very international game,' said the adjutant getting up from the table. 'Seven o'clock then. Here. Black tie for you, I think.'

Eva Brücke sat in the small study of her second-floor apartment on Kurfürstenstrasse in central Berlin. She was at her desk wearing just a slip under a heavy black silk dressing gown with gold dragon motifs and a woollen blanket over her knees. She was smoking, playing with a box of matches and thinking of the new poster that had appeared on the billboard of her apartment building. It said 'German women, your leader and your country trust you.' She was thinking how nervous and unconfident that sounded – the Nazis, or maybe just Goebbels, subconsciously revealing a deep fear of the unquantifiable mystery of the fairer sex.

Her brain slid away from propaganda and on to the nightclub she owned on the Kurfürstendamm, *Die Rote Katze*. Her business had boomed in the last two years for no other reason than she knew what men liked. She could look at a girl and see the little triggers that would set men off. They weren't always beautiful, her girls, but they'd have some quality like big blue innocent eyes, or a narrow, long, vulnerable back, or a shy little mouth which would combine perversely with their total availability, their readiness to do anything that these men might think up.

Eva's shoulders tightened and she pulled the blanket off the back of the chair around her. She'd begun to feel dizzy because she'd been smoking too fast, so fast that the end of her cigarette was a long, thin, sharp cone. This only happened when she was irritated, and thinking about men irritated her. Men always presented her with problems, and never relieved her of any. Their job, it appeared, was to complicate. Take her own lover. Why couldn't he do what he was supposed to do and just love her? Why did he have to own her, intrude on her, occupy her territory? Why did he have to take things? She chucked the matches across the desk. He was a businessman, and that, she supposed, was what businessmen did for a living – accumulated things.

She tried to get her mind off men, especially her clients and their visits to her office at the back of the club where they'd sit and smoke and drink and charm until they'd get to what they really wanted which was something special, something really special. She should have been a doctor, one of those new-fangled brain doctors who talked you out of your madness, because as the war had worn on she'd noticed the tastes of her clients had changed. Normally, these days, as she'd found out to her cost, to include pain – both inflicting it and, perhaps to redress the balance, receiving it. And then there was one man who'd come and asked of her something that even she didn't know whether she'd be able to supply. He was such a quiet, insignificant, enclosed man, you wouldn't have thought . . .

There was a knock at the door. She crushed her cigarette, threw off the blankets and tried to plump some life into her blonde hair but lost heart when she caught sight of herself in the mirror with no make-up. She refolded the dressing gown across herself, pulled the belt tight and went to open the door.

'Klaus,' she said, producing a smile. 'I wasn't expecting you.'

Felsen pulled her over the threshold and kissed her hard on the mouth, desperate after two days in the barracks. His hand slid down to her lower back. Her fists came up and she pushed herself away from his chest.

'You're wet,' she said, 'and I've only just woken up.'

'So?'

9

She went back inside and hung up his hat and coat and led him back to her study. He followed with his slight limp. She never used the living room, she preferred small rooms.

'Coffee?' she asked, drifting over to the kitchen.

'I was thinking . . .'

'The real thing. And brandy?'

He shrugged and went into the study. He sat on the client side of the desk, lit a cigarette and picked the flakes of tobacco off his tongue. Eva came in with the coffee, two cups, a bottle and glasses. She stole one of his cigarettes which he lit for her.

'I was wondering where that was,' she said, tugging the lighter out of his grip, annoyed.

She was wearing lipstick now and had brushed her hair. She pulled the telephone plug out of the wall, so that they could talk privately.

'Where've you been?' she asked.

'Busy.'

'Trouble at the works?'

'I'd have preferred that.'

She poured the coffee and tipped some brandy into hers. Felsen stopped her doing the same to his.

'After,' he said. 'I want to enjoy the coffee. They've been making me drink tea for two days.'

'Who's they?'

'The SS.'

'They're so brutal those boys,' she said, irony on automatic, unsmiling. 'What do the SS want from a sweet little Swabian peasant like you?'

The smoke curled under the art deco lamp. Felsen tilted the shade downwards.

'They're not saying, but it feels like a job.'

'Lots of questions about your pedigree?'

'I told them my father ploughed the strong German soil with his bare hands. They liked it.'

'Did you tell them about your foot?'

'I said my father dropped a plough on it.'

'Did they laugh?'

'It's not a very humorous atmosphere down there.'

He finished his coffee and poured brandy over the dregs.

'Do you know someone called Gruppenführer Lehrer?' asked Felsen.

'SS-Gruppenführer Oswald Lehrer,' she said, becoming very still. 'Why?'

'I'm playing cards with him tonight.'

'I've heard he's in charge of running the SS or rather the KZs as a business . . . making them pay for themselves. Something like that.'

'You know everybody, don't you?'

'That's my business,' she said. 'I'm surprised you haven't heard of him. He's been in the club. This one and the old one.'

'I have. Of course I have,' he said, but he hadn't.

Felsen's mind raced. KZs. KZs. What did that mean? Were they going to assign him some cheap concentration camp labour? Switch his factory over to munitions production? No. Job. It was for a job. He felt the cold in his bones suddenly. They weren't going to make him run a KZ, were they?

'Drink some brandy,' said Eva, sitting on his lap. 'Stop guessing. You've got no idea.'

She ran her fingers over his bristly head and thumbed one of his cheekbones as if he was a child with a mark. She tilted his head and planted some fresh lipstick on his mouth.

'Stop thinking,' she said.

He slipped a large hand up under her armpit and cupped one of her firm, braless breasts. He eased another hand under the hemline of the slip. She felt him hardening under her. She stood, wrapped herself in the gown again and knotted the belt. She leaned in the doorway.

'Am I seeing you tonight?'

'If they let me go,' he said, shifting in his seat, his erection troubling him.

'Didn't they ask how come a Swabian farmboy speaks so many languages?'

'Yes, they did, as a matter of fact.'

'And you had to give them a guided tour of all your lovers.'

'Something like that.'

'French from Michelle.'

'That was French was it?'

'Portuguese from that Brazilian girl. What was her name?'

'Susana. Susana Lopes,' he said. 'What happened to her?'

'She had friends. They got her out to Portugal. She wouldn't have lasted long in Berlin with that dark skin,' said Eva. 'And Sally Parker. Sally taught you English, didn't she?'

'And poker and how to swing.'

'Who was the Russian?' asked Eva.

'I don't speak Russian.'

'Olga?'

'We only got as far as *da*.'

'Yes,' said Eva, '*niet* wasn't in her vocabulary.'

They laughed. Eva leaned over him and tilted the lampshade back up.

'I've been too successful,' said Felsen, failing to look sorry for himself, trickling more brandy into his cup.

'With women?'

'No, no. Drawing attention to myself . . . all this entertaining I do.'

'We've had some good times,' said Eva.

Felsen stared into the carpet.

'What did you say?' he asked suddenly, looking up at her, surprised.

'Nothing,' she said, leaning over him to stub her cigarette

12

out. He breathed her in. She stepped back. 'What are you playing tonight?'

'Sally Parker's game. Poker.'

'Where are you taking me with your winnings?'

'I've been advised to lose.'

'To show your gratitude.'

'For a job I don't want.'

Outside a car drifted through the slush down Kurfürstenstrasse.

'There is one possibility,' she said.

Felsen looked up, sun perhaps breaking through the cloud.

'You could clean them out.'

'I've thought of it,' he said, laughing.

'It could be dangerous but . . .' she shrugged.

'They wouldn't stick me in a KZ, not with what I'm doing for them.'

'They stick anybody in a KZ these days . . . believe me,' she said. 'These are the people who cut down the lime trees on Unter den Linden so that when we go to the Café Kranzler all we have are those eagles on pillars looking down on us. Unter den Augen they should call it. If they can do that they can stick Klaus Felsen, Eva Brücke and Prince Otto von Bismarck in a KZ.'

'If he was still alive.'

'What do they care?'

He stood and faced her, only a few inches taller but nearly three times wider. She put a slim white arm, the wrist a terminus of blue veins, across the door.

'Take the advice you've been given,' she said. 'I was only joking.'

He grabbed at her, his fingers slipping into the crack of her bottom which she did not like. He went to kiss her. She twisted and yanked his hand away from behind her. They manoeuvred around each other so that he could get himself out of the door.

'I'll be back,' he said, without meaning it to sound a threat.

'I'll come to your apartment when I've closed the club.'

'It'll be late. You know what poker's like.'

'Wake me if I'm sleeping.'

He opened the door to the apartment and looked back down the corridor at her. Her dressing gown had been rucked open. Her knees, below the hem of her slip, looked tired. She seemed older than her thirty-five years. He closed the door, trotted down the stairs. At the bottom he rested his hand on the curl of the bannister and, in the weak light of the stairwell, had the sense of moorings being loosed.

At a little after six o'clock Felsen was standing in his darkened flat looking out into the matt black of the Nürnbergerstrasse, smoking a cigarette behind his hand, listening to the wind and the sleet rattling the windowpane. A slit-eyed car came down the road, churning slush from its wheel-arches, but it wasn't a staff car and it continued past him into the Hohenzollerndamm.

He smoked intensely thinking about Eva, how awkward that had been, how she'd needled him bringing up all his old girlfriends, the ones before the war who'd taught him how not to be a farmboy. Eva had introduced him to all of them and then, after the British declared war, moved in herself. He couldn't remember how that had happened. All he could think of was how Eva had taught him nothing, tried to teach him the mystery of nothing, the intricacies of space between words and lines. She was a great withholder.

He pieced their affair back to a moment where, in a fit of frustration at her remoteness, he'd accused her of acting the 'mysterious woman', when all she did was front a brothel as a nightclub. She'd iced over and said she didn't play at being anything. They'd split for a week and he'd gone whoring with nameless girls from the Friedrichstrasse, knowing she'd hear about it. She ignored his reappearance at the club and then wouldn't have him back in her bed until she was sure that he was clean, but . . . she had let him back.

Another car came down Nürnbergerstrasse, the sleet diagonal through the cracks of light. Felsen checked the two blocks of Reichsmarks in his inside pockets, left the window and went down to join it.

SS-Brigadeführers Hanke, Fischer and Wolff and one of the other candidates, Hans Koch, were sitting in the mess taking drinks served by a waiter with a steel tray. Felsen ordered a brandy and sat amongst them. They were all commenting on the quality of the mess cognac since they'd occupied France.

'And Dutch cigars,' said Felsen, handing round a handful to all the players. 'You realize how they used to keep the best for themselves.'

'A very Jewish trait,' said Brigadeführer Hanke, 'don't you think?'

Koch, still as pink-faced as he had been at fourteen, nodded keenly through the smoke of his cigar which Hanke was lighting for him.

'I didn't know the Jews were involved in the Dutch tobacco industry,' said Felsen.

'The Jews are everywhere,' said Koch.

'You don't smoke your own cigars?' asked Brigadeführer Fischer.

'After dinner,' said Felsen. 'Only cigarettes before. Turkish. Would you like to try one?'

'I don't smoke cigarettes.'

Koch looked at his lit cigar and felt foolish. He saw Felsen's cigarette case on the table.

'May I?' he said, picking it up and opening it. The shop's name was stamped on the inside. 'Samuel Stern, you see, the Jews *are* everywhere.'

'The Jews have been with us for centuries,' said Felsen.

'So was Samuel Stern until Kristallnacht,' said Koch,

sitting back satisfied, synchronizing a nod with Hanke. 'They weaken us every hour they remain in the Reich.'

'Weaken us?' said Felsen, thinking this sounded like something verbatim from Julius Streicher's rag, *Der Stürmer*. 'They don't weaken *me*.'

'What are you implying, Herr Felsen?' said Koch, cheeks reddening.

'I'm not implying anything, Herr Koch. I was merely saying that I have not experienced any weakening of my position, my business, or my social life as a result of the Jews.'

'It is quite possible you have been . . .'

'And as for the Reich, we have overrun most of Europe lately which hardly . . .'

'. . . possible you have been unaware,' finished Koch shouting him down.

The double doors to the mess thumped open and a tall, heavy man took three strides into the room. Koch shot off his chair. The Brigadeführers all stood up. SS-Gruppenführer Lehrer flicked his wrist at waist height.

'*Heil Hitler*,' he said. 'Bring me a brandy. Vintage.'

The Brigadeführers and Koch responded with full salutes. Felsen eased himself slowly out of his chair. The mess waiter whispered something to the dark, lowered head of the Gruppenführer.

'Well, bring me a brandy in the dining room then,' he shouted.

They went straight into dinner, Lehrer fuming because he'd wanted to stand in front of the fire, warming his arse, with a brandy or two.

Koch and Felsen sat on either side of Lehrer at the dinner. Over a nasty green soup Hanke asked Felsen about his father. The question Felsen had been waiting for.

'He was killed by a pig in 1924,' said Felsen.

Lehrer slurped his soup loudly.

Sometimes he used a pig, other times a ram. What he

didn't do was tell the truth, which was that as a fifteen-year-old, Klaus Felsen had found his father hanging from a beam in the barn.

'A pig?' asked Hanke. 'A wild boar?'

'No, no, a domestic pig. He slipped over in the pen and was trampled to death by a sow.'

'And you took over the farm?'

'Perhaps you know this already, Herr Brigadeführer. I worked that farm for eight years until my mother died. Then I sold it and joined the Führer's economic miracle and I've never looked back. It's not something I enjoy doing.'

Hanke sat back after that, shoulder to shoulder with his protégé who smiled pinkly. Lehrer slurped on. He knew it all anyway. Except for the pig, of course. That had been interesting, not true, but interesting.

The soup bowls were removed and replaced by plates of overcooked pork with boiled potatoes and a sludge of red cabbage. Lehrer only ate it for something to do while Koch gave him the party line. He shovelled food faster and faster into his face. In a momentary lull he leaned over to Felsen and said:

'Not married, Herr Felsen?'

'No, Herr Gruppenführer.'

'I've heard,' he said, nibbling at a hangnail, 'that you have a reputation with women.'

'Do I?'

'How does a man who's never been south of the Pyrenees speak Portuguese?' asked Lehrer, valuing his earlobe with thumb and finger. 'And don't tell me that that's what they're teaching you down in Swabia these days.'

Lehrer arched his eyebrows in a parody of innocence. Felsen realized that Susana Lopes had moved in higher circles than even he'd known about.

'I used to go riding with a Brazilian around the Havel,' he lied, and Lehrer's stomach grunted.

'Horses?' he asked.

After dinner they moved into an adjoining room. They each bought a hundred RM of chips and sat at a green baize table. The waiters moved a wooden trolley with drinks and glasses alongside, served brandies and left. Lehrer loosened off his tunic and drew on the cigar Felsen had given him, blowing the smoke on to the ember.

The light above the table, stratified by smoke, lit only the players' faces. Koch, even pinker now with the wine and brandy. Hanke with hooded unreadable eyes, the shadow of his dark beard already showing through. Fischer with pouches under his eyes and his skin taut and scraped raw as if he'd been half the night in a blizzard. Wolff, blonde and blue-eyed, impossibly young for a Brigadeführer, in need of a duelling scar to lend experience to the face. And Lehrer, the big man, with jowls fully formed, hair grey on the wings, dark eyes, wet and glistening with the anticipation of joy and further corruption. If Eva had been there, thought Felsen, she'd have told him that this was a man who liked to spank.

They played. Felsen lost consistently. He dumped hands which had any excitement in them and bluffed with no will to back it up. Koch lost flamboyantly. They both bought more chips and transferred them to the SS officers who showed no inclination for the process to stop.

Then Felsen started to win. There were comments about the cards turning. Hanke and Fischer were quickly burned out. Koch was stripped clean, going down for 1600 RM. Felsen concentrated on Wolff and began to lose to the man consistently on bluffs. Felsen was down to 500 RM when Lehrer cleaned Wolff out with four of a kind to a full house. Wolff looked as if he'd been speared to his chair. Lehrer was enormous behind his stacks of chips.

'You might wish to replenish your stocks if you want to take me on,' said Lehrer. Felsen poured himself a brandy

18

and sucked on his cigar. Lehrer beamed. Felsen reached into his pocket and took out 2000 RM.

'Will that be enough?' he asked and Lehrer licked his lips.

They played for an hour with Lehrer, now stripped to his shirt, losing lightly. Wolff, out of the light, watched the game with the intensity of a falcon. Hanke and Koch colluded on the sofa while Fischer slept noisily.

Just after 1.30 a.m. Lehrer declined to draw on a hand. Felsen thought for a full three minutes and drew two which he looked at and laid face-down on the table. He moved 200 RM into the centre of the table. Lehrer matched him and raised him 400 RM. Felsen likewise matched and raised. They stopped and checked each other. Lehrer was trying to find the light, the narrow crack, the hairline fissure that was all he needed. Felsen knew then that his strongest card wasn't face-down on the table in front of him and allowed himself a tiny smile in the pit of his stomach. It was enough for Lehrer who matched Felsen and raised him 1000 RM. Felsen moved his remaining 500 RM into the centre and drew a block of 5000 RM out of his pocket and threw it on top.

Wolff was up to his chest at the table burning holes in the green baize. Hanke and Koch shut up. Fischer stopped snoring.

Lehrer smiled and drummed the table with his fingers. He asked for a pen and paper. He pushed his remaining 2500 RM into the centre and wrote a note for 2500 RM.

'I think we should see each other now,' he said.

'You first,' said Felsen, who'd have been happy to go on.

Lehrer shrugged. He turned over four aces and a king. Koch was gritting his teeth with fury at how Felsen had bought the job from under him.

'Well, Felsen,' said Wolff.

Felsen turned over his draw cards first. The seven and

ten of diamonds. Wolff sneered but Lehrer leaned forward. The next two cards were the eight and nine of diamonds.

'I hope that last one's not a jack,' said Lehrer.

It was the six.

Lehrer tore his tunic off the back of his chair and left the room.

Perhaps, thought Felsen looking at the deflated men leaving around him, that had been a step too far. Beating four of a kind with a low straight flush – that could be seen as humiliation.

The sleet had turned back to snow. Then it became too cold for snow and the air froze still. The black ruts in the white roads iced over and the staff car taking Felsen back to Berlin fish-tailed its way up Nürnbergerstrasse.

Felsen tried to tip the driver, who refused. He limped slowly up the stairs to his apartment. He let himself in, threw off his coat and hat and slapped his money on the table. He poured himself a brandy, lit a cigarette and, despite the cold, stripped off his jacket and hung it off the back of a chair.

Eva was asleep in a wool coat, a blanket over her legs, on the chaise longue. He sat in front of her and watched her eyes fluttering under their lids. He put his hand out to touch her. She woke up with a small cry that sounded as if it came from the night rather than her throat. He took his hand back and gave her a cigarette.

She smoked and stared at the ceiling and stroked his knee without thinking about it.

'I was dreaming.'

'Badly?'

'You'd left Berlin, I was on my own at a U-bahn station and where the tracks should have been there were crowds of people looking up, as if they were expecting something of me.'

'Where'd I gone?'

'I don't know.'

'I doubt I'll be going anywhere after tonight.'

'What did you do?' she asked, mother to small boy.

'I cleaned them out.'

Eva sat up.

'That was stupid,' she said. 'You know Lehrer . . . he's not so nice. You remember those two Jewish girls?'

'The ones who got washed up in the Havel . . . yes, I do, but that wasn't him was it?'

'No, but he was there. He was the one who'd ordered the girls.'

'He knew about me too,' said Felsen sipping the brandy. 'He knew about me and Susana Lopes. How do you think he knew that?'

'It's the nature of the regime isn't it?'

'It was years ago.'

'It was a totalitarian state before the war too,' she said, swinging her knees round to between his legs and taking the brandy glass from him. 'Is that why you beat him at cards?'

'What do you mean?' he asked, annoyed to have sounded defensive.

'You were jealous, weren't you? I can tell,' she said. 'Of him and Susana.'

Her hands found the front of his trousers and rubbed the thick material.

'I beat him because I didn't want to leave Berlin.'

'Berlin?' she asked, toying with him now.

She undid the front of his trousers and unbuttoned his fly. He slipped out of his braces and she tugged his trousers down to his thighs and yanked his undershorts out and over his erection.

'Not just Berlin,' he said, and gasped as her hands enclosed the stem of his penis.

'Sorry,' she said, without meaning it.

He swallowed. His penis felt extremely hot in her small,

21

cold, white hands. She moved her fists up and down, painfully slowly, without taking her eyes off his face. His neck juddered and he pulled her forward on to his lap, pushing the coat open and drawing her dress up over her stocking tops. He tugged the gusset of her knickers aside and she had to grab at the arms of the chair to save herself from falling. She found him and lowered herself down on to him feeling the slow burn creeping into her.

At dawn the heavy black curtains were crushing the iron-grey light back outside. The white linen bedclothes were stiff with cold. Felsen's head came off the pillow at the second crash, which came with the noise of a length of wood splintering. Boots thundered over wooden floors, something fell and rolled. Felsen turned, his shoulders hardened by the frost, his brain grinding through the gears, drink and tiredness confusing the double declutch required. The two huge panes of mirrored glass in the double doors of the bedroom shattered. Two men in calf-length black leather coats stepped through the door frames. Felsen's single thought – why didn't they just open the doors?

Eva came out of sleep as if she'd been stabbed. Felsen slid out of the bed and crouched naked. A leather heel from a black boot hit him on the side of his cloth-filled head and he went down.

'Felsen!' roared a voice.

Felsen murmured something to himself, things slopping in his head, the room full of Eva shouting hobnail German.

'You! Shut up!'

He heard a dull smack, something delivered with a closed fist, and then quiet.

Felsen sat with his back against the bed, his genitals shrinking back from the cold polished wooden floor.

'Get dressed!'

He stumbled into clothes. Blood trickled, warm behind

his ear. The men took a shoulder each. They crunched over the broken glass, opening the doors this time, polite on the way out.

A green padlocked van was the only colour in a crevasse of snow-covered gunmetal buildings, whose street was frozen into arctic maps of white, fringed grey and black. The door of the van opened. They heaved Felsen into the darkness and pant of fear.

Chapter II

16th February 1941, 8 Prinz Albrechtstrasse, RHSA Head-quarters.

The van doors opened to an inarticulate shriek from an armed soldier. Felsen took a sideswipe from a rifle butt on the shoulder. He lowered himself into the ankle-deep black slush and staggered up the steps out of the courtyard into the grim stone Gestapo building. He was one of four prisoners. They were led straight down into the cellars, into a long narrow corridor with cells on either side. Most of the light came from an open door from which came the moaning of a man post-coitus. The two men ahead of Felsen looked into the light and switched their heads away fast. A man in shirt sleeves wearing a stiff, grossly stained, brown apron was attending to a man strapped into a chair.

'Shut the door, Krüger,' he said, in a tired, long-suffering voice. A man with a full day's work ahead of him and none of it easy.

The corridor darkened with a bang to a sodium-lit gloom. Felsen was put in a stinking unlit cell with a pallet and full bucket for company. He put his hands up against the damp wall and tried to breathe away the cold clamminess he felt on the inside of his rib cage. He *had* gone too far. He knew that now.

They came for him after several hours, took him past the shut door of the horror room up to the first floor and into an office with tall windows in which a man in a dark suit sat at a desk cleaning his glasses for an absurdly long time. Felsen waited. The man told him to sit.

'Do you know why you're here?'

'No.'

The man fitted his face into the glasses and opened a file which he tilted away from Felsen, who stared at the precision of the man's parting.

'Communism.'

'You're joking.'

The man looked up but didn't comment.

'You are pro-Jewish.'

'Don't be ridiculous.'

'You also knew a woman called Michelle Duchamp.'

'*That* is true.'

'My colleagues have been talking to her for a week in Lyons. She's been remembering things about the time she spent in Berlin back in the thirties.'

'Before the war . . . when I knew her, you mean.'

'But not before politics. As you know, she's been working for the French Resistance movement for over a year.'

'I'm not political and no, I didn't know that.'

'We are all political. Party member number 479,381, *Förderndes Mitglied* to SS unit . . .'

'You know as well as I do that there is no life outside the Party.'

'Is that why you joined, Herr Felsen? To grow your business? Improve your prospects? Just hitching a ride on us are you, while the going's good?'

Felsen sat back from the desk and looked out of the window at the bleak Berlin sky, realizing that this could happen to anybody and did . . . every day.

'That's a nice jacket,' said the man. 'Made by your tailor . . .'

'Isaac Weinstock,' said Felsen. 'That's a Jewish name in case . . .'

'You know it's forbidden for Jews to buy yarn.'

'I bought the cloth for him.'

It was snowing again. He could just make out the grey

25

flakes against the grey sky through the grey glass over the grey filing cabinet.

'Olga Kasarov,' said the man.

'What about her?'

'You know her.'

'I went to bed with an Olga . . . once.'

'She's a Bolshevik.'

'She's a Russian, I do know that,' said Felsen, 'and anyway, I didn't know you could catch communism from fucking.'

That seemed to snap something inside the man who stood up and tucked the file under his arm.

'I don't think you understand your situation very well, Herr Felsen.'

'You're right, I don't. Perhaps you would be good enough . . .'

'Some rehabilitation is, perhaps, in order.'

Felsen suddenly felt the runaway vehicle he was on lurch down a steeper slope.

'Your investigation . . .' he started, but the man was moving towards the door. 'Herr . . . Herr . . . wait.'

The man opened the door. Two soldiers came in and heaved Felsen to his feet and took him out.

'We're sending you back to school, Herr Felsen,' said the dark-suited man.

They took him back down to his cell where they kept him for three days. Nobody spoke to him. They gave him a bowl of soup once a day. His bucket wasn't emptied. He sat on his pallet surrounded by his piss and faeces. Screams would occasionally penetrate his darkness, sometimes faint, other times horrifically close and loud. Terrible beatings took place in the corridor outside his cell. More than one man called for his mother under the crack of his door.

He spent the hours and days preparing himself. He tutored his brain into a state of excessive politeness and his demeanour into one of submissive timidity. On the fourth day they came for him again. He was stinking and feeble with fear. They didn't take him to the horror room and they didn't take him upstairs for another meeting with the man in the dark suit. They handcuffed him and took him straight out into the courtyard, the snow falling in soft large flakes but packed hard underfoot by boots and tyres. They loaded him into an empty van with a large and still tacky stain on the floor. The doors shut.

'Where's this going?' he asked the darkness.

'Sachsenhausen,' said the guard outside.

'What about the law?' said Felsen. 'What about the process of law?' The guard hammered on the side of the van. The driver slammed it into gear and sent Felsen cannoning against the doors.

Eva Brücke sat in her office in *Die Rote Katze* smoking cigarette after cigarette and trickling more brandy into her coffee cup until it was all brandy, no coffee. The swelling on her face had gone down with the daily application of a little snow and she was left with a blue and yellow mark which disappeared under foundation and the white powder she used.

The door to her office was open and she had a clear view of the empty kitchens. She heard a light tapping on the back door and stood to answer it. At that moment the telephone went off louder than a stack of china hitting the floor. She jumped and steadied herself. She didn't want to pick it up, but the noise was shattering and she snatched it to her ear.

'Eva?' asked the voice.

'Yes,' she said, recognizing it. 'This is *Die Rote Katze*.'

'You sound tired.'

'It's a job with long hours and not much opportunity for rest.'

'You should take some time off.'

'Some "Strength through Joy" perhaps,' she said, and the caller laughed.

'Do you have anybody else with a sense of humour?'

'It *does* depend on who's telling the jokes.'

'No, well, I mean . . . someone who appreciates fun. Unusual fun.'

'I know people who can still laugh out loud.'

'Like me,' he said, laughing out loud to prove it.

'Perhaps,' she said, not laughing with him.

'Could they come and see me for an evening of amusement and wonder?'

'How many?'

'Oh, I think three is a merry number. Would three be all right?'

'Could you drop by and give me a better idea of what . . . ?'

'It's rather inconvenient at the moment.'

'You know, I worry after . . .'

'Oh, no, no, no, don't be concerned. The theme is food. What could be more joyous than food in this day and age.'

'I'll see what I can do.'

'Thank you, Eva. Your service is appreciated.'

She hung up and went to the back door. The small, enclosed man she'd been expecting was there in the snow-packed alley. She let him in. He shook the snow off his hat and stamped his boots clean. They went to the office. She pulled the telephone plug out of the wall.

'Do you drink, Herr Kaufman?'

'Only tea.'

'I have some coffee.'

'Nothing, thank you.'

'What can I do for you?'

'I was wondering if you'd have room for two visitors?'

'I told you . . .'

'I know, but it's an emergency.'

'Not here.'

'No.'

'How long?'

'Three days.'

28

'I might be going away,' she said, off the top of her head, inspired by the telephone call.

'They can manage on their own.'

'I told you before that this would be . . . it would have to be . . .'

'I know,' he said, folding his hands into his lap, 'but the circumstances are unusual.'

'Won't they always be unusual?'

'Perhaps you're right.'

She lit a cigarette and sighed the smoke out.

'When are they coming?'

Sachsenhausen was an old barracks turned concentration camp thirty kilometres north-west of Berlin in Oranienberg. Felsen knew of the place only because he'd taken on a political and two Jews to sweep the factory floors. They'd been released from there in 1936 just before the Olympics. They didn't have to say anything about the conditions in the KZ, the two tendons at the backs of their necks stood out sharply from under their shaved heads – they were fifteen kilos underweight minimum.

It was an unnerving drive on snow-covered roads from Berlin. The van skidded and slewed across the road. At Sachsenhausen he heard the gates opening and a thunderous pummelling on the panels of the van. The van seemed to run a gauntlet for a hundred metres until Felsen's nerve was completely shattered. Then silence and only the creak of tyres on snow. The van stopped. The wind moaned. The driver coughed in his cab. The doors opened.

Felsen got to his feet, felt the stickiness on the edges of his hands which were stained russet from the drying blood on the floor. He stumbled to the back of the van. Outside was a vast white expanse with just two lines across it from the wheels of the van. Far off, perhaps two hundred metres away, it was difficult to judge over the snow's squinting glare, were trees and buildings.

29

The van took off, throwing him out on to the ankle-deep snow. The doors flapped and banged shut and he put his hands up over his head, confused by the sudden noise. At the edge of the enormous flat expanse of snow-covered ground a figure stood at ease. Felsen nosed forward, eyes creased shut. The figure, grey and indiscernible, didn't move. Felsen flinched at a noise behind him, the sound of sharp metal slicing through snow. He whipped round. There were three men in black SS greatcoats and helmets. The hems of their coats rested on the surface of the snow. One carried a wooden club, the next a spade which he swung in an arc, the blade singing against the crystalline snow. The third held a metre length of steel cable, frayed at the end. Felsen looked back to the figure, as if he might help. The figure had gone. He got to his feet. The men were eyeless beneath their helmets. Felsen's legs were shaking.

'*Sachsengruss*,' said the guard with the club.

Felsen put his hands on his head and began doing knee-bends. The Saxon Greeting. They kept him at it for an hour. Then they told him to stand to attention for an hour, until his body was shaking with cold and his ears full of the swish from the cable, the slicing of the spade, the tamping of the wooden club. The guards trod a circle around him.

They removed his handcuffs. The spade flew through the air at him. He caught it in fingers which he expected to shatter like porcelain.

'Dig a path to the building.'

They walked behind him over the vast area as he dug hundreds of metres of paths. Tears streamed down his face, the snot ran in freezing rivulets from his nose, the steam poured off him thick as bull's breath. It began to snow. They told him to reclear the paths he'd already made.

They worked him for six hours until it was completely dark, no light coming from the blacked-out buildings. They faced him out into the darkness and gave him another hour's *Sachsengruss* while they told him how he was going to have to clear it all again tomorrow. In the last ten minutes he dropped to the floor twice and they kicked him back up on to his feet. He was glad to be kicked. He knew something from the kicking. He knew they weren't going to beat him to death with the club, cable and spade.

They stood him to attention after that until a thin reed of music came floating through the pitch black. They told him to march into the building. He fell over. They dragged him backwards inside. His feet trailed damp lines over the polished floors.

The warmth of the building seemed to unfreeze his mind and tears poured out of his head, water leaked out of his nose and ears. The music grew louder. He knew it. Mozart. It had to be. All those notes. Voices and laughter came over the music. A familiar smell. The guards' boots rolled over the polished floors. Felsen's feet came back to a life of pain but he was grinning. He was grinning because he knew now what he'd suspected before out in the snow – he wasn't in Sachsenhausen.

They arrived in a room with chairs and carpets, newspapers and ashtrays – unimaginable civilization after Prinz Albrechtstrasse. They stopped. The guards got him standing. One of them knocked and they took him backwards into the room. A girl giggled. The talking subsided, only the music remained.

'Does the prisoner like this music?' asked a voice.

Felsen swallowed hard. His legs trembled. His humiliation stiffened his neck.

'I don't know whether I should like it, sir.'

'You have no opinion?'

'No, sir.'

'This is Mozart. *Don Giovanni*. This has been banned by the Party. Do you know why?'

'No, sir.'

'The libretto was written by a Jew.'

The music was cut.

'Now what did you think of the music?'

'I didn't like it, sir.'

'Why are you here?'

'I've been sent back to school, sir.'

Felsen's feet throbbed in his ruined shoes, the blood thumping through them.

'Why are you here?' asked a different voice.

He thought for a long minute.

'Because I'm lucky at cards, sir,' he said, which screwed the tension down in the room so that the girl tittered. 'Sorry sir, because I *cheat* at cards, sir.'

'Prisoner, turn around and stand at ease.'

He didn't see who was sitting at the table at first. His watering eyes took in the gross quantities of food before anything. Then he saw Wolff, Hanke, Fischer and Lehrer, two other men he didn't know and a young woman who was smoking through lipstick already smudged.

Lehrer was smiling. The Brigadeführers were all amused. Fischer broke first and roared and drummed the floor with his boots. They all laughed, banging the table, even the girl, who didn't know why she was laughing.

'Is the prisoner permitted to laugh?' asked Hanke.

They roared again.

'Prisoner Felsen. Laugh!' shouted Fischer.

Feslen smiled and started to blink, conjuring mirth from relief. His shoulders began to shake, his stomach pumped and he laughed, he laughed himself helpless, he laughed himself to a retching standstill. He laughed the SS officers silent.

'The prisoner will stop laughing now,' said Lehrer.

Felsen's mouth clamped shut. He returned to 'at ease'.

'There are some clothes for you in there. Change.'

He went into the kitchens, stripped and got into a dark suit which hung off him. He rejoined the table.

'Eat,' said Lehrer.

He laid waste to the table in his immediate vicinity more

32

thoroughly than a retreating army. The officers talked amongst themselves except Lehrer. 'Don't think I'm a bad loser,' he said.

'I don't think that, sir.'

'What *do* you think?'

'I think you are what your name implies . . . a teacher, sir.'

'And what have you learned?'

'Obedience, sir.'

'We're giving you this job you don't want for a number of reasons. You can organize things. You are ruthless and aggressive. But you must not be insubordinate, Felsen. In your business you might lose an hour's production because somebody didn't follow your orders. In the business of war it could be a thousand lives or more. There's no place for the maverick. Control is the key. And I am in control,' he said, swilling the brandy in his glass. 'So why don't you want this job?'

'I don't want to leave Berlin, sir. I have a factory to run.'

'At least it's not a girl.'

'I've produced quality goods and I've shown my appreciation.'

'Don't start on a different question. What's in Berlin for a Swabian like you apart from your factory? We're not talking about Paris or Rome. It's not a city you can fall in love with. Not like Nuremberg, my city. And Berliners? . . . My God, they think the world owes them a living.'

'Maybe I like their sense of humour.'

'Yes, well, you've always been a bit dry down in Swabia.'

'I don't follow you, sir,' said Felsen, touchy.

'Trampled to death by a pig. What was that?'

Felsen didn't respond.

'Do you think I don't know about your father?' said Lehrer.

'Yes, well, there you have two examples of Swabian humour.'

'It gave me a problem, Hanke thought you were psychologically unsuitable.'

'I should have tried harder with him.'

Lehrer leaned across the table, his face flushed with wine, his breath sour and cigar-streaked.

'This job is a big opportunity for you . . . a big opportunity . . . You will thank me for it. I know you will thank me.'

'Then why don't you tell me about it, sir?'

'Not yet. Tomorrow. You'll come to Lichterfelde. I'll have you sworn in first.'

'Into the SS?'

'Of course,' said Lehrer, until he saw Felsen's frozen face. 'Don't worry, you're going west, not east.'

They drove slowly north through the fresh snow back to Berlin. That familiar smell had been the Lichterfelde barracks. On the few occasions a car passed in the other direction Felsen could see the shadows of the officers in the car in front, passing the girl between them. Lehrer didn't speak. It stopped snowing. They cruised into Berlin and the first car peeled off to the Tiergarten and Moabit. Lehrer ordered the driver to do a small circuit of the city. Felsen stared out into the dark, the black parks, the flak towers, the lightless houses, the silent Anhalter station.

'It's the nature of war,' said Lehrer, 'that things happen. More things happen than could possibly happen in peacetime. In that respect it's the most exciting time of a man's life. One moment you're running a factory, making more money than you could ever dream of as a farmer in Swabia. You dance with girls in the Golden Horseshoe, watch the shows in the Frasquita, walk the Kufu with all the other monied bastards. And the next moment . . .'

'I'm in Prinz Albrechtstrasse.'

'A new and radical regime must protect itself. Strength through fear.'

'And the next moment . . . go on.'

'Think international. Germany is not just Germany any more. Germany is the whole of Europe. A world power. Political and economic. Don't be small-minded.'

'It's my peasant mentality. It's how I get things done for the money.'

'That's good, but see the big picture too. The Reichsführer Himmler wants the SS to be an economic power in its own right within the new Germanic Reich. Think about that.'

The car finally turned into Nürnbergerstrasse and pulled up outside Felsen's apartment. He got out and went up the two flights of stairs and found his front door repaired. He let himself in and lit one of his own cigarettes. He looked from behind the blackout and found the car gone. He put on a coat and hat and went out into the night.

It was a short walk to Kurfürstenstrasse. He walked in the street where it was easier. There was nobody out. The temperature had dropped sharply.

Felsen went down the small lane at the side of Eva's apartment building and in through the gate. The mounds of earth and rubble taken out of the cellar were covered in thick snow. The door was locked. He hammered on it and stepped back and up on to one of the mounds to see if there were any cracks of light around the windows. He roared her name. After a few moments someone opened a window and told him to shut his drunken talk.

He went back home, soaked in a bath and got into bed. It was 2.30 a.m. He'd call her in the morning, he thought, as he drifted into his first hour's sleep. He came awake four times, each time with a rush and a crack in his head as if he'd been hit with a brick. There was the smell of shit in his nostrils, and the last frames of his dream stayed with him; the white of the widening parade ground lengthening out for ever. He had to put the light on after that.

Chapter III

26th February 1941, SS Barracks, Unter den Eichen, Berlin-Lichterfelde.

Felsen sat in the polished corridor outside Lehrer's office, watching two soldiers in vests and fatigues cleaning the corners with brushes too small for the job. Twice in the last fifteen minutes a sergeant had dropped by to kick their arses and salute Felsen, who was sitting uncomfortably in the uniform of an SS-Hauptsturmführer.

An adjutant came out of Lehrer's office and waved him in. Felsen saluted the Gruppenführer. Lehrer nodded him into in a high-backed chair on the other side of a desk with black leather inlay. Felsen took out his cigarettes, screwed one in his mouth and Lehrer reminded him that permission was required to smoke in front of a superior officer.

'You'll get used to it,' said Lehrer. 'You'll even grow to like it.'

'I'm not sure how.'

'The greatest burden . . .' he said, fixing him with the glare of his full authority, 'the *true* burden, which is responsibility, is the cast-iron yoke across *my* shoulders. *Your* actions are an added weight. You, on the other hand, have the lightness of being of a man unencumbered in the field.'

'Following orders.'

'You'll find yourself with more of a free hand than most.'

'Now that I'm a fully paid up member of the SS . . .'

'It's only a mark a month off your salary and it all goes into the *Spargemeinschaft-SS* so you can draw interest-free loans and . . .'

'A mark a month isn't my problem. What am I being paid to do? Am I allowed to know yet?'

'I wasn't trying to bore you Hauptsturmführer Felsen, I was merely trying to give you a practical instance of what I've been talking about . . . what I mentioned in the car last night.'

'The SS as an economic power in the new Germanic Reich, spreading from the North Cape of Scandinavia to the Pyrenees and the tip of the Brest Peninsula to Lublin.'

'Don't leave out Great Britain, the Iberian Peninsula, the Ukraine, the Black Sea states and on and on and on,' said Lehrer. 'The big picture, remember.'

'I'll settle for a thumbnail sketch for the moment. It's the peasant brain, sir.'

'You probably know the SS runs various businesses.'

'I've only supplied couplings to the railways which are heavily used by the SS, but I don't know much about their other business interests.'

'We have brickworks, quarries, potteries, cement factories, building material plants, soft drinks factories, meat processing plants, bakeries and, of course, military armaments and munitions factories. There are a lot of other enterprises, but that gives you the idea.'

'I don't see where my expertise fits in, sir.'

'Let's talk about munitions. What's the difference between this war and the last one?'

'It's an aerial war, an aerial bombardment war.'

'All Berliners think about is air raids,' Lehrer sighed. 'I'm talking about the war. The offensive.'

'There are no static fronts. It's a mobile war. *Blitzkrieg*.'

'Exactly. It's a mobile war. It requires machinery, machine tools, artillery. It's also a tank war. Tanks have armour. To stop a tank you have to penetrate the hardened steel of its armour and that requires what is known as solid-core ammunition.'

'The shell heads are hardened with an alloy – tungsten,

37

I believe . . . so are the machine tools, the gun barrels and tank armour.'

'Otherwise known as wolfram or wolframite,' said Lehrer. 'Do you know where that comes from?'

'China . . . most of it, and Russia. Sweden has some, not much, even though they invented the word tungsten, and . . .' Felsen slowed as the cogs clicked, '. . . the Iberian Peninsula.'

'You know your stuff.'

'I learnt a lot from Wencdt.'

'Wencdt?'

'My General Manager, he's a metallurgist,' said Felsen. 'You mentioned the Ukraine and the Black Sea states earlier.'

'Ah . . .' said Lehrer leaning back, steepling his fingers, savouring his own lips, 'the bigger picture.'

'I was under the impression that we had signed a non-aggression pact with Stalin in 1939. I'm not expecting you to confirm that that pact will be broken, but it hasn't escaped the Berliners' attention that factories are churning out massive amounts of material and it's all heading in one direction.'

'Let's hope Stalin's not as perspicacious as the Berliners.'

'All he'd have to do is hang around the *Bierstuben* and *Kneipen* of Kreuzberg and Neukölln and offer to buy a few beers and he'd get all the military intelligence he needs.'

'A worrying thought,' said Lehrer, totally unconcerned. 'Keep talking, Herr Hauptsturmführer, you're doing very well.'

'The wolfram we're getting from China . . . does it come via Russia?'

'Correct.'

'And when we break the non-aggression pact we'll be cutting ourselves off from the biggest wolfram suppliers in the world.'

'Now you understand why I wanted you in uniform before I told you about the job.'

'Susana Lopes,' said Felsen, nodding at Lehrer. 'You want me to use my lover's Portuguese to buy wolfram.'

'Portugal has the largest reserves in Europe and you didn't get the job just because you speak Portuguese.'

'What was wrong with Koch?'

Lehrer fanned the name away like a nasty fart.

'Not subtle enough,' he said. 'This job requires finesse, an understanding of people, a sort of games-playing skill, you know, a genius for bluff, a talent for dissimulation, that kind of thing. Skills of yours we have already seen in action. And anyway, he wasn't what Susana would call *simpatico* was he?'

'Am I buying this wolfram for the SS?'

'No, no, you're buying it for Germany, but the Supply Department is headed by Dr Walter Scheiber who, apart from being a great chemist, is an old Party member and a true SS man. In this way, the Reichsführer Himmler wants to make sure that the SS gets the credit for the campaign *and* in return we'll take more of the munitions production. That is nothing to do with you. Your task is to get your hands on every kilo of uncontracted wolfram there is.'

'*Uncontracted* wolfram? What's already under contract?'

'The biggest mine is British. Beralt – production 2000 tons per annum. The French own the Borralha mine – production 600 tons. The United Kingdom Commercial Corporation signed a contract with Borralha last year but we are being successful, through the Vichy government, in preventing it from working. We control a small mine called Silvicola, maximum production a few hundred tons. The rest is on the open market.'

'And how much do we need?'

'Three thousand tons for this year.'

A clock ticked behind Felsen's head. Snow shifted on the roof overhead and dropped in a flurry past the window.

'May I smoke now, sir?' asked Felsen, Lehrer nodded. 'Didn't you just say that the biggest mine produced two thousand tons a year?'

'I did. And that's not the least of your problems. The UKCC will institute pre-emptive buying offensives. You will have to manage vast quantities of "free" labour as well as your own men and any associated Portuguese agents. You will have to secure stockpiles, arrange shipments. You will have to be . . . how shall I put it . . . unconventional in your methods.'

'Smuggling?'

Lehrer stretched his fattening neck out of his collar.

'You will need information about your competitors' movements. You will need to stiffen your labour force's resolve, keep foreign agents in line.'

'And the Portuguese Führer – Dr Salazar – how does he . . . ?'

'He has a tightrope to walk. He is ideologically sound but there's a long history of cooperation with the British which they are keen to invoke. He will find himself torn but we will prevail.'

'And when do I leave for Portugal?'

'You don't, not yet. Switzerland first. This afternoon.'

'This afternoon? And what about the factory? I haven't organized a damn thing. That's totally impossible, out of the question.'

'These are orders Herr Hauptsturmführer,' said Lehrer icily. 'No order is impossible. A car will pick you up at one o'clock this afternoon. You will not be late.'

Felsen stood outside his apartment building at exactly 1.00 p.m. He was in uniform but with one of his own coats over the top and watching grimly as an overalled worker pasted a huge black and red poster on to the wall by the pharmacy opposite. It said 'Führer, we thank you'.

He'd phoned Eva all morning and got no reply. Finally,

after he'd packed and finished talking things over with Wencdt, he'd run round to her apartment and banged and shouted outside her windows until the same man who'd told him to shut up the night before stuck his head out to do so again. He stopped short on seeing the uniform under the coat and became excessively polite. He told him in sticky sweet German that Eva Brücke had gone away, that he'd seen her getting into a taxi with suitcases yesterday morning, Herr Hauptsturmführer.

An old woman who'd been working her way up the frozen pavements of Nürnbergerstrasse drew level with the huddled Felsen and saw the poster and the sick look on his face. She gave the *BerlinerBlick* up and down the street and pointed her cane across to the pharmacy.

'What have we got to thank *him* for?' she said, emphasizing her clouds of breath with her spare fur-cuffed gloved hand. 'The National Socialist coffee bean? How to bake cakes with no eggs? The only thing we've got to thank him for is that the *Völkischer Beobachter* . . . it's softer than the National Socialist toilet paper.'

She stopped as if she'd been knifed in the throat. Felsen's coat had fallen open and she'd seen the black uniform. She ran. Her feet suddenly as sure as a speed skater's on the sheet ice of the pavement.

Lehrer arrived in a chauffeur-driven Mercedes. The driver loaded the cases into the boot. They drove past the skittering old lady who still hadn't made it to the Hohenzollerndamm and Felsen mentioned her.

'She's lucky she didn't meet someone more severe,' said Lehrer, whacking his gloved hands together. 'Perhaps *you* should have been more severe. You'll need to be.'

'Not with old ladies in the street, Herr Gruppenführer.'

'Selective severity weakens the whole,' he replied, and wiped the window with the back of his fat black finger.

They headed south-west out of Berlin to Leipzig and then

across the whitened countryside to Weimar, Eisenach and Frankfurt. Lehrer worked out of a briefcase all the way, reading documents and drafting memos in a spidery unreadable hand. Felsen was left to think about Eva but couldn't find any discernible change in the pattern of things – long nights drinking and laughing and listening to jazz – bouts of lovemaking in which she couldn't seem to wrap her arms around enough of his body – terrible arguments which started because he wanted to have more of her but she wouldn't give it, and which only stopped when she threw things at him, normally her shoes, never the china unless she was in his apartment and there was some Meissen available.

There was nothing . . . except for the incident with the Jewish girls. For days after she'd found out about them, she'd been like the sole survivor from a direct hit – pale, vacant and fluttery. But it had passed, and anyway it didn't have anything to do with him, with them. He looked across at Lehrer who was humming to himself now and staring out of the window.

They arrived at a *Gasthaus* on the other side of Karlsruhe just as the light was failing. Felsen lay down in his room while Lehrer borrowed the manager's office and made telephone calls. At dinner they were alone but Lehrer was distracted until he was called to the telephone. He came back in an expansive mood and demanded brandy in front of the fire.

'And coffee!' he roared. 'The real stuff, none of this nigger sweat.'

He rubbed his thighs and warmed his arse. He took in his surroundings as if it had been far too long since he'd been in a simple roadside inn.

'I've never seen you in the *Rote Katze* before,' said Felsen, testing some untrodden ground.

'I've seen you,' said Lehrer.

'Have you known Eva long?'

42

'Why do you ask?'

'I just wondered how you knew about my old girlfriends. She introduced me to all of them . . . including the poker player.'

'Who was that?'

'Sally Parker.'

'She didn't mention her.'

'If she had you wouldn't have proposed the game.'

'Yes, well . . . I've known Eva for some time. Since she had that first club. Where was it now, *Der Blaue Affe?*'

'I've never heard of it.'

'Back in the twenties when she first started out.'

Felsen shook his head.

'Anyway. Your name came up. I recognized you. I asked Eva, who spoke very highly of you which she knew very well was not what I wanted. Then, of course, she was as discreet as she could be but, I'm an SS-Gruppenführer and . . . and that's it,' he said, taking the brandy off the tray.

'You weren't . . . ?'

'What?'

'Fräulein Brücke wasn't one of the reasons you didn't want to leave Berlin, was she?'

'No, no,' said Felsen, annoyed at himself for snatching at it.

'I was going to say . . .'

The wood hissed in the fire. Lehrer moved his hands over his buttocks to warm them.

'What were you going to say, sir?' asked Felsen, unable to stop himself.

'Well, you know, Berlin clubs . . . the women . . . it's not . . .'

'She wasn't a hostess,' said Felsen, tamping his anger.

'No, no, I know that, but . . . it's the culture. It's not conducive to . . .' he waited to see if Felsen would fill in the word for him and reveal some more of himself, but he didn't, '. . . stability. Very artistic. Very free. Very easy.

43

Permanent attachments are rare in a night-time culture.'

'Wasn't the most famous Party rally of all time held at night?'

'*Touché*,' roared Lehrer, throwing himself into an armchair, 'but that was just so the camera wouldn't pick up the fat sods in the *Amtswalter* and make the Party look like a bunch of Bavarian pigs. And, may I remind you, Herr Hauptsturmführer, that glibness is not an approved National Socialist attitude.'

They went to bed shortly after that, Felsen feeling outmanoeuvred and sick. He lay on his cot and stared at the ceiling smoking through his cigarettes, turning over Eva's dismissal of him, the slickness with which she'd set him up and pulled it off.

'Ah well,' he said out loud, crushing his last cigarette into the ashtray on his chest, 'just another in a long line.'

It took him two hours to go to sleep. He couldn't get rid of a picture in his brain and a thought. The sight of his father's bare feet and ankles, swaying minutely at eye height, and why did he take his shoes and socks off?

27th February 1941.

They wore suits to breakfast. Lehrer's was single-breasted thick wool, dark blue and heavy. Felsen felt flashy in his Parisian cut, double-breasted bitter chocolate suit and a regrettable red tie.

'Expensive?' asked Lehrer, his mouth full of black bread and ham.

'Not cheap.'

'Bankers don't believe you unless you wear dark blue.'

'Bankers?'

'The bankers of Basel. Who did you think we were going to see in Switzerland? You can't buy wolfram with chips.'

'Or Reichsmarks apparently,' said Felsen.

'Quite.'

'But Swiss francs . . . dollars.'

'Dr Salazar was a professor of economics.'

'And that entitles him to be paid differently to everybody else?'

'No. It just entitles him to the opinion that in wartime it's best to have strong gold reserves.'

'You're sending me down to Portugal with a consignment of *gold*?'

'A problem is developing. The Americans are being difficult about letting us have our dollars so we've started paying for what we want in Swiss francs. Our suppliers in Portugal exchange those Swiss francs for escudos. Eventually, through the local banks, the Swiss francs find their way to the Banco de Portugal. And once they've accumulated enough, they use them to buy gold from Switzerland.'

'I don't see the problem.'

'The Swiss don't like it. They're worried about losing control of their gold reserves,' said Lehrer. 'So, we are experimenting.'

'How do we move this gold?'

'Trucks.'

'What sort of trucks?'

'Swiss trucks. There'll be armed soldiers with you all the way. It's taken some organization I can tell you. You don't think I enjoy having my head in my briefcase all day, do you?'

'I didn't realize gold was physically moved. I thought it was accounted for on paper by national banks.'

'Perhaps Dr Salazar likes . . . physically . . . to sit on his gold,' said Lehrer, thinking some more, but he left it at that.

'Whose gold is this?'

'I don't follow your question.'

'Wouldn't German gold be held in the Reichsbank?'

'Now you're asking me questions which I can't . . . which I don't have the knowledge to reply to . . . or the authority. I am merely an SS-Gruppenführer, after all.'

By 11.00 a.m. they had drawn up outside an unmarked building in Basel's business district. There was nothing inside or out to indicate what happened in this building. There was a handsome woman in her thirties sitting behind a desk with a single telephone on it. A large marble staircase spiralled behind her. Lehrer talked to the woman quietly. Felsen only heard a single word – 'Puhl'. The woman picked up the telephone, dialled a number and spoke briefly. She stood and set off on strong legs up the stairs. Lehrer indicated that Felsen should wait while he followed the legs.

Felsen sat in a densely packed leather armchair. The woman returned and sat at her desk without looking at him. She folded her hands and waited for the next high point in her day. It took Felsen half an hour and several cubic feet of charm to find out that he was in the lobby of the Bank of International Settlements. The name meant nothing to him.

At one o'clock Felsen and Lehrer were sitting at a table in a restaurant called Bruderholz. Only other men in dark suits ate in this place and at tables well-spaced from each other. There were four *petits poussins* between the two men and a flat plate of *boulangère* potatoes. Lehrer was holding a glass of Gewürztraminer and rolling the stem between his thumb and forefinger.

'It's so good to have Alsace back in the German fold, don't you think? What magnificent country, magnificent wine. The meat of the *poussin* will be a little delicate for this, we should have ordered goose or pork, hearty Alsatian fare, but I can't have too much fat, you know. Still . . . the fruits of summer in the dead of winter. Your health.'

'Was that a particularly successful meeting, Herr Gruppen-führer?'

'Tell me what you think of the Gewürztraminer?'

'Spicy.'

'I'm sure you can do better than that. I was always told that you were very appreciative of the good things in life.'

'Boldly fruity, but clean and dry. The spice holding from the top to the bottom, as long as an Atlantic cruise.'

'Where did you get that from?' Lehrer laughed.

'It's not true?'

'It's true . . . but not as boring or as dangerous as an Atlantic cruise,' said Lehrer. 'I think a heavenly *brioche* is called for after this.'

They ate the *poussins* and drank two bottles of the Gewürz-traminer. The restaurant emptied. They ate the *brioche* with a half-bottle of Sauternes. They ordered coffee and cognac and sat in the fading light of the darkening afternoon with cigars growing inches of concertinaed ash. The staff left them and the bottle and retired. The two men were well loosened up. Lehrer's cigar arm swung off the back of his chair and Felsen's legs were spread wide, a foot on either side of the table legs.

'A man,' said Lehrer heading for some pontification, pointing Felsen up with his cigar, ash still intact, 'must always do his important thinking alone.'

'What's a man's important thinking?' asked Felsen, lick-ing his lips.

'Where he wants to be, of course . . . in the future,' he sifted through the air for some more words, 'I mean, on your way you must gather your intelligence, you may ask opinion, but when you are determining your own place in the world . . . this is your private, your secret thinking . . . and if you are to be a man . . . a man of difference, then this thinking must be done alone.'

'Is this the start of an essay entitled "How to become an SS-Gruppenführer"?'

Lehrer waggled his cigar in the negative.

'That is my position only. A badge of the success of my thinking but it is not the ultimate purpose. A small example. You won the poker game the other night because your ultimate purpose was greater than mine. The adjutant told you to lose because I like to win. You wanted to stay in Berlin . . . ergo you win. My intelligence, as you indicated to me last night, was not good enough to have played that game with you.'

'But you *did* win. I'm here. You lost a little money, that's all.'

Lehrer smiled broadly, his eyes glistening with drink, amusement and triumph.

'Perhaps you're thinking now why you're so important to me,' he said. 'Don't. My ultimate purpose should be no concern of yours.'

Except that it involves me, thought Felsen, but he said: 'Perhaps I should have one of my own.'

'My point entirely,' said Lehrer shrugging massively.

'This Russian campaign . . .' Felsen started and Lehrer held up his hand.

'You will get your intelligence by degrees,' he said. 'Let me ask you something first. What happened in the skies over England last summer?'

'I'm not sure we can read the precise truth in the *Beobachter* or the *12-Uhr Blatt*.'

'Well, the precise truth,' said Lehrer leaning over and whispering into his brandy, 'is that we *lost* a great air battle. Goering will tell you otherwise. Goering has *told* me otherwise, but we all know how *he* keeps his distance from reality . . .'

'Excuse me, sir?'

'Nothing,' said Lehrer, straightening himself with a belch. 'The loss of a great air battle. What does that mean to you?'

'But we haven't been bombed in Berlin for nearly two months.'

'Berliners,' said Lehrer, despairing, 'even new Berliners, my God, man, believe me, we lost it. Now come on, tell me what that means.'

'If it's true, then we are exposed.'

'In the west and in the air.'

'So if we open up on an Eastern . . .'

'That's enough. I think you've understood something.'

'What is England with the Channel in between,' said Felsen. 'They're no threat.'

'I'm not being defeatist,' said Lehrer, 'no, no, no. But listen. We let them get away at Dunkirk. If we'd smashed them on the beaches then we'd be having this meal in London and we'd have nothing to worry about. But the English are determined. They have a friend across the Atlantic. The biggest economic force in the world. The Führer doesn't believe that, but it's true.'

'Perhaps we'll all join forces and smash the Bolsheviks.'

'That's a hopeful reading of the situation. Here's another,' said Lehrer putting down his glass and screwing his cigar in between his teeth. He chopped down his left hand on the table and said: 'The United States and England.' He removed his cigar, chopped down his right hand and mouthed the word: 'Russia.' He pressed them together. 'And all that's left is a thin scraping of liverwurst in the middle.'

'Totally and utterly fantastic,' said Felsen. 'You're forgetting . . .'

Lehrer guffawed.

'That's the thing about intelligence. It's not always what you want to hear.'

'But do *you* believe that?'

'Of course I don't. It's just a thought. Don't trouble yourself with it. We will win the war and you will be in a perfect position to become one of the most powerful businessmen in the Iberian Peninsula. Unless, of course, I've misjudged you and you're a complete fool.'

'And if we lose, as you've suggested we possibly might?'

'If you're in Berlin and you listen to the Berliners, you'll be jam in the bottom of a bomb crater. But out there on the edge of the continent you will be far away from the disaster . . .'

'Then I have every reason to thank you for forcing this job on me, Herr Gruppenführer.'

Lehrer raised his glass and said: 'Prosperity.'

They'd drunk the best part of half a bottle of cognac and when the fresh evening air hit the older man he breathed it in deeply, backed himself into the rear of the Mercedes and collapsed with his head thrown forward on to his chest. Felsen tried to think his way through their conversation while listening to the air whistling in and out of the other man's nose. It was like piecing together a jig-saw with too much sky and it wasn't long before his cheek was picking up the indent of the piping round the leather upholstery.

They woke up in the Bundesplatz in central Bern. Lehrer was groggy and on the verge of ill temper. They passed the parliament building and the Swiss National Bank before leaving the square and pulling up outside the Schweizerhof. A doorman and two bellboys rushed the car.

Their rooms were on different floors and as they went up in the lift Lehrer told Felsen he had business to attend to that night and he could have the evening to himself.

'You'll need it to read these,' he said giving him a folder from his briefcase.

'What are they?'

'Your orders. I go back to Berlin first thing in the morning. You may have some questions. Prepare them. Goodnight.'

Felsen ran a bath and flicked through his orders which started at the Swiss National Bank at 8.00 a.m. He soaked in the bath but still felt dull from the lunch. He dried off, redressed and went out into the sub-zero temperature to walk off his head. In a few short minutes he was freezing. A bar next to the railway station looked warm and he saw it contained Lehrer's driver.

He bought two beers and joined the driver.

'I envy you,' said Felsen, chinking glasses. 'You'll be back in Berlin by tomorrow night.'

'Not quite.'

'You've got the whole day, once you get on the autobahn . . .'

'We go down to Gstaad first for a few days. He likes the mountain air and . . . other things.'

'Oh yes?'

'When they're away they always like to play . . . even Himmler and you wouldn't think anyone would want to play with him. Power,' said the driver staring into his beer, 'it does it for the ladies, I can tell you.'

Felsen finished his drink and headed back to the Schweizerhof. Lehrer was still in his room. Felsen sat in the bar until he saw him coming through the reception and going out into the night. He decided to gather his own intelligence, rather than let Lehrer serve it to him in portions, and fell in behind him. They walked through the streets of the old city. There were few people about but it was easy to follow him down the dark pavements overhung by the green sandstone houses. Finally Lehrer turned down a street and when Felsen arrived at the corner there was nothing but a single lit sign which said *Ruthli* in red. He felt foolish. It meant nothing that Lehrer had a girlfriend in Bern. But curiosity drew him on.

He went into the club, handed over his hat and coat and took a table in the dark. A fat man with black brilliantined hair was playing the piano while a girl with a long red wig stood in a spotlight and sang something sad in Swiss German. He ordered a cognac. He couldn't see Lehrer. The cognac arrived and a few minutes later a girl sat down next to him. They spoke in French. His eyes got used to the dark and he found Lehrer sitting at a table close to the stage with a woman who was blocked out by the big man's shoulders.

The club filled up. The girl asked him to buy her a drink. It arrived in a bucket of ice. She was very young and too thin for his taste. She moved closer with her drink and stole one of his cigarettes. The red-wigged girl slipped off the stage with her sad song and fat pianist. There followed a drum roll and spotlights flashed around the club catching people unawares. One spot hit Lehrer's companion full in the face. She closed her eyes to it and turned her head but not quick enough. It brought Felsen out of his seat and tipped the girl's glass across the table. Cymbals clashed. The audience faded to black. The spotlights stilled on a red curtain which split and revealed a man in a top hat and tails. But there was no mistaking what Felsen had seen. The white face in the spotlight had been Eva Brücke's.

Chapter IV

Friday, 12th June 199–, Paço de Arcos, near Lisbon.

'Ladies and gentlemen,' said the mayor of Paço de Arcos, 'may I present to you Inspector José Afonso Coelho.'

It had been a hot day with a perfect blue sky and now a soft lick of a breeze was coming off the ocean to mess with the poplars and pepper trees in the public gardens. The faded pink disused cinema's walls drank in the evening light, a small girl squealed, rocking on a happy dinosaur, a big man smoked and sucked beer next to her, women greeted each other with kisses, their dresses rippled in the cool. Cars flashed past on the Marginal, a light aeroplane sputtered out to sea over the sand bank. The air was redolent of grilled sardines and a bureaucrat had a microphone.

'Zé Coelho,' said the mayor, using my more recognized name, but still not squeezing out much more interest from the *festa de Santo António* crowd which included my sixteen-year-old daughter, Olivia, my sister and brother-in-law and four of their seven children.

The mayor talked on, elaborately explaining the event in rococo Portuguese to a robustly inattentive public consisting mostly of my neighbours, who were well apprised of the bare facts which were: my wife died a year ago, I put on weight, to encourage me to take it off my daughter arranged this charity event with money pledged against each kilo lost and if I was a single gram over eighty kilos I was to have my perfect, neatly-clipped beard of twenty years shaved off in front of this rabble.

My daughter waved at me, my brother-in-law gave me a thumbs-up. I weighed in that morning at seventy-eight kilos, my stomach hadn't been as hard and flat since I was eighteen and I'd been cycling 250 kilometres a week with the police trainer. I was feeling supremely confident . . . until the mayor had started talking. There was something mannered about the crowd's insouciance, something insincere about my brother-in-law's encouragement, even my daughter's wave. I had a part to play, I knew it at that moment.

A fat man, balding with a heavy moustache, wearing a blazer, grey slacks and a wild tie arrived at my daughter's table. He kissed her on both cheeks and squeezed her shoulder. One of my nieces made room for him and after shaking everybody's hands he sat down.

There was a sudden silence. The mayor had arrived at the money. There was respect for the money.

'Two million, eight hundred and forty-three thousand, nine hundred and eighty escudos.'

The crowd went up like a flight of fantails. That . . . even I had to agree, was a hell of a lot of money for seventeen kilos of lard. I held up my hand and took the applause like a returning monarch.

The band on the stand behind me cut in on my dignity and played a jaunty little number as if I was a *toureiro* who'd just executed a blinding move against the bull, and a group of small girls in traditional costume broke out into disorganized, elephantine dancing. Two local fishermen lifted a set of scales up on to the platform. The crowd left their seats by the bar and rushed the stage. The fat man sitting next to my daughter had his pen out and was writing. The mayor was fighting people off who wanted a go with the microphone which he'd stuffed inside his suit and the speakers were carrying the crunching explosions from his armpit.

Calm was restored by my doctor mounting the podium. He balanced a pince-nez on his nose and explained the rules like an oncologist who'd been asked to give a terrible prognosis without holding back on the details. He introduced my barber who'd crept up behind me with a cloak and scissors.

I stepped out of my shoes and on to the scales. The doctor adjusted the top scale to eighty and counted down from eighty-nine. The crowd joined in. I held my head up, gave them the full force of my brand-new bridgework, closed my eyes and thought: – soufflé, helium-filled soufflé.

At eighty-three I heard the crowd wavering. I was levitating like a Brahmin. At eighty-two, my eyes snapped open, the scales middled out and the doctor gravely announced major surgery. I was outraged. The crowd roared.

The two fishermen pressed me into a chair. I lashed out. The girls in national costume fled. Did I overdo that? I remonstrated and allowed myself to be pinioned. My barber stropped his razor and looked at me out of the half-closed lids of a casual killer. The mayor shouted his eyes clean out of his head until he remembered the microphone.

'Zé, Zé, Zé,' he said, bringing forward the fat, bald, moustachioed man who'd been sitting with my family, 'this is *Senhor* Miguel da Costa Rodrigues, Director of the Banco de Oceano e Rocha. He has something to tell you.'

The man's skin texture clearly indicated he was earning five times my monthly salary per hour even when he was eating lobster on the beach.

'It gives me great pleasure, on behalf of the Banco de Oceano e Rocha to make the following offer. If Inspector Coelho will accept the doctor's ruling and allow his beard to be shaved, this cheque made out for a total of three million escudos will join the sum already pledged for charity making a total fund of nearly six million escudos.'

You'd have thought Sporting had lifted the European

55

Cup by the noise the crowd made. There was nothing to be done. Grace was imperative. Fifteen minutes later I looked like that rare thing – a Portuguese badger.

I was pretty well passed overhead to the bar *A Bandeira Vermelha* which was run by an old friend, António Borrego, who billed himself as the last communist in Portugal. The bank director was pressed in there with me, along with my daughter and the rest of my family and even the mayor found his way to my side with the microphone still in his top pocket.

António assembled the beers in glass-frosted ranks. He was a man who needed a meal, a lifetime of meals. The sort who couldn't put on weight if you sat a pig in his lap. He had a concave, white, hairy chest, eyes sunken deep into his head and untrained eyebrows off the leash. His forearms were as wiry and covered in hair as a monkey's and he had a past I didn't know the half of.

Olivia, the fat man and myself took a beer each. António had his Polaroid out to record the event for his wall of bacchanalia.

'I wouldn't know you any more,' he said to me. 'I need a reference.'

I raised my glass. Tears rolled down the side. The emotional beer.

'With my first drink for 172 days,' I said, 'I propose a toast to the health and generosity of *Senhor* Miguel da Costa Rodrigues of the Banco de Oceano e Rocha.'

Olivia told me how she knew the banker. She was at school with his daughter and cut clothes for her mother. He was wearing one of her ties. He'd even offered to set her up in the fashion business. I told him I wanted her to finish her education. An expensive international school in Carcavelos paid for by her English grandparents who didn't want a granddaughter who couldn't speak their language. The banker sighed at a missed opportunity. Olivia sulked for show. We all had parts to play.

'A toast,' said *Senhor* Rodrigues, getting into the spirit, 'to Olivia Coelho for making all this possible.'

We drank again and Olivia planted a red 'O' on my new white cheek.

'One more thing,' I said to the packed bar buzzing with beer, 'who fixed the scales?'

There were two seconds of frost-brittle silence until I smiled, a glass smashed and the barber came in with a plastic bag which he presented to me.

'Your clippings,' he said weighing it with a kiss. 'A two-kilo bed for your cat.'

'Don't tell me that now.'

'It must have been what you had living in there that weighed,' said the mayor. We all looked at him. He fingered his microphone. António put three more beers on the counter. Olivia and I turned into each other.

'Me?' I said to her quietly. 'I think it was the past all tangled up in it.'

She licked a finger and wiped the lipstick off my cheek, her eyes brim-full for a moment.

'You're right,' said António, suddenly between us, 'history's a weight, a dead weight too . . . isn't that right *Senhor* Rodrigues?'

Senhor Rodrigues belched politely into his hand, not used to proletarian drink.

'History repeats itself,' he said and even António laughed – the communist who can smell the pork meat of a capitalist when they're roasting him as far away as the Alentejo.

'You're right,' said António. 'History's only a weight to those that lived it. For the next generation it's no heavier than a few school books and forgotten with a glass of beer and the latest CD.'

'Eh, António,' I said, 'have a beer yourself. It's Friday night, tomorrow's your saint's day, the poor people of Paço de Arcos are nearly six million better off and I'm back on the drink. The new history.'

António smiled and said: 'To the future.'

We all went out to eat that night, even *Senhor* Rodrigues who might not have been used to the metal tables and chairs but appreciated the food. It was the meal my stomach had growled over for six months. *Ameijoas à Bulhão Pato*, clams in white wine, garlic and fresh coriander, *robalo grelhado*, grilled sea bass caught off the cliffs at Cabo da Roca that morning, *borrego assado*, Alentejo lamb cooked until it's falling apart. Red wine from Borba. Coffee as strong as a mulatto's kiss. And to finish *aguardente amarela*, the yellow fiery one.

Senhor Rodrigues left for his house in Cascais at the *aguardente* stage. Olivia went to a club in Cascais with a bunch of her friends soon after. I gave her the taxi fare home. I drank two more *amarelinhas* and went to bed with a litre of water inside me and two aspirins, the pillow soft and cool against my my naked burning cheeks.

I woke in the night for ten seconds, confused in the darkness and feeling as big and as solid as the central pillar in a motorway bridge. I'd dreamt luridly but one image stuck – a cliff-top walk in the dark of an evening, a sheer drop close by somewhere, the sea roar out there, its saltine prickle bursting up from the rocks below. Fear, apprehension and excitement rose up and I fell into more sleep.

It was at about that time that a girl started to make her dent in the sand no more than a few hundred metres away from where I was sleeping. Her eyes wide open, she moonbathed to a night full of stars, her blood slack, her skin cold and hard as fresh tuna.

Chapter V

Plates were crashing on to a marble floor. Plates were crashing and smashing and endlessly shattering on the marble floor. I surfaced into the brutal noise, the harshest reality there is, of a phone going off in a hangover at 6.00 a.m. I wrenched the handset to my ear. The blissful silence, the faint sea hiss of a distant mobile. My boss Eng. Jaime Leal Narciso gave me a good morning and I tried to find some moisture in my beak to reply.

'Zé?' he asked.

'Yes, it's me,' I said, which came out in a whisper as if I had his wife next to me.

'You're all right then,' he said, but didn't wait for the reply. 'Look, the body of a young girl's been found on the beach at Paço de Arcos and I want . . .'

Those words trampolined me off the bed, the phone jack yanked the handset from my grip and I cannoned off the door frame into the hall. I thundered down the distressed strip of carpet and wrenched the door open. Her clothes lay in a track from the door to the bed – clumpy big-heeled shoes, black silk top, lilac shirt, black bra, black flares. Olivia was twisted into her sheet face down, her bare arms and shoulders spread, her black hair, as soft and shiny as sable, splashed across the pillow.

I drank heavily in the bathroom until my belly was taut with water. I snatched the phone to my ear and lay down on the bed again.

'*Bom dia, Senhor Engenheiro,*' I said, addressing him by his degree in science, as was usual.

'If you'd given me two seconds I'd have told you she was blonde.'

'I should have checked last night but . . .' I paused, synapses clashed painfully, 'why are you calling me at six in the morning to tell me about a body on the beach? Throw your mind back to the weekend roster and you'll find I'm off duty.'

'Well, the point is you're two hundred metres from the situation and Abílio, who *is* on duty, lives in Seixal which as you know . . . It would be . . .'

'I'm in no condition to . . .' I said, my brain still blundering around.

'Ah yes. I forgot. How was it? How are you?'

'Cooler about the face.'

'Good.'

'More fragile in the head.'

'They say it could get up to forty degrees today,' he said, not listening.

'Where are you, sir?'

'On my mobile.'

A good answer.

'There's some good news, Zé,' he said, quickly. 'I'm sending someone to help you.'

'Who's that?'

'A young guy. Very keen. Good for leg work.'

'Whose son is he?'

'I didn't catch that?'

'You know I don't like to tread on anybody's toes.'

'This line's breaking up,' he shouted. 'Look, he's very capable but he could use some experience. I can't think of anybody better.'

'Does that mean nobody else would have him?'

'His name is Carlos Pinto,' he said, ignoring my question. 'I want him to see your approach. Your very particular approach. You know, you have this ability with people. They talk to you. I want him to see how you operate.'

'Does he know where he's going?'

'I've told him to meet you in that communist's bar you like so much. He's bringing the latest missing persons printout.'

'Will he recognize me?'

'I've told him to look for someone who's just had his beard shaved off after twenty-odd years. An interesting test don't you think?'

The signal finally broke up. He knew. Narciso knew. They all knew. Even if I'd been a stick insect those scales would still have come out at eighty-two kilos. You can't trust anybody these days, not your own daughter, not your own family, not even the *Polícia Judiciária*.

I showered and dried off in front of the mirror. Old eyes, new face looked back at me. Having just levered myself over forty maybe I was too old for this kind of change and yet, just as my wife had said I would, I looked five years younger without the beard.

Sunlight was beginning to colour the blue into the ocean just visible from the bathroom window. A fishing smack pushed through it and for the first time in a year I had that same surge of hope, a feeling that today could be the first day of a different life.

I dressed in a white long-sleeved shirt (short sleeves lack gravitas), a light grey suit and a pair of black brogues. I selected one of the thirty ties Olivia had made for me, a quiet one, not one that a pathologist would like to trap in a petri dish. I went to the top of the shabby wooden stairs and had a momentary feeling of a man who's just been told to take a grand piano down on his own.

I left the house, my crumbling mansion which I inherited from my parents at a peppercorn rent, and headed for the café. The plaster was flaking off the garden wall which was reckless with unpruned bougainvillea. I made a mental note to let the riot continue.

61

From the public gardens I looked back at the faded pink house whose long windows had lost all their white paint and thought that if I didn't have to go and inspect bludgeoned, brutalized bodies I could persuade myself that I was a retired count whose annuity was in a vice.

I was nervous, part of me willing this day not to proceed to my first meeting with a new person and my face naked – all that sizing up, all that accommodation, all that . . . and no mask too.

A corner of pepper trees in the gardens whispered to each other like parents who didn't want to wake the kids. Beyond them, António, who never slept, who hadn't slept, he once told me, since 1964, was winding down his red canvas awning which sported only the name of his bar and no advertising for beer or coffee.

'I didn't expect to see you before midday,' he said.

'Nor did I,' I said. 'But at least you recognized me.'

I followed him in and he started the coffee grinder which was like a wirewool scrub on my eyeballs. Yesterday's Polaroid was already up on his memorial wall. I didn't recognize myself at first. The young-looking one between the fat man and the pretty girl. Except that Olivia wasn't looking very girlish either, more . . . more of a . . .

'I thought you were off today,' said António.

'I was but . . . a body's been found on the beach. Anyone been in yet?'

'No,' he said, looking out vaguely in the direction of the beach. 'Washed up?'

'The body? I don't know.'

Standing in the doorway wearing a dark suit which had been cut in Salazar's time and had knuckle-brushing sleeves was a young guy. He approached the bar stiffly as if it was his first time on TV and asked for a *bica*, the one-inch shot of caffeine which adrenalizes a few million Portuguese hearts every morning.

He watched the black and tan mixture trickle into the

cups. António turned the grinder off and the golfball cleaner effect on my eyeballs eased.

The young guy put two sugar sachets into his coffee and asked for a third. I flicked him one of mine. He stirred it lengthily to a syrup.

'You must be Inspector *Senhor Doutor* José Afonso Coelho,' he said, not looking at me but glancing up at the hammer and sickle António kept behind the bar. His relics.

'*Engenheiro* Narciso will be pleased,' I said, glancing around the empty bar. 'How did you guess?'

His head flicked round. He must have been mid-twenties but he looked no different than he had done at sixteen. His dark brown eyes connected with mine. He was irritated.

'You look vulnerable,' he said, and nodded that into me for effect.

António's eyebrows changed places.

'An interesting observation *agente* Pinto,' I said grimly. 'Most people would have commented on the whiteness of my cheeks. And there's no need to call me *Doutor*. It doesn't apply.'

'I thought you had a degree in Modern Languages.'

'But from London University, and there you don't get called a doctor until you have a PhD. Just call me Zé or Inspector.'

We shook hands. I liked him. I didn't know why I liked him. Narciso thought I liked everybody but he had that confused in his mind with 'getting on with people' which he couldn't do himself because he was colder and rougher-skinned than a shark with blood on its radar. The fact was, I'd only ever loved one woman and the people I'd call close were in single figures. And now Carlos. What was it about him? That suit? Old-fashioned, too big and wool in summer said no vanity . . . and no money. His hair? Black, durable, disobedient, short as a trooper's, said, to me anyway: serious and dependable. His irritated look said: defiant, touchy. His first words? Direct, candid, perceptive said: uncompromising. A difficult combination for a policeman. I could see why nobody else would have him.

'I didn't know about London,' he said.

'My father was over there,' I said. 'So what *do* you know about?'

'Your father was an army officer. You spent a lot of time in Africa. In Guinea. You've been seventeen years on the force, eight of them as a homicide detective.'

'Have you accessed my file?'

'No. I asked *Engenheiro* Narciso. He didn't tell me everything,' he said, sucking in his thick coffee. 'He didn't say what rank your father was for instance.'

António's eyebrows switched back again and a glint of partisan interest came from deep in his eye sockets. A political question: was my father one of the younger officers who started the 1974 revolution, or old guard? Both men waited.

'My father was a colonel,' I said.

'How did he end up in London?'

'Ask him,' I said, nodding to António, no appetite for this.

'How long have you got?' he asked, gripping the edge of the bar.

'No time at all,' I said. 'There's a dead body waiting for us on the beach.'

We crossed the gardens to the Marginal and went through the underpass to a small car park in front of the Clube Desportivo de Paço de Arcos. There was a dried-fish and diesel smell amongst the old boats lying on their sides or propped up on tyres amongst rusted trailers and rubbish bins. A halved oil drum was smoking with two planks of wood burning to heat a pan of oil. A couple of fishermen I knew were ignoring the scene and sorting through the marker buoys and crab and lobster pots in front of their corrugated-iron work shacks. I nodded and they looked across to the crowd that had already formed even at this early hour.

The line of people that had gathered at the low stone balustrade on the edge of the beach and along the harbour wall were looking down on to the sand. Some broad-backed working women had taken time out to distress themselves over the tragedy, muttering through their fingers:

'*Ai Mãe, coitadinha.*' O mother, poor little thing.

There were four or five *Polícia de Segurança Pública* boys ignoring the total contamination of the crime scene and talking to two members of the *Polícia Marítima*. Another two hours and there'd be girls on the beach to chat up and then not even the *Polícia Marítima* would have had a look in. I introduced myself and asked them who'd found the body. They pointed to a fisherman sitting further along the harbour wall. The position of the body above the flattened sand of the highest tide mark told me that the victim hadn't been washed up but dumped, thrown, from just about where I was standing, off the harbour wall. It was a three-metre drop.

The *Polícia Marítima* were satisfied that the body hadn't been washed up but wanted it confirmed from the pathologist that there was no water in the lungs. They gave me authority to start my investigation. I sent the PSP men along the harbour wall to move the onlookers back to the road.

The police photographer made himself known and I told him to take shots from above as well as down on the beach.

The girl's naked body was twisted at the waist, her left shoulder buried in the sand. Her face, with just a single graze on the forehead, was turned upwards, eyes wide open. She was young, her breasts still high and rounded not far below her clavicles. The muscle of her torso was visible below the rib cage and she carried a little puppy fat on her belly. Her hips lay flat, her left leg straight, the right turned out at the knee, its heel close to her buttock and

65

right hand which was thrown behind her. I'd put her at under sixteen and I could see why the fisherman hadn't bothered to go down to look for life. Her face was pale apart from the cut, the lips purple and her intensely blue eyes vacant. There were no footprints around the body. I let the photographer down there to take his close-ups.

The fisherman told me he'd been on his way to his repair shack at 5.30 a.m. when he saw the body. He knew she was dead from the look of her and he didn't go down on to the beach but straight along the Marginal, beyond the boatyard of the Clube Desportivo, to the *Direcção de Farois* to ask them to phone the *Polícia Marítima*.

I squeezed my chin and found flesh instead of beard. I looked dumbly at my palm as if my hand was in some way responsible. I needed new tics for my new face. I needed a new job for my new life.

Dead girl on the beach, the seagulls screeched.

Perhaps being exposed was making me more sensitive to the minutiae of everyday life.

The pathologist arrived, a small dark woman called Fernanda Ramalho, who ran marathons when she wasn't examining dead bodies.

'I was right,' she said, her eyes coming back to me after I'd introduced Carlos Pinto, who was writing everything down in his notebook.

'The best kind of pathologists always are, Fernanda.'

'You're handsome. There were those who thought you were hiding a weak chin under there.'

'Is that what people think these days,' I said, running for cover, 'that men grow beards to hide something? When I was a kid everybody had a beard.'

'Why *do* men grow beards?' she asked, genuinely perplexed.

'The same reason dogs lick their balls,' said Carlos, pen poised. Our heads snapped round. 'Because they can,' he finished.

Fernanda enquired with an eyebrow.

'It's his first day,' I said, which annoyed him again. Twice in less than an hour. This boy had shingles of the mind. Fernanda took a step back as if he might start lapping. Why didn't Narciso tell me the kid wasn't house-trained?

The photographer finished his close-ups and I nodded to Fernanda who was standing by with her bag open wearing a pair of surgical gloves.

'Check your list,' I said to Carlos, who'd disassociated himself from me. 'See if there's a fifteen/sixteen-year-old girl, blonde hair, blue eyes, 1.65 metres, fifty-five kilos . . . Any distinguishing marks, Fernanda?'

She held up her hand. Muttering into her dictaphone she inspected the abrasion on the girl's forehead. Carlos flicked through the missing-persons sheets, plenty of names in the black hole. More cars flashed by on the Marginal. Fernanda minutely inspected the girl's pubic hair and vagina.

'Start with the ones who've gone in the last twenty-four hours,' I said. Carlos sighed.

Fernanda unrolled a plastic sheet in front of her. She removed a thermometer from the girl's armpit and eased her over on to her front. Some rigor mortis had already started. With a pair of tweezers she picked her way through a mash of hair, blood and sand at the back of the girl's head. She reached for a plastic evidence sachet and fed something into it and marked it up. She sheafed the girl's hair and kissed the dictaphone again. She looked down the length of the girl's body, parted the buttocks with finger and thumb speaking all the time. She clicked off the dictaphone.

'Mole at the back of the neck, in the hairline, central. Coffee-coloured birthmark inside left thigh fifteen centimetres above the knee,' she shouted.

'If it was her parents who reported it, that should be enough,' I said.

'Catarina Sousa Oliveira,' said Carlos, handing me the sheet.

An ambulance arrived. Two paramedics walked to the back. One pulled out a stretcher, the other carried the bodybag. Fernanda stood back from the body and brushed herself off.

I walked down the harbour wall to the sea. It was barely 7.15 a.m. and the sun already had some needle in it. To my left, looking east, was the mouth of the Tagus and the massive pillars of the 25th April suspension bridge which floated footless in a heavy mist. With the sun higher the sea wasn't so much blue any more as a panel-beaten silver sheet. Small fishing boats, moored off the beach, rocked on the dazzling surface in the morning's breeze. A passenger jet came in low above the river and banked over the cement works and beaches of Caparica south of the Tagus to make its approach into the airport north of the city – tourists arriving for golf and days in the sun. Further west and out to sea, a tugboat pulled a dredger alongside the Búgio lighthouse, Lisbon's scaled-down, antique Alcatraz. At the end of the wall a fisherman reached back with his rod, took two steps and sent his hook out into the ocean with a violent whip of his shoulders and flick of his wrists.

'She was hit hard on the back of the head,' said Fernanda, behind me. 'I can't say what it was yet but something like a wrench, a hammer or a piece of pipe. The blow propelled her forward and her forehead connected with a solid object which I'm ninety percent certain was a tree but I'll do some more picking around back at the Institute. The blow must have knocked her unconscious and would have killed her in time but the guy made sure with his thumbs on her windpipe.'

'The guy?'

'Sorry, my assumption.'

'It didn't happen here, did it?'

'No. Her left clavicle was broken. She was dropped from the harbour wall and I found this in her hair, in the wound.'

The sachet contained a single pine needle. I called a PSP officer over.

'Sexual assault?'

'There's been sexual activity but no evidence of assault or violent entry but I'll be able to tell you more later.'

'Can you give me a time of death?'

'About thirteen to fourteen hours ago.'

'How do you work that out?' asked Carlos.

His aggression got the full reply.

'I checked with the meteorological office before I came out. They told me the temperature didn't get much below 20°C last night. The body would have cooled at around 0.75 to 1°C per hour. I recorded her body temperature at 24.6°C and found rigor mortis in the smaller muscles and just beginning in the bigger ones. Therefore my deduction, based on experience, is that you're looking for someone who murdered her between five and six yesterday afternoon but it's not an exact science as Inspector Coelho knows.'

'Anything else?' I asked.

'Nothing under her nails. She was a nervy type. Hardly anything left of them. The nail on the index finger of the right hand was torn, by that I mean bloody . . . if that's any help.'

Fernanda left followed by the ambulance men who were staggering across the beach and up the steps of the harbour wall, the body zipped up in its bag. I asked the PSP men to search the car park and then take a squad up the Marginal towards Cascais to the nearest pine trees. I wanted clothing. I wanted a heavy metal object or tool.

'Give me your ideas, *agente* Pinto,' I said.

'Knocked unconscious in some pine woods, stripped, raped, strangled, thrown in a car, driven down the Marginal, ultimately from Cascais direction, which is the only way in to this small car park, and dumped off the harbour wall.'

69

'OK. But Fernanda said no violent entry.'

'She was unconscious.'

'Unless her murderer had the foresight to bring his own lubricant and condom there would be evidence . . . abrasions, bruising, that kind of thing.'

'Wouldn't a rapist think of that?'

'He hits the girl from behind, smacks her head against a tree with a blow hard enough to kill her but he strangles her for good measure. My gut tells me that he was intending to kill rather than rape but I may be wrong . . . let's see what Fernanda says in her lab report.'

'Murdered or raped they took some risks.'

'They? Interesting.'

'I don't know why I said that . . . fifty-five kilos isn't that much.'

'You're right though . . . why dump her here? In full view of the Marginal . . . cars going up and down all night. Not that this part is particularly well lit . . .'

'Somebody local?' asked Carlos.

'She's not a local girl. The contact addresses for Catarina Oliveira are Lisbon and Cascais. And anyway, what's local? There's quarter of a million people living within a kilometre of where we're standing. But if she did come here and meet a creep, why kill her in the pine trees and dump her on the beach? Why kill her in any pine woods in the Lisbon area and bring her here to this spot?'

'Is it relevant that *you* live near here?'

'I suppose you don't know why you said that either?'

'Possibly because you were thinking it.'

'And you can read my thoughts . . . all on your first day?'

'Maybe you're revealing more than you think now your beard's gone.'

'That's a lot to read off any man's cheeks, *agente* Pinto.'

Chapter VI

Saturday, 13th June 199–, Paço de Arcos, near Lisbon.

We worked the boatyard next to the harbour and came up with nothing. We crossed the Marginal using the underpass and talked to the people who were clearing up last night's mess in the *Bombeiros Voluntarios* tent but none of them had been working the night shift. The restaurant/café in the gardens was closed. We walked up to the pine woods to see how the PSP men were getting on. They had the usual array of used condoms, syringes and bleached and tattered pornography. No such thing as an innocent pine wood in this area. I told them to bag the lot and send it up to Fernanda at the Institute of Forensic Medicine in Lisbon. Carlos and I went back to António and had some toast and more coffee.

At 08.30 I put a call in to Dr Aquilino Dias Oliveira who I assumed was the girl's father and, given his two addresses in Lisbon and Cascais, was not engaged in the great financial struggle that the rest of us were. It was a Saturday so I tried the Cascais number first and thought I was wrong until he picked it up at the twelfth ring and groggily agreed to see us in half an hour's time. We got into my black 1972 Alfa Romeo, which was not, as many thought, a classic car, just an old car, and it started without having to draw on any reserves of bravery. We headed west on the Marginal with Carlos pinned to his seat by the belt that was stuck at one length and for a girl Olivia's size.

There were big fans of Cascais but I wasn't one of them. It used to be a small fishing village with houses falling

71

down steep cataracts of cobbled streets to the harbour and port. Now it was a townplanner's nightmare, unless you were one of the townplanners who'd passed the numerous development projects in which case you'd be living in a dream elsewhere. It was a tourist town with an indigenous population of women who dressed to shop, and men who shouldn't be allowed out of a nightclub. Real life had been stripped out and replaced with an international cosmopolitanism which appealed to a lot of people who had money, and about as many again who wanted to ease it away from them.

We rolled in past the supermarket, the railway station and an electronic signboard which told us that it was 28°C at 08.55 and we should get some insurance. The fish market was wrapping up for the morning. The lobster and crab pots were piled high in front of the Hotel Bahia. The fort, square and ugly, out on the point, dominated. I drove up a cobbled street at the back of the town hall and turned into a tree-lined, heavily-shaded square, cool and sombre with wealth, in the old part of town. Dr Oliveira's traditional villa on two floors was large and silent in the breathless morning. Carlos Pinto sniffed like a dog that's picked up the whiff of the first possible scrap of the day.

'Pine,' he said.

'The pine needle angle could be a lot of work in this area, *agente* Pinto.'

'There's a pine tree in the back garden,' he said looking down the side of the house.

We let ourselves in by the front gate and went past a pillar of red bougainvillea to the back of the house. The pine tree was huge and shut out the light to the garden. The floor beneath it was a perfect brown carpet of dried needles.

'Put your foot on that,' I said.

Carlos' foot crunched through a couple of inches of needles.

'I don't think you could kill someone on that and leave it . . .'

'*Bom dia, senhores*,' said a voice behind us. 'And you are . . . ?'

'We were admiring your pine tree,' said Carlos, electing to be the idiot.

'I'm going to cut it down,' said the thin, tall, erect man with white brilliantined hair, combed in rails off a high forehead and curling at the collar. 'It kills the light in the back of the house and makes the maid feel gloomy. You are the *Polícia Judiciária*, I take it?'

We introduced ourselves and followed him into the house. He wore a lightweight, English checked shirt, grey slacks with turn-ups and brown loafers. He walked with his hands behind his back and stooped a little like a thoughtful priest. The parquet-floored corridor was lined with portraits of ancestors depressed at being cooped up in the dark. His study had more parquet flooring and Arraiolos carpets of some quality and antiquity. His desk was large and made out of walnut and had a brown leather chair behind it which was shiny where he'd buffed it with his back. Four lamps, supported by polished women carved from jet, provided light. The red bougainvillea outside had eclipsed the sunshine. He sat us down at a three-piece suite in a book-lined corner of the room. Only a lawyer would have so many books in the same bindings. An ormolu clock ticked as if each tick was going to be its last.

Dr Oliveira was in no hurry to talk. As we sat down he fitted his dark-skinned face into a pair of bifocals and searched his desk for something he didn't find. The maid came in and laid out coffee without looking at us. There was a photograph of the dead girl on a shelf squeezed in between some old paperbacks, thrillers, written in English.

Catarina Oliveira was smiling at the camera. Her blue eyes were wide open but they didn't match what her mouth was doing. Something tightened in my chest. I'd seen the same look in Olivia's eyes after I'd told her that her mother was dead.

'That's her,' said Dr Oliveira, his white eyebrows jumping over the frames of his bifocals.

He was old for the father of a fifteen-year-old girl – late sixties in his body and more than that in the lines and creases of his face and neck. He should have been trying to remember the names of his grandchildren. He leaned forward and picked out a small cigar from a jade box on the desk top. He licked his lips which became the colour of pig's liver and screwed the cigar between them. He lit it. The maid rattled a coffee cup down in front of him and reversed out of the room.

'When did you last see her?' I asked, putting the photograph back.

'Thursday night. I left my Lisbon house early on Friday morning. I had to get to my office to prepare for a day in court.'

'What sort of law do you practise?'

'Corporate law. Tax. I've never done criminal work if you think that's relevant.'

'Did your wife see Catarina on Friday morning?'

'She dropped her off at school and came down here. It's what she does in the summer at the weekends.'

'And Catarina makes her own way here after school . . . on the train . . . from Cais do Sodré?'

'She's usually here by six or seven o'clock.'

'She was reported missing at nine.'

'I got back here at about half-past-eight. My wife had been here about an hour worrying, we phoned everybody we could think of and then I reported her missing at . . .'

'Does she have any particular friends? A boyfriend?'

'She sings in a band. She spends most of her spare time with them,' he said, leaning back with his coffee. 'Boyfriends? None that I know of.'

'Is that a school band?'

74

'They're all at the university. Two boys – Valentim and Bruno – and a girl. The girl is called . . . Teresa. Yes. Teresa, that's it.'

'All of them a lot older than Catarina.'

'They must be twenty, twenty-one, the boys. The girl, I don't know. Probably the same but she wears black and uses purple lipstick so it's difficult to tell.'

'We'll need all their details,' I said, and Dr Oliveira reached for a pad and began leafing through his address book. He scribbled down names and addresses. 'Is she your only child?'

'From this marriage, yes. I have four grown-up children. Teresa . . .' he let the name drift with his cigar smoke, his eyes glanced at a photograph on his desk.

'Is that your current wife?' I asked, and looked at the same photograph, which was of the four children from his previous marriage.

'My *second* wife,' he replied, annoyed with himself. 'Catarina's her only child.'

'Is your wife here, *Senhor Doutor*?' I asked.

'She's upstairs. She's not well. She's sleeping. She takes . . . she's taken something to help her sleep. I don't think it would be a good idea . . .'

'Is she a nervous woman . . . ordinarily?'

'When it comes to Catarina, when it comes to her only daughter missing the whole night, when it comes to a phone call from the *Polícia Judiciária* first thing in the morning . . . then yes, she becomes . . .'

'How would you describe their present relationship? Catarina and your wife.'

'What?' he said, looking across to Carlos as if he might be able to clarify this sort of question.

'It's not always a simple relationship – mother and daughter.'

'I don't know what you're driving at,' he said, coughing a half-laugh.

'The Chinese character for "strife" is represented by two women under the same roof.'

Dr Aquilino Oliveira supported himself with the heels of his palms on the edge of the desk and looked out at me over the rims of his glasses. His dark brown eyes reached in.

'She's never run off without a word before,' he said, quietly.

'Does that mean they have been known to disagree?'

'Strife,' he said, ruminating over the word. 'Catarina has been practising at being a woman, yes, I see what you mean. That's very interesting.'

'By "practising", *Senhor Doutor*, you mean sexual experimentation?' I asked, easing myself down on to some of my own eggshells.

'It has been a concern of mine.'

'Do you think she might have got out of her depth?'

The lawyer sucked himself in and then sagged to one side of his chair. Was it acting or real? It was surprising the number of people who resorted to soap in times of stress . . . but a lawyer of this calibre?

'Last summer, Teresa, my wife, doing the usual Friday routine forgot something in the Lisbon house. She drove back around lunchtime and found Catarina in bed with a man. There was a big fight . . .'

'Catarina would have been fourteen then, *Senhor Doutor*. What did you make of it?'

'I think that's what kids do given half the chance . . . less than half the chance. But, for me, it's different. I've had four children already. I've been through all that. I've made mistakes. I've tried to learn. It's made me more understanding . . . more liberal. I didn't get angry. We talked. She was very straight, very candid, even brazen as they are, kids, these days . . . showing off that they're adult too.'

Carlos had been sitting with his coffee cup ten centimetres from his mouth for the last two minutes, transfixed by the exchange. I shot him a look and he ducked into his coffee.

'When you said "man", your wife "found Catarina in bed with a man", that sounds as if her companion was older than . . . than one of the "boys" in the band for instance. Was that the case?'

'You're a careful listener, Inspector Coelho.'

'How old was he, Dr Oliveira?' I asked, volleying his flattery straight back at him.

'Thirty-two.'

'That's very precise. Did Catarina tell you that?'

'She didn't have to. I knew the man. He was my wife's younger brother.'

The ormolu clock nearly missed a tick.

'Didn't that make you very angry, Dr Oliveira?' I said. 'You don't have to be a lawyer to know that your brother-in-law broke the law – that's child abuse.'

'I'm hardly going to run him in, am I?'

'I didn't mean that.'

'I'm a mixture, Inspector Coelho. I was an account-ant before I became a lawyer. I'm sixty-seven years old now and my wife is thirty-seven. I married her when I was fifty-one and she was twenty-one. When she was fourteen . . .'

'But she wasn't, *Senhor Doutor*, when you knew her. You weren't taking advantage of a minor.'

'That's correct.'

'Perhaps, after this incident, Catarina, in your talk with her, gave you some reason to be tolerant with your brother-in-law?' I said, struggling with the sentence as if it was a giant octopus.

'If, by that, you mean, she wasn't a virgin, Inspector Coelho . . . you would be right. You might also be shocked to know that she admitted to seducing my brother-in-law,' he replied, copying my syntax.

'Do you think she was telling the truth?'

'Don't imagine that they're thinking like we were when we were fourteen.'

'Did drug-use come up in this conversation?'

'She admitted to smoking hashish. It's very common as you know. Nothing more. She wouldn't . . . I know,' he faltered. 'I'm beginning to see from your expression, Inspector Coelho, that after a conversation like that you think I should have locked her in a tower until she was twenty.'

I wasn't thinking that. I was thinking a whole turmoil of things but not that. I've got to get this face under control.

'Perhaps you're a more advanced ethical thinker than most Portuguese, *Senhor Doutor*.'

'We're nearly a generation beyond the dictatorial age and prohibition makes for a criminal society. I don't call that advanced . . . just observant.'

'You said she wouldn't have admitted to using anything more than hashish . . .'

'My son's a heroin addict . . . *was* a heroin addict.'

'Catarina knew him?'

'She still knows him. He lives in Porto.'

'He's off it?'

'It wasn't easy.'

I remembered his stooped clerical walk. With these burdens he should have been bent double.

'You're still a practising lawyer.'

'Not so much now. Some corporate clients keep me on a consultative basis and I represent a few friends on tax points.'

'In these calls on Friday night, did you speak to any of her teachers?'

'The one I wanted to speak to, the one who taught her on Friday afternoon, wasn't available. You know . . . it was Santo António . . .'

He wrote down her name, address and number without my asking.

'I'd like some shots of your daughter and I think we should speak to your wife now, if possible.'

'It would be better if you came back later,' he said, and tore off the sheet of paper and handed it to me. 'My mobile number's on there too, if you hear anything.'

'You gave your daughter a lot of freedom, would she have gone to the Santo António celebrations without telling you?'

'Friday night we always have dinner together and she likes to go down to the bars in Cascais afterwards.'

We left the house. He didn't see us out. The maid watched us from the end of the corridor. It was hotter outside after the chill of the house. We sat in the car with the windows down. I stared into the square beyond the line of trees seeing nothing.

'Shouldn't you have told him?' asked Carlos. 'I think you should have told him.'

'A complex individual, the lawyer, don't you think?'

'His daughter is *dead*.'

'I just had a feeling that by not telling him we might learn more,' I said, giving Carlos the paper. 'My decision.'

Fifteen minutes later a flame-red Morgan convertible, containing the lawyer in dark glasses, eased into the street. We followed him around the square, past the fort, through the centre of Cascais and back on to the Marginal heading for Lisbon. The day seemed to be taking shape.

'See if he looks at the beach when we pass Paço de Arcos,' I said.

Carlos, braced as an astronaut for lift-off, didn't blink but the lawyer's head didn't turn. It didn't turn until we cruised into Belém past the Bunker, or the new Cultural Centre as it is sometimes known, and the gothic intricacies of the Jerónimos monastery. Then, it suddenly snapped to the right to catch the ship's prow monument to the Discoveries – Henry and his men looking out across the Tagus at a gigantic container ship nosing out into the well-known, or maybe it was the blonde in the BMW overtaking him in the inside lane.

'Well?' asked Carlos.

I didn't answer.

The mist had cleared from around the bridge, the cranes being used to sling the new rail link underneath it saluted Cristo Rei, the massive Christ statue on the south bank, whose outspread arms reminded us that it could all be possible. I didn't need reminding. I knew it. Lisbon had changed more in the last ten years than in the two and a half centuries since the earthquake.

It had been like a mouth that hadn't seen a dentist for too long. Rotten buildings had been yanked out, old streets torn up, squares ripped out, centuries of plaque scraped off, façades drilled out and filled with a pristine amalgam of concrete and tile, gaps plugged with offices and shopping centres and apartment blocks. Moles had tunnelled new stretches of Metro and a brand-new intestine of cabling had been fed into the root canals of the city. We'd wired in new roads, built a new bridge, extended the airport. We're the new gnashers in Europe's Iberian jaw. We can smile now and nobody faints.

We thundered over the patchy tarmac at Alcântara. An old tram dinged past the Santos station. To the right the steel hulls of freighters flashed between the stacks of containers and advertisements for Super Bock beer. On the left office blocks and apartment buildings climbed up the hills of Lisbon. We ran the light at Cais do Sodré as a new tram, a mobile hoarding for Kit Kat, hissed behind us. I lit my first cigarette of the day – SG Ultralights – hardly smoking at all.

'Maybe he's just going to his office,' said Carlos. 'Do a bit of work on a Saturday morning.'

'Why speculate when you can call him on his mobile?'

'You're kidding.'

'I'm kidding.'

The yellow façade and the massive triumphal arch of the Terreiro do Paço sucked us away from the river towards the grid of the Baixa valley between the hills of the Fort of São Jorge and the Bairro Alto. The temperature hit thirty degrees. Fat, ugly bronzes loafed in the square. The lawyer's Morgan cut right down the Rua da Alfândega and left into Rua da Madalena which climbed steeply before dropping away into the new-look Largo de Martim Moniz with its glass and steel box kiosks and disinterested fountains. We skirted the square and accelerated up the slope of the Rua de São Lázaro past the Hospital de São José and into the square dominated by the pedimented, pillared façade of the Institute of Medicine. We parked close to the statue of Dr Sousa Martins, his plinth heaped with stone tablets of thanks, wax limbs and candles. Dr Oliveira was already parked and walking down the hill to the Institute of Forensic Medicine. Carlos took his jacket off and revealed a long dark stripe of sweat-soaked shirt.

By the time we arrived in the Institute the lawyer was using all his training to get what he wanted – the staff, however, were more difficult to impress than a judge. I left him with Carlos and arranged for the body to be displayed. An orderly brought in Dr Oliveira, who had removed his dark glasses and now wore the bifocals. The assistant drew the sheet back. The lawyer blinked twice and nodded. He took the sheet from the assistant and pulled it back to see the whole body which he inspected closely. He drew the sheet back over her face and left the room.

We found him standing outside in the cobbled street. He was cleaning his sunglasses endlessly and wearing an expression of extreme determination.

'I am sorry for your loss, *Senhor Doutor*,' I said. 'I apologize for not telling you earlier. You have every right to be angry.'

He didn't look angry. The initial determination had flagged and the confusion of emotions that had followed had left his face strangely flaccid. He looked as if he was concentrating on his breathing.

'Let's walk up here and sit in the gardens in the shade,' I said.

We walked on either side of him through the cars, past the good doctor's statue which rather than being imbued with the success of the cured was, in its pigeon-shit-spattered state, infused with the sadness of those who'd been lost. The three of us sat on a bench in surprising cool some distance from the pigeon-feeders and the coffee-drinkers idling in plastic chairs around the café.

'You may be surprised to know that I am glad that you are investigating the murder of my daughter,' said the lawyer. 'I know you have a difficult job and I also realize that I am a suspect.'

'I always start with those closest to the victim . . . it's a sad fact.'

'Ask your questions, then I must go back to my wife.'

'Of course,' I said. 'When did you finish in court yesterday?'

'About half-past-four.'

'Where did you go?'

'To my office. I keep a small office in the Chiado on Calçada Nova de S. Francisco. I went by the Metro from Campo Pequeno, changed at Rotunda and got off at Restauradores. I walked to the Elevador, took that up to the Chiado and continued on foot to my office. It took me maybe half an hour and I spent half an hour there.'

'Did you speak to anybody?'

'I took one call.'

'From who?'

'The Minister of Internal Administration asking me up to the Jockey Club for a drink. I left my office just after half-past-five and as you may know it's only a two-minute walk to Rua Garrett from there.'

I nodded. It was cast-iron. I asked him to write down

the names of the people who were with him at the Jockey Club. Carlos gave him his notebook for the purpose.

'Can I talk to your wife before you tell her what's happened?'

'If you follow me back there, yes. If not, I won't wait.'

'We'll be right behind you.'

He gave me the paper and we walked back towards the cars.

'How did you know to come here, *Senhor Doutor*?' I asked, as he threaded his way back to his Morgan.

'I spoke to a friend of mine, a criminal lawyer, he told me that this is where they bring the bodies of those who have died in suspicious circumstances.'

'Why did you think she'd died like that?'

'Because I'd already asked him about you and he told me you were a homicide detective.'

He turned and walked across the cobbles to his car. I lit a cigarette, got into the Alfa, waited for the Morgan to pull away and followed.

'What did you make of that?' I asked Carlos.

'If it had been my daughter in there . . .'

'You were expecting more distress?'

'Weren't you?'

'What about numbness? Trauma leaves people numb.'

'He didn't seem numb. The look he had on his face when we came out, he was galvanized.'

'Concerned about himself?'

'I couldn't say . . . you know, I only saw him from the side.'

'So you can only tell me what I'm thinking about when you look at me head-on?'

'That was just a bit of luck, *Senhor* Inspector.'

'Was it?' I said, and the boy smiled. 'What did you think of Dr Oliveira's accountancy? The mathematics between him and his wife.'

'I thought he was a bloodless son of a bitch.'

'Strong feelings, *agente* Pinto,' I said. 'What does your father do?'

'He was a fitter with LisNave. He installed pumps in ships.'

'Was?'

'They lost some contracts to the Koreans.'

'Your politics might be to the left of centre perhaps?'

He shrugged.

'Dr Aquilino Oliveira is a serious man,' I said. 'He's high calibre ordnance . . . 125 mm cannon, no less.'

'Was he a colonel in the artillery, your father?'

'The cavalry. But listen. The lawyer has used his brain all his life. It's his job to use his intelligence.'

'That's true, so far he's one step ahead of us all the way.'

'You saw him. His instinct was to check the body. His brain always operates in front of his emotions . . . until, perhaps, he remembers he's supposed to have feelings.'

'And then he leaves the room to go and collect them.'

'Interesting, *agente* Pinto. I'm beginning to see why Narciso put you on to me. You're an odd one.'

'Am I? Most people think I'm very normal. They mean boring.'

'It's true you haven't said a word about football, cars or girls.'

'I like the way you see the order of things, *Senhor* Inspector.'

'Maybe you're a man of ideals. I haven't seen one of those since . . .'

'Nineteen-seventy-four?'

'A little after that, in the mess that followed our glorious revolution there were lots of ideas, ideals, visions. They petered out.'

'And ten years later we joined Europe. And now we don't have to struggle on our own any more. We don't have to sweat at night thinking where the next escudo is coming from. Brussels tells us what to do. We're on the payroll. If we . . .'

'And that's a bad thing?'

'What's changed? The rich get richer. The ones in the know go higher. Of course, it's trickled down. But that's the point. It's a trickle. We think we're better off because we can drive around in an Opel Corsa which costs us our entire living wage to run while our parents house us, feed us and clothe us. Is that progress? No. It's called "credit". And who benefits from credit?'

'I haven't heard anger like that since . . . since FC Porto came down here and put three past Benfica.'

'I'm not angry,' he said, cooling his hand out of the window. 'I'm not as angry as you are.'

'What makes you think I'm angry?'

'You're angry with him. You think he killed his daughter and he's given you the best possible alibi a man can have . . . and you're angry about it.'

'Now you're reading my face in profile. Next it'll be the back of my head.'

'You know what annoys me?' said Carlos. 'He makes out he's some kind of liberal thinker but you think about this. He's nearly seventy years old. He must have worked the best part of his life under the Salazar regime and you know as well as I do that you didn't work in those days unless you were politically sound.'

'What's happening here, *agente* Pinto? I've spent the last twenty years of my life not thinking about the revolution other than the fact we get a holiday on 25th April. I've been with you less than half a day and we've talked about it three or four times. I don't think it's any way to start a murder investigation by going back twenty-five years and looking . . .'

'It was only talk. He was projecting himself as a liberal. I don't believe him . . . and that's one of the reasons why.'

'Guys like that are too intelligent to believe in anything. They change . . .'

'I don't think they do. Not this late on. My father's forty-eight, he can't change and now he's scrap in the breaker's yard along with all his old pumps.'

'Don't get fixed ideas about people, *agente* Pinto. It'll cloud your vision. You don't want to ram somebody into a life sentence just because they're politically disagreeable, do you?'

'No,' said Carlos, innocent as his hair, 'that wouldn't be fair.'

Chapter VII

Saturday, 13th June 199–, Dr Aquilino Oliveira's house, Cascais.

We were shown into the sitting room which, judging by the furnishings, was not Dr Oliveira's side of the house. There was natural light in the room, fancy ceramics and no dark corners of books. The art on the walls was the sort that demanded comment unless you happened to be a police inspector from Lisbon in which case your opinion didn't matter. I took a seat on one of the two caramel leather sofas. Above the fireplace was a portrait of a skeletal figure in an armchair as seen through lashes of paint. It was disturbing. You had to be disturbed to live with it.

Under the thick plate glass of the coffee table was *Senhora* Oliveira's more human side. Magazines like *Caras*, *Casa*, *Máxima* and the Spanish *¡Hola!*. There were plants in the room and an arrangement of lilies but just as the eye relaxed it came across a dark metal figure scrabbling out of the primordial slime or a terracotta head, open-mouthed, screaming at the ceiling. The safest place to look was the floor which was parquet with Persian rugs.

Dr Oliveira showed his wife in. She was probably the same height as her daughter but her hair gave her another ten centimetres. It was big, pumped-up and blonde. Her tanned face looked tight, still puffy from barbiturate sleep and she'd tried to mask it with heavy eye make-up. Her lips were pink and she'd added an extra dark line to the rim of her mouth. She wore a cream blouse and a bra that created cleavage where none naturally existed. Her short

87

silk skirt was five shades off matching her blouse and she was chained with gold about the waist. We shook hands. The jewellery felt crusty.

'We'd like to talk to your wife alone, *Senhor Doutor*.'

He was going to make a stand, a man in his own home, but the side of his wife's face said something to him which I missed and he left the room. We sat. Carlos took out his notebook.

'When did you last see your daughter, *Dona* Oliveira?'

'Yesterday morning. I took her to school.'

'What was she wearing?'

'A white T-shirt, a mini-skirt, light blue with a yellow check. Those big clumpy shoes they all wear these days studded with rhinestones. She also had a thin leather lace choker with a cheap stone strung on it.'

'No tights in this weather?'

'No, just bra and pants.'

'Any particular make?'

She didn't answer but squeezed her bottom lip between her thumb and forefinger and then rubbed them together to disperse the grease.

'Did you hear the question, *Dona* Oliveira?'

'I just . . .'

Carlos leaned forward and the sofa creaked underneath so he stopped halfway. *Senhora* Oliveira blinked her slightly enclosed brown eyes.

'Sloggi,' she said.

'Did something else occur to you then, *Dona* Oliveira?'

'A horrible thought . . . when you asked about the underwear.'

'Your husband's already told us that Catarina has been sexually active for some years.'

Carlos sat back. She dabbed at her smudged lower lip with a finger.

'*Dona* Oliveira?'

'Was there a question, Inspector Coelho?'

'I wondered if you'd tell us what's on your mind, it might help.'

'It's every mother's fear that their daughter might get raped and killed,' she said, automatically, as if that hadn't been what she was thinking.

'How have you been getting on with your daughter over the past couple of years?'

'He's told you . . .' she started, and held herself back.

'What exactly?' I asked.

She darted a look at Carlos who didn't help.

'How we haven't been getting on.'

'Mothers and daughters don't always . . .'

'. . . compete,' she finished for me.

'Compete?' I asked, and she picked up on my surprise.

'I don't think this will help you find Catarina.'

'I'd like to know more about her psychological state. If she was likely to get herself into a difficult situation. She's a confident girl. That could have been the start of the . . .'

'Why do you say she's confident?'

'She fronts a band . . . that needs something.'

'It wasn't a very successful band,' she said, and switched. 'Yes, it's true, she can appear older than she is.'

'Is that what you meant by competing?'

Our eyes connected but she couldn't hold mine for more than a few seconds. She seemed to steady herself against the coffee table, rapping it with her ringed fingers.

'I didn't . . . I'm wondering what he's told you now,' she said, glancing at the door.

'Just tell me what happened.'

'Did he tell you I found Catarina in bed with my brother?'

'Why would you see that as competitive?'

'He's thirty-two years old.'

'But he's your brother.'

'I don't see any reason to be discussing middle-age female paranoia with someone investigating my daughter's disappearance. The fact is if she can get him she can . . .'

'Your husband said that too.'

'This is hopeless.'

'Maybe your brother's the one to help us with . . .'

'I don't know why he has to do this . . . now of all times.'

'He?'

'I didn't find Catarina in bed with my brother. She was with my lover,' she said, coolly, now that she'd given up the pretence.

'Do you still see this man?'

'Are you insane, Inspector?'

'And your daughter?'

Silence.

'I don't know,' she said, after a while.

'I'll need to speak to him,' I said.

Carlos handed her the notebook. She scribbled fiercely and finished with a pile-driving dot that must have gone through to the cardboard.

'How did your husband find out?'

She pushed up her chin like a boxer who could take anything now. Truth, part truth and lies passed behind her eyes.

'You can imagine the atmosphere in this house . . . between me and Catarina. My husband talked to her. He's good with words. He wrung it out of her.'

'Did she seduce your lover . . . Paulo Branco?'

'The delicacy of young flesh is difficult to resist so I'm told.' She said it in a way that particularly pained her.

'She was a drug-user. Your husband knows about hashish. Were you aware of her taking anything stronger?'

'I wouldn't know the difference. I've never taken drugs.'

'But you know how you feel when you've taken a sleeping pill, *Senhora* Oliveira?'

'I go to sleep.'

'In the morning, I mean.'

She blinked.

'Doesn't it give you an insulated feeling, the real world kept at a distance? Did you ever notice Catarina in that state or perhaps the opposite, nervous, hyperactive, wired . . . I think they call it?'

'I really don't know,' she said.

'Does that mean you didn't notice or . . .'

'It means that, of late, I haven't cared.'

It was a long silence in which the unheard air conditioning made its presence felt.

'How did she get her money?' I asked.

'I gave her five thousand escudos a week.'

'What about clothes.'

'I used to buy her clothes until . . . until last year,' she said.

'Did you buy the clothes she was wearing?'

'Not the skirt. I wouldn't have bought her anything that short. It barely covered her knickers but then that's the fashion so . . .'

'Was she doing all right at school?'

'I didn't hear anything to the contrary.'

'No attendance problems?'

'We would have been told, I'm sure. Whenever I dropped her off she walked in there like a lamb.'

'One minute,' I said, and left the room.

I found Dr Oliveira in his study smoking a cigar and reading the *Diário de Notícias*. I told him I wanted to break the news to his wife and asked him if he'd prefer to do it. He said he'd leave it to me. We went back into the room. *Senhora* Oliveira was talking animatedly to Carlos. She was sitting sideways on the sofa and her skirt had crawled up her legs. Carlos was as stiff as his hair. She saw us and froze. Her husband sat next to her.

'At a quarter-to-six this morning, *Dona* Oliveira,' I started, and her eyes looked into me avid and horrified. 'The body of your daughter, Catarina Oliveira, was found on the beach in Paço de Arcos. She was dead. I am very sorry.'

She said nothing. She stared into me hard enough to see the texture of my organs. Her husband took her hand and she absentmindedly removed it from his grip.

'*Agente* Carlos Pinto and myself are conducting the investigation into your daughter's death.'

'Her death?' she said, astonished and coughed out an appalled laugh.

'We are very sorry for your loss. I apologize for not telling you earlier but there were certain questions I had to ask which needed a clarity of mind.'

Her husband made another attempt on the hand. She left it there this time. She was speared rigid by what I'd said.

'We believe that she had been murdered elsewhere and her body taken to the beach in Paço de Arcos and left there.'

'Catarina has been murdered?' she said, incredulous, as if this was what happened to riffraff on television only. She slumped back into the sofa, stunned. She tried to swallow but couldn't, couldn't gulp down the dreadful news. I realized we weren't going to get any further today. We shook hands and left. At the garden gate we heard a long unrestrained wail from the house.

'I'm not sure I understood all of that,' said Carlos.

'It was . . . very disappointing.'

'I thought it was . . .'

'It was very disappointing for someone of your youth and optimism to have to look at that sort of behaviour.'

'Why did we have to know anything about this affair with the brother or the lover . . . what was Dr Oliveira's game with all that?'

'That was what was so disappointing,' I said. 'He was using us . . . he was using our investigation into his daughter's murder to punish his wife's infidelity. What we saw in there was a master class in humiliation. Now you've observed the intelligence of the lawyer.'

'But the wife,' said Carlos, agitated, 'the wife . . . when

you left the room she didn't ask one question about her daughter's disappearance. Not one. She chatted. She asked me things about the stupid paintings, how long I'd been in the *Polícia Judiciária*, did I live in Cascais . . .'

'Yes, well, there was a couple of things about those two in there. First, Dr Oliveira kept a photograph of his previous family on his desk while Catarina was up on a bookshelf with some dog-eared paperbacks. The second, was that both of them had brown eyes.'

'I didn't notice,' he said writing it down in his notebook.

'And brown eyes plus brown eyes don't often make blue, and Catarina Oliveira had blue eyes.'

Chapter VIII

2nd March 1941, South-west France.

It was a perfect morning. The first perfect morning for days. The sky was pristine, cloudless and of such a blue that only pain could come from looking at it. To the south the mountains, the snow-capped Pyrenees, were just catching the first rays of the rising sun and the thin, spiky cold air up there sharpened the white peaks and deepened the blue of the sky close to them. Felsen's two Swiss drivers couldn't stop talking about it. They were from the south and spoke Italian and they knew mountains, but only the Alps.

They didn't talk to Felsen unless he spoke to them first which was infrequently. They found him cold, aloof, abrupt, and on one occasion brutal. In the few moments he fell asleep in the cab they heard him grinding his teeth and saw the muscles of his jaw bunching under the skin of his cheek. They called him 'bone-crusher' when he was visible and at some distance. That was the only risk they were prepared to take after witnessing the excessive kicking he'd given a driver who'd accidentally reversed into a gatepost in the barracks outside Lyons. They were Italian-Swiss after all.

Felsen hadn't noticed. He didn't care. He was treading a well-trodden circle, going over and over the same ground so that if he'd walked his thoughts he'd have been in a circular trench up to his shoulders. He'd smoked hours of cigarettes, metres of them, kilos of tobacco while he dissected his every living moment with Eva searching for *the* moment. And when he couldn't find *the* moment, he came at Eva from a different angle sizing all the sentences, all the phrases, weighing every word she'd ever said to him and all the ones she hadn't as well, which was a bigger task because Eva was a between-the-lines talker. She left the sayable unsaid and said what she meant without saying it.

He played over the scene of the first time she ended up in his bed after four years of knowing each other, after four years of being friends. She'd sat astride him in her black silk stockings and suspenders running her hands over and over his chest.

'Why?' he'd asked.

'Why what?'

'After all these years . . . why are you here?'

She'd pursed her lips and looked at him out of the corner of her face measuring the question for its long-term prospects. Then she'd suddenly gripped his penis with both hands and said:

'Because of your big Swabian cock.'

They'd laughed. It hadn't been it, but it would do.

Now as he came to that point, for the hundredth time, where Eva had diminished him, he all but writhed in his seat with the torment of his sexual jealousy. He saw the heavy-waisted, pink-skinned, uncontoured-buttocked Gruppenführer squeezing and pumping between her slim white thighs, her heels encouraging him, her breath coming out in jolts, his trembling grunts into the corner of her neck, her clawing fingers on his flabby back, his greedy hands, her rising knees, his deeper thrusts . . . Felsen would shake his head. No. And he would go back to Eva again sitting astride him in her black . . . Why?

'Power does it for the ladies,' Lehrer's chauffeur had said, 'even Himmler . . .' That's what Felsen had thought as he watched Lehrer eat his breakfast the morning after he'd seen him in the club with Eva. That's what he'd thought as he strolled through the dark morning to the Swiss National Bank, as he'd signed the release documents, as he'd supervised the loading of the gold, as he'd shaken hands with

Lehrer and watched him walk back to the Schweizerhof, to his three days in Gstaad with Eva.

He could barely remember crossing the border. He couldn't think of any moment in France apart from the stupid driver. He'd lived inside his head until the cloud had lifted off the Pyrenees that morning and the Swiss wouldn't stop talking about it.

He got drunk that night with a Standartenführer of a Panzer division in Bayonne who'd told him his tanks would be in Lisbon before the end of the month.

'We got to the Pyrenees in four weeks. We'll reach Gibraltar in two, Lisbon in one. We're just waiting for the crack of the Führer's starting pistol.'

They drank claret, a Grand Cru Classé from Château Batailley, bottle after bottle of it as if it was beer. He slept in his clothes that night and woke up in the morning with his face hurting and his throat sore from snoring like a hog. They crossed the border into Spain and picked up an army escort sent with a personal instruction for their safety from General Francisco Franco himself. By nightfall they were still grinding up the hairpins of the Vascongadas as if they were dragging Felsen's hangover behind them.

Now that there was no threat of Allied air attack they drove through the night and they were glad to be able to keep the engines running because once they came out of the mountains and on to the *meseta* there was nothing to stop the wind which drove a bleak mixture of freezing rain and ice into the sides of the trucks. The drivers stamped their feet on the metal floors to keep them from going numb. Felsen, hunched behind the collar of his wool coat, stared into the darkness, the swerving road, the headlights arcing across the trees. He didn't move. This had become his kind of temperature.

They refuelled in Burgos, a bleak and frozen place with disgusting food laced, no, swimming in the acrid urine of the poorest quality olive oil which burnt through the bowels of

96

the drivers so that they shat all the way to Salamanca. They shat so frequently that Felsen refused them permission to stop and they just hung their bare arses out of the doors and let the icy wind take it wherever.

Refugees appeared on the road, most of them on foot, some with a cart between them and occasionally an emaciated mule. They were dark people with faces hollowed out by fear and hunger. They walked automatically, the adults grim, the children blank. These people silenced the drivers, who stopped complaining about the food and the cold. As the trucks ground past them not a head turned, not a single homburg altered its course. The Jews of Europe tramped through the empty wilderness of Spain with their cardboard suitcases and knotted sheets, seeing no further than the next wind-blasted oak on the skyline.

Felsen looked down on them from the cab. He'd expected to find some pity for them as he had for the two men from Sachsenhausen who'd swept his factory floor after their release at the time of the Berlin Olympics. He found nothing. He found he didn't have room for anything else.

They drove through Salamanca. The golden stone of the cathedral walls and the university buildings was dull under the white dome of the frozen sky. There was no fuel. The drivers managed to buy some *chorizo* and weevil-riddled bread. The convoy moved on to Ciudad Rodrigo and the border town of Fuentes de Oñoro. The Spanish army escort harassed the columns of refugees who shifted off the road on to the barren rock-strewn plain without even a raised gesture.

The twenty whitewashed hovels on the rocky treeless site that made up Fuentes de Oñoro were frozen in a piercing wind that kept the inhabitants indoors and the refugees huddled behind boulders and upturned carts. The drivers blundered amongst them looking for food and found everyone in a worse state than themselves. A woman in the only shop offered them lumps of pork fat in what looked like the same rancid oil they'd had in Burgos. They named the dish *Gordura alla Moda della Guerra* and didn't touch it.

The customs formalities on the Spanish side were brief. The officials left their less lucrative work of minutely inspecting the jittery refugees' papers and their reductions of a lifetime's possessions and came to get their bonuses. Felsen, who knew that this was the border post that would see most of his business, had prepared himself for the crossing with French brandy and *jambon de Bayonne*. His drivers were furious. The deal was sealed with shots of cheap *aguardente* and the convoy moved across to the Portuguese side at Vilar Formoso.

The Portuguese army escort had not arrived. There was a member of the German legation who'd already dispatched a messenger to Guarda. They arranged for the drivers to park the trucks in the square outside the ornately tiled railway station, which showed framed scenes of all the major towns in Portugal. The square was packed with more wild-eyed people. The drivers went looking for food again. They found a soup kitchen which had been set up by firms from Porto but it was for British passport-holders only. They tried talking to the refugees. The women, collapsed under coloured shawls, wouldn't look at them, and with the men, in long mud-rimmed coats with furry hats jammed down over thick black matted hair and faces blanked out and ragged with beards, they could find no common language. There were Poles and Czechs, Yugoslavs and Hungarians, Turks and Iraqis. They tried the less picturesque – men in creased three-piece business suits who stood above exhausted women and howling children but they were Dutch or Flemish, Rumanians or Bulgarians and in no mood for sign language, especially of the sort which involved pointing a finger into the mouth. Even the young were uncommunicative – the boys shifty, the girls cringing and babies either wailing or mute and vacant. When the engine of one of the approaching Portuguese army motor-cycles back-fired, this massed driftwood of war ducked and flinched as one.

Felsen worked on the customs officials using charm and some supplies that the member of the German legation had brought with him. The Portuguese responded with cheese, *chorizo* and wine and were very helpful with the reams of bureaucracy that needed to be filled out to allow the trucks to move freely in the country. When the convoy moved off the *chefe* of the *alfândega*, the customs, came out to wave and wish him a speedy return because he could see that this was the auspicious start of what could be years of graft.

They crossed the River Côa and spent a night at an army post in Guarda where they ate an enormous meal whose four courses all tasted the same and drank a lot of wine from five-litre flagons. Felsen had already begun to feel himself coming round. He knew because he was interested in seeing the women in the kitchens. Since moving to Berlin he'd barely gone forty-eight hours without sex and now it had been more than a week. When finally he saw the women he hoped they'd been especially selected to keep the soldiers' ardour at bay. They were all tiny with no more than an inch of forehead between their dark eyebrows and the scarves around their heads. Their noses were sharp, their cheeks sunken and their teeth gone or rotten. He went to bed and slept badly on a flea-ridden mattress.

In the morning they began driving through some of the places they'd seen depicted on the blue and white *azulejos* in the station at Vilar Formoso. The drivers realized what had been missing from the designs, or perhaps bad roads, poverty and filth looked different in their own colours. They rounded the pine-forested, rock-strewn mountains of the Serra da Estrela on the northern boundary of the Beira Baixa which, as Felsen already knew, was going to be his home for the next years of his life. Where schist and granite meet was where the black, shiny crystalline wolfram occurred, and

Felsen could see from the grey/brown block stone houses and slate roofs that this was the right country.

They crossed the Mondego and Dão rivers to Viseu and headed south to Coimbra and Leiria. The air changed. The dry cool of the mountains disappeared and a warm humidity took over. The sun was hot even in early March and they stripped off their coats. The drivers rolled up their shirt sleeves and looked as if they might sing. There were no refugees on the road. The representative from the German legation told them that Salazar was making sure that no more came into Lisbon – the city was already full. They spent a last night on the road at Vila Franca de Xira and got up early the next morning to deliver the gold to the Banco de Portugal before normal office hours.

It was first light as they turned away from the Tagus into the Terreiro do Paço and the trucks made their way behind the arcaded eighteenth-century façade into the grid system of the Baixa, purpose-built by the Marquês de Pombal after the Lisbon earthquake in 1755. They drove along Rua do Comércio, behind the massive triumphal arch at the head of the Rua Augusta, to the conglomeration of buildings including the church of São Julião that made up the Banco de Portugal. They waited for the gates to open in the Largo de São Julião and one by one the trucks reversed in to unload.

In the bank Felsen was met by the Director of Finance and another, more senior and taller, member of the German legation who greeted his offered hand with a spring-loaded salute and an incongruous '*Heil Hitler*'. This did not appear to disturb the bank's finance director who, he found out later, was a member of the Portuguese Legion. It had confused Felsen who only managed a half-wave in return, like a bad attempt at getting a waiter's attention, and the words '*Ja, ja.*' He also missed the tall, Prussian-looking man's name. It wasn't until the gold had been unloaded and accounted for that Felsen saw the man signing the endless documentation with his left hand in the name of

Fritz Poser. He noticed that the right hand was a gloved prosthesis.

By 11.00 a.m. the business was completed. The junior member of the legation had taken the drivers to an army barracks on the outskirts of the city and Poser and Felsen were sitting in the back of a flagged Mercedes driving down Rua do Ouro towards the river. The pavements were packed with people, mostly men in dark suits, white shirts, dark ties and hats a size too small for their heads who swerved past barefooted boys selling newspapers. The few women were smart and dressed in tweed suits with hats and furs even though it wasn't cold. The faces flashed by as the car picked up speed in the empty street, one woman hatless and blonde stared at the car, the small swastika flapping on the bonnet, mesmerized. Then her head flicked away and she buried herself in the crowd. Felsen turned in his seat. A boy was running alongside the car waving the *Diário de Notícias* in his face.

'Lisbon is full,' said Poser. 'It's as if the whole world is here.'

'I saw them at the border.'

'The Jews?'

Felsen nodded, tired now after the anxiety of the journey.

'There's a more eclectic mix down here. Lisbon can cater for all tastes. It's one long party for some.'

'So there's no rationing.'

'Not yet and not for us anyway. It will come though. The British are mounting their Economic Blockade and the Portuguese are beginning to suffer. Fuel could start to be a problem, they don't have any of their own tankers and the Americans are being difficult. Of course you can eat well if you like seafood and drink their wine if your palate's not too French. There's still sugar at the moment and the coffee is good.'

They turned right out of the Praça do Comércio and followed the Tagus past the docks. At Santos there was a huge brawling mass of people, men, women and children fighting outside the offices of the shipping lines.

'This is the more distasteful end of Lisbon,' said Poser. 'You see that ship, the *Nyassa*, in the docks there. They all want to get on the *Nyassa* but it's full. It's been full for weeks. In fact it's been filled twice over but these morons think that because it's there they can get on it. Most of them don't have any money which means they don't even have American visas. Ah well, the *Guarda Nacional Republicana* will be along in a moment and break them up. Last week it was the same with the *Serpa Pinto*, next week it will be the *Guiné*. Always the same.'

'We seem to be leaving Lisbon,' said Felsen, as the driver accelerated away towards the green outskirts of the city.

'Not yet. This evening perhaps. We're going to the Palácio do Conde dos Olivais in Lapa where we've installed the German legation. You'll see we have the best location in Lisbon.'

They came into Lapa from Madragoa and drove up the Rua São Domingos à Lapa. Halfway up the Union Jack hung limply off a long pink building with tall white windows and a central pediment which made up about fifty metres of the street's façade. The Mercedes thundered past on the cobbled street.

'Our friends, the British,' said Poser, waving his prosthetic hand.

The driver turned first left into Rua do Sacramento à Lapa and after a hundred metres a cuboid palace in its own grounds appeared on the left. Bougainvillea spilled over the iron railings, the leaves of the phoenix palms rattled in the light breeze and the three red, white and black swastika flags snapped gently. The gates were opened, the car swung away from a sea view and up a short gravel drive and stopped in front of the steps. A doorman opened the car.

'Early lunch?' asked Poser.

They sat in the dining room with the sun throwing short

102

rectangles of light across the empty tables. They waited for soup. Felsen tried to remember a time when he'd felt such calm. It was before the war, before the Olympics, in his old apartment on . . . he couldn't remember where his old apartment was . . . the windows open in summer, lying on the bed with Susana Lopes, the Brazilian girl.

'You like it?' asked Poser, erect as if his spine was in a brace.

'Excuse me?'

'Our legation. Our *palácio*.'

'Magnificent.'

'The Baixa,' said Poser, wrinkling his nose, 'all the refugees, you know, it's very enervating. Lapa is so much more civilized. You can breathe.'

'And the war seems such a long way away,' said Felsen, stonily.

'Quite so. Berlin, I believe has not been so much fun,' said Poser trying to hit a more businesslike tone. 'We'll be having a small reception for you this evening and a dinner so that you can meet some of the people you'll be working with. It will be formal. Do you . . . ?'

'Yes, I do.'

'Afterwards I thought perhaps you'd like to go out of town to Estoril. There's a room for you at the Hotel Parque. The casino's out there and there'll be some dancing. I think you'll find it very agreeable.'

'I'd like to have some sleep at some stage. I haven't had much on the road this last week.'

'Of course, I didn't mean to be presumptuous. I just wanted you to be sure of some comfort and entertaining company after the more serious occasion.'

'No, no, I'd be happy to. A few hours this afternoon will be fine.'

'I have a cot in a room next to my office. You can use that if you wish.'

The soup arrived and the two men worked their way through it.

'This Hotel Parque . . . ?' started Felsen.

'Yes. We have the Hotel Parque and the British have the Hotel Palácio. We're next to each other. The Palácio is bigger but the Parque has the waters . . . if you like that sort of thing.'

'I was going to ask . . .'

'It's a very international crowd as I said. One long party. From the conversations you hear up there you'd think they were still having court balls in the Palace of Versailles. And the women out there, so I'm told, are a lot more progressive in their attitude than the natives.'

The soup plates were removed and replaced by a split grilled lobster.

'Did I answer your question?' asked Poser.

'Perfectly.'

'Your reputation precedes you, Hauptsturmführer Felsen.'

'I didn't know I had one that could be of much interest.'

'You'll find the foreign women in Estoril very accommodating, although I should . . .'

'You're well-informed, Herr Poser. Are you with the Abwehr?'

'Although I should warn you that there are two currencies in this city. The escudo and information.'

'Which is why you're here.'

'Everybody's a spy in Lisbon, Herr Hauptsturmführer. From the lowest refugee to the highest members of the legations. And that includes maids, doormen, waiters, bar staff, shop owners, businessmen, company executives, all women, whores or not, and royalty, real or fake. Anybody with ears to overhear can make a living.'

'Then there must be a lot of rumour as well. You've said yourself that the city is full, probably with a lot of people with nothing better to do than talk. It passes the time after all.'

'That is true.'

'Who does the winnowing?'

'Ah yes, your agricultural background coming out.'

Felsen stripped the white flesh out of the shell of his lobster.

'So where do the real spies pass their time?' asked Felsen.

'The ones who give us advance information on Dr Salazar's thinking about wolfram exports, you mean?'

'Does he do any thinking about that?'

'He's beginning to. We think he's beginning to perceive an opportunity. We're working on it now.'

Felsen waited for Poser to continue but instead the Prussian began dismantling his lobster claws with some difficulty given the stiffness of his gloved right hand.

'How many people know what I'm doing here?'

'Those you will meet this evening. No more than ten people in all. Your work is very important and, as you've probably realized, somewhat complicated by a very delicate political situation which, at the moment, we are winning. It is our people here who will make your work on the ground easier.'

'Or more difficult if you start losing.'

'We have good relations with Dr Salazar. He understands us. The British are relying on the strength of their old alliance, 1386 I think it was, you wonder which century they're living in. We, on the other hand, are . . .'

'. . . frightening him?'

'I was going to say that we are providing him with what he needs.'

'But he's aware of the Panzer divisions in Bayonne, I'm sure.'

'And the U-boats in the Atlantic,' said Poser. 'But if you want to play the harlot and bed both sides you might expect to get slapped about. Sweet?'

'Excuse me?'

'The lobster.'

'Very sweet.'

'Portuguese lobster . . . small but perfectly sweet. The best in the world.'

'I thought I'd go for a walk after my nap.'

'The Jardim da Estrela isn't far and it's very pleasant.'

It was 5.00 p.m. and the Chave do Ouro café in the Rossio square at the top end of the Baixa grid, in the heart of the city, was full to capacity. It was still warm and the windows were all open. Laura van Lennep sat by one of these open windows and looked into the square repeatedly. She fingered the single coffee she'd ordered in the hour and a half she'd been sitting there, but the waiters didn't bother her. They were used to it.

She was half-listening to a table of refugees speaking French with thick accents. The two men had seen army trucks in the Baixa first thing that morning and were expounding some fantastic invasion theory. It did nothing to calm Laura van Lennep down. She couldn't bear the inertia of these people, who she knew came from a *pensão* three houses down from her own in the Rua de São Paulo behind Cais do Sodré. She'd heard them in the street correcting each other about aristocrats they'd met at parties as if it had been only last week, when it had been in a different country, in a different decade. She was desperate with no cigarettes and the man who was going to change her life, who'd promised that he could change her life, wouldn't arrive.

A man appeared at the top of the stairs and looked around. He walked slowly around the room and finished up at her table. He wasn't short but his width and bulk made him look shorter than he was. He had short dark hair, cut *en brosse* and blue-grey eyes. He made her tremble inside. She looked away into the Rossio again, to the same groups of dark-suited men standing about on the black and white *calçada*, to the same lines of taxis, to the same kiosk where the cabbies drank coffee and talked about football. Sporting were going to be champions this year. She knew that by now. She turned back and he was still there. She felt those eyes on her. She gripped her handbag which contained her papers. Was he the police? She'd been told about the plain-clothed ones. He didn't look Portuguese but he had something of authority about him. She rearranged her claret dress which did not need rearranging but should have been thrown away last year.

'Could I join you?' asked the man in French.

'I'm waiting for someone,' she said, also in French, letting her blonde head slip around to the window again.

'There's nowhere else to sit and I only want a coffee. You're a single person sitting at a table for four.'

'There's someone coming.'

'I'm sorry,' he said. 'I didn't mean to . . .'

'No, no, please,' she said suddenly, her nerves setting her hands off like the pigeons in the square.

He sat opposite her and offered her a cigarette. She refused but had to hold on to her hand to do it. He lit one for himself and seemed to enjoy more than the smell of his own smouldering tobacco. The waiter came to his side.

'Your coffee looks cold, may I . . . ?'

'I'm fine, thank you.'

He ordered one for himself. She looked out into the square again. He'd spoken in Portuguese but not Lisbon Portuguese, more open, like slow Spanish.

'He won't come any quicker, you know,' said the man.

She smiled a sort of relief that she'd begun to feel that he wasn't going to ask to see her papers.

'I can't bear waiting,' she said.

'Have a cigarette, some warmer coffee . . . it'll pass the time.'

She took a cigarette. He looked at her empty ring finger and the tense shake in her hand. She puffed on it and left a red mark on the white end. She blew out the strange, strong smoke.

'From Turkey,' he said.

107

'You can get anything here if you can pay,' she said.

'I wouldn't know. I brought these with me. My first day in Lisbon.'

'Where have you come from?'

'From Germany.'

That's why he'd made her tremble.

'Where are you going?'

'I'm staying here for a while and then . . . who knows? And you?'

'From Holland. I want to go to America.'

Her blue eyes flickered out over the balcony again and then searched the room behind where the man was sitting. His coffee arrived. He ordered one for her. The waiter took her old stained cup away. Her eyes settled back on to him.

'He'll come,' he said, with a reassuring wink.

The four refugees on the table behind had started running down the Portuguese. How uncivilized they were. How uncouth. How all the food tasted the same and have you tried to eat that *bacalhau*? Lisbon, oh Lisbon was so boring.

She'd heard it all before and she leaned away from them. She knew it could be dangerous to speak to the man, but after three months in the Lisbon refugee world she thought she'd developed some instinct.

'I can't bear not knowing,' she said.

'Like the waiting.'

'Yes. If I know . . . if I knew . . .' she drifted off. 'You don't know what it's like yet, you've only just arrived.'

'Where are you staying?'

'In the Pensão Amsterdão on Rua de São Paulo. And you?'

'I'll find somewhere.'

'Everywhere's full.'

'So it seems. Perhaps I'll go out to Estoril.'

'It's more expensive out there,' she said, shaking her head.

He didn't seem bothered by that. She let her head fall over

her shoulder again to look out of the window. This time she leapt to her feet and started waving. She dropped back into her seat and closed her eyes. Her table companion twisted around to view the top of the stairs. A man in his early twenties with blonde, reddish hair came striding through the tables. He faltered when he saw the older man but pulled a chair out and pushed it close to the girl. Her eyes snapped open. Her face fell. He took her hands. She stared into the tablecloth as if her own blood was growing a stain in the middle of it. He leaned into her ear and whispered in English.

'I did everything I could. It's just not possible without . . . The woman in the visa office . . .' he stopped as the waiter put a coffee down in front of her, he looked across at the man at their table who was looking out of the window. 'It takes money. A lot of money.'

'I haven't got any money, Edward. Do you know how much the tickets are now? You used to be able to get one for $70, now it's $100. I was there today at the ticket office. A man paid $400 to get on the *Nyassa*. The longer I stay here . . .'

'I got as far as the guichet . . . but then *she* comes to the window. *She* doesn't recognize me. *She* doesn't know me. *She* won't even take the application unless . . . unless you can come up with the money, or the right invitations, or . . .'

The German called for the waiter and paid for the two coffees. He stood and looked down at the young couple. The Englishman was suspicious. The woman had a different look than before – a hungry intensity in her face. The German put on his hat and tipped it at her.

'Thank you for the coffee,' she said. 'You didn't tell me your name.'

'You didn't say yours. I don't think we got that far.'

'Laura van Lennep,' she said. 'And this is Edward Burton.'

'Felsen,' he said. 'Klaus Felsen.'

He put out his hand. The Englishman didn't shake it.

109

Chapter IX

8th March 1941, the German legation, Lapa, Lisbon.

The ambassador didn't make the reception or the dinner that night. Felsen sat between two wolfram exporters, a Portuguese with three concessions in the Trancoso area in the Beira Alta, and a Belgian aristocrat who wouldn't tell him anything other than that it was his group who was providing a shell company through which Felsen was going to export his wolfram.

The members of the legation, who were without their ambassador to remind them of their own insignificance, spent too much of their time extending their own importance into areas which were none of their business. Felsen was left with the impression that all the real work would be done in the corridors of power and hotel lounges of Lisbon rather than in the bleak mountain ranges of the north. He didn't improve his popularity by asking how their oblique bargaining was going to translate into tons in trucks crossing the border. They patronized him back. They hinted at intricate negotiations but offered no substance. They said that he would feel the results. Felsen reinterpreted all this to himself. The *Abwehr* and Supply Department resented the intrusion of the SS into their territory. He was on his own.

After dinner, as they gathered on the steps waiting for the cars to take them out to Estoril, Felsen still couldn't help being unnerved by the unembarrassed flagrance of light everywhere. All the windows of the *palácio*, each one or two metres high, glowed from reckless chandeliers of glittering incandescence. As he'd left the Baixa by taxi in the evening the *Nyassa* was still at anchor, unconcerned in the heart of the docks, blazing with light as the loading continued. Berlin had been widowed for two years. You could end up in a concentration camp for lighting a cigarette in the street after dark. Cars moved around at night with slit eyes, blind as moles. The rest of Europe was like a coal hole and Lisbon its furnace mouth.

A crack and crump of small-arms fire started up around the city. One of the younger legation members with a glass too much of wine inside him shouted: 'The invasion!' and roared.

The Portuguese was stone-faced as they got in the cars. Felsen sat with Poser again in the back of the leading Mercedes. They dropped down the steep hill to Alcântara and headed west out of town.

'What was "the invasion"?' asked Felsen.

'A nightly reminder of who's in charge,' said Poser, looking out of the window as if he was expecting crowds. 'Salazar only allows the Lisboans to beat their carpets after nine at night.'

They drove through Belém, past lit buildings and monuments.

'Not used to the light yet, Herr Hauptsturmführer?' said Poser. 'Still jittery after Berlin, the flak towers and the air raid warnings? This is last year's Expo site. While London burned and France fell, Lisbon showed off its eight hundred years of sovereignty to the world.'

'I'm not sure what you're getting at, Herr Poser.'

'You went walking today.'

'You told me to go the gardens in Estrela and I just kept going, over the top of the Bairro Alto, down to the Chiado and then into the Baixa.'

'Ah, the Bairro Alto,' said Poser. 'And did you see the market in Praça da Figueira – it doesn't smell too bad at this time of the year; and that rat hole – the Mouraria, or the stinking, crumbling Alfama?'

111

'I walked up to the Castle of São Jorge and took a taxi back.'

'So you've seen some of Lisbon,' he said. 'Now when you see Salazar's capital after dark perhaps you understand my point about the harlot. Lisbon's a whore, a peasant Arab whore, who wears a tiara at night.'

'Perhaps you've been here too long, Poser.'

'Ach, Salazar, he says one thing, he does another, he leans one way and sticks a foot out the other. He takes our Swiss francs and gold bars and then extends unlimited credit to the British. He rails at them for blocking his imports from the colonies and ... ach ... The man's a Moor and he's making the beast with two backs with anyone he pleases,' Poser finished bitterly.

'Now you're thinking that because you pay the whore she should be faithful. Next you'll be wanting her to fall in love with you.'

'Quite so, Felsen,' said Poser, coolly. 'I forgot your expertise in these matters.'

They hit the new coast road, the Marginal. The lights of the dormitory villages of Caxias, Paço de Arcos, Oeiras, Carcavelos and Parede glittered by the black heave of the unseen Atlantic. Poser was still sulking as they pulled up outside the lit façades of the Hotels Parque and Palácio. The high heads of the Washingtonian palms in the gardens in front were just out of the light. Poser pointed out the Casino at the top of the long square which sloped several hundred metres down to the sea front. Music came from the low modern building. Queues of cars stretched down the side of the gardens. The bellboy fetched the bags from the boot and Felsen and Poser went through the high Roman arch which made up the front of the Hotel Parque.

'There's somebody you should meet,' said Poser, heading for the concierge's position.

'This is Felsen,' he said to the sharp-faced man behind the counter.

The concierge flicked through his register. He rattled something off to the bellboy without taking his eyes off the book.

'You don't need to tell him anything,' said Poser, of the concierge. 'He knows it before you do. Isn't that right?'

The concierge didn't say anything but Felsen could tell from his attentive stillness that he was a man of some hotel experience.

'Install yourself in your rooms, Felsen, and I'll show you around,' said Poser, and laughed looking at the concierge. 'Don't talk to the flowers. Or use the phone. Isn't that right?'

The concierge blinked once, slowly.

Felsen rejoined Poser in the bar. They left the boorish company of the other members of the legation and walked up the gardens in the balmy night to the Casino.

'The concierge knows when we talk like that it's what we want everybody to hear.'

'Is that why the bar's empty?'

'You'll see, it'll fill up as the night wears on.'

'Maybe they should make themselves more interesting – invite some women across, they all seem to be going in here.'

They entered the lobby of the Casino at the same time as a small, dark-haired, highly-manicured woman who slid out of a fur coat and an expensive hat before being escorted to the bar by two men, younger and firmer than herself. She wore nylons and more than half the room turned as she came in.

'Is she the Queen of somewhere?' asked Felsen.

'That's the Queen of Lisbon,' said Poser.

'The daughter of the Arab whore?' asked Felsen, and Poser roared.

'Her name is Madame Branescu. She runs the guichet of the visa office at the American consulate. You saw all those people who wanted to get on the *Nyassa* this evening?'

113

'She took a percentage off every one of them.'

'You wouldn't have recognized her eighteen months ago. She was half the size and you could read a newspaper through her clothes but . . . she speaks fourteen languages and, I don't know whether you walked past the American consulate, but she needs those fourteen languages and a few more besides.'

They went into the bar. The waiter was already standing at her table as the woman and her blonde escorts sat down. Despite the clothes, the coiffure and the make-up she was not an attractive woman. Felsen saw her in a previous life, in the office of an important lawyer. A short, plain woman in grey clothes, ignored by all but, like the Hotel Parque's concierge, she missed nothing and had learned everything – the languages, the control, the art of power. And here she was, an improbable, little person conferring life or despair on the thousands atticked in Lisbon's *pensions*. Men and women approached her and spoke small obsequious words, bowing from the waist. Some were allowed to brush their lips across the dimpled knuckles of her puffy hand, others scuttled back to their seats blanched and quivering.

Felsen excused himself from Poser and presented himself at her table. The escorts' eyes bored into him. He asked her in perfect English if she wanted to dance. Her eyes roved over his face trying to work out if she knew him, then glanced down at his clothes and footwear, expert on quality.

'I've heard Madame Branescu is an excellent dancer. I am too. I think we should lead the way.'

She tried to give him her steely look but he seemed like a man who had access to one himself. She smiled and gave him her hand.

'You're not English, are you?' she said, as they made their way to the dance floor, everybody watching. 'And you limp.'

'You won't be disappointed.'

114

'Are you Swiss, or maybe an Austrian? I can hear something in your accent.'

'I'm German.'

'I don't like Germans,' she said, switching to his language.

'We haven't arrived in Bucharest yet.'

'If what the Germans do to countries is "arrive", then you must be the *arrivistes* of the century.'

'Perhaps that is why you're here?'

'Because the Germans who aren't murderers are brutes. That's why I'm here.'

'I don't know what calibre of German you've been meeting.'

'Austrian Germans. I used to live in Vienna.'

'But you are Rumanian, aren't you?' asked Felsen.

'Yes, I am.'

'Allow me to show you our less brutal side.'

She looked at the Swabian ploughboy with some doubt in her mind but he whisked her into a swing number that left her breathless and amazed. Felsen had been a little worried when he'd heard the swing, he didn't know whether Madame Branescu's hips could cope, but the woman knew how to move her pork. They danced three numbers and left the floor to some light applause.

'I didn't think Hitler approved of swing,' said Madame Branescu.

'He's afraid it will unhinge our goose step.'

'You should be careful talking like that,' she said. 'You wouldn't be the first German to be taken off the streets. Did you know that the PVDE are Gestapo-trained?'

'The PVDE?'

'*Polícia de Vigilância e de Defesa do Estado* – Salazar's security police,' she said. 'And their jails are not so nice unless you can afford a good one.'

'I don't think there's anything that anybody can tell the Germans about jails.'

She excused herself to the powder room. Felsen calculated an extra inch of swing in her hips. Poser drew alongside.

'Most surprising, Felsen,' said Poser in his ear.

'An American taught me before the war.'

'I meant your taste . . . your choice of partner.'

'That's my agricultural background, Poser,' said Felsen. 'It comes from chasing piglets round the yard.'

Poser smiled and moved off. Madame Branescu reappeared having brought the flush down in her cheeks. He walked her back to her table. The escorts stood. She flapped them back into their seats.

'You're new in Lisbon, aren't you Herr . . . ?'

'Felsen. Klaus Felsen. And yes, I'm fresh in today.'

'You don't talk like somebody who needs to get to America.'

'Because I don't need to go.'

Her eyes narrowed.

'Perhaps you're here to work?'

'On the contrary, I'm here to dance which I hope we can do again.'

He bowed and she let him brush her dimples with his lips before returning to her seat.

Felsen found Poser with his nose navigating the inside of a brandy glass.

'You seem to have the measure of this place already,' said Poser, leaning back from the fumes.

'I don't think so, Poser. It's just that you and I see things differently. You're a diplomat who wants to know what everybody's thinking. I'm an opportunist who wants to know what everybody's doing. Madame Branescu's another. We recognized each other, that's all.'

'But what could you possibly do for each other?'

'You'll see, you'll see,' he said, and moved off.

More people drifted into the casino – a mixed crowd, some happy and smiling in spectacular evening dress, others hunched and furtive in borrowed clothes. Felsen shouldered his way through to the cashier and made straight for the roulette table. Only fools played roulette.

He came across the usual sights and smells of the inside of a casino but this time their distinction was sharper and more poignant. The tables were lit by the normal harsh glare of avarice – an unblinking, hard-swallowing need. But the air in between was layered with cigarette smoke and a fear, so pungent, it cut the back of Felsen's throat like steaming vinegar. Occasionally carefree elation broke out of the canopy like tropical birds from the forest, but all the time, crouching lower and lower, a grim desperation sweated will into cheap shirts and shored-up evening dresses. The hopes riding on the clicking, chattering, hopping ivory ball were either nothing or everything. The backing for each milled chip on the green baize was either a banknote from the top of the next block or the last family jewel in the case. The faces closest to the table, the most avid, were ones that would either pale to translucence at a jaunty jump of the ball or, like the costive patient, would momentarily flood with relief at a perfect movement.

Felsen stood back from the crowd on the roulette table, only his starched shirt-front picking up the edgy light. An American talked loudly over his shoulder at anyone who'd listen, while slapping down the maximum bet on a number he didn't have to think about. He stopped only to glance at the ball and to cheer when he won and shrug when he lost. Next to him, seated and humped with age, bathing in the sunny warmth of his stacked chips, was an elderly, spectral, threadbare aristocrat, probably Russian, who gripped her minimum-stake chips with a tight, white-knuckled, sinewy hand. An Englishman, impeccable in his stiff wing collar, looked down his nose at the turning wheel and disdained all winning numbers until his collar was all the stiffness left in him. His mouth had already taken on the sneer of someone who'd have to face bread and horse mackerel for lunch until the next remittance. In front of Felsen a minute Portuguese woman, who wore the rosette of the Legion of Honour, was smoking cigarettes through a six-inch holder and wore gloves to her armpits. She played for amusement and gave cigarettes to a young woman sitting at her side who smoked them too quickly with her chest pressed against the wood of the table as if she might influence the turn of the wheel. The young woman had a single minimum-stake chip which had scored red marks on to the palm of her hand. It was a confused chip that could look confident on its own square right up until the call for last bets, when it would have to join other chips on nearby squares, before suffering the indignity of being taken back. It survived five turns of the wheel like that, until it found a home on number five, which had come up twice in ten minutes. The wheel turned, the ivory ball span and clicked, the white hand came out.

'Madame,' said the croupier severely, and the hand shot back.

The ball settled in twenty-four and the hot chip was raked in. The young woman's head dropped. The Portuguese lady's hand found her back and patted it. She gave her another cigarette. The woman stood and turned and she found Felsen's eyes on her. She smiled.

'Mr Felsen, isn't it?'

'That's right, Miss van Lennep,' he said giving her a stack of chips. 'Would you put these on red for me?'

The transfusion had an instant effect. The anaemia was gone. Blood thumped again. Red came up. She turned.

'Put them all on even,' said Felsen.

Even came up. He split the chips and gave her half.

'Those are for you. If you have to play, play fifty/fifty but remember there's a zero on the wheel which always tips the odds away from you, so . . .'

She'd already turned back to the table before she realized that the last piece of advice was the most important.

'So what?' she said.

'So don't play when it matters, only for fun.'

The Portuguese woman, who was the same size standing as the young woman was sitting, nodded agreement. Laura van Lennep put the chips in her handbag. Felsen offered her his arm. They went to the Wonderbar and drank whisky which she diluted with soda. They danced on the lighted dance floor until Felsen collided with one of Madame Branescu's escorts who was hauling her around as if she was a cast-iron stove. They nodded and Felsen left the floor with his partner. They sat at a front table and ordered more whisky.

'You didn't say why you were in Lisbon, Mr Felsen.'

'What happened to your friend? Edward, I think, Edward Burton.'

'He had to go up north. He's one of these Anglo-Portuguese from up there around Porto. The Allies use them a lot for buying things, you know, they understand the people. He told me it was all very important, but I think he might be a bit silly,' she said, diminishing him for her nearer purpose.

'Why did you ask him to help you?'

'He's young and good-looking and well-connected . . .'

'But not with the lady in the American consulate visa office.'

'He tried. She likes them young and good-looking.'

'But with money.'

She nodded dismally and looked back at the gaming rooms. The band released Madame Branescu from the next number and she walked past Felsen and gave him a little roll of her eyes.

'Who was that?' asked Laura van Lennep.

'Madame Branescu,' said Felsen. 'She runs the visa office in the American consulate.'

Something like love came into her face.

An hour later Felsen was removing the pearled stud from

his throat and stripping away the collar from his shirt. He unthreaded his monogrammed gold cufflinks and put them on the dressing table next to a letter he'd written on Hotel Parque stationery for the attention of Madame Branescu. He undid a shirt button.

'Let me do that,' said the girl.

Her borrowed evening dress lay on the chaise longue where she'd thrown it with her small, tight purse. She knelt up on the bed in her black slip and stockings. He stood in front of her with the first tingle of adrenalin shivering up his legs in his voluminous black trousers. She undid his shirt, drew the braces down off his shoulders and tugged the tails out of the waistband of his trousers. He eased her towards him and felt her stiffen against his front. She undid his trousers which dropped straight to the floor. Her head trembled on her neck at the jib of his undershorts. She drew them out and over, and put her fingers to her lips. She was flushed crimson and not with whisky and soda.

In the bathroom she found something among the bottles of perfumes and unguents provided by the Hotel Parque that would suit her purpose. Jasmine oil. Back in the room Felsen stood in his opened shirt. Her careful and thorough lubrication of him brought out the desperation of a chased man. He frightened her as he pulled her round on the bed, rucked up her slip and tore at the already flimsy lace-edged knickers.

'Careful,' she said nervously, and stretched back a hand to try and slow him down.

He stood between her bald heels showing out of the holes of her overused silk stockings. She shouted out as he entered her and her elbows collapsed. Felsen grabbed at her haunches and pulled her back on to him. Her hand flailed behind. Her face was screwed up with pain, her throat contorted by the way her head bent under her as he drove in.

Felsen was shocked to find himself thrilled by her every

wince, at her fingers stretching out to push him back, at the white knuckles of the other hand which gripped the rucked counterpane on the bed. He didn't last long.

They lay on the bed in the light and cold air from the open windows. She was under the covers huddled and shivering and trying not to cry. This part always made her cry. The shame of it. How many times had this been in three months?

Felsen smoked. He'd offered her one but she hadn't answered. He was irritated because he'd expected satisfaction, but in emptying himself he'd done just that, and found his head full of Eva.

He slept badly and woke early, alone in the room which was now freezing and damp from the sea air. He closed the window. The letter he'd written for the girl addressed to Madame Branescu had gone and the pair of gold KF cufflinks Eva had given him on his last birthday weren't on the dressing table.

Later in the day he caught a lift into Lisbon and went to the Pensão Amsterdão in Rua de São Paulo. At the front desk they'd never heard of Laura van Lennep and no one answered to the description he gave of her. He worked the other *pensions* in the street and drew a blank. He went to the American consulate and walked the line of faces but there were no single women. Finally he went down to the shipping offices but they were closed and the docks were empty. The *Nyassa* had gone.

Chapter X

It had been raining in Guarda all night. It rained throughout breakfast and it rained during the strategy meeting Felsen had convened with his fellow-agents to decide on the necessary tactics if they were to buy and ship in the region of three hundred tons of wolfram per month for the rest of the year.

The size of his task had only just crystallized in his head on seeing the British Beralt mine in Panasqueira, near Fundão in the south of the Beira. The mine and buildings were extensive, the colossal slag already part of the landscape. To have created that quantity of slag there had to be a small city of hundred-metre-deep shafts and kilometres of galleries under his feet. There was nothing remotely comparable in the rest of the Beira. This feat of engineering was ripping two thousand tons of thick horizontal wolfram veins from the earth each year. All the other mines in the area were nothing but scratches and nicks on the earth's crust by comparison. His only hope was total motivation of the people. The galvanizing of thousands to the task of gleaning the surface. And, of course, theft.

The strategy meeting had started off badly. These men were already working at full stretch and had never achieved anything close to three hundred tons in a month. They started off by complaining that the Portuguese concession-holders had sensed which way the market was going and were stockpiling. Then they railed against the British who had instituted some pre-emptive buying operations which had forced the price up and encouraged the Portuguese to sit tight.

'Price is no longer an issue,' said Felsen, which quietened the meeting. 'Our job now is to get our hands on the product by any means we can. My intelligence briefing in Lisbon indicates that the UKCC has a slow decision-making process, that they are active in the market only for short periods, that they are frightened of high prices because their managers are cautious and are buying with borrowed money. They have shot themselves in the foot. They've driven the prices up and now they've started to lose labour from their own mines. Their miners have begun to see that they can earn more fossicking than by taking wages to go underground. We don't have any of these problems. We have money. We can be aggressive. We can be consistent.'

'What do you mean by consistent?'

'It means we never fail to buy. The British can't do that. They work in fits and starts. They disappoint. We will never disappoint. We'll develop close relationships with people on the ground, people who control the local communities and we'll make them loyal to the German buying cause.'

'And how do we make them loyal?' roared one of the agents. 'The British give them tea and cakes and kiss their children. Do we have time for that, chasing three hundred tons a month?'

'They're only loyal to one thing in the Beira,' said another agent, grimly.

'That's not true,' said the first agent. 'There are concession-owners who will *only* sell to the British, some of them have British blood. They will never come over to us.'

'You're both right,' said Felsen. 'First – I've seen the people here, the ordinary men. They are living like we did in the Middle Ages. They have nothing. They walk twenty miles with fifty kilos of charcoal on their back to sell in

123

town. They make enough money to fill their stomachs so they can make it back to their villages. These are very poor people. They can't read or write. They have a hard life ahead of them. And it is these people who will scour the Beira for us and bring in every rock of wolfram they can find. In time, people will see how easy the money is up here and more will come up from the south. The Alentejo is full of the same victims of poverty, and they'll work for us too.'

'And what about the mines who sell to the British whatever the price?'

'My second point – the people who work in those concessions live in villages. We will move into the villages and encourage them to do some night shifts. We will buy from them at market rates.'

'You mean stealing?'

'I mean distributing wealth. I mean taking from the enemy. I mean waging war in the Beira.'

'They're difficult people in the Beira.'

'They're mountain people. Mountain people are always difficult. They have hard, cold lives. Your job is to understand them, to like them, to befriend them . . . and to buy their wolfram.'

Felsen divided the region up, putting a group of agents in Viseu, Mangualde and Nelas, another group in Celorico and Trancoso, one further south in Idanha-a-Nova and he took for himself the area south of Guarda to the Serra da Malcata from the foot of the Serra da Estrela in the west to the Spanish border. Most of the product would travel on the Guarda/Vilar Formoso road and cross the border at that point. He needed the *Guarda Nacional Republicana* in one pocket so that the trucks would get there and the *alfândega* in the other so that it would cross the border into Spain without any trouble. The town of Guarda was the central point of the wolfram area. It was the obvious headquarters.

The rain had stopped by the time he'd finished the conference. His driver came in to say that he'd delivered the two bottles of brandy to the *chefe* of the GNR and that he should go to the GNR post now, preferably before lunch, for a meeting.

The *chefe* of the GNR had recently been transferred to this post from Torres Vedras. He was a big man with a small face encased by a fat head. His moustache was thick, black and luxuriant as mink with ends tweaked to points, making him look as if he was permanently delighted, which most of the time he was. His hand felt small and soft in Felsen's peasant grip and not one that was in the habit of coming down with the full force of the law. Felsen sat on the other side of the man's desk which looked as if it had seen heavy skirmishing during the Peninsular Wars. The *chefe* thanked him for his gift and offered him a glass of absinthe. He poured the green liquor into two small glasses. Felsen's mouth crinkled at the bitterness of the wormwood as he laid a piece of newspaper down in front of the *chefe*. He tapped an article near the bottom of the page. The *chefe* read it, sipping his absinthe and thinking about lunch. He took one of Felsen's cigarettes.

'You're making the front page in Lisbon,' said Felsen.

'Murder,' said the *chefe* looking out of the window at the clearing sky, 'is very common now in this area.'

'This is the third murder in two weeks. The bodies were all found in the same area and they were all stripped, bound and bludgeoned to death.'

'It's the wolfram,' said the *chefe*, as if it was nothing to do with him.

'Of course it's the wolfram.'

'They've all gone crazy. Even the wild rabbits are collecting wolfram.'

'How is your investigation coming along?'

The *chefe* shifted in his seat and drew on the strange Turkish tobacco. The fire hissed in the chimney.

'There's since been a fourth death,' he said.

'One of your officers?'

He nodded his head and refilled the glasses. The absinthe was smoothing the creases out in his fat face so that the schoolboy was beginning to come back into it.

'Are you pursuing the matter?'

'A state of lawlessness exists in the land,' he said, dramatically, sweeping his hand over his desk. 'We have found the body.'

'In the same area?'

The nod was slower this time.

'Where did the officer start his enquiries?'

'In a village called Amêndoa.'

'Perhaps you will be going up there with a larger force?'

'The area I have to cover is large. The present circumstances – difficult.'

'So you'd like this lawlessness to stop without using up your manpower.'

'This is unlikely,' he said, sadly, 'there's a lot of money at stake here. These people have been living on five *tostões* here, five there. For them a single escudo is a fortune. When a small rock of wolfram is worth seventy-five, eighty, a hundred escudos, it's like a fever in their brains. You can't imagine. They go mad.'

'If I could ensure that your law is upheld, that there'll be no more violence, perhaps you'd be able to help me with some of my difficulties?'

'No more violence,' he said, repeating this back to his glass of absinthe as if it had put the idea to him. 'None?'

'None,' said Felsen, repeating the lie.

'What would be the nature of your difficulties?'

'As you know, there'll be a lot of my trucks moving product around the mining areas and out to the border at Vilar Formoso.'

'Customs is a separate organization.'

'I understand that. Where you can help is with the

papers, the *guias* that we have to present when we're moving the product around.'

'But the *guias* are very important for the government. They have to know what's going where.'

'That is true and ordinarily there would be no problem . . . but the bureaucracy.'

'Ah, yes, the bureaucracy,' said the *chefe*, suddenly feeling trussed in his uniform. 'You're a businessman. I understand. Businessmen like to do what they want, when they want.'

They lapsed into silence. From the *chefe*'s facial expressions it appeared that there was some internal struggle going on, as if there was something indigestible going down or a painful wind ballooning in his bowel wanting to get out.

'I'll find out what happened to your officer too,' said Felsen, but that wasn't it. The *chefe* was not wildly overconcerned at that.

'The *guias* are a very important government mechanism. This would be a serious breach of . . .'

'There will, of course, be a commission for you on every ton we move,' said Felsen, and he realized he'd hit the point. The creases unfurled. The belly quietened. The *chefe* took another of Felsen's cigarettes and skewered him with a look at the same time.

'But without the *guias*,' said the *chefe*, 'how will I know how many tons you have moved? How will my commission be calculated?'

'You and I will have a meeting with customs once a month.'

The *chefe*'s smile was extended another foot by the joy of his moustache. They shook hands and finished their drinks. The *chefe* opened the door for him and clapped him on the shoulder.

'If you go up to Amêndoa,' he said, 'you should talk to Joaquim Abrantes. He's a very influential man in that area.'

127

The door closed behind Felsen, leaving him in the gloom of an unlit corridor. He walked slowly out of the building contemplating his first lesson in underestimating the Portuguese. He got into his car and instructed the driver to take him up to Amêndoa in the foothills of the Serra da Estrela.

There was no road up to Amêndoa. It was a rough track of beaten earth with slabs of granite showing through, lined on either side by broom and heather, and then later and higher, pine forest. The rain had stopped but the cloud was still hanging and drifting lower down the mountains to the treetops until it sucked in the car itself. The driver rarely got out of second gear. Men appeared on the track. Cowled like monks, they wore split sacks over their heads. Grey and silent, they moved to the side, without turning.

Felsen sat in the middle of the back seat feeling every metre between himself and the rough civilization of Guarda lengthening behind him. He'd mentioned the Middle Ages in the conference but this was more like the Iron Age or earlier. He wouldn't have been surprised to see people hoeing with bone. He hadn't seen a mule or a donkey yet. All the carrying was done on the shoulders by men, and on the head by women.

The car came up on to the flat. There was no sign announcing Amêndoa. Granite block houses appeared out of the mist, a woman in black shuffled across the road. The driver pulled over at the only house on two levels in the village. They got out. There was an open door at street level. An old woman was working amongst sacks of grain, boxes for salting hams, cured cheeses, racks of potatoes, bunches of herbs, buckets and tools. The driver asked for Joaquim Abrantes. The woman left her work, locked the door with knobbed and crooked fingers, and took the two men up the granite steps on the outside of the house to a porch supported by two granite pillars. She left them there and went into the house.

A few minutes later she reopened the door and Felsen ducked into the dark house. The driver went back to the car. A fire was smoking heavily in a large fireplace emitting no heat. As his eyes got used to the lack of light he began to pick out an old man sitting in the fireplace. There were *chouriços* hanging along a pole above his head. The woman had taken a rag out of her pocket and was wiping the old man's eyes. He moaned quietly as if disturbed from sleep and coming into a world of pain. She left the room. A throat, somewhere in the house, coughed and spat. The woman returned with two small clay lamps burning olive oil. She put one on the table and pointed Felsen into a chair. Some of the slate tiles were visible through the laths between the rafters of the roof. She left the other lamp in a wall niche, wiped the old man's eyes again and left. The two windows in the room were permanently closed up to the weather by heavy wooden shutters.

After some minutes the double doors behind Felsen shuddered open and a short and very wide man engineered himself through the gap sideways. He roared something to the back of the house and then offered his hand which gripped Felsen's with a mechanical hardness. He sat resting his forearms across the table, the rough hands, with split nails, hung off square wrists. The body under the heavy jacket was thick-boned and powerful. Felsen recognized something in him, and knew from that first moment, that this was the man who was going to help him control the Beira.

A girl in a headscarf brought in a bottle of *aguardente* and two glasses. The Portuguese's face was still in the glow from the oil lamp and as big as a landscape opencast-mined. His hair was swept back in a thick black and grey lava flow, his brow and nose like an escarpment with an exposed ridge of granite, his eye sockets and cheekbones like craters. The whole geography of the face was hardened to bleakness by years of cold dry wind. It was impossible to tell his age – anything from thirty-five to fifty-five. But whatever the minerals he had in the bones of his face, they were not extended to his teeth, which were blackened and worn, sheered off and yellowing or just missing. Joaquim Abrantes poured the pale alcohol into the glasses. They drank.

The girl returned with bread, cured ham, cheese and *chouriço*. She laid a knife in front of Abrantes. The girl's face was very young, her eyes light-coloured, blue or green, it was difficult to say in the yellow oily light. A strand of blonde hair hung down from her headscarf. She was prettier than anything Felsen had seen since leaving Lisbon, but young, no older than fifteen, but strangely, with the body, the full form, of a grown woman.

Abrantes watched the German looking at the girl. He moved the ham in front of him and handed him the bread and knife. He ate. The ham was perfectly sweet.

'*Bolotas*,' said Abrantes, acorns. 'They make the meat sweet, don't you think?'

'I haven't seen many oak trees around here. It's all broom and pine.'

'They have them away from the mountains. I bring them up here. I have the sweetest pigs in the Beira.'

They ate and drank more. The *chouriço* was lumpy with chunks of fat. The cheese soft, sharp and salty.

'I heard you were coming to see me,' said Abrantes.

'I don't know how.'

'News gets through to us up here. We've even heard about your war.'

'So you know why I'm here.'

'To investigate murder,' said Abrantes, his shoulders shaking, metal chinking in his jacket. The man laughing.

'Murder interests me, that's true.'

'I don't know why you should be interested in the death of a few Portuguese peasants.'

'And the GNR officer.'

'That was an accident. He fell off his horse. These things happen on difficult terrain,' said Abrantes. 'And anyway, what's interesting? Isn't there enough killing in your war to keep you occupied without having to come to the Beira?'

'It's interesting because it means that someone is controlling the situation.'

'And this is a situation you would, perhaps, like to control yourself.'

'This is your country, *Senhor* Abrantes. They are your people.'

The glasses were refilled. Felsen offered a cigarette. Abrantes refused, not ready to accept anything yet. Felsen admired the psychology.

'*Senhor* Abrantes,' said Felsen. 'I'm going to make you a very rich man.'

Joaquim Abrantes turned his glass on the wooden table as if he was screwing it in. He didn't respond. Maybe he'd heard it before.

'You and I, *Senhor* Abrantes, are going to corner the market in every scrap of uncontracted wolfram in this area.'

'Why should I work with you when I do very well myself and . . . if you can make me rich, can't the British do the same? Perhaps I'd prefer to play the market. It has only one direction as far as I can see.'

'The British will never be in the market for as much tonnage as us.'

'They still buy. They buy to close you out.'

'What do you think of the wolfram price now?' asked Felsen.

'It is high.'

'Are you buying?'

Abrantes rearranged himself in his seat.

'I have stocks,' he said. 'The price is going up.'

'If, as you say, the wolfram price has one direction, then you're going to sell high to buy higher . . . that is, if you want to stay in the market.'

Abrantes' darker eye, the one away from the light, looked over the granite ridge of his nose.

'What are you proposing *Senhor* Felsen?'

'I'm proposing to increase your capacity to trade wolfram for my account.'

'You have the money, I have no doubt, but do you have any idea how you can do it?'

'Perhaps you know the country better than I do.'

Abrantes thumbed a lump of bread and cheese into his mouth and swilled it back with the *aguardente*.

'A lot of the wolfram that's brought to me is not pure,' he said. 'There's always quartz and pyrites in it. If we set up companies to clean the wolfram we will attract more of the mineral and guarantee the quality.'

Felsen nodded.

'I'd want financial control,' said Abrantes. 'I don't want to have to ask permission for every rock I buy and I'd want a share of the profits and if there are no profits a guaranteed percentage of the turnover.'

'How much?'

'Fifteen percent.'

Felsen stood and went towards the door.

'You might be able to make that on your own account with small volume but I can't offer anywhere near that for the volumes I'm talking about.'

'What are these volumes?'

'Thousands rather than hundreds of kilos.'

The Portuguese balanced that in his head.

'If I go with you I'm out of the market . . .'

'I'm not stopping you from trading for your own account.'

'How long will you be in the market? I have no guarantee that you'll . . .'

'*Senhor* Abrantes. This war . . . this war that we need all this wolfram for, will change everything. Do you know what's happening in Europe? Germany controls everything from Scandinavia to North Africa, from France to Russia.

132

The British are finished. Germany will control the economy of Europe and, if you work with me, you will be a friend of Germany. So to answer your question, *Senhor* Abrantes, we will be in the market for your lifetime, the lifetime of your children and theirs and more.'

'Ten percent.'

'That's not a percentage that the business can bear,' said Felsen and reached for the door.

'Seven.'

'I don't think you understand where this business is going, *Senhor* Abrantes. If you did, you'd know that a single percent would make you the richest man in the Beira.'

'Come, sit down,' he said. 'We can discuss this. We must eat. You must know how important it is for us to eat by now.'

'I know it,' said Felsen and sat down.

The girl brought in a thick stew of pork, liver and black pudding. She put more bread on the table and a jug of red wine. The two men ate alone. Abrantes told Felsen the dish was called *Sarrabulho* and that it was the best thing the girl had learnt from her mother.

Joaquim Abrantes might have been a peasant once but he wasn't one any more. This didn't mean, as Felsen found out during their discussion towards an agreement on volumes and percentages, that he could read or write. It meant that his father had farmed land and between them they'd acquired more. He had the house which was joined to two others at the back and to the side. They had livestock. He appreciated good food and drink. He had his young wife. He was a strange brute. On the few occasions that their eyes met, Felsen had the same feeling as he did looking into a bull's head. There was something big, private and planetary going on inside the man's brain. He understood surprising things about business and numbers but had no concept of maps or distances unless he'd travelled them. He had an instinct for power. He didn't like anybody except his old, half-blind father. Women did not speak to him.

After lunch he excused himself. Felsen stood and stretched. Through the double doors he saw into a parlour where the mother was crocheting and beyond that into the kitchen. Abrantes was standing behind the girl who was leaning with both hands on the table. He had his hand up her skirt. He straightened the front of his trousers and looked down as if he might mount her there and then. He thought better of it and went outside and down the back stairs.

Chapter XI

3rd July 1941, Guarda, Beira Baixa, Portugal.

Felsen was sweating at his small table by the shuttered window in the airless restaurant, which had fans but not working ones. The shutters kept out the devastating heat, which blasted off the cobbles and stone façades of the buildings, but did not improve the stuffiness in the room. The restaurant contained fifteen men split between two tables near the door, and him alone at the other end. The men were loud, *volframistas*, with too much money from their mineral finds and too much brandy in their guts. They all had *chapéus ricos*, which were the same as poor man's hats but more expensive and they all had pens in their jacket breast pockets even though they were illiterate to a man. The restaurant had been quiet enough until they'd run out of the best wine in the house and the *volframistas* had taken to drinking brandy in the same quantity as wine. Their rivals on the next table matched them bottle for bottle. The insults were piling high, like washing-up in the sink, and they were threatening to soak blood into the bare, rough wooden floors.

Joaquim Abrantes came in and shouted at the table of fat sweating men nearest the door. They calmed. The other *volframistas* continued a one-way trade in insults. Abrantes turned his head slowly on them and gave them a smile with some brand-new dentures. They were more sinister than the wrecking rocks he'd had before and the men shut up.

Abrantes sat down opposite Felsen in his new suit. He was learning the value of a smile in business with northern

Europeans, but he hadn't quite mastered the new dentures he'd had fitted in Lisbon at Felsen's expense the month before.

Felsen had just flown back from Berlin having had a meeting with the uglier side of Gruppenführer Lehrer. On the 20th June Lehrer had been to see Fritz Todt, the Armaments Minister, who had been sick and grey with worry at the consequences for his production line of the invasion of Russia, which was due to start on 22nd June. Lehrer had told Felsen that the wolfram stocks were pitiful and gave him a vivid description of another meeting he'd had with the SS-Reichsführer Himmler, who'd trampled his balls into the carpet. Felsen doubted this. He'd seen Himmler at a rally in Munich before the war. The man was more of a bean-counter than a ball-trampler.

There was a net result of this bad lunch meeting. Wolfram was required at any price. He was to look at tin as well and there were other markets – sardines, olive oil, cork, hides, blankets for instance.

'Does that mean we're going to take on the Russians in their own winter?' Felsen had asked.

'Russia is a large place,' Lehrer had replied, slowly and quietly. 'Our little delay was not . . . timely.'

'It takes time to conquer Yugoslavia, Greece, Rumania, Bulgaria . . .'

'The champagne has been flowing in the Hotel Parque no doubt,' said Lehrer, cutting him off savagely.

'I wouldn't know, Herr Gruppenführer.'

The Riesling had gone down like acid.

Felsen had flown back to Lisbon and looked to the *Abwehr* for some intelligence help that would give him an edge against the British, who had matched his new prices and taken a fifty-ton contract from under his nose. They were not helpful. Felsen was now back in the Beira looking to do some kicking himself.

Abrantes sucked the soup between his new dentures.

Felsen, two courses ahead, toyed with a large lump of pork but had no appetite.

'There's going to be a car,' said Abrantes, 'on a small road between Melos and Seixo tomorrow afternoon between two and four o'clock.'

'With a British agent?'

Abrantes nodded.

'Do we know anything else?'

'No. Except the road is in pine forest.'

'Who told you?'

'The driver.'

'Is he reliable?'

'He cost a thousand and he wants a job. We'll have to look after him.'

'Reliability's getting expensive.'

Abrantes nodded over his shoulder at the *volframistas*.

'They won't eat bread any more, it's too cheap. They have wristwatches, but can't tell the time. They cap their rotten teeth with gold, but still sleep over their sheep. The Beira's a place for madmen now. A whole village came to see me yesterday. A whole village! Four hundred people from somewhere outside Castelo Branco. They've heard the prices. Two hundred escudos for a little rock and they earn fifty times their daily wage. They're calling it black gold.'

'It can't go on.'

'They'll buy cars next, then you'll see. We'll all be dead men.'

'I mean Dr Salazar won't allow this to carry on. The government won't let people leave their homes, stop tending their crops. They won't let wages and prices get out of control. Salazar knows about inflation.'

'Inflation?'

'It's a plague of the pocket.'

'Tell me.'

'It's a disease that kills money.'

'Money is paper, *Senhor* Felsen,' said Abrantes, flatly.

'Do you know what cancer is?'

Abrantes nodded and stopped working on his *bacalhau*.

'Well, there's cancer of the blood too. It looks the same, it's still red, but there's something growing inside it. You look at your ten-escudo note one day and the next day it's a hundred escudos and the day after that a thousand escudos.'

'And this is not good?'

'The money still looks the same but it has no value. The government is printing money just to keep up with price and wage rises. Your thousand-escudo note buys you nothing. We know about inflation in Germany.'

Joaquim Abrantes' knife and fork still hovered over his *bacalhau*. It was the only time Felsen ever saw him scared.

4th July 1941, Serra da Estrela, Beira Baixa, Portugal.

It was hot. Unbearably hot and still. Even up in the foothills of the *serra* where there should have been some breeze there was only this bleaching, drying heat so dense that Felsen could feel it searing his throat and lungs. He sweated in the back seat of the Citroën with the window open and the furnace air bellowing over him. He drank warm water from a metal flask. Abrantes sat next to him with his jacket on, not a drop of sweat on him.

They'd driven up from Belmonte where there'd been crowds of people out in the baking wilderness. So many people that Felsen had thought that there must have been some miracle, another vision such as the one outside Fátima in 1917, and people were hurrying to catch their sight of the Blessed Virgin. But it was wolfram that had brought them out. Black, shiny crystallized magma blasted up from the centre of the earth a million years ago.

He'd been the start of this new cult, and it fascinated and

horrified him. People had left their lives on one side. Small-town mayors, bureaucrats, lawyers, cobblers, stonemasons, charcoal-makers, tailors . . . they'd all left their work to go scratching at the hills, tearing at the heather, gouging up the earth, their minds teeming with the virus of wolfram. If you'd wanted to die, there was nobody to organize your funeral for you, no one to make a coffin for you.

The blond Englishman felt sick. He lay sprawled in the back seat of his wreck of a car, trying to get some coolness on his fair skin, on his red arms and pink face. It had been a long, brutal drive from Viseu with nothing going right. He'd stopped thinking about wolfram after the first puncture and drifted off into a mild delirium where he was married to a blue-eyed Dutch girl, having children and making wine.

The road jolted him out of his fantasy, the driver finding the deepest potholes with instinctive genius. Snatches of reality riddled through his brain. Why did she want to go to America? There was no talking to the woman. Should he feel guilty? Maybe he should. Maybe he should have at least gone to the US consulate, at least tried to talk to the woman in the visa office, but why cut off your own nose to spite your face? God, this heat, this strange light. Dust from the desert, the driver had said. The man was a bloody idiot, and insolent too. These Beira people, he'd never get the hang of them. Why had they brought him down from the Minho? It never got that hot up there and the people were easier. Wolfram. And he'd never even kissed her.

Felsen's car dropped down the hillside into the pine forest, through the hairpins to the valley floor and then back up the other side. A small truck followed with four men and a driver. They reached the bend in the road they'd found the day before and got out. The car and the truck moved off further up the hill and stopped.

Two men dragged the pine tree, which they'd dug out and

pushed over yesterday, across the road. Another with an axe set off round the hairpin and up the hill. Felsen, Abrantes and the rest went into the susurrating heat of the pine forest. Abrantes gave each of the men a wooden cudgel. They all sat on a crust of dried pine needles. Abrantes straightened a leg and eased out a Walther P48 from his waistband. Felsen lit a cigarette and hung his head between his knees. He'd drunk too much the night before and this heat was getting closer and the light was reddening at the edges as if something terrible was going to happen, something unnatural, like an earthquake. The men whispered behind him, their heels dug into the hillside.

'Shut up,' he said, to the ground.

The men fell silent.

Felsen tried to rearrange his undershorts around his genitals, which were sore from last night's whoring. He shuddered at the memory of the woman's vast, dimpled buttocks, her thick, black bush and her garlic, sewery breath. The disgust stuck in his throat and he couldn't swallow. Flies settled on his sweaty shirt and needled him so that he lashed out over his shoulder. He was hitting another low. He tried to let his mind drift off, but it came aground again on the same rocks. Eva, Lehrer, and the gold KF cufflinks the girl had stolen.

The men were whispering again. It maddened him and he leapt to his feet tearing his own gun from his pocket. He pointed it at each of them in turn.

'Shut up. Shut up. Shut up.'

Abrantes held up his hand.

They all heard the car on the valley floor at the same time. It changed gear and started up the gradient. The men were still as owls on a branch. Felsen sat down and looked through the trees to the man with the axe, who was waiting above them on the side of the road fifty metres up from the fallen tree. He held up his hand. The car worked its way up through the hairpins, the driver disdaining the clutch and crunching through the gears. The sharp stink of resin began to tickle the back of Felsen's dry throat.

'You're going to shred that gearbox if you don't use the clutch,' shouted the Englishman from the back seat.

The driver didn't turn a hair. He stirred the pudding with his gearstick and screeched the shift through the gate as if he enjoyed the sound of grating metal. The Englishman slumped back as the car shuddered round the next hairpin. What would it be like to kiss her lips? He'd felt the corner of it just on the edge of his lip once, and the newness of it had shot through him. Months ago. Would she still be there? He took out his wallet and eased her photograph out with his thumb. He felt the car slow down.

'What is it?'

'Fallen tree,' said the driver, revving the engine, desperate not to stall.

'Is it fallen or cut?' asked the Englishman looking around him through the pine forest, slipping his wallet back.

'It's fallen . . . you can see the roots.'

'How does a pine tree fall at this time of the year?'

The driver shrugged. No expert. No expert on anything, not even driving.

'Get out and take a look,' said the Englishman.

The driver blasted the accelerator again.

'No, wait,' he said, nervous now, suspicious.

Nobody got out of the car for a full two minutes. The driver gunned the engine until it died abruptly. They all sat in the cicada-broken, resinated silence of the forest. The driver got out and gave the tree the benefit of his indolence. He went to the back of the car, opened the boot and rummaged about without looking. He shut it and leaned into the rear window.

The English agent got out. He was tall, dressed in khaki trousers and a white shirt, sleeves rolled up. A revolver

141

hung from his right hand. He looked over the roof into the trees. He checked the base of the pine tree. He went back to the car, laid the gun on the roof, stripped off his shirt and tossed it through the rear window. He was in a white vest now, his arms red to his elbows and white above.

Felsen dropped his arm and the man with the axe over the crook of his elbow set off down the road to the tree.

'*Boa tarde*,' he said to the two men in the road.

The agent tore his gun off the roof and pointed it at the peasant whose hands shot into the air. The axe clattered to the floor. The agent beckoned him over the tree. The peasant looked at his axe. The Englishman shook his head.

'*Não, não, anda cá, anda cá*,' he said.

The peasant told him in a thick accent that he didn't want to leave his axe there on the floor. The driver repeated it for the agent's benefit. The agent told him to pick it up and hand it over. The peasant held out the smooth wooden handle. The agent gave it to the driver and told him to get on with it.

'Let him do the work,' said the driver.

'I want you to do it. We don't know him.'

The driver shook his head and walked away. The Englishman was angry but in a situation now. He shoved the revolver in his waistband and set to work on the tree. The driver sat on the front bumper and wiped the sweat off his forehead. The peasant looked at the agent with the mildness of expression that a working man's face takes on when he sees someone who doesn't know how to use a tool. The agent was in a lather in seconds. At first he stopped to wipe the sweat, then he just flicked his head to keep it out of his eyes. The peasant's hands itched.

'Leave him be,' said Felsen under his breath, easing himself down the hillside to the edge of the road. 'Let him do it.'

Felsen and Abrantes walked on either side of the car past

the driver on the bumper. Felsen nodded to the peasant.

'*Posso?*' the peasant asked the Englishman. May I?

The agent handed him the axe and felt Felsen's warm Walther P48 in the hollow behind his right ear. Abrantes removed the Englishman's revolver. The agent's legs were trembling in his trousers. He turned slowly and couldn't stop the flicker of recognition across his eyes as he saw the German.

This one, thought Felsen, whose eyes were hot in his head, Laura van Lennep's friend. The one who wouldn't shake his hand. What was this one's name? Edward Burton.

Abrantes told the Englishman's driver to help the men move the tree off the road. The driver had different ideas. He wasn't a labourer any more, this wasn't his type of work, and where was his thousand escudos? Abrantes tightened his hat down on his head. Felsen, already on the brink, snapped. He ripped one of the men's wooden cudgels out of his hands and ran at the driver. The driver went on to his back foot, his mind changing fast, but it was too late. Felsen fell on him like a pile of logs, swiping and slashing and chopping. The driver went down in the first mad chaos of blows from the cudgel. Felsen with his heart blasting in his chest, dropped to his knees and hammered, and hammered and hammered until he didn't know what he was hammering any more.

The other men stopped their work and watched him through their sweat.

Felsen wiped his forehead on his shoulder and stained it dark. He rubbed his eyes but couldn't get the dimmed edges of his vision to brighten. He was panting, still down on his knees, his head thumping and his vision pulsing with it. He looked down at the piece of meat in front of him and felt his guts rise. He got to his feet on shaky legs, the bloody club hanging loosely from his hand. The Englishman was vomiting.

The light sickened further, the high red dust scarfing the sun.

The men hadn't gone back to work and Felsen thought he might join the Englishman until he saw their faces. They were confused and afraid of the power of a man who could do such a thing for nothing at all. Felsen had seen them like this before, but only around Abrantes.

'Now you see,' he said, pointing at them with the cudgel, still breathing heavily. 'Now you understand the importance of obedience. Isn't that right *Senhor* Burton?'

The use of his name jerked the agent up straight from his retching, but he couldn't get any words out. His lips had gone white in his pale face. He sweated fatly from the forehead as if he'd been touched by cholera.

'Bury him,' said Felsen, and threw the cudgel at the feet of the men.

Abrantes led Burton to the back seat of his car while Felsen got behind the wheel. They stopped at Abrantes' house and picked up a chair, some rope, and a bottle of cool *bagaço* from the back of the cellar. They drove to a disused mine in the hills near Amêndoa, one where the wolfram vein had run out after about thirty metres. In the boot of the car was a brazier and some charcoal and a few *chouriços*. Abrantes sprinkled the raw alcohol of the *bagaço* over the coals and started a fire. In Burton's briefcase Felsen found bundles of notes amounting to 500,000 escudos and an unsigned contract for eighty tons of wolfram with a mining concession down in Penamacor. His throat still felt dry, but there was no water so he chugged the cold *bagaço* and wiped his mouth on his sleeve.

'Did you ever see Laura again?' asked Felsen in English, flicking through the contract.

'The Chave d'Ouro,' said Burton on automatic.

'Did she get her precious visa?'

Burton stared into his past as if it was his own country disappearing over the horizon. Felsen took another blast of alcohol trying to stop the needle from scoring the inside of his cranium. The cool alcohol burnt all the way down.

'Did she?' he asked again, and Burton looked up wild-eyed but didn't answer.

Felsen frisked the Englishman's pockets and came up with the wallet. He fingered through the currency and came across the photograph. He held it up to the terracotta light of the afternoon.

'Did you get what you wanted?' asked Felsen. 'At least tell me that.'

'I didn't *want* her to get a visa.'

'In that case you probably didn't get what you wanted.'

'What did I want?'

'You mean . . .' Felsen stopped. 'To fuck her, Mr Burton. Didn't you want to fuck her?'

'Laura?' he said.

'Ah,' said Felsen. 'A misunderstanding.'

'I don't follow.'

'Laura's deal. You didn't know Laura's deal? You get me a visa. No. You look as if you can get me a visa . . . and you can fuck me. Just the word "visa" brought love into her eyes. It was there for everyone to see, Mr Burton. I was not the first, I can assure you, not by a long way.'

Felsen turned the photograph over.

'To Edward, with love,' he read, and for some reason it made Felsen crueller. 'Come on Edward, don't tell me . . . I mean she was doing things you'd be hard pressed to get a Friedrichstrasse whore to do . . .'

Burton was off his chair and on him, his scrawny arm around the German's bull neck. He drove his boy's fist into the man's kidney. Felsen's thick elbow kicked back like a steam piston. The boy went down. Abrantes fanned the charcoal white.

Felsen secured Burton to the chair. He took another shot of the *bagaço*. His head felt better, clearer, smoother. He shook the contract at the Englishman.

145

'You're on my territory, Edward. This is my wolfram you're taking. Who else are you talking to down there?'

Burton shut down his brain. He didn't listen to the German. He didn't smell the acrid charcoal. He didn't feel the hot pant of Abrantes' fan. He didn't see the red clouds boiling in the strange sky.

Felsen found a length of wire in the boot of the car. Abrantes began roasting the *chouriços*, turning them with fingers suddenly dainty. Felsen pushed more questions at the English agent, his tongue thick in his mouth, the alcohol telling now. The alcohol reminding him of Laura, the stolen cufflinks, Eva, Lehrer, the whore in Guarda last night. Burton was silent, forcing the gross smell of the spitting pork fat out of his mind.

'That fat Rumanian sow in the visa office told me Salazar's police were Gestapo-trained,' said Felsen. 'My colleagues told me it was Kramer. He's a KZ commandant now. They know how to treat you in a KZ. We all hear about it, Edward, we all know . . . but there's nothing like learning from actual experience. I've never been in one which means I've only learnt at second-hand, so you might find my methods a little unrefined.'

Felsen tucked the wire into the coals. He removed the agent's belt and using Abrantes' knife cut away the man's trousers and undershorts. He found a leather glove, fitted his hand into it and removed the hot wire. He stopped, feeling a rush of wind at his back, he looked out of the mine at the chemical sky, then stepped towards the Englishman.

The peasants who'd been burying the body of the driver in the pine forest arrived back in Amêndoa a little after five in the afternoon. The day was at its hottest. Their eyeballs stung in their sockets and their mouths were full of thick, rancid saliva. They went to the spring, drank heavily and dipped rags from their pockets into the water and cooled their necks and faces. They stopped only when they heard the animal for the first time. A strange animal, of a type they'd never heard before, and in terrible pain.

They walked to the edge of the village. A scream came from a hole out in the hills and suddenly they recognized it. They put their hats on and straightened them. They went back to the cool of their granite houses and lay down on their wooden cots, heads on elbows, the balls of their palms in their ears.

The weather broke. The thunder roused Felsen from his drunken sleep. He didn't know where he was. His head ached so that he thought he must have fallen, and his mouth tasted sour as cheese. He rolled over to see the Englishman slumped in his chair and it shocked him. He was going to check him, but he saw the gun on the floor and the blood over the man's chest and . . . how had that happened?

Rain began falling darkly. Felsen went out into it to wash his hands. He leapt back and fell staggering into the mine, crashing over Abrantes' supine body. His hands and shirt stained red, his arms flecked with more red. He kicked at the rocks on the floor to get away from the crude opening of the mine. It was raining blood out there. He roared at Abrantes who'd come awake and put his hand out into the rain and squeezed it in his fist.

'This happened before,' he said, and wiped his hand clean on his trousers. 'My father told me that it rained like this forty years ago. It comes through the red desert dust. It's nothing.'

They folded the agent's body into the boot of the car and backed up the track to Abrantes' house. They unloaded Burton into the yard. Felsen drove the car back and as deep into the old mine as it would go. The storm had brought night on early. When he dimmed the headlights in the mine there wasn't a scrap of ambient light. He gripped the steering wheel and pressed his forehead to it. The sound of shattering glass came to him, the *bagaço* bottle on the wall of the mine, the neck of it now forming the handle of a primitive tool. How could that have happened?

Abrantes was waist-deep in a hole in the yard, the girl watching him. She was big, pregnant, halfway through her term. She poured Felsen a glass of cool white wine and went into the house.

'Congratulations,' said Felsen, reconnected now with the world.

Abrantes wondered what he meant. Felsen nodded to the house.

'It had better be a boy,' said Abrantes.

'Isn't she young for children?'

'More likely to produce boys.'

'I didn't know that.'

'It's what the *Senhora dos Santos* says, our local wise woman.'

Abrantes shovelled earth, a cigarette in the corner of his mouth.

'How old is the girl?'

'I don't know.'

The girl came into the yard with olives, cheese and meats. She laid them on the table next to the wine.

'How old are you?' asked Abrantes.

'I don't know,' she said.

They buried the body and went to bed. Felsen dreamt vividly. He woke up, his bladder swollen tight. He mistakenly stumbled into the main house to relieve himself and heard the sound of Abrantes' animal grunting and the girl making a kind of hissing sound as if she'd cut herself with a knife. He went back out into the yard and then to the edge of the village where the air was now fresh and the earth smelling rich after the rain. He pissed a twenty-metre length of barbed wire. Tears coursed down his face. That whore in Guarda. The pain was excruciating.

Chapter XII

16th December 1941, SS Barracks, Unter den Eichen, Berlin-Lichterfelde.

'So,' said Gruppenführer Lehrer, summarizing the wolfram campaign to Brigadeführers Hanke, Fischer and Wolff, 'we have received 2200 tons here in Germany. There's 300 tons in transit and there are 175 tons of stocks in Portugal. By my mathematics that makes a total of 2675 tons which is 325 tons below the 3000-ton target for the year.'

Silence from the four men. Felsen sat smoking in a chair about three metres adrift from Lehrer's desk.

'Our Intelligence in Lisbon inform us that the British exported 3850 tons.'

'You probably haven't seen the Beralt mine, sir,' said Felsen. 'It's a colossal operation . . .'

'Intelligence goes on to say that 1300 tons of that was "free" wolfram, uncontracted wolfram. As I see it that's 1300 tons that should have come to Germany. My God,' said Lehrer, rifling through the papers on his desk, 'the money we're paying for this . . .'

'660,000 escudos per ton,' said Felsen.

'That doesn't mean anything to me.'

'Six thousand pounds per ton,' said Wolff.

'Exactly,' said Lehrer. 'Huge money.'

'It's over seven thousand pounds a ton in Spain and product is moving across the border to take advantage of that,' said Felsen. 'In a market like this it's not always easy to persuade people to sell. The British moved out of the market in October and you saw the price fell by a quarter. Now they're back in.'

'That shouldn't stop you from buying.'

'We have to accept that when the British are in the market they will always have their contacts. These are people who cannot be persuaded to sell to us, not with money and not with fear.'

'Fear?'

'We are conducting our own war in the Beira, it's just not as well covered as the Russian campaign.'

'Blankets,' said Hanke, in a knee-jerk reaction to the word Russia.

'Not now, Hanke,' said Lehrer.

'It might make you happier to know that the British are paying more for their wolfram,' said Felsen. 'Salazar introduced a 700 pounds per ton export tax in October. All the British product goes out by sea so they have to declare every kilo in the ports. I've shipped more than 300 tons without paying any tax.'

'Smuggling?' asked Fischer.

'It's a long and difficult border.'

'We understand that Salazar wants to reduce the wolfram production. All this money we're pouring into his country is worrying him . . . inflation, that sort of thing.'

'That's why he brought in the export tax,' said Felsen. 'Now he's put a special department of the Metals Corporation in position which is designed to buy all wolfram and tin . . .'

'Yes, yes, yes, we know all this,' said Hanke. 'Our legation in Lisbon will now have to persuade Salazar that Germany deserves the lion's share of the "free" wolfram ahead of the British.'

'I will carry on buying and smuggling,' said Felsen, 'but from now on the big tonnage will be settled in the government offices in Lisbon and not out in the fields of the Beira. It will take time though . . .'

'Why?'

'Ask Poser. He thinks Salazar's the trickiest bastard since Napoleon.'

'What's Salazar after?' asked Wolff.

'Gold. Raw materials. No trouble.'

'We have gold. We can probably lay our hands on some good steel and if he doesn't like that we can hurt him,' said Lehrer.

'How?' asked Fischer.

'We sank the SS *Corte Real* back in October, Fischer. Don't you remember anything? There's no reason why we shouldn't torpedo another one.'

'Oh, I see what you mean,' said Fischer, who'd had something more personal in mind.

'Now . . . blankets, Hanke,' said Lehrer.

The meeting and dinner afterwards went on until 11.00 p.m. Lehrer had accompanied him to his waiting car, jolly, drunk and dangerous.

'The Americans are in now, Felsen. How about that?' he'd said and run his finger back and forth over his palm as if he was spreading something. Then he'd clapped his hands. 'Don't forget the liverwurst.'

Felsen didn't react. Lehrer shook with laughter.

The car started its slow mole-crawl back to his apartment in Berlin. Felsen hadn't said anything in the meeting, but those figures had bothered him. He knew his campaign hadn't made the 3000-ton target, but he also knew he was a lot closer than 325 tons adrift. There must have been something wrong with the way the stocks had been calculated in Portugal. He smoked a cigarette in about three drags, thinking about it.

The car dropped him off just before midnight. He waited for it to leave and then he set out for Eva's club on the Kurfürstendamm.

He took a small table on his own in an alcove with a

151

view of Eva's office door. A girl with short jet-black hair, and bare white arms, was singing badly up on the stage, but getting away with it because her legs were long, slim and perfect in nylon. He ordered a brandy and looked at all the women in the house. No Eva. A girl came to his table and asked if he wanted company. She was boyish, with no hips and a starved bottom. He shook his head without speaking. The girl shrugged her bony shoulders.

Felsen took out his cigarettes, the silver case slipped out of his hand. He fished around under the table. There was another hand there. He surfaced. Eva was putting one of his cigarettes in her mouth. She lit it, then Felsen's, and polished the case on her dress.

'I thought it was you,' she said. 'I still don't recognize you in uniform. I mean I can't distinguish men in uniform. Shall I join you for a bit?'

She swung her legs under the table and her knee touched his. There was a spark of recognition, a pulse that travelled, and brought back a time and two people who'd known something of each other.

'What happened to you?' she asked, giving him back his case, touching his hand, the familiar hair, tough hair, strong as pig bristle. 'You've lost your Berlin pallor.'

'You were always the pale one,' he said.

'Recently, I've become translucent,' she said. 'It's the diet and the fear.'

'You don't look scared.'

'The only reason I have a full house tonight is because of the cloud cover. Some nights it's just me and the girls . . . and our friends from across the water dropping Christmas turkeys.'

'The girls are looking scrawnier,' said Felsen, not seeing Eva's stick-thin arm.

'Me too,' she said, showing him an arm stringy with muscle.

He played with his glass and made a perfect cone of the

152

ember of his cigarette. How to get started? Nine months out of Berlin, and he'd lost the veneer, the hard-dried varnish of cynicism and wit, that got the Berliners through their days.

'I saw you in Bern,' he said, to the ashtray.

She frowned and her cheeks sank as she drew on her cigarette.

'I've never been to Bern,' she said. 'You must have . . .'

'I saw you in a nightclub in Bern . . . back in February.'

'But, Klaus . . . I've never even been to Switzerland.'

'I saw you there with him.'

He was completely still and looking at her with the intensity of a hungry wolf down from the mountain. She returned the look, back-lit, the smoke curling around her head. No backing down from the lie.

'You've changed,' she said, and took a sip from his brandy glass.

'I spend a lot of time outdoors.'

'We've all changed,' she said, and her knee disconnected from his. 'There's been a human hardening.'

'We all end up doing things we don't necessarily want to do,' he said. 'But it's not as if there's no opportunity.'

'Just that there's not always the choice.'

'Yes,' he said, and had a hot stink of memory from a July afternoon in a disused mine when there had been a choice and something had gone wrong.

'What *happened* to you, Klaus?' she asked, the different emphasis jolting him, as if he'd been wearing something on his face he shouldn't have.

'Some things can't easily be explained.'

'That is very true,' she replied.

The girl who'd come by earlier drew up next to Eva.

'Nobody wants me to sit with them,' she said.

'Sit with Klaus,' said Eva. 'He wants you to sit with him.'

They looked at him. He nodded to the empty space. The

153

girl wriggled in, happy now. Eva leaned over and put her cheek next to his.

'It's been nice,' she said, 'to have a little talk.'

She left no scent, only the feeling of her warm breath.

'My name is Traudl,' said the girl.

'We met before,' he said and turned the brandy glass around on its coaster. He put it to his lips where Eva's had been. She still wore the same lipstick.

He took Traudl back to his apartment. She talked for the two of them. He hung his coat up, poured himself a drink and found that she'd gone. He was relieved until she called him from the bedroom. He told her to come back into the living room.

'It's cold,' she said.

She was naked walking on tiptoe across the polished floor, the tendons and sinews in her thin legs visible. The unfilled flaps of her breasts with shrivelled nipples hung off the racked ribs of her chest. She hugged them to herself. He took off his tunic and loosened the braces off his shoulders. She shivered with her fists under her chin. He saw her back view reflected in the glass doors of the bedroom – the sad bottom with hip bones protruding. He nearly lost all enthusiasm for the project. He sat down and asked her to massage the front of his trousers. Her teeth chattered. His penis wouldn't stir.

'You're cold, go back to bed,' he said.

'No,' she said, 'I want to.'

'Go back to bed,' he said, with a little blade in his voice and she didn't argue.

He sat in the dark and drank *aguardente* that he'd brought back with him for Christmas. It tasted like hell. He circled over his meeting with Eva looking for scraps. There were none. In the early hours he decided there was nothing left for him in Berlin and he'd take the next flight back to Lisbon.

*   *   *

He flew back the next day via Rome and spent only enough time in Lisbon for Poser to tell him that something had happened. He didn't know what it was, he had men working on it, but Salazar was not happy.

'He's frothing at the mouth,' said Poser, relishing it, 'completely rabid with fury. Magnificent rage. And the Allies are catching it . . . just in time for our negotiations with the Metals Commission.'

Felsen drove up to the Beira and spent the afternoon of the 19th December with the accountant in Guarda. He made a small circuit of his territory and three days before Christmas appeared in Amêndoa on a wind-whipped frozen morning. There was no sign of Abrantes. The old woman was there with her husband, Abrantes' father, sitting in his customary winter position in the fireplace, crying from the smoke. The girl was there too with her son, Pedro, who was four months old. Felsen asked her where her husband was, and she looked embarrassed, which she was only rarely in his company now that she was used to him. Her fingers were ringless. She wasn't married.

Felsen stroked the baby's downy head which fitted neatly into his palm. The girl offered him food and drink and flipped the baby on to her hip.

'Let me take him,' said Felsen.

She hesitated and searched the German's face with her lime-green eyes. Foreigners. She gave him the baby and went to the kitchen. She'd never regained her girlish form. Her bosom had stayed full and her hips swung in her calf-length skirts. When she turned she found Felsen looking at her in that way and she nearly smiled. He tickled the baby. Pedro grinned and Felsen had a cameo of Joaquim Abrantes with his dentures out.

She brought him some wine and *chouriço*. He gave her the baby who reached for her breasts.

'Is he out on his land?' asked Felsen, thinking Abrantes

might be fossicking his twenty hectares now that the wolf-ram price had peaked.

'He left this morning. He didn't say,' she said.

'Do you expect him back?'

She shrugged – Abrantes didn't talk to any of the women in his house. Felsen drank two glasses of the rough wine and ate a couple of chunks of *chouriço* and went out into the cold morning. He drove into the next valley and found someone to take him to Abrantes' piece of land. He was right, they were working it. But no Abrantes.

There was a small granite and slate house on the property. Half its roof was fallen in, the unbroken slates stacked in rows on the floor, the shattered ones in a pile of grey shards. A woman was cooking in there out of the wind, stirring a pot on a rusted brazier. She was filthy and haggard, her face sunken with toothlessness.

The door was rotten on the other side of the house. People were living in there. There was a rag-covered pallet and some chipped clay jars. The place smelled of damp earth and urine. Something small was shivering under the rags.

One of Abrantes' peasants from Amêndoa came around the side of the house and stopped, surprised to see Felsen. He removed his hat and came forward, bowing. Felsen asked after Abrantes.

'He's not here,' said the peasant looking at the ground.

'And the others? Where are they? Why aren't they here?'

No answer.

'And who are these people living out here on the land of *Senhor* Abrantes like this?'

The woman left her pot and began talking to the peasant in toothless Portuguese and at some length using her wooden spoon for emphasis.

'What is she saying?'

'It is nothing,' said the peasant.

The woman railed at him. The peasant looked away. Felsen directed his question at the woman. She gave him a very long answer during which the peasant cut in with the short words:

'She is the wife of *Senhor* Abrantes.'

'And this child in here?'

The peasant beckoned Felsen away from the old crone around to the back of the house where there were three mounds of grass unmarked.

'The children of *Senhor* Abrantes,' said the peasant. 'A sickness of the lungs.'

'And the one inside?'

The peasant nodded.

'All girls?'

He nodded again.

'Where is *Senhor* Abrantes?'

'Spain,' he said without taking his eyes from the mounds.

The peasant's name was Alvaro Fortes. Felsen put him in the front seat next to the driver and they went to the border at Vilar Formoso. Felsen drank *aguardente* from the same metal bottle he used for water in the summer and ran his thumb over the calculations he'd made – 28 tons from Penamacor, 30 tons from Casteleiro, 17 tons brought over from Barco, 34 tons up from Idanha-a-Nova. All missing – which was why the Portuguese stocks were 109 tons lower than they should have been.

At the border he drank with the *chefe* of the *alfândega* who was pleased to give him the information that the British had been tracking German shipments through the border all last month, and there'd been rumours that Lisbon were going to issue orders to hold up his consignments of wolfram. Felsen gave the man a bottle of brandy and asked after Abrantes. The *chefe* hadn't seen him in a week.

It started to rain as they drove south along the border to Aldeia da Ponte and then on to Aldeia do Bispo and

157

Foios at the foot of the Serra da Malcata, whose vast low, lynx-patrolled hills crossed the border. Here there was a *contrabandista* who was going to run a pack mule operation through the *serra* for him if Dr Salazar decided to make life difficult.

'Have you ever made the journey across to Spain?' he asked the back of Alvaro Fortes' head. No answer.

'Did you hear me?'

'Yes, *Senhor* Felsen.'

'Have you done it before?'

Again no answer.

'When was the first time?'

Alvaro Fortes answered by not answering. Felsen began to feel the heat of his missing tonnage as the wind strafed the car from the north. They drove through the village to the house and stables of the man who kept the mules. The *serra* was invisible under low cloud.

At the mule-owner's house Felsen went to the boot and unlocked a small metal trunk. He removed his Walther P48 and loaded it. He told Alvaro Fortes to get out of the car. They went to the back of the granite house, into the stableyard, which had a warehouse at one end, chained and padlocked. There were no mules. Alvaro Fortes jiggled about like a man with a full bladder.

Felsen banged on the door at the back of the house with the heel of his hand. No response. He made Alvaro Fortes hammer continuously, and they heard the old man's voice from inside.

'*Calma, calma, já vou,*' he said. I'm coming.

The rain was slanting across the yard as he opened the door on the German standing in a thick leather coat with his hands clasped behind his back. He knew he was in trouble well before a hand came out and put a gun in his face.

'No mules,' said Felsen.

'They're out working.'

158

'Who's with them?'

'My son.'

'Anybody else?'

The old man's eyes flicked across to Alvaro Fortes who was no help.

'Have you got the key to that warehouse?'

'It's empty.'

Felsen put the barrel of the gun right up to the man's eye so that he could smell the oil, see the narrow, dark, escape route from life. The old man produced the key. They walked across the puddled yard. He opened the padlock and ripped the chain out. Alvaro Fortes opened the doors. The warehouse was empty. Felsen went down on his haunches and pressed his finger on to the dry floor and came back up with fine black chips embedded in his skin. He stood up.

'Kneel, both of you,' he said.

He fitted the gun barrel under the occipital bulge at the back of the old man's head.

'Who is with your son and the mules?'

'*Senhor* Abrantes.'

'What are they doing?'

'Running wolfram to Spain.'

'Where do they take the wolfram?'

'A warehouse in Navasfrias.'

He pressed the gun into Alvaro Fortes' head.

'What happens to the wolfram?'

'He sells it.'

'To who?'

'To the highest bidder.'

'Has he sold to the British?'

Silence. The rain lashed the yard and the roof overhead.

'Has he sold to the British?'

'I don't know who he sells to. *Senhor* Abrantes doesn't talk of such things.'

159

Felsen went back to the old man.

'When will he return?'

'The day after tomorrow.'

'Will you tell him I have been here?'

'No, *Senhor*, I will not . . . if you don't wish it.'

'I don't wish it,' said Felsen. 'If you do tell him I will come back here and kill you myself. I will shoot you in the head.'

To show a level of seriousness he let off a round past the old man's ear that would leave him deaf for a week. The bullet ricocheted around the slate and granite warehouse. Alvaro Fortes threw his hands over his head and fell to one side. Felsen grabbed him by the scruff and threw him into the yard.

They went back to the car. Felsen sipped liquor from his bottle while Alvaro Fortes shivered with his hair plastered to his white forehead.

He ordered the driver to take them back to Amêndoa and as the wind drove the rain over the hills and through the chestnut trees and oaks and on to the granite walls, rather than wolfram or Abrantes he found himself thinking of Eva. A few nights ago he'd been a civilized man sitting with a woman in a Berlin club. She'd lied to him. There'd been a betrayal before the lie, but he hadn't been able to drag up any anger. Out here in this rock-shambled, wind-blasted place, where the houses were carved out of the ground, he could only find a single-minded brutality to drive him through to the next day. He was a primitive, a man stripped down to the essentials.

And now he was going to have to kill Joaquim Abrantes.

It was dark when they arrived back in Amêndoa. The girl and Abrantes' parents were eating. He joined them. The rain had stopped and only the wind was left, shifting the tiles on the roof. The old man wouldn't eat. His wife brought the food to his mouth but he wouldn't take it.

She ate her own food, wiped her husband's eyes and took him to bed. The girl waited on Felsen. She wouldn't sit with him. He asked after the baby. The baby was sleeping. She offered him apples, but he hadn't finished the stew. He listened to her skirts as she moved around him. He thought about Abrantes grunting over her and that hissing sound she made.

She looked at him while he was eating. Every chance she had. Even when she was behind him he knew she was looking. He was different to look at. He asked for coffee, which they'd never had in the house before the German came. He drank it and poured *aguardente* on to the grounds and sank that. He said goodnight. She brought him a flat, metal pan of hot coals to take the edge off the cold in his bare room across the courtyard where they used to keep the hay for the animals.

He lay on his bed and smoked cigarettes by the light of the hurricane lamp. After an hour he got up and crossed the courtyard. He went to the girl's room which had just a curtain across the door. She was sleeping. He put the lamp on the floor. She woke up with a gasp. He clamped his hand over her mouth and pulled back the covers. The baby was sleeping at her back. He eased the child to one side. He rolled her on to her back trapping her arms underneath. He pushed his hand up her woollen-stockinged legs. Her thighs were clamped shut. He jammed his hand between them and prised them open by making a fist. Her eyes darted left and right over his hand. He tugged her drawers down to her knees and undid his trousers. He was surprised to slide into her easily and their eyes connected in the leopard light from the lamp on the floor. He was slow and gentle with the baby in the bed. After some minutes she closed her eyes and he felt her heel on his left buttock. He took his hand away from her mouth. She began to tense and shudder against him and the other heel began to kick at his right buttock. He quickened. Her eyes sprang open and

161

he emptied himself into her and stayed there, rammed to the hilt and quivering.

The next day she gave him breakfast. It was no different to any other day except that she looked at him straight, with no shyness.

He stayed out all day, overseeing the loading of a cargo of wolfram into rail cars. He went back to Abrantes' house at nightfall. After dinner the old couple went to bed. The girl remained sitting at the table with Felsen. They didn't talk. He got up to go to bed. She gave him the pan of coals. He asked her name, and she told him Maria.

An hour later she joined him. This time, without the baby in the bed, he could be more robust with her but he was aware that she never hissed in the way that she did when Abrantes was covering her.

In the morning he dressed and checked the Walther P48, which he tucked into his waistband. Her muddy footprints had dried on the floor.

At breakfast he asked her to clean his room. Then he sat in the darkness of the main house, listening to the rain and waited for Abrantes.

Chapter XIII

Saturday, 13th June 199–, Cascais, Portugal.

Carlos and I stood outside the apartment block of the lawyer's wife's ex-lover. It was brand-new, finished in nasty
yellow, with a sea view over the railway line, over the
Marginal, over the car park of the supermarket. Not perfect,
but good enough to be way beyond what a policeman could
ever afford.

There was a chain across a forecourt of *calçada* on which
was parked a brand-new jeep called something like a
Wrangler, with chrome and black roll bars and a high
polish finish. It was a lot of jeep to go pavement-hopping
in Cascais. Under the apartment building there was a small
garage with a silver 3 series BMW and a jet-black Kawasaki
900 motorbike. These all belonged to Paulo Branco, the
ex-lover and only occupier of any of the apartments in
the block. A salesman's foot wedged open the door to the
building while he fitted in his last two metres of bullshit
to a young couple leaving. We walked past them and up
to the penthouse.

We got Paulo Branco out of bed. He came to the door in
shorts and smelled of a recent sexual encounter although
we didn't see much of her – a tanned arm over a sheet, a
brown foot dangling. He was good-looking in a way that
hundreds of guys are – black hair swept back, dark brown
eyes, square jaw with regular cleft and a gym-worked phy-
sique. Bland but confident, until he saw our identification.

We went into the open-plan living room with a floor-
to-ceiling arched window and the view. We sat around a

table scattered with photographs and four coloured mobile phones.

'You know *Senhora* Teresa Oliveira?' I asked.

He frowned.

'She's the wife of Dr Aquilino Dias Oliveira, a lawyer. They have a house here in Cascais,' I reminded him.

'Yes, I know them.'

'How?'

'I sold him a computer last year.'

'Is that your business?'

'It was then. Now I'm at Expo. I installed most of the equipment there.'

'The stuff that didn't work?' asked Carlos, getting his needle in early.

'We had some teething problems.'

'Made some money though?'

The photographs on the table showed a farmhouse in the Alentejo by the look of the land – the cork trees and olive groves. Another fashion accessory.

'This yours too?' asked Carlos.

He nodded. So did we.

'We understand you became intimate with the lawyer's wife. When did that happen?'

He looked over his shoulder at the bedroom door, open a crack.

'May,' he said. 'I think it was May, last year. I'd like some coffee . . . would you like some?'

'We won't keep you long,' I said. 'Why did you become intimate with Teresa Oliveira?'

'What sort of a question is that?'

'One of the easier ones,' said Carlos.

He leaned across the table to take us into his confidence.

'She wanted sex. She said the old guy wasn't up to it any more.'

'Where?' asked Carlos.

164

'In the usual place,' he said, pulling some cockiness together, now that he knew this wasn't a fiscal investigation.

'Geographically.'

He gave Carlos his best false smile.

'In her Lisbon house.'

'Not here?'

'Once or twice when I was home early on a Friday evening she'd come over . . . but it was mainly in Lisbon. I'd go out on a sales call and drop by her house. That was it.'

'And the daughter,' I said, 'Catarina?'

He looked like a man whose parachute had just failed to open.

'The *daughter*?' he said.

'Her name was Catarina.'

'*Was?*'

'That's what I said.'

'Now look, I haven't seen Catarina for . . . for . . .'

'Go on . . . for how long?'

He swallowed hard and put his hand through his styled hair.

'We heard you went to bed with her,' I said. 'When was the last time?'

He slapped his thighs, stood up, shouted something inarticulate and strode across the room gesticulating. Suddenly we were in soap opera.

'Sit down please, *Senhor* Branco,' I said, getting out of my seat and pointing at his.

He was stunned. The door to the bedroom clicked shut – the girl probably looking for her underwear by now. Paulo Branco sat down and viced his head between his hands, not wanting to hear any more.

'I want a lawyer,' he said.

'You've got the number of one here in Cascais,' said Carlos, enjoying himself too much.

'We're not going to charge you with having sex with an underage girl . . . or child abuse as it's more commonly known, *Senhor* Branco,' I said. 'But if you murdered her. That's a different thing. Maybe you *should* get a lawyer.'

'Me?' he said, his sunny day suddenly gone very black. 'I didn't kill her. I haven't seen her for . . . for . . .'

'When was that last time?'

'Months ago.'

'How did you meet her?'

'In the house in Lisbon.'

'How? *Senhor* Branco . . . not where.'

'I came out of the bedroom . . .'

'Whose bedroom?'

'Her mother's . . . Teresa's bedroom. She was standing in the corridor.'

'When?'

'It was a lunchtime . . . June, July last year.'

'What happened?'

'I don't . . . she had her shoes in her hand. She walked down the stairs. I was leaving. I looked back at her mother and followed her. We met again in the street. She was putting her shoes on.'

'Did she say anything?'

'She told me to be there the next Friday lunchtime.'

'You took that from a fourteen-year-old girl?'

'Fourteen! No, no. That's not possible. She said . . .'

'Don't waste our time, Paulo,' I said. 'Let's have the rest of it.'

'I turned up the next Friday. Teresa wasn't there. She went to Cascais on Fridays.'

'We know.'

'I had sex with her,' he said, and shrugged.

'In the mother's bed?'

He scratched the side of his head and nodded.

'Anything else?'

'She took five thousand escudos off me.'

'You allowed that?'

'I didn't know what to make of it. I wasn't sure what she could do.'

'Don't give me this shit,' I said. 'You're a grown man compared to her.'

'You didn't even have to turn up,' said Carlos.

He sized us up for the big schoolboy admission.

'We can take it,' I said.

'I got a kick out of it,' he said. 'Having sex with the mother and the daughter in . . .'

'Big deal,' I said. 'Now how many times did this happen before Teresa found out?'

'Three. She came in on the fourth.'

'Anything unusual about that day?'

His face weakened to a six-year-old's. He giggled with nerves.

'Shit,' he said, and squeezed the bridge of his nose, 'there was something different. That was the first time Catarina seemed to be enjoying it.'

'She didn't put it on all the time?' asked Carlos.

Paulo stared into the table determined not to rise to it.

'She was shouting, and kind of smiling, but not up at me . . . over my shoulder. I looked round and Teresa was standing by the door.'

'What did Teresa do?'

'I got off the bed. Catarina sat up . . . didn't even close her legs, just looked at her mother and smiled. Teresa ran at her and smacked her across the face, shit, it was like a rifle shot.'

'Did Catarina say anything?'

'In a baby-girl voice she said, "Sorry, mummy."'

'And you?'

'I was out of there and down the stairs.'

'You never saw Teresa again.'

'No.'

'And Catarina?'

167

He glanced back at the bedroom door again and spoke quietly.

'She came round a few times. The last time was . . . March. Yes, March . . . a couple of days after my birthday, the seventeenth.'

'She came round for sex?'

'It wasn't conversation.'

'You didn't talk?'

'She walked straight in there and took her clothes off.'

'Do you think she was on drugs?'

'Maybe,' he ducked his head.

'Did she take money from you?'

'Yes, until I hid my wallet.'

'Did that annoy her?'

'She didn't comment.'

'How many times did she come here?'

'Ten, twelve times.'

'And why didn't she come back after the nineteenth of March?'

'She did. I just didn't let her in.'

He nodded back at the bedroom door and we looked over there too.

We left a little after that and sat in the car outside. The girlfriend came out a few minutes after us, taking strides far too long for her legs, her stacked heels wobbling on the *calçada*. Carlos nodded, satisfied that the girl had seen what he had.

'That guy,' he said, '*novo rico*.'

We drove back to the lawyer's house. I had a couple of questions for Teresa but Dr Oliveira wouldn't allow it until she came into the corridor and beckoned us in. She was moving like an old woman and her speech was slow and drifting at the edges.

'The day you found Catarina in bed with Paulo Branco . . . why did you go back to the house?'

'I don't remember.'

168

'Weren't you already here?'

'I was.'

'It must have been something important to go all the way back into Lisbon.'

She didn't say anything. I apologized and stood to leave. Her face had sagged. Pouches that hadn't been there before appeared below her eyes.

'I went back,' she said, so tired she could hardly get it out, 'because Catarina called me. She said she'd hurt herself at school.'

The three of us exchanged looks. She held her hands open to show us how life could be.

'That was the end of me and Catarina,' she said.

We drove back to the *2ª Circular* around Lisbon in silence. I liked Carlos for this. No need to ask questions for which neither of us had any answers. He was contemplative. A different man to the edgy one he'd revealed on the beach and in Paulo Branco's flat. I doubted he had many friends.

I was feeling sick at how a family like the Oliveiras could go so wrong. The family. The strongest unit of Portuguese currency. Our gold. Our greatest asset. The pure element that keeps our streets mostly clean. Nobody in Europe understands the value of family better than us and it's not just leftover Salazarist propaganda. Was this where society's cracks started to appear?

We were heading for a massive development on the north edge of Lisbon called Odivelas. We skirted one of our present glories – Colombo, the biggest shopping centre in Europe – opposite one of the older ones – Benfica stadium, toying with bankruptcy. We curved off and back under the *2° Circular* and headed uphill. At the top we had the best view there was of Odivelas – twenty square kilometres of distressed tower blocks, covered in a frazzled hair of clustered television aerials. It was a hellish vision, a construction company's Elysium. They built these things in weeks – concrete skeleton bones, skin walls with no fat – they were baking in the summer and freezing in the winter. I've never been able to breathe in them, the air's been re-used too much.

We walked up the stairs to the fourth floor of a block which was part of a development within another development. This block was one of the originals, the rest clones. The lift didn't work. Tiles were broken and missing underfoot, and the concrete walls had encrustations from dried damp. Televisions squabbled between floors. Music and the smell of lunches piped down the stairwell. A couple of kids bounced off the walls and squeezed past us.

We knocked on a cardboard door where we were hoping to find the lead guitarist from Catarina's band. The man who opened the door was thin, with what looked like a badly applied moustache of the same lank texture as the dark hair on his head. He wore a purple short-sleeved shirt open all the way down. His hand was on his chest where he stroked the hair around his nipples with the two fingers he used for smoking. He knew we were police.

'Is Valentim Mateus Almeida in?' I asked.

He turned without speaking. We followed him down the narrow corridor. He tapped on a door as he was passing.

'Valentim,' he said. 'Police.'

He carried on into the kitchen where an overweight woman with bleached hair, who'd squeezed herself into a turquoise skirt, was clearing away lunch. She asked him who'd been at the door. He told her, and she sucked in her stomach. We knocked on Valentim's door again. The place smelled of fried fish.

Valentim invited us in but didn't look up from where he was sitting on the bed playing an electric guitar, unplugged. He had a huge thick swag of long dark brown ringlets, sheafed down the length of his back. He wore a T-shirt and jeans. He was thin, olive-skinned with big dark eyes

170

and hollow, underfed cheeks. Carlos closed the door of the narrow room which had a bed, a desk but no bookcase. The books were piled on the floor. Some of them were in English and French.

'Your father's not too concerned about the quality of your visitors.'

'That's because he's not my father, not even my stepfather. He's just the resident asshole who keeps my mother from getting lonely . . . and don't worry, I've told her.'

'What?' asked Carlos.

'That it's better to be lonely than live with a tick, but then . . . she'd scratch him off and get another one in its place. That's the nature of ticks and those they feed on.'

'Are you reading zoology?'

'Psychology,' he said. 'Zoology's something I live with. It creeps under my door.'

'You know a girl called Catarina Sousa Oliveira?'

'I know her,' he said, going back to his fingerwork on the guitar.

'She's dead. Murdered.'

His fingers stopped. He took the guitar by the neck and leaned it against a chair at the end of the bed. He was thinking, composing himself, but shocked too.

'I didn't know.'

'We're reconstructing her last twenty-four hours.'

'I haven't seen her,' he said, quickly.

'Not for twenty-four hours?'

'No.'

'Did you speak to her?'

'No.'

'When did you last see her?'

'Wednesday evening.'

'What happened?'

'The band met to talk about the weekend gig and rehearsals for Friday and Saturday.'

'Yesterday was Friday,' said Carlos.

171

'Thanks for reminding me. One day's like the next in Odivelas,' he said. 'The band also bust up on Wednesday. There was no rehearsal, there will be no gig.'

'Why did you bust up?'

'Musical differences,' he said. 'Teresa, she's the keyboard player . . . she's fucking some guy who plays the saxophone, so she thinks we suddenly need a saxophonist. She thinks we need to do more instrumental stuff. I said . . .'

'Less emphasis on the lead singer?' said Carlos.

Valentim turned to me for an opinion.

'I can't help you there,' I said. 'Nothing's happened in my life since Pink Floyd.'

'How musical were these differences?' asked Carlos.

'That's your first decent question and you go and answer it yourself.'

'What about Bruno, what does he play?'

'Bass.'

'Were either you or Bruno going out with Catarina?' I asked.

'Going out?'

'Were you fucking her?' said Carlos, picking up words as we went along.

'We had a "no relationships" agreement in the band.'

'The saxophonist didn't have a chance.'

'I don't suppose he did.'

'The meeting. Where did it take place?'

'In a bar called Toca. It's in the Bairro Alto.'

'And you didn't see her after that – not on Thursday, nor Friday?'

'No.'

'Do you know what she was doing yesterday?'

'She went to school, didn't she?'

'Where were you?'

'In the Biblioteca Nacional . . . all day . . . until seven, seven-thirty.'

I gave him a card and told him to call me if he remembered anything. Valentim's mother was looking down the corridor from the kitchen when we came out. I gave her a good afternoon which brought the tick to her shoulder.

'Where was Valentim yesterday?' I asked.

'He was out all day and most of the night,' said the tick. 'Didn't get in until three in the morning.'

The woman looked despondent behind the make-up she'd just put on. The tick wanted us to take the kid away right now. We left and got back in the car, which was too hot to touch. I lit a cigarette and put it out after two drags.

'He's lying,' said Carlos. 'He saw her.'

'Let's go and talk to the keyboards,' I said, starting the car.

'Don't we get lunch on this job?'

'English lunch.'

'I don't like the sound of that.'

'You wouldn't. You're Portuguese.'

'They said . . .' he pulled up.

'What did *they* say?'

'They said you were married to an Englishwoman.'

'Was that supposed to explain something to you?'

'I think . . . I was surprised when you said Pink Floyd back there.'

'I was in England in the seventies.'

He nodded.

'What else did *they* say?' I asked, surprised that people bothered to talk about me when I wasn't there.

'They said you weren't . . . normal.'

'Why do you think they put you to work with me?' I asked. 'Get all the weirdos off in one corner?'

'I'm not weird.'

'Just boring . . . you still haven't talked about girls, cars or football. You're twenty-seven years old. You're a policeman. You're Portuguese. What do you think *they* make of that?'

173

'Sporting,' he said, to satisfy requirements.

'They're a good team.'

'I can't afford a car.'

'Not the point.'

'I worked in a garage. I only know about old cars that don't work. Like Alfa Romeos.'

'Girls?'

'I don't have a girlfriend.'

'Still not the point. Are you gay?'

You'd have thought I'd slipped a sharpened screwdriver between his ribs.

'No,' he said, mortally wounded.

'Would you have told me if you were?'

'I'm not.'

'Do you think any of our colleagues talk to each other like this?'

He looked out of the window.

'That's why they put us together,' I said. 'We're the outsiders, we're weird.'

Chapter XIV

We lunched on *bifanas*, a sandwich but with a hot slice of pork as a filling – an Anglo-Portuguese solution to lunch. I teased Carlos back round to me, cooled his temper. We ordered coffee. I handed over my sugar without a word. He asked me about my wife – something nobody ever did. He asked me what it was like being married to an Englishwoman.

'What was the difference, you mean?' I asked, and he shrugged, not that sure what he meant. 'The only differences we had were on how to bring up Olivia, our daughter. We had fights about that. She had fights about that with my parents. It was a cultural thing. You know how it is in Portugal.'

'We're pampered every inch of the way.'

'And adored. Maybe we have a romantic vision of child-hood, that it should be a golden time with no respon-sibilities, no pressure,' I said, remembering all the old arguments. 'We cosset our kids, we let them know they're a gift to us, we encourage them to think they're special. And, for the most part, they come out confident, happy people. The English don't think like that. They're more pragmatic and they don't indulge . . . well, my wife didn't anyway.'

'So what's she like . . . Olivia?' he asked, getting used to the name.

'As it turned out the English upbringing was the best thing. She's a sixteen-year-old girl going on twenty-one.

She can take care of herself. She can take care of me. She *has* taken care of me – that was how she managed her grief. She's socially adept too. She can handle situations on her own. She does things. She's a brilliant seamstress. It was my wife's hobby. The two of them spent all day running up clothes, talking to each other all the time. But I still don't know whether it was what I would call a childhood. It drove me crazy sometimes. When Olivia was a little girl my wife wouldn't listen to her unless she talked sense. If she wanted to talk little kid's rubbish she had to come to me . . . And, you know, sometimes that comes out . . . she has a need to prove herself all the time, to be good at things, to always be interesting. She can't always live up to her own high standards. Look, you've started me off now. I'll shut up, or you'll get this for the rest of the day.'

'How did your wife like the Portuguese?'

'She liked us,' I said. 'Most of the time.'

'Did you tell her?'

'That we're not so nice to each other? She knew. And anyway, the English hate each other even more, but at least – *she* said this – the Portuguese like foreigners, which the English don't. She also said I had a jaded view of my countrymen from talking to liars and murderers all the time.'

'She couldn't have liked *everybody*.'

'She didn't like bureaucrats, but then I told her they were specially trained. It's all that's left of the Inquisition.'

'What did she really hate about the Portuguese? There must have been something she really hated.'

'The television programmes never came on time.'

'Come on. She could do better than that.'

'She hated Portuguese men in their cars, especially the ones who accelerated when they saw they were being overtaken by a woman. She said it was the only time she saw us macho. She always knew she was going to die on the roads and she did.'

176

Silence. He wasn't satisfied though.

'There must have been something else. Something worse than that.'

'She used to say: the quickest way to get trampled to death is to come between the Portuguese and their lunch.'

'Not the lunch we've just had . . . and anyway that just means we're hungry. Come on . . . what else?' said Carlos, that inferiority complex of his trying to push me to further extremes.

'She thought that we didn't believe in ourselves.'

'Ah.'

'Any more questions?'

None.

Teresa Carvalho, the keyboards player, lived with her parents in an apartment building in Telheiras, which is not far from Odivelas on the map, but a steep climb on the money ladder. This is where you come when your first cream has risen to the top of your milk. Insulated buildings, pastel shades, security systems, garage parking, satellite dishes, tennis clubs, ten minutes from the airport, five minutes from either football stadium and Colombo. It's wired up but dead out here, like pacing through a cemetery of perfect mausoleums.

The Carvalhos had the penthouse. The lift worked. An Angolan maid kept us outside while she took our IDs in to *Senhor* Carvalho. She showed us into his study. He sat behind his desk with his elbows and hairy forearms braced. He wore a red YSL polo shirt with more hair pouring up out of the neck. His head was nut-brown with not a strand of hair across it. His moustache was strong enough that he must have trimmed it with bolt cutters. He tilted his head forward so that he looked at us from under where the boss of his horns should have been. He was less friendly than a bull with six *bandarilhas* in its back. The maid closed the

177

door with the faintest click as if the slightest thing could draw the big bad bull's attention.

'What do you want to talk to my daughter about?' he asked.

'This wouldn't be your first visit from the *Polícia Judiciária*,' I said. 'Has your daughter been in trouble before?'

'She's never been in any trouble, but that doesn't stop the police from trying to push her into some.'

'We're Homicide, not Narcotics.'

'But you knew.'

'A guess,' I said. 'What are they talking to her about?'

'Manufacture and supply.'

'Of what?'

'Ecstasy,' he said. 'Her chemistry lecturer at the university is being held for questioning. He gives out names to make his life easier. One of them was my daughter's.'

I explained our business and he slowly released himself from the harness of his anger. He went to get his daughter. I called Fernanda Ramalho on my mobile. The pathologist might have been a marathon runner, but she gave her information out in one-hundred-metre sprints.

'Things you might be interested in,' she said. 'Time of death: near enough six or six-thirty p.m. on Friday. Cause of death: asphyxiation by strangulation, pressure applied by gloved thumbs to the windpipe (no nail marks on her neck). The blow to the back of the head: she was only hit once by something very hard and heavy, not an iron bar – the shattered cranium and the area of contusion suggest something like a sledgehammer. She was definitely unconscious when asphyxiated. I can't find any evidence of a serious struggle, no abrasions apart from the one on her forehead which was caused by contact with a pine tree. There was bark in the wound. She had nothing under her fingernails. Sexual activity: you're not going to like this. She had been penetrated both vaginally *and* anally. Condoms were used. No semen deposits. There

178

were traces of a water-based lubicrant in her rectum and
the damage to her sphincteral muscle would suggest that
she had not practised anal sex before. Blood: her blood
group is unusual, AB negative, and there were traces
of three, four methylenedioxymethamphetamine . . . also
known as E or Ecstasy. She had also smoked cannabis and
there were traces of caffeine.'

'Anything in her stomach?'

'She hadn't eaten anything for lunch.'

'Is that it?'

'Something, even this quick, is never enough for you
guys.'

'Fernanda,' I said. 'You know it's appreciated.'

She hung up.

Teresa Carvalho had long purple hair, dark purple eye
make-up, lipstick and nail varnish. She wore a black vest,
a black short skirt, black tights and purple calf-length Doc
Martens. She sat in an armchair in the corner of her
father's study and crossed her legs. *Senhor* Carvalho left
the room and we sat in the silence left over from Teresa's
gum-chewing.

Senhor Carvalho's shoes did not move off. Teresa didn't
look at either of us but focused on a point above Carlos'
head. I opened the door and told *Senhor* Carvalho that I'd
like to talk to him again later. He moved off like a bear
back into its cave. There was a micron of trust in Teresa's
eyes when I sat down again.

'Nothing said here has to go further than this room,' I
said.

'Dad says you're Homicide. I haven't killed anyone so
I'm cool,' she said, cracking her gum at us.

'Have you spoken to any members of your band since it
broke up on Wednesday night?' I asked.

That opener made it look as if there was plenty more
ammunition in the magazine and I could see the implications fidgeting behind her eyes.

'No, I haven't. There wasn't much point.'

'Was that the last time you saw Catarina?'

'Yes it was,' she said. 'Has something happened to her?'

'Why do you ask?'

'Anything could have happened to her.'

'Any reason?' asked Carlos.

'She looks innocent enough, doesn't she?'

'The blonde hair and blue eyes, you mean.'

She cracked her gum again, and brought one of her Doc Martens up on to the edge of the chair.

'Go on, Teresa,' I said, 'tell us what you thought of Catarina.'

'She was badly fucked-up in the head.'

'What does that mean? Crazy, neurotic, drugged-out?'

'I don't think she's even sixteen, is she?'

'That's right.'

'You might find some thirty-year-old *putas* with her experience but I . . .'

'I hope this isn't cat talk, Teresa.'

'It's guys' talk. Go out on the campus and ask.'

'You didn't like her.'

'No.'

'Did you envy her?'

'Envy?'

'Her voice, for instance.'

She snorted.

'The fact that guys went for her.'

'I told you, she was no better than a *puta*.'

'What about Bruno and Valentim?'

'What about them?'

'Just answer the question,' said Carlos.

'Where is it?'

'The band,' I said, trying to steady Carlos who didn't seem to like this one either, 'how did the band break up?'

'I didn't like the music any more.'

'I meant, how. Did you all have a row and split in different directions? Did some of you side with others . . .'

'I don't know what they did. I met up with a friend in the Bairro Alto.'

'That wasn't the saxophonist was it?' I asked, and she went still.

'No, it wasn't,' she said it so quietly we had to lean in.

'What else does he do apart from play the saxophone?'

She didn't answer. Her hand was up by her mouth, and a thumbnail between her teeth.

'This saxophonist . . . is he your lecturer at the university?'

She nodded. Fat tears formed in her purple eye make-up. She studied her knee.

'You weren't with him the night the band bust up?'

She shook her purple head.

'Did you see him?' I asked.

Her eyes closed and purple tears eased down her face.

'Maybe you saw him with Catarina Oliveira later that night?'

'She stole him,' she blurted along with some snot. 'She stole him from me.'

'Is that why Narcotics got a phone call about a university lecturer manufacturing and supplying Ecstasy?'

She sprang out of the chair and grabbed some tissues from her father's desk and smeared her face around so she looked as if she'd taken a heavy beating.

'Where were you last night?'

'In the Alfama at the *festa*.'

'When?'

'I was here most of the afternoon working in my room . . . friends picked me up about seven o'clock.'

I told her to write down the names and phone numbers of her friends.

'You still haven't told me what's happened to Catarina,' she said.

'She was murdered last night.'

'*I* didn't do anything to her,' she said quickly, the pen hovering.

'Do you think either Valentim or Bruno were involved with her sexually?'

'I'm sure Valentim was . . . he found her. Not Bruno. He was scared of Valentim.'

'Found her?'

'Heard her voice, brought her into the band.'

'So why do you think they were having sex?'

'That was Catarina's way.'

'But you never saw anything that confirmed it?'

She looked up to see how the truth would go down.

'No,' she said. 'I didn't see anything.'

We got up to leave.

'You're not going to tell the drug squad about my phone call,' she said.

'If your lecturer's innocent I am,' I said. 'Is he?'

She shook her head.

'Are you?'

'They're trying to say I lab-assisted for him but I didn't.'

'What about supplying?'

'No,' she said, her mouth clamped shut.

'Catarina had traces of E in her blood the day she died.'

'Not from me. *I* didn't give her anything.'

'What about Valentim or Bruno?'

'No,' she said, a terse, hard, rock-sure lie.

I gave her a long look which she couldn't hold. She was thinking how she could salvage something from the situation, how she could make me like her. The unpopular girl. The fraud. The conservative playing in purple and black.

'If you wanted to understand Catarina,' she said, 'you had to hear her sing. She had a direct line to pain.'

We drove through an empty Lisbon on the first hot Saturday afternoon of the summer. We went straight down the normally clogged arterial avenues through Campo Grande to Saldanha, to the huge roundabout at Marquês de Pombal and on to Largo do Rato which baked silently in the heat. Carlos was talking like a man with a mouthful of nails who couldn't spit enough of them out.

'The world can do without *chatas* like Teresa Carvalho,' he said. 'Little *senhorinha rica* with no personality, playing at being a grunge artist but all the time nurturing and cultivating those piss-weak, middle-class Salazarist values. She's the kind who's always had what she's wanted and when she can't get it, because she's too much of a *chata*, she makes sure nobody else can have it. She rats on people to save her own ass. She's a liar. She checks you all the time to make sure she's telling you what you want to hear. She dumps on her lecturer, trashes Catarina and then she gives us . . .' he put on a whiny voice, ' "If you wanted to understand Catarina, you had to hear her sing, she had a direct line to pain," and you can bet that she didn't think that up herself. Gah! They're all the same.'

'Who?'

'Middle-class girls. Nothing to them. Chickens without giblets.'

'Was Catarina a chicken without giblets?'

'She must have had more to her than the rest put together . . . which is why they're all queueing up to shit on her and tell us what a little *puta* she was, but so far we haven't met anybody associated with her who's worth more than five *tostões*.'

'So you *do* want to find her killer?'

'Yes I do. Anything wrong with that?'

'Just checking.'

'But if she was a *chata* like Teresa Carvalho . . .'

'As a matter of interest, do you like black people?' I asked.

He checked to see which side of the field I was coming from.

'I'm not racially prejudiced, if that's what you mean,' he said slowly.

'But if you had a daughter and she wanted to marry a black guy . . . ?'

'Maybe that should be my question to you.'

'I wouldn't like it,' I said. 'There . . . you found me out.'

'The good old racist Portuguese policeman.'

'That doesn't mean I think that black people are all criminals,' I said. 'I lived in Africa, I know Africans, and a lot of them I liked. What it means is that there are plenty of people out there who are racially prejudiced and I wouldn't want my daughter to have to face any of that if she didn't have to.'

The dark gardens of the Jardim da Estrela slipped by looking cool and soporific. I cut up by the side of the Basílica and climbed the hill up to Lapa. This is embassy land, an old money haven overlooking the docks of Alcântara, probably so the rich could see their money coming in. We parked in a central square outside an old apartment block with a view over an old and decrepit *palácio* which had scaffolding around it and a building licence from the town hall on the front gate.

We rang the bell. No answer. A gardener hacked away at some undergrowth on the other side of the railings.

'That's the Palácio do Conde dos Olivais,' I said to Carlos. 'It's been locked up and in ruins since I can remember.'

'Looks like they're doing it up.'

I shouted over to the gardener, an old dark-skinned guy with a face like a mule. He stopped work and leaned against the railing and removed the cigarette from his mouth that had gone out some time ago.

'It's going to be a bordello,' he said.

'Is that right?'

'You know what you need for a good bordello?'

'Nice girls, perhaps.'

'Plenty of rooms. This place is perfect,' he said and set off on an asthmatic laugh. He wiped his face off with a soiled rag. 'No. It's going to be one of those exclusive clubs for rich people with too few ideas on how to spend all that money they've got under their mattresses.'

Carlos grunted a laugh and rang the bell again. No answer. The gardener relit his cigarette.

'This is where the Nazis lived in the war,' he said. 'Then the Americans took it over when they lost.'

'It's a big place for a club.'

'They're serious people . . . the rich. That's what they tell me anyway.'

We got an answer. A very faint one. A spindly female voice too frail to comprehend. She let us in on the fifth explanation. We walked up the stairs to the second floor. A woman in a thick green cardigan and a tweed skirt answered the door. She'd forgotten who we were already and when we re-explained she said she hadn't called the police, that nothing had happened. She began to close the door with a shaky Parkinson's hand.

'It's OK, Mum,' said a voice behind her. 'They're here to talk to me. It's nothing to worry about.'

'I sent the maid out for something . . . and they always come when she's out, and I have to get up and answer the bell, and I can never hear anything from that . . .'

'It's OK, Mum. She'll be back soon.'

We followed the woman who shuffled into the living room on her son's arm. The walls were floor-to-ceiling with books and the air space was mostly taken up with racks of drawings, paintings, sketches and watercolours. The boy sat the woman down at a table which had a large diameter glass on it and a decanter of what might have been tawny port.

The boy, in regulation T-shirt and jeans, took us into another room. He had long straight dark hair parted in the middle and a sad face with a limited range of expression.

His mouth barely opened when he spoke. The walls of this room were covered in more drawings and sketches, none of them framed.

'Who's the artist?' asked Carlos.

'My mother was a gallerist . . . this is what's left of her stock.'

'She looks sick.'

'She is.'

'Have you spoken to Valentim?'

'He called.'

'When did you last have sex with Catarina?' I asked, and Carlos flinched as if he'd have to answer the question.

Bruno stepped back and brushed his hair over his shoulders with his two hands flapping like a startled bird.

'What!' he said, his mouth opening two millimetres more than a clam's, which was a Munch's *'Scream'* for him.

'You heard.'

'I wasn't . . .'

'Teresa Carvalho says you were. You, Valentim and half the university.'

He looked broken already, as if he was a spider wearing his skeleton on the outside. Valentim might have prepared him for something but not this. He swallowed.

'We don't want to hear Valentim's script either,' I said. 'This is a murder investigation so if I think for two seconds that you're lying and obstructing the course of justice, I'll take you down to the *tacos* for the weekend. Have you ever been there before?'

'No.'

'Do you know what they are?'

No answer.

'Pimps, prostitutes, druggies, drunks, pushers, pickpockets and other assorted punks too violent to be allowed home. No daylight. No fresh air. Pig slop for food. I'll do it to you, Bruno. The maid will look after your mother, so I won't feel bad about that. So, forget Valentim . . . and let's have it.'

He stood by the window and his head slid round to look over the *palácio* to the patch of the River Tagus visible through the trees. It didn't look as if he was going to have to do too much thinking.

'Friday lunchtime,' he said to the windowpane.

'Where?'

'The Pensão Nuno ... it's near the Praça da Alegria somewhere.'

'What time?'

'Between one and two.'

'Were drugs involved?'

Bruno came away from the window and sat on the bed. He leaned forward with his elbows on his knees and spoke to the floor.

'We took a tab of E each and smoked a joint.'

'Who supplied?'

He didn't answer.

'We're not doing anybody for possession or supply of drugs,' I said. 'I just want to have the picture straight in my head. I want to see every minute of that day clearly as if it were my own. Was it Teresa Carvalho?'

'Valentim,' he said.

'Valentim was there as well?' asked Carlos.

The boy nodded to the floor.

'The two of you were there together ... having sex with the girl?'

Bruno gripped his forehead trying to squeeze the memory out.

'How did this happen?'

'Valentim said she was into it.'

'Was that true?'

He opened his hands and shrugged.

'So which of you sodomized her?' I asked.

He coughed, a half sob, half retch. He wrapped his hands over his head and leaned over in the plane-crash position as if expecting some terrible impact.

Chapter XV

Saturday, 13th June 199–, Odivelas, Lisbon, Portugal.

I dropped Carlos and Bruno off at the PJ building in Rua Gomes Freire so that Carlos could take down his statement, and went back to Odivelas to pick up Valentim.

There were a few things different about Valentim's apartment block. Life had moved on a centimetre, there were different TV programmes raging, techno music ricocheted down the stairwell, heat came off the walls as if the building was running a fever.

The tick answered the door and turned without a word. He delivered the same passing knock on Valentim's door and went into the kitchen where he picked up an open bottle of Sagres.

'Police,' he shouted over the bottle-top and began chugging beer.

Valentim's mother appeared in the door frame. I hammered on the cardboard door until Valentim tore it open.

'We're leaving,' I said. 'You won't need anything.'

'Where are you taking him?' said the mother, screechy now.

'Lisbon.'

'What's he done?' she asked, bouncing off the door frame, coming down the corridor at me.

The tick stayed in the kitchen, sipping beer, spreading his weak moustache with a forefinger and thumb, looking well-pleased.

'He's going to help us with our enquiries into the murder of a young girl.'

'Murder?' she said, moving to embrace him as if he'd been condemned already.

'Let's go,' he said, turning away from her.

We got in the car. Valentim rested an elbow on the window ledge, and played drum solos on the roof with his fingers as we drove back into town in the highest heat of the day.

'Where's your father?' I asked.

'He pulled out years ago, I don't remember him.'

'How old were you.'

'Too small to remember.'

'You did all right to get to university.'

'Not if you look at the *chatos* in my class.'

'How do you like your mother?'

'She's my mother . . . that's it.'

'How old is she?'

'What do you think?'

'I don't know. It's difficult to say . . .'

'With all the make-up?'

'The guy she's with looks young.'

'She's thirty-seven. OK?'

'But do you like her?'

He stopped tapping on the roof.

'Where did they find you?' he asked. 'Winged on the motorway?'

'I'm one of the few people you'll meet in my world with an interest in other human beings . . . but that doesn't mean I'm sweet all the time. Now tell me what you think of your mother.'

'This is shit,' he said, enunciating each word with precision.

'You're the one reading psychology at university.'

He sighed, bored to his hair roots.

'I think my mother's a beautiful person with a strong moral and ethical purpose, profoundly concerned with . . .'

'You've answered the question,' I said. 'Now . . . do you have a girlfriend at the moment?'

'No.'

'You've had girlfriends?'

'Occasionally. Temporarily.'

'What attracted you to these girls?'

'Do you write for *Cosmopolitan* in your spare time?'

'It's either this or the elbow in the face.'

'The girls always came to *me*.'

'All that highly-charged magnetism of yours.'

'I was stating a fact. I did not pursue them. They came to me.'

'What sort of girls?'

'Middle-class girls from well-off families who wanted to be different, who wanted to be cool, who wanted to have a go with someone who wasn't a trussed-up jerk with a mobile phone that never rang.'

'But you were too strong for them. Too rich. No. Wrong word. Too gamey.'

'They're not real people, Inspector. They're just kids dressing up.'

'And Catarina . . . was she like that?'

He nodded and smirked as if he'd seen my thread.

'You're forgetting something,' he said. 'Catarina was never my girlfriend.'

'But it was interesting wasn't it,' I said, 'because you found her.'

'Found her?'

'Discovered her voice. Brought her into the band. You pursued her. She didn't come to you.'

'That doesn't mean she was . . .'

'But it was different wasn't it?'

He drummed on the roof again.

I had a small fight to get into the PJ building with the policeman on the door who knew me well, but didn't believe who I was until I showed him some ID with my bearded self on it. Was this the start of a good old-fashioned identity crisis?

I left Valentim at the front desk and went upstairs to find Carlos and Bruno sitting in my office, both silent. I read the statement and told Bruno to sign it.

'Did Valentim have an arrangement to see Catarina after school on Friday?'

'She always went back to Cascais on Fridays.'

'Did you see Valentim on Friday night?'

'Yes. We met up in Alcântara around ten o'clock.'

'What was he doing between two and ten o'clock?'

'I don't know.'

'Was he agitated when you saw him?'

'No.'

'Teresa said Catarina had been promiscuous around the university. Is that true?'

'Not if Teresa said it. That would not be reliable.'

'She says she saw Catarina with her chemistry lecturer in the Bairro Alto later on Wednesday night after the band bust up.'

'I wouldn't know.'

'Where did you go after the band meeting?'

'Home. I worked late on a paper I had to deliver on Thursday morning.'

'And Valentim and Catarina?'

'I left them in that bar, Toca, in the Bairro Alto.'

We went to the stairs and I told him to wait five minutes before he went home. Carlos and I took Valentim to the Pensão Nuno which was on Rua da Glória, a narrow road that ran between the Praça da Alegria and the funicular from Restauradores up to the Bairro Alto. There weren't many hookers around in the street at this time of day. A few older and sadder ones looked out of the bar windows sitting over coffee. Valentim's face in the rear view was straight out of the mould, solid.

The reception was on the second floor of a four-storey nineteenth-century building with a tiled façade up to the first-floor balcony. The staircase was wide, wooden and

191

musty with a strip of blue lino up the middle. A guy in his sixties was standing behind the reception bar, a newspaper in front of him, his finger on his tongue. A strip of neon lighting on the wall above his grey head lit cobwebs and other high grime. He was unshaven and smoked a cigarette unconsciously. He looked as if he had been fat and then lost it and been left with useless folds of skin that sagged in his shirt.

He glanced up at us, and I saw it in his eyes that he knew he was looking at two policemen and a suspect.

He stood up straight and put a hand under his armpit. He ran a thumbnail through the bristles below his bottom lip. The smoke made him close an eye. His skin looked grey as if ingrained by dust from some previous work such as mining.

'Are you Nuno?' I asked.

'He's dead.'

'Who are you?'

'Jorge.'

'You run this place?'

He smoked and nodded.

'I know who you are,' he said.

'So you don't need to see any ID.'

'You can still show it to me.'

We laid our cards out. He inspected them closely without touching.

'You look better without,' he said to me.

'You know this kid?' I asked.

Jorge's eyes went sleepy in his head as if he was a python who'd eaten a horse and was finding the hooves difficult to digest. He smoked some more, stubbed out the cigarette with a grimace and showed us a set of yellow teeth that hadn't met floss.

'You're going to tell me he's been here before and I'm going to have to believe you but . . .' he trailed off, took out his reservations book and flicked through empty pages.

'Maybe you should get the "rooms by the hour" edition out.'

'If they occupy . . .'

'We want to take a look at a room on the top floor. Are they all free?'

'If they're locked they're occupied.'

'Are you busy?' I asked, and Jorge made some calculations. 'I'm going into every room, locked or not.'

He hitched his trousers and slid out from behind the bar. He was wearing flip-flops and his yellow toenails, thick as tile, matched his teeth. I followed the dead skin on his crusty heels up to the top floor.

'How many rooms up here?'

'Four,' he said, economical now that the stairs were taking his puff.

At the top he coughed himself to a tremulous silence and spat into a handkerchief.

'Well?' he said, waving a finger at Valentim.

'Don't ask me,' said Valentim. 'I don't know what I'm doing here.'

'You remember what I said about the elbow in the face?' I asked.

'You heard that?' he said to Jorge. 'That was a threat.'

'I don't see you. I don't hear him,' said Jorge. 'All my senses got worn down years ago.'

Valentim looked at one of the doors and Jorge opened it up with a flourish from his hand like a nineteenth-century doorman.

Inside Valentim took up a position on the other side of the bed from me. Carlos sat on a sciatic chair by the door which he'd just closed. I washed my hands in the sink, looked at Valentim in the mirror and dabbed my face cool with wet palms. I shook my hands dry, straightened my tie and took my jacket off. It was hot in the room even with the shutters closed.

'Let's have it, Valentim.'

'You know what happened.'

'So now, suddenly, you know why you're here,' I said. 'But I want to hear it from you. You set it up. You told Bruno that Catarina liked this sort of thing. You tell it your way.'

'She said she wanted to try it . . . but only with someone she knew.'

'She said that? She made the proposal to you. A fifteen-year-old to a twenty-one-year-old?'

'Twenty-two,' he said, and waited two beats. 'That's made you think, hasn't it, Inspector?'

'That your mother was fifteen when she had you? So what? That's not three in a bed. That's a young girl's mistake.'

The hate came across the room in slivers from the boy who'd started life as a mistake. He dropped his head and when it came back up again his eyes were smiling.

'Maybe girls are older these days,' he said. 'You wouldn't know, Inspector.'

'I have a daughter . . . not much older than Catarina.'

'And you know what runs through her perfect virginal head?'

'It's not three in a bed.'

'You must have talked about it to be that certain.'

'Shut up,' I said, feeling my lid boiling.

'At least you must know that girls aren't so confused these days . . . about what they want.'

'What did they used to think they wanted?' asked Carlos, rescuing me.

'Romance.'

'And now?'

'Now they know that sex can happen without love and they're interested in it,' said Valentim. 'I'm not a pre-revolutionary kid like the Inspector. I wasn't spoon-fed Catholicism, Salazarist family values, no women in the workplace, no tits and bums on the street . . .'

194

'If this is a justification,' said Carlos, 'get to it.'

'It's not a justification, just an opinion as to why girls these days, a girl like Catarina, who was not by any means a virgin, could make the proposal she did, and also why the Inspector should doubt it.'

'Why is it that the next generation always believe they invented sex.'

'Not invented it, just revolutionized it.'

I had a trickle of sweat at the back of my neck inching under the collar, ready to career down my spine. Valentim, like the best mango fly in Guinea, was getting under my skin.

'So what was it that you heard in Catarina's voice that made you run after her?'

'Talent.'

'There must have been something else for the great Valentim, who's always pursued by girls, to go running after . . .'

'She had blonde hair and blue eyes. That's not a common Portuguese look. I was interested in something different.'

Silence for some time. Valentim raised his eyebrows.

'I want you to think about that question a little more while you tell us what happened in this room. You're clever enough to do that, aren't you?'

'Where do you want me to start?'

'When did you take the drugs?'

'As soon as we got in here. Bruno had a joint. We smoked it. I had some pills. We took a tab each. E . . . to save you from asking.'

'Where did you get the E?'

'Off the street.'

'Not Teresa,' I said.

'Well, I'm sure Teresa has been helpful to you in your enquiries already so I'll give her to you. Yes, Teresa supplied.'

'What effect did the E have?' asked Carlos.

'It makes you uninhibited, in love with the ones you love.'

'So you end up fucking yourself,' said Carlos, happy with that resolution.

'Maybe *you* would, *agente*,' said Valentim.

'Does the room look the same now as it did yesterday?'

'That chair was ten centimetres to the right,' he said.

Silence, while I rolled up my sleeve to bare a brown-skinned, pointed elbow.

'OK, OK,' he said, holding up his hands, 'we moved the bed.'

'Show us.'

He manoeuvred the bed in front of the mirror.

'Your idea?'

'She said she wanted to see herself.'

'Did she?'

'See herself?'

'Did she say that that was what she wanted?'

'I just told you.'

'I'm having trouble believing you.'

He shrugged.

'Carry on.'

'We took our clothes off.'

'How did that happen?'

'We took our shoes off first, like good little boys.'

That got Carlos off his chair, thin-lipped with rage.

'*Eh pá*,' said Valentim, '*calma*.'

'Did you strip her?' I asked.

'She was naked by the time we'd moved the bed.'

'Now she's running the show.'

'I told you it was her idea,' he said. 'She knelt in the middle of the bed. She told Bruno to kneel in front and me behind. She told me to use a condom. She had to work on Bruno . . . he was nervous. I put on the condom and that was it.'

'You forgot something.'

196

'I don't think so.'

'The lubricant.'

'She didn't need any.'

'I believe it's normally used to sodomize someone and the pathologist said there were traces of it in her rectum.'

'I did *not* sodomize her. No way. That is not my kind of thing at all.'

'That's not what Bruno said.'

'What did he say?' said Valentim. 'Tell me what he said.'

I nodded at Carlos who leafed through his copy of Bruno's statement. He read:

'. . . she masturbated me and sucked my penis while Valentim had sex with her from behind. I did not penetrate her vaginally nor anally and I did not ejaculate.'

'That doesn't mean I sodomized her . . . and I didn't. What Bruno says is true. He was nervous, and I did have sex with her, and I was behind her, but I penetrated her vagina. You can use your famous elbow on me all you like, Inspector, but I won't say anything different.'

'So how do you explain the pathologist's report?'

Silence while Valentim shifted the swag of his heavy hair and passed a finger across his forehead. He flicked a hank of sweat on to the floor.

'There must have been somebody else,' he said.

'When did you leave here?'

'Around two o'clock.'

'Bruno says he went home and you walked off towards the funicular with Catarina.'

'That's true.'

'Where did you go?'

'We walked down to Avenida da Liberdade and took a 45 bus. She got off at Saldanha to go back to school. I stayed on until Campo Grande and went to the Biblioteca Nacional.'

'How long did you spend there?'

197

'I was there until well after seven. Plenty of people saw me.'

'Have you got a car?'

'You're joking, Inspector.'

'Have you got access to one?'

'My mother's boyfriend has one. Do you think he'd lend it to me?'

'Let's go back to my first question about why you took Catarina into the band.'

'I told you.'

'What was special about her, Valentim? What did she have that particularly interested you?'

He licked his lips which had dried on him. He didn't seem to have any spit.

'She wasn't a happy girl was she, Valentim?'

'Happy?' he asked, sneering, as if this was a questionable state.

'Did you like that, Valentim? Did you like a bit of vulnerability to work with, some real suffering to get your teeth into?'

'Next you'll be telling me I hate my mother,' he said, on the end of a high-pitched laugh. 'Do they teach Freud at police college now?'

'Ask *agente* Pinto, I haven't been in police college for some time,' I said. 'I wouldn't be needing Freud anyway, after eighteen years talking to people like you.'

He looked at Carlos sniffing for a softer target.

'Have you got any bullshit for me, *agente*?'

'You're not a nice guy,' said Carlos, quietly on the end of a direct look.

'If you were a nice guy,' I said, 'and a fifteen-year-old girl proposed three in a bed with some sodomy thrown in . . .'

'I did not sodomize her!' he shouted.

'. . . you wouldn't go ahead with it, would you? You'd think there was something wrong with the girl. You're a psychology student. You'd know that it wasn't normal behaviour. If you were a nice guy you'd help the girl. Talk to her parents. Get her some therapy. But you're not, are you, Valentim? You're a piece of shit. You look at someone like that and think: I can *use* that. I can *abuse* that . . . and it'll make me feel better.'

'And all because I didn't say I loved my mother . . . you're a radical, Inspector. You're a fucking radical.'

'But that's why you arranged this little rendezvous yesterday wasn't it, Valentim? To bring Catarina down to your own level, suck her into your own swamp. Now all I've got to find out is whether you wanted to take it one step further and kill the girl.'

'Then you've got a lot of work ahead of you.'

'In the meantime you can spend the weekend in the *tacos* . . . see if that refreshes your memory. And I'll get a search warrant for your room.'

Valentim ran a thumb and forefinger down his nose and flicked the sweat on the floor. He shook his head and I saw that he was worried and not about spending a few nights in the *tacos*.

Chapter XVI

Saturday, 13th June 199–, Pensão Nuno, Rua da Glória, Lisbon, Portugal.

A police car arrived to take Valentim. I sent Carlos with it to start work on the search warrant. Jorge stripped off the cellophane to what must have been his third pack of the day. I took out the photograph of Catarina.

'You're still not finished?' he said, lighting up a cigarette.

'You lost a lot of weight recently, Jorge?'

'I was sick. They thought I had lung cancer.'

'What was it?'

'Just some pleurisy.'

'Good to get the weight off though.'

'You don't have to be nice to me, nobody else is.'

'You know about people don't you, Jorge?'

'The whole world's been past this front desk.'

'Have you always done this work?'

'Probably.'

'Ever been inside?'

'If I was, it was before I can remember whether I've been doing this job all my life.'

'That memory of yours must be famous.'

'I've got a room full of industrial awards for it,' he said. 'You should drop by some time, when I'm not so busy, and I'll show them to you.'

'Do you remember this girl?' I asked, snapping the photograph down on the bar. 'She was in here with that kid and another one Friday lunchtime.'

If anything Jorge's eyes got rheumier. He barely looked at the shot.

'Look, Inspector, I've got a reputation to keep up. If it gets out that my particular brain disease cleared up and I got on a quiz show with the *Polícia Judiciária* I'll have an empty place.'

'Emptier than this?' I said. 'The floors aren't exactly shaking.'

'You take my point.'

'Maybe this place is due an inspection.'

'Why's it so important that I remember her?'

'Five hours after she left this place she was dead. Murdered.'

Jorge's eyebrows left his head for a moment.

'When?'

'This is ridiculous . . . I just told you. Friday six, six-thirty in the afternoon.'

'Here in Lisbon.'

'Maybe. She was found dumped on a beach in Paço de Arcos.'

He nodded, wiping his cheeks with the back of his hand feeling the rasp of the bristles.

'She was in here Friday lunchtime. You must know that by now after talking to the kid. She was with another one as well . . . a student.'

'How do you know?'

'This is the gateway to heaven, Inspector. The whole world comes before me . . . even police officers.'

'Can I use your telephone?'

I called the home number of Catarina's teacher. She answered as if she'd been sitting there waiting for the phone to ring. I made an appointment for an hour's time. She said she wasn't going anywhere. I refitted the telephone, an old heavy Bakelite piece of work that took me back to my father's army headquarters in Africa. I headed for the stairs, Jorge's eyes on me all the way. I stopped two steps down and heard him sigh.

'The girl,' I said, 'had she been in here before?'

Jorge turned the page of his newspaper, kissed his cigarette again.

'Did you hear me, Jorge?'

'I heard you,' he said. 'I heard that phone call too. She's a schoolgirl.'

'Not even sixteen, Jorge.'

He shook his head, not that amazed at what the world had come to.

'She's been coming in here pretty regularly Friday lunchtimes, since March, April, something like that.'

'She was a hooker?'

'She wasn't going up there on her own for a nap, if that's what you mean,' he said, lighting another cigarette from the butt of the last. 'Girls these days, they're different. Clean, nicely dressed, polite. They come in here to make spending money for the weekend because they don't want to have to explain to daddy why they need 30,000 escudos for a decent Saturday night. The regular girls know it too. You go out there and watch. If they see a girl in a short skirt hanging around too long, they'll kick her half to death. If you ask me, and not many people do these days, Inspector, it's the heroin.'

'Did you know any of her clients?'

Jorge gave me a sad sorry look and tapped the side of his head.

'How many times have you been closed down?'

'Never . . . unless it was before . . .'

'That's enough, Jorge. You're boring me now.'

'Look, Inspector, I cooperate as much as I can . . . in the end.'

'How about doing some cooperating now?'

He thought about it, wanting to get me off his back.

'I'll tell you something, it's not much but if it'll get you down the stairs . . .'

'I won't promise you.'

'You're not the first guy to ask me about the girl . . . I mean in an investigative way.'

'What are we talking about . . . another cop?'

'Could be.'

'Get it out, Jorge. One go. Like pulling a tooth.'

'He looked like a cop but he wouldn't show me any ID and I wouldn't tell him anything.'

'What did he ask you?'

'He made out he was a punter and interested in the girl. I didn't believe him. He told me he was *Polícia Judiciária*. I asked for ID. He wouldn't show. I told him to stop wasting my time and he left.'

'When are we talking about?'

'Not long after she became a Friday lunchtime regular.'

'April, May?' I asked, and he nodded. 'Tell me what he looked like.'

'Short, stocky, and the bit of hair I saw was grey. He wore a small, brimmed hat, black, which he never took off, a grey tweed jacket, white shirt, tie, grey trousers. No moustache, no beard. Brown eyes. That's it.'

'I'm going down the stairs now, Jorge.'

'Don't rush,' he said. 'I wouldn't want you to fall.'

I went out into the dark narrow street. It had been cool in Jorge's windowless reception and I stripped off my jacket and slung it over my shoulder. There were more girls outside now and I walked down the street towards the funicular asking the odd one here and there whether they'd seen Catarina. A couple of mulatto Brazilian girls remembered her, but not from yesterday. A bleach-blonde girl, standing on one leg while she repaired the heel of her shoe, tapped the photograph and nodded but couldn't remember when she'd seen her.

I asked the funicular driver, who I reckoned must take an interest in life around him rather than looking endlessly at the same old two hundred metres of rail up and down his hill, but he shrugged me off. I walked back down Rua da Glória, got into my car and drove back to the bus stop at Saldanha. It was mostly newly developed office buildings around here and they were all shut but I found a few little places open to ask my question.

'*Boa tarde*, did you see this girl yesterday around two, two-fifteen? No. Thank you. *Adeus*.'

It's a stomach thing for me, police work. For a lot of my colleagues it's brain work. They have the suspects, the clues, the statements, the witnesses, the motives, and they reason them all together. I do that too but I have something in my stomach as well, something that tells me if I'm right. António Borrego once asked me what it was like and the only thing I could think of was 'love' and he told me to be careful because, as anybody knows, love is blind. Good point. It's not like love, but that's the strength of it.

'*Boa tarde*, did you see this girl yesterday around two, two-fifteen? No. Thank you. *Adeus*.'

People ask me why I do this job, as if I have some choice in the matter, as if I could finish with it now and run off and be an avant-garde poet in Guatemala. I got into this thing because, back in 1978 when my father and I crept back into the country, that was the only job I could find, and in those days money was as scarce as a job. When I came out of the Rossio station after five years in London I knew what I'd been missing. The poverty bustle, I call it. There's a lot of it in Africa, which is why I recognized it. It's a nervous freneticism brought about by insufficient economic activity to ensure that everybody gets fed. It's the agitation of hunger and it's gone now. The streets are calm like any other European city. Now there's only the stress left, but that's not the same as hunger, that's just neuroticism.

'*Boa tarde*, did you see this girl yesterday around two, two-fifteen? No. Thank you. *Adeus*.'

So I do this job because over the years I've come to believe in it. The hunt for the truth or the teasing out of the truth, anyway. I like the talk. I marvel at the natural genius humans have for deception. If you think footballers are pretty good at cheating and diving and deceiving, you should see murderers perform. Mind you, they get a lot of practice lying to themselves every minute of the day. Our prisons are full of innocent people. But that's the nature of the murderer. It's the ultimate human weakness. The most radical solution to the inability to resolve, and the shame of that weakness is the inadmissible guilt. But the lies . . . the lies keep the job alive. I'm like a couturier appreciating cloth, enjoying the texture, the finery of a brilliant tapestry, a fabulous, gold-threaded brocade, a silky smooth damask, a dark, rich, impenetrable velvet. But I never underestimate the value of a light, strong denim, a hard-wearing drill, a tough fine-ribbed poplin. That doesn't mean I don't get the moth-eaten taffeta, or the well-worn flannel, or wispy tissues of voile, it's just that I have the developed taste of a connoisseur.

'*Boa tarde*, did you see this girl yesterday around two, two-fifteen? No. Thank you. *Adeus*.'

We've seen some liars today. The lawyer, the wife, her lover, the psychology student, the little *nouvelle riche* girl, the old money kid. But take the *pensão* landlord. Jorge. The one you'd expect to be a liar. The one who looked like a liar. But he wasn't. He was an elider, an omitter, an excluder, an editor, but he wasn't guarding his own secrets. That was the difference. Now Valentim. He's got potential. Plenty of practice. He's been at it since his father left, probably. He doesn't trust anybody. Not even his mother. He's got the makings of the finest brocade that one. Then there's the one I missed out. The victim. She must have done some lying in her time, but what interests me about her is the game she played on her mother. What was that? Phoning her up. Getting her to come over. So that what? So that she could show her that she knew? So that she could show her that she was better? So that she could punish her?

'*Boa tarde*, did you see this girl yesterday around two, two-fifteen? No. Thank you. *Adeus*.'

My stomach's told me something. Watch the lawyer. So far that's all. I don't know about Valentim. That's a hard thing, to admit that you sodomized a young girl. Still shaming, even for him. Maybe there was someone else. Another creep who did that to her, shamed himself and killed her for the feeling she'd given him. But it's a job, this one. Jorge said she'd been coming in there for months doing tricks for pocket money. The lover said she took money off him after sex. Teresa Carvalho said she's been sleeping around the university, even with her lecturer. Bruno said that wasn't reliable. None of them know her. They know bits of her. Only Valentim has got inside, but then he knew what he was looking for.

'*Boa tarde*, did you see this girl yesterday around two, two-fifteen? Yes. You did?'

I was in a café now on Avenida Duque de Ávila, a few buildings down from Catarina's school, the Liceu D. Dinis.

'She came in here sometime after two o'clock,' said the barman. 'I've seen her before. She's at the school. She buys a coffee, drinks it, leaves . . . just like everybody else.'

'Was there any particular reason you remembered her?'

'I came on at two, she came in a few minutes later. She was the only person in the place.'

'Was she with anybody?'

'No. She stood at the counter, like I said. Blonde hair, blue eyes, white top, short skirt, nice legs, big shoes with shiny stones in the heels.'

'You took a good look at her.'

'Why not?'

'Any reason?'

He leaned on the stainless-steel counter, drummed his fingers on the edge of it, looked up into his head, went through a long list of pros and cons and balanced it all out. I didn't take my eyes off his face. He stopped fooling around.

'You're joking,' he said.

'I'm not.'

'Because,' he said, flipping his thumbs up on the counter, 'I wouldn't have minded fucking her. She had a very nice ass. OK? Now, who are you?'

'Police,' I said. 'Have you got a phone?'

'Down the end of the bar.'

I called Carlos who still hadn't got the search warrant. I told him to wait for me in the office when he got it, that I was going to talk to the schoolteacher for no more than an hour, and then we'd search Valentim's room together. I hung up, slapped some coins on the bar and left.

Catarina's teacher lived at the top of a smart, renovated four-storey apartment building in Rua Actor Taborda, which was just on the other side of Saldanha from the school and not far from the *Polícia Judiciária* building. It was after seven o'clock and still light with a little way to go but the heat was backing off now.

First thing. She didn't look like any schoolteacher I'd ever had or met. She had short, dark, shiny hair, fashionably cut. She wore earrings which looked like two bent coffee spoons and lipstick . . . even for the police. She had green, penetrating eyes that never left my face and perfect, white hard-looking teeth. She was wearing a lightweight, very short blue shift with the four inches of sleeve rolled over her shiny shoulders to keep herself cool. She was my height with long slim legs and long slim arms. Her name was Ana Luísa Madrugada.

'But I use Luísa,' she said. 'Ice tea? Homemade.'

I nodded.

'Take a seat.'

She went into a galley kitchen and opened the fridge. I sat in the dark room, the shutters partly closed to the light and heat outside. She'd been working. There was a table lamp on over piles of books and papers, some typed, some in longhand. A computer with text on the screen flickered in the corner. She handed me the ice tea and slumped into a chair opposite. She stretched out a long, tubular arm, not muscular but taut. She placed her glass elegantly on a side table, where there was an ashtray with two cigarette butts which had been smoked right down to the filter as if they were an allowance. She was hardly sitting, almost lying with her back on the seat of the chair and her legs so far out in front that her knees were almost touching mine.

She was careless with her limbs which was why I looked at them so much. I mentioned her work. She told me she was working on a doctoral thesis on a subject that did not snag in my brain. I found myself too concerned by the shift which was working its way up her thigh at her every movement, so that I thought I was going to see something that was none of my business, but I wanted it to be. A few seconds later I realized they were culottes and she could afford to be negligent. I could relax. My eyes drifted back up to her shiny shoulders and the bent spoons. I wished I'd brought Carlos along with me now. There would have been someone else to ask and answer questions while I did some idle watching without the pressure of having to pay attention.

I wanted to know how old she was. I tried to look at the back of her hands, but she wouldn't keep still. She looked anywhere between twenty-five and thirty-five. She kicked me on the leg, and put her hand on my knee to say sorry. I felt plugged in, the blood zipping around me like quicksilver. How did it go? What were the words to use? Where were the words?

'Inspector?'

'Yes,' I said, seeing her head on one side, waiting for an answer. 'It's been a long day, *Senhora Doutora*.'

'Luísa,' she said. 'I've been talking too much. When I work all day and it gets to night-time I just need to talk.

Having you here is a luxury. Normally I have to go down to the café and try to engage the barman, but they're surly down there and hard work. I give it to them anyway, my whole day's worth of nonsense. I'm doing it again. I'm talking too much. It's your turn.'

'I wouldn't mind some more nonsense myself,' I said. 'I don't get enough nonsense. Too much senselessness, not enough nonsense.'

'I got up at eight. By nine I was working. It was perfect. Everything was coming out just right. Then I heard some kids playing in the street, but there's no traffic, and I remember it's Saturday and that's why I'm working and not teaching. Then I think: What are kids doing in the city on the first hot day of summer? What am I doing in the city? Why aren't I having lunch with somebody out on the beach? Why isn't someone taking me out to lunch on the beach? Why am I sitting indoors writing learned rubbish that only five people will ever read? I can feel the pointlessness beginning to break like a tidal wave, so before it does I go back to work. I work all afternoon . . . and nobody calls me. They're all out at the beach.'

'Mine's the only call you get.'

'My saviour.'

'The police.'

She laughed.

'That is your job, isn't it?'

I ducked out of that one. I haven't been in the saving business for years. I've been in the picking-up-the-pieces business.

'I was lucky you were in,' I said. 'One other phone call and you'd have been gone.'

'I was always going to be in,' she said, a little melancholy creeping into the room.

'Not just work?'

'No,' she said and took a careful look at me, then shrugged. 'I split up with a boyfriend recently and fell

209

off the edge of the earth. But anyway, that's not nonsense, that's deadly, seriously boring.'

'A long-term relationship?'

'Too long. So long we didn't get married,' she said, and then caught me on the hop. 'What about you?'

'What about me?' I said, defensive, only used to dealing the questions, nobody ever asking *me* anything personal.

'Are you married?'

'I was for eighteen years.'

'Police work probably isn't that good for marriage.'

'She died.'

'I'm sorry.'

'About a year ago,' I said and then thought of something which I said out loud, 'which means, in fact, that I was married for seventeen years, I suppose. I just still . . .'

It had grown darker in the room. We were sitting out of the restricted light from the table lamp and were now upright on the edges of our chairs, trying to see each other's faces in the warm dusk.

'I've been coming to the surface,' I said, stirred by the intimacy present in the room, and then disturbed by it, I pulled out. 'But that, too, is probably deadly, seriously boring.'

'And this is what happens to us.'

'What?'

'The deadly, seriously boring people end up working on Saturday afternoons. It's the only thing that makes us feel worth something.'

'I have a daughter. That helps. And I'm working only because a faceless man on the end of a mobile phone assigns things to me and I obey.'

'What sort of an assignment could bring you to my door? Is one of my kids in trouble?'

'You've had no calls today?'

'Don't rub it in.'

'Which of your kids do you think would be in trouble?'

'Boy or girl?'

'Girl.'

'Catarina Sousa Oliveira.'

'First time.'

'I thought somebody would be coming to talk to me about her in the end.'

'What about?'

'Drugs, probably.'

'I'm with Homicide.'

She put her hands up to her face. The word had chilled her. She went over to the window and opened a shutter to let more light in and some of the day's residual warmth.

'What's happened?' she asked.

'She was murdered yesterday, late afternoon,' I said. 'I'm surprised nobody's called you. Dr Oliveira said he tried last night.'

'I was out with my sister in the Alfama.'

'You were expecting trouble with drugs,' I said.

'I see it as part of my job to look for signs. Needle rash, dilated pupils, poor concentration, loneliness.'

'How many of those did Catarina have?'

'Everything except the needle rash.'

'Did you talk to her about it?'

'Of course. I talk to all the suspect kids.'

'Why was she lonely?'

'That doesn't mean she wasn't popular. You know how it is. She had talent. It attracted a lot of attention. She had a great voice and the blonde hair and blue eyes. A lot of the kids liked her and wanted to be like her . . . but she didn't have any friends amongst them . . . too far ahead for that.'

'You heard her sing?'

'It wasn't a beautiful voice, nothing clear or sweet about it but it could raise the hairs on the back of your neck. She could do *fado* but what she really liked was black music, the blues numbers . . . Billie Holiday. She loved doing Billie Holiday.'

211

'And *she* had plenty to cry about,' I said. 'What about mood swings?'

'She hasn't been so bad this term. She went through a patch of incredible anger. She'd go puce and look as if she was going to toss her desk out of the window, then she'd calm down just as quickly and go morose. I talked to her mother and things got better almost instantly.'

'She didn't have any medication in her blood.'

'Maybe she stopped taking whatever was causing the trouble.'

'She was sexually active in an extreme way for a girl her age. Were you aware of any relationships within the school?'

'Nothing happens in that place without the whole world knowing about it, but sometimes rumour is more exciting than the truth, and it's not so easy to distinguish, so I don't talk about what I hear.'

'I'm only interested in what you've seen.'

She came back from the window and sat on the edge of her chair again.

'I'll put it another way,' I said. 'I've retraced her steps from a *pensão* in Rua da Glória to the café down the street from the school, La Bella Italia, at around two-fifteen. She went to school, I presume. She wouldn't have come all this way not to.'

'She was in my class until close to four-thirty.'

'Then what?'

She wrung her hands and looked into the floor.

'I saw her leave the building. She was with this guy, a young guy who's teaching English Language. He's Scottish. Jamie Gallacher. He was talking to her on the corner of the street and she wasn't talking back. Then she walked off up Duque de Ávila and he followed . . . that's all I saw.'

'Was that unusual?'

'If you listened to the rumour there was something going on there. I heard that Catarina would go back to

212

his apartment after school sometimes. But that is not reliable and shouldn't appear in any of your reports. It's girl talk.'

'What do you make of Jamie Gallacher?'

'He's OK, but he's like a lot of these English people. He likes to drink and he drinks heavily . . . and then he's not such a nice guy.'

Chapter XVII

20th December 1941, Serra da Malcata, Beira Baixa, Portugal.

The mule train had split up. Abrantes had sent the younger man on ahead. He was cursing himself for overloading the mules but there was no sense in leaving just a few hundred kilos behind for another trip. Two of the mules had broken down, one lame, the other with a snapped girth. They'd tried to spread their loads out over the other mules, but it was impossible, they risked losing more. There'd been no let-up in the weather which had turned colder, bringing ice in the rain on the back of a fierce north-easterly, while black clouds crowded the hills.

Abrantes and one of his men, Salgado, unloaded the mules. While Abrantes worked on one mule's hoof, Salgado did his best to repair the torn leather strap of the other. They were down by the river when they heard them. Men on horseback. The *guarda*. One of the regular border patrols. The two men looked at the wolfram, over two hundred kilos of it, nearly one hundred and fifty thousand escudos' worth. They pinched their cigarettes out and calmed the animals.

Abrantes jerked his head at Salgado and they picked up a sixty-kilo sack of wolfram each and staggered to the edge of the freezing river. Salgado wanted to drop his in at the edge but Abrantes urged him out into the faster flowing water in the middle. They went back. Salgado couldn't manage the second one, so they picked up the next two sacks between them and waded out. They went back to the mules and coaxed them into the water and back out

214

again. They could still hear the horses of the *guarda* closer now but not making progress, assessing the situation.

They didn't see them at first, the acoustics of the river valley playing games with the sound of the hooves on the rocks. The *guarda* appeared directly above them, their peaked caps silhouetted against the lighter distant sky. One of the men pointed down to their position. Two of the *guardas* unholstered their sidearms, the third took out a rifle from the back of his saddle. They shouted down to them. The rifleman levelled his weapon and aimed. Abrantes and his man put up their hands. The two *guardas* with pistols galloped along the ridge and came down into the gully. Their horses trod carefully over the rocks towards the two mules. The *guardas* dismounted. The man on the ridge lowered his weapon, stuck it back in his saddle, and reined his horse round to join the party down by the river.

The *chefe da brigada* approached the two men still with their hands up. He adjusted the grip on his gun in his gloved hand. He looked over the mules.

'What are you doing out here?'

'We've had trouble with the mules,' said Abrantes. 'This one's lame and the other's girth has broken.'

'Where's your cargo?'

'We don't have one.'

'Where have you come from?'

'Penamacor.'

'Where are you going?'

'Foios,' said Abrantes. 'We're taking the mules back to their owner. They've been used for work outside Penamacor.'

'What sort of work.'

'Transport.'

'Transporting what?' said the *guarda*, getting frustrated.

'You know, working around the mine.'

'Wolfram?'

'I think so. I think that's what it was.'

'Were you carrying any wolfram?'

215

'No, we're just taking the mules back.'

'You're wet. Up to your waist, you're wet.'

'We've just brought the animals across the river.'

The *chefe* pointed them over to the mules with his pistol. He slapped the mules' bellies, satisfied himself that they were wet. He went to the riverside. The *guarda* with the rifle arrived and dismounted. He tore a branch from a tree and joined the *chefe*. They walked along the side of the river dragging the branch along under the water.

It was late afternoon now and the light was failing. Abrantes didn't know where the *guarda* were from, but they had a two-hour ride ahead of them, wherever. The *chefe* and the rifleman talked out of earshot. They came back to their horses, all three mounted and rode back out of the river valley without exchanging another word.

Abrantes brought Salgado to his side and they sat and watched the river for some minutes, the rain driving into their backs. He took out his Walther P48 and checked that it was loaded and still dry. They made a fire. Abrantes worked on the mule's hoof again, Salgado repaired the girth. Night fell and they slept around the fire, having eaten some stale bread and ham.

In the morning they were up at first light wading into the river to bring out the sacks of wolfram. It took some time, as the river had swollen some more during the night, and they could only bring them out one at a time. They loaded the sacks on to the mules, giving the lame mule the lighter load. The rain had stopped, but the cold wind was still blowing and there was more on its way down from the *meseta*. They moved out of the gully and up on to the ridge to start the climb across the *serra* to Spain. That's where they were waiting for them, on the other side of the ridge.

The *chefe de brigada* raised his gun and told the men to stop. Abrantes fell to one side as if he'd taken a bullet in the side of the head. The *chefe* instinctively squeezed the trigger

216

and Salgado open-mouthed took the bullet high in his chest where it shattered his clavicle. Salgado's mule took off. The second bullet hit Salgado in the stomach before he'd reached the ground.

Abrantes dragged his mule down to the floor, he tore the gun from his waistband and shot the *chefe* in the chest under the armpit. The man fell to the ground. The rifleman was trying to keep his rearing horse calm and Abrantes let off two shots, the second hitting him in the head. The third *guarda* wheeled his horse round in time to take a bullet between his shoulderblades. He fell backwards with a crack and his horse ran back down into the gully.

Abrantes tethered his mule and approached the *chefe* who was still breathing but bubbling blood out of his mouth. He shot him in the head. The rifleman was already dead. The third *guarda* had a broken neck. Abrantes went to Salgado who was lying on his back so flat that it was as if the ground had already claimed him. He was panting, scared and in pain, his lips and face white. Abrantes tore open the man's coat and shirt and saw the mash of bone and flesh at his clavicle and the dark hole in his stomach. Salgado whispered something. Abrantes put his head down to his mouth.

'I can't feel my legs,' he said.

Abrantes nodded at him, stood back and shot him in the eye.

The *chefe*'s horse had stayed. Abrantes loaded two *guardas* on to it and took them down to the river. The other two horses were down there and he tethered them to a tree. He went back and loaded the *chefe* and Salgado. He filled the dead men's clothes with rocks and dragged each one of them out into the river.

Riding the *chefe*'s horse he picked up his own mule and found Salgado's grazing in a hollow, still fully loaded with the wolfram. He spread the loads from the mules over

217

the *guardas'* horses and set off once more across the *serra* for Spain.

It was the afternoon of Christmas Eve and Felsen was still in Abrantes' house, waiting with his cleaned and loaded pistol. It had been a long wait and one he had not been prepared for. There was only so much time he could spend thinking about Abrantes, the missing wolfram, and how he was going to manoeuvre the Portuguese across the border and leave him out there, amongst the rocks and broom, with a bullet in his brain.

Occasionally Maria came in with coffee and then later food and drink. She wanted his attention but he wouldn't give it to her. Her presence irritated him. She triggered strands of thought that he'd rather have left dormant. He remembered a look she'd given him when they were burying the Englishman in the courtyard, and that would start him thinking about that afternoon in the old mine, and he'd have to shake his head and pace the room to get rid of it. He wondered why he'd had her now. How could it have been to spite Abrantes when he was going to kill the man anyway?

At that moment she'd appear again, and the word 'rape' would climb into his brain, and he'd remember the thrill as he rammed gently into her, her eyes darting afraid above the knuckles of his hand over her mouth. But then it had turned into something else. He'd felt that heel on his buttock. She'd come back the next night and it had sickened him. He told her to stay in the kitchen.

He thought about other women. He thought about the first woman. A girl who was supposed to be out in the field working for his father, but who he'd caught sleeping in the barn. She'd seen the way he'd looked at the flesh between her stocking top and skirt, and had let him have her to keep him quiet.

She was still the only one by the time he arrived in Berlin

as a young man. A girl picked him up in the railway station. He'd thought that this was all part of the wild city life until he'd finished, and she'd demanded her money. He'd asked, what for? And her lips had hardened to chisel tips. She'd called the pimp, who'd taken one look at the size of the farmboy and produced a blade. He'd paid and backed out and then heard the pimp beating the girl. *Wilkommen in Berlin*.

The weather closed in again over Amêndoa. The rain raked the tiles. Felsen smoked and continued to amuse himself by trying to remember all the women he'd ever had in the right order. If he missed one he had to start again. It took him some time to work his way to Eva.

He didn't want to think about her, but in the near darkness of the house and after their brief encounter back in Berlin, he found he couldn't prevent his mind from drifting back over the shards of the affair like gunsmoke over a battlefield. He began to discern her slow dismantling of their relationship. From the moment she'd taken him back in after they'd split up over his accusation that she was acting, to that last sexual act in his apartment before the Gestapo removed him in the morning. But even in that period he could still find moments when they'd reconnected, and he could still feel that point of contact when their knees had touched under the table in the club only a few nights ago. He rubbed it as if it was still burning.

He lit a cigarette and the draught in the room battered the smoke this way and that, whipping it away to nothing. He asked himself if this was what love was – this strange acid in the stomach that burns a constant ulceration, this airlock in his pipes that could send shudders around his system and stop the flow of everything. But that was not how he'd ever heard love described and, like a man taking a short leap over a high drop to white water, he lurched to a sudden conclusion. He'd gone from intimacy to loss without ever having experienced love. It choked him and

219

he had to pace the room again to try and free himself of the notion. He took long hard draws on his cigarette until he was dizzy with nicotine and he reeled to the door and let himself out into the blustery afternoon.

The wind gusted needles of sleet into his face. He breathed it in as if it would somehow clean him out. He had no idea how long he stood there. The afternoon had already darkened with the weather and his face had instantly numbed. The only way he knew that there was ice in the rain was the way it spiked his tongue.

When finally he turned to go back into the house he saw that he wasn't alone in the street. Some way off two figures approached, heads bowed against the wind. Felsen came level with the steps up to the house. One figure split away and headed for the side of the house as if for cover. In profile now, he saw it was a mule. The other figure came doggedly forward and he knew from the gait and the hat that it was Abrantes. He felt the hardness of the gun in his waistband. He unbuttoned his coat in the middle. The figure didn't hesitate until he was about five metres away.

Felsen's fingers flipped open another button. Hands appeared from the clothing of the man opposite. Felsen slid his hand into the opening of his coat and gripped the handle of the gun. Abrantes' left hand came up and removed the scarfing from his face. The right hand hung limply. When it happened it was quick, too quick for Felsen to move. Abrantes covered the five metres in a fraction of a second, threw his arms around the German and smacked two hands on his leather back.

'*Bom Natal*,' he said. Happy Christmas.

Abrantes guided Felsen back up the stairs and into the house. He shouted for Maria and told her to take care of the mule. She disappeared out of the back of the house. They went into the parlour room and Abrantes threw logs on to the fire. Felsen's face came back to life, raw and

220

aching. Abrantes went into the kitchen and came back with a bottle of *aguardente* and two glasses. He poured the liquor and they drank to Christmas. He was happier than Felsen had ever seen him.

'I heard you were in Foios,' he said, as if Felsen had dropped round there for a drink and found nobody in.

'The *chefe* at Vilar Formoso said we could be in for a hard time. I thought I'd take a look at the mules.'

'And you saw that I'd been running them for months.'

'Months?'

'I've got more than fifty tons over there.'

'Where?'

'In a warehouse in Navasfrias.'

'You should have told me. I've had a hard time explaining the shortfall in Berlin.'

'I'm sorry for that. I was only reacting to rumours.'

'Which rumours?'

'That now you've invaded Russia and that campaign is . . . continuing, Dr Salazar is not so concerned about an invasion here. The Germans are too stretched, they say.'

'You remember the *Corte Real* going down in October?'

'And the *Cassequel*,' said Abrantes. 'The *Cassequel* was one of our best ships, seven thousand tons.'

'So you don't think this is a Lisbon problem?'

'I think we should go to Vilar Formoso tomorrow,' said Abrantes. 'Take the *chefe* another Christmas present.'

'I was there only a few days ago.'

'They have short memories,' he said.

'And we could cross over and take a look at the product in Navasfrias,' said Felsen. 'Is it secure?'

'It's secure.'

Secure meant men with shotguns. Felsen suddenly saw himself lying amongst the rocks and broom with his face blown apart, but he couldn't back down from Abrantes now. He nodded and checked Abrantes, but all he saw was weathered skin stretched over large bones with eyes concentrated on the task of pouring more alcohol.

What was it Poser had said to him, or someone else in the legation, about the Portuguese? Two things. The first, that there wasn't a law in Portugal that couldn't be got around, and the second, was that the Portuguese never came at you head-on. They got you looking straight ahead and then they stuck you from behind. It had been Poser. He remembered pointing it out to him that this, of course, would never happen in Germany and the Prussian had walked off sick of his irony.

The two of them ate a Christmas dinner of a large hen and some roasted *bacalhau*. They drank two bottles of pre-war Dão which left the warm, rounded taste of a less complicated summer at the back of the mouth.

Felsen went to bed early and smoked and drank *aguardente* from his metal flask in the dark. He kept his gun under his pillow. After an hour he went across the courtyard and listened at the door of the house with the gun dangling from his hand. He heard Abrantes' familiar grunt and Maria's strange hiss.

In the morning he drank coffee and smoked a cigarette and ignored the stone-faced girl. He had a problem. He didn't want to cross the border with Abrantes and walk into a team of shotguns in Navasfrias. At nine o'clock, this problem was solved by a driver who'd come up from Guarda with a telegram from Lisbon: *Dutch and Australian troops invade E. Timor. Return to Lisbon immediately. Poser.*

He liked Poser's use of the word 'invade'. He knew that Salazar would see it exactly like that, an invasion of Portuguese sovereignty.

'Is there a problem?' asked Abrantes, suddenly anxious.

'Our border difficulties are over,' said Felsen. 'The Allies have made a mistake. I have to go to Lisbon now. You will

222

arrange for the one hundred and nine tons you have stored in Navasfrias to go to the compound in Ciudad Rodrigo and no more smuggling until I authorize it.'

'One hundred and nine tons?'

Felsen gave him the calculations. The numbers flickered through Abrantes' head, his face impassive and grey as hoar frost from not shaving. At that moment Felsen realized what Abrantes had been doing. He hadn't been stealing, but playing the price difference over the border. Selling high in Spain to come back and buy cheap in Portugal and pocket the difference. But he'd been caught out, the price in Spain had dropped, maybe there were no buyers at the time. He didn't have the money to replace the stock in Foios. All he could do was try to recoup the situation by underestimating the tonnage he'd smuggled. The good mood of last night had been the start of a bluff, a man playing for time to control his losses.

'When do you want the product moved?' asked Abrantes, anxiety showing through.

'It's supposed to be in last year's accounts which should be finalized by the end of January.'

Felsen went into the kitchen. Maria was there holding her baby, looking pathetic. He strode past her, crossed the courtyard and packed his clothes.

In the back of the Citroën he wrote a note to the manager of the compound in Ciudad Rodrigo and gave it to the driver. As they drove down the hill they caught up with a procession. There were men he recognized carrying a body wrapped in cloth and women walking behind. He dropped the window.

'Who has died?' he asked.

The men didn't answer. A woman spoke up.

'It is Alvaro Fortes,' she said, 'and this is his widow and son.'

Felsen blinked and told his chauffeur to drive on.

27th December 1941, German legation, Lapa, Lisbon.

'Salazar,' said Poser, who hadn't referred to him as a
cheating Arab for over twenty-four hours now, 'was in
such a lather . . . still is . . . about the invasion, that we
thought it expedient to open our wolfram negotiations
for 1942 immediately. It's been a marvellous sight. Sir
Ronald Campbell, the British ambassador, has been staggering about like a concert pianist with broken fingers.
The good doctor has spent the whole year in a state of
irritation with the British, who've put an arm around his
shoulder and whispered the old alliance in his ear and
taken advantage of his credit, while with the other they
blockade him and sweep troops into Dili. We, on the other
hand . . .'

'. . . have been sinking his ships.'

'True. Minor, but necessary, corrective measures or should
we say reminders of his neutral status.'

'As far as Salazar's concerned, Christmas happens once
a year and he gets all the presents. What are you offer-
ing?'

'Steel,' said Poser, brimming with confidence. 'Steel and
fertilizer. We'll be making an offer in two weeks' time.
Salazar will give us guaranteed export licences for 3000
tons and, once we have that, these other negotiations
about who will get what from the Metals Corporation will
be immaterial. We will get what *we* want and the British
can learn about sweating for 1942.'

'And do I continue my operations?' asked Felsen.

'Of course you do, unless you receive orders to the
contrary. I think a more clandestine approach might be
in order, but you should have an open field.'

'Where's this intelligence from?'

'Not intelligence, just an observation about British character. You probably don't know much about cricket, do you? Nor do I. But I'm told it's all about fair play. They'll play by the book and report all your indiscretions to Salazar like the good boys they are. And Salazar . . . if we keep stroking his fur the right way, will ignore them.'

Poser took one of Felsen's offered cigarettes, lit it and stuck it in his prosthetic hand. He sipped his coffee, licked his lips and applied his handkerchief to them as if they were sore. He sat back patting his chest as if that was where he had his winnings.

'Is that it?' said Felsen. 'You brought me all the way down from the Beira just to tell me how brilliant you are?'

'No,' said Poser, 'just to smoke some of your cigarettes. I like the brand.'

Felsen checked him over.

'Yes,' confirmed Poser, 'I've been learning from you, Felsen. A joke. A rare thing in diplomatic circles.'

'When are you and Salazar getting married, Poser?'

'The wedding, I fear, is still some way off,' he said, grinning.

'Happy Christmas, Poser.'

'And to you, Felsen,' said the Prussian, raising his prosthetic hand in a half salute. 'And by the way, there's someone to see you in my office.'

For an irrational moment, caught up in Poser's good humour, Felsen thought that it would be Eva. But he was distracted by the smell of burning in his nostrils and Poser tearing the cigarette out of his prosthetic hand, the glove burnt through and ruined.

'Shit,' said Poser.

'Another rare thing in diplomatic circles?' asked Felsen.

In Poser's office, sitting with his back to the door and his feet up on the window sill, looking out at the weak, winter sunshine filtering through the Phoenix palms in the gardens, was Gruppenführer Lehrer.

'*Heil Hitler*,' said Felsen. 'What a surprise, Herr Gruppenführer, what a wonderful surprise.'

'Don't waste any of that Swabian charm on me, Herr Sturmbannführer.'

'Sturmbannführer?'

'You've been promoted. So have I. Now I'm Herr Obergruppenführer if you can manage that. And as from next March we'll be operating under the auspices of the *Wirtschaft-und Verwaltungshauptamt* or the WHVA if that means anything to you?' said Lehrer, who paused for a sign. 'Clearly not.'

'Now we get promoted for failing to achieve our targets . . .'

'No, for getting close to impossible ones. The circumstances have not been easy, I know, and you haven't had full control of the campaign, but despite all this you've made considerable progress and more important, the Reichsführer Himmler has been able to shine in front of the Führer and annoy Fritz Todt. The latter being the most gratifying.'

'I can only thank you for coming all this way to confer the honour, sir.'

Lehrer whipped his feet off the sill and swivelled his chair to face Felsen. Promotion had worked on him, there was a greater and harder authority emanating from under the black eyebrows.

'Do you know what temperature it is in Russia?'

'Now?' asked Felsen, unnerved. 'Well below zero, I imagine.'

'Minus twenty if you're in Moscow. Minus thirty if you're out in the wilderness somewhere . . . and it's going down not up. It's not so easy to remember that in plus fifteen with the blue sea and the Estoril casino and the champagne . . .'

'The blankets . . .'

226

'Forget the damned blankets. The quality was complete shit anyway. I'm glad, you know this, I'm *glad* the British pre-emptive campaign was so successful. Now they've got all those blankets rotting in their own warehouses instead of them stinking out ours.'

'And Poser seemed so cheerful.'

'What you don't know about Poser is that he has a prosthetic head. Nothing in there is real,' said Lehrer. 'You know who they've got fighting our boys out there on the eastern front?'

'Russians?'

'Siberians. Flat-faced, slit-eyed Siberians. Those people, they sleep in the summer, it's too warm for them. They only wake up when the temperature drops below minus ten. That is their operating temperature. Our troops are still in their summer tunics. They haven't even got gloves. And they're faced with those barbarians who dance because it's so beautifully cold, who rub rancid pig fat on to their bayonets so that when they stick our half-frozen soldiers the wound will be hopelessly infected and they'll die in agony. If their screams could carry as far as Berlin we'd be out of there tomorrow.'

'Why are you telling me this?'

'The reward for failure is a posting to the Russian front. What does that tell you?'

'We are not experiencing total victory.'

'The real winter has just started, but it's been damn cold for two months. Our supply lines are stretched over thousands of miles. The Russians have retreated and left us nothing. They've razed everything to the ground. There isn't a single thing we don't have to transport. You know what we do with our Russian prisoners of war? We stick them behind barbed wire and watch them starve and freeze to death. We can't give them anything. We can't supply ourselves. Grim, is an unimaginably slight adjective for the situation out there.'

'The first half of the liverwurst sandwich?'

'Have you been out in the Beira with your head up a pig's arse? What happened on 7th December?'

'Pearl Harbor.'

'We already have the makings of the sandwich.'

'The way we see it here, we're twenty-five kilometres from Moscow. We're in the suburbs, for God's sake. The Americans are on the other side of the Atlantic. They've still got to invade Europe. Let's be reasonable, Herr Obergruppenführer.'

'I'm hopeful, Herr Sturmbannführer, but we must have contingency,' said Lehrer. 'Now . . . that peasant you work with up there in the Beira.'

'Abrantes.'

'Can he read or write?'

'No,' said Felsen, 'but he has a signature.'

'Is he under control?'

'He's under control,' said Felsen, thinking how close it had been. 'As long as he's making money he's happy. He does well enough out of the wolfram cleaning companies we set up.'

'This is a different thing altogether. Those cleaning companies are nothing, they don't have significant assets. You remember what I said to you at the beginning of the year . . . about private thinking.'

Their eyes connected and achieved an understanding.

'In the event of unlikely disaster . . .' Felsen allowed the sentence to drift.

'What I have in mind . . .' said Lehrer, 'we're going to open a bank, a Portuguese-owned bank.'

'Portuguese-owned?'

'If it comes to it . . . the completion of the sandwich, I mean. I can assure you the Allies will be vengeful. No German assets will survive in Europe. This bank will be Portuguese-owned with significant, but very discreet, German shareholders.'

'And who are they going to be?'

'You and me for the moment,' said Lehrer. 'This is our private enterprise. No one, and certainly not that Prussian idiot, should know about it.'

'Is this an SS thing?'

'In a manner of speaking,' said Lehrer, trying to get a clearer reading from Felsen. 'But I hope you understand the importance of Abrantes in this. He must be reliable . . . he must be a friend.'

'He's a friend,' said Felsen, holding Lehrer's adamantine look.

'Good,' said Lehrer, easing himself back into his chair. 'Now all we need is a name. A good Portuguese name. What does "felsen" translate as in Portuguese?'

'*Rochedo, rocha.*'

'*Rocha*. That sounds reliable, but I think we should have something big and encompassing to go with it.'

'The sea is probably the most important Portuguese icon,' said Felsen.

'What's "sea" in Portuguese?'

'*Mar.*'

'No, no. *Mar e Rocha* sounds like a bad restaurant.'

'*Oceano e Rocha?*'

'I think that could be it. Banco de Oceano e Rocha,' said Lehrer, looking out into the gardens. 'I'd put my money in that.'

Chapter XVIII

Eva Brücke sat in the study in her apartment. She smoked cigarette after cigarette and took sips of brandy from a glass she held with white hands in which she could see the blue veins working clearly. Her face had so little colour in it she thought her teeth might be visible through her cheeks if she stood in front of the light. Her insides? She didn't have any insides. She felt like a plucked and drawn bird, freezing too.

There were two of them in the apartment, nameless of course, Hänsel and Gretel, Tristan and Isolde. The two were practised, expert at not being there – quieter than insects but not so silent that the tension in the rooms became palpable. They'd been at it around Berlin for months and this was their last stop.

Eva had been getting ready to go out, had just got to the point of applying a nub end of a lipstick to her mouth when there'd been a knock at the door, a polite knock. She put the lipstick away. She didn't want to fluff it and break up the valuable nub end. The next knock was a roll of thunder, a heart-stopping pounding on the door followed by the dread three-syllable word that could jelly the thighs of a Berlin bartender.

'Gestapo!'

It was loud enough that the two in the back of the apartment would have heard and hidden themselves. She had no time.

'I'm coming,' she said, getting it out clear first time with no croaks and adding a slightly irritable intonation. The pounding continued. She shrugged into her overcoat and opened the door.

'Yes,' she said, efficient, a slight divot of a frown on her forehead. 'I was just on my way out.'

The two men pushed past her into the living room. They both wore black leather coats and black hats which neither of them removed. One was thin. The other a brute.

'Come in,' she said.

'Your papers?'

She took them out of her handbag and handed them over, straight-armed, on the confident side of impertinent.

'Eva Brücke?' said the thin one, not reading the papers.

'I think you'll find that's who I am.'

'You've been reported.'

'For what and by whom?'

'Harbouring illegals,' he said. 'Your neighbours.'

'I don't have any neighbours, I'm surrounded by rubble.'

'We're not necessarily talking about people who live next door. Neighbours could be those who overlook from the back, for instance.'

'They were bombed out last week,' she said.

'You don't mind if we have a quick look around.'

'I was on my way out,' she said, verging on the desperate.

'It won't take long,' said the thin one, sniffing the air.

'As long as you don't mind giving me the names of the neighbours, the names of your superior officers so that I can report those neighbours for nosiness when your superiors come to my club tonight, and your names too.'

'So that what? So that you can report us too?' asked the brute, hanging his face in front of her.

'Müller,' said the thin one pointing to his own chest, 'and

231

Schmidt. Do you want to write those down? Can we get on with it now?'

'The back of the apartment is still unsafe from the bombing. I will not be responsible if you hurt yourselves. And if a wall falls out because of your carelessness and I'm left to freeze this winter I'll . . .'

'. . . sleep in this room,' finished Schmidt, his eyes gone sleepy, his nose broken and bent to the right.

'No. I will ask my friends, your superiors at the RHSA, to pay for the reconstruction.'

'In a pig's arse,' said Schmidt crudely. Nobody was sure what he meant.

They stared into her. She'd overdone it on the haughtiness and the name-dropping. Nerves. Müller gave her back her papers.

'Perhaps I'll go first,' he said. 'If Schmidt's hundred kilos starts slipping he'll take the whole of the side of the building away with him.'

He smiled as if his mouth was a recent cut, turned away from her and sniffed the air again. She didn't like him. He seemed a little too intelligent for Gestapo. What happened to the dolts, or did they all get sent to Stalingrad?

Eva sat down in the living room and jammed her hands into her coat pockets. Schmidt leaned against the door jamb and watched Müller's progress down the corridor.

'Tell him it's the last two rooms he has to watch out for. He'll feel it in the floorboards.'

Schmidt glanced at her, nodded and looked back without saying a word. She wanted to smoke but didn't dare take her hands out of her pockets. She knew from the state of her stomach they'd be shaking.

'He smells them first,' said Schmidt after a few minutes.

'What?'

'Jews,' said Schmidt. 'He says they smell of rancid cheese.'

'Tell him I've got some in my kitchen.'

'Jews?' he asked, as a matter of fact.

'Cheese,' said Eva. 'I don't want him to smash the place up just because I've got a piece of Gruyère somebody gave me six weeks ago.'

'Doesn't it keep?' he asked. 'Gruyère.'

'Where do they find you people?'

He jolted himself off the door jamb and moved across the room at an alarming pace, as if pleasantries were over and the usual tools were to be applied. He clamped his meaty hands on to the arms of her chair and leaned his face into hers so that she could see each nascent bristle above his top lip.

'You've got nice legs,' he said.

'Unlike your manner.'

'I hope we get you down at Prinz Albrechtstrasse,' he said, glancing down at her lap and then back to her eyes. 'We can do anything we like down there.'

'Schmidt!' shouted Müller, from the back of the apartment. Eva jumped. 'Get down here!'

Schmidt smiled and pushed himself away from the chair. He went down the corridor. Eva pressed one of her hands, still in her pocket, between her legs and clamped her thighs in case she pissed herself. Her bowels were trembling and liquid.

'Take hold of my belt,' said Müller.

'This floor's completely fucked,' said Schmidt, with a construction engineer's precision.

Eva forced herself out of the chair and down the corridor.

'For God's sake be careful,' she said. 'It's a seven-metre drop to the street. The fall will kill you if the rubble doesn't.'

'She's concerned for you, Müller.'

Müller strained forward, craning his neck around the door. Schmidt held on, smiling, and winking at Eva.

'I think she must like them slim,' he added.

'Shut up, Schmidt, and pull me back up.'

Schmidt, without taking his eyes off Eva, twitched his forearm and Müller sprang back and thumped into his chest. Schmidt put an arm around him.

'You know what you have to do,' said Schmidt. 'You have to be totally confident. You can't piss about. You just have to do it.'

He took two steps down the corridor and went into the bedroom on the left. The whole floor lurched. Beams groaned. Plaster and masonry broke off and powdered. There was a loud crack. Schmidt reappeared ashen-faced, his head wobbling on his neck. A line appeared in the plaster work above their heads.

'You fucking idiot,' said Müller, springing back down the corridor.

'There's nobody in there,' said Schmidt, walking tightly, buttocks squeaking.

'We're going now.'

'Didn't you smell anything?' asked Schmidt, recovering his cool.

'Only the shit you've got in your pants.'

Eva led them back to the living room. Müller was tight-lipped, furious and thwarted. Schmidt opened the door and looked back at Eva.

'What's in that,' said Müller, pointing at an old chest she'd moved up from the damaged room. It wasn't a big chest. It couldn't have taken a grown man.

'Books,' said Eva. 'Try lifting it.'

Müller tried the lid. It was locked.

'Open it,' he said.

'I haven't opened it in years. I don't even know where the key is.'

'Find it.'

'I don't . . .' Eva stopped. Schmidt had opened his coat and taken out a Walther PPK. 'What are you doing?'

'Best Jew detector I've ever known,' he said.

234

'And if there isn't a Jew in there you're prepared to give me six months of your salary?'

'Six months?'

'That's a seventeenth-century chest and the books are valuable too. Why do you think I moved it up from the bedroom?'

Schmidt regripped the gun and turned it on Eva.

'You know the penalty for harbouring illegals?'

'I imagine it involves some years in a KZ.'

'Boom!' he said.

'Let's go,' said Müller.

They left. Eva went straight to the lavatory and let out a thin stream of diarrhoea. She lit her first cigarette with her dress and coat still up around her waist.

She had to force herself out of the house. She had said she was going out so she had to do it. She knew they'd be sitting there in their car waiting for her. She finished the fourth cigarette, dropped the last of the brandy, swilled her mouth out with water and goaded herself out on to the street. She walked in the road. The pavements were covered in piles of rubble and there were always Poles and Czechs carting more of it out of the half-collapsed buildings. The Gestapo car pulled alongside and Schmidt rolled down his window.

'Want a lift?' he said. 'We must be going your way.'

'I'll walk thanks.'

'See you again. Number Eight Prinz Albrechtstrasse.'

She arrived at her club on the Kurfürstendamm. It had been cold in the street but she was in a sweat. Traudl was in her office lying on a camp bed behind a curtain. She lived there when she couldn't find men to take care of her, which was most of the time. She was thin and white, her facial bones as clear and as fragile as porcelain. Eva sent her out to clean the bar and sat back with another brandy and more cigarettes. Her body, which had begun to feel as dislocated as a cubist's idea of one, slowly came back together. Her insides warmed and filled, her guts firmed. She did the September accounts and put Hänsel and Gretel to the back of her mind.

At 7.30 p.m. she left for home to change into her evening wear. It was a cold night. Small groups of Jews, all with the yellow stars they'd been required to wear by law since the beginning of September, trotted past her making for home before the 8.00 p.m. curfew – armaments factory workers, they were all legal.

Before turning down her cobbled street off Kurfürsten-strasse she looked up at the starry night. She sniffed the air. It was clean and there were no obvious Gestapo cars in the street. The bombers would be out though. It had been a terrible summer. First Lübeck, then Cologne, Düsseldorf, Hamburg, Osnabrück, Bremen and, of course, Berlin. Putrefaction had clogged the air. Only the rats were fat. But tonight was clean. She went up to the apartment, let herself in and checked each room.

'It's safe,' she said, quietly.

Gradually there was movement from the end room. A young man inched around the door, his face contorted from the stiffness of his body.

'Where's the girl?' asked Eva.

The girl appeared behind her.

'Where were you?'

'In the chest,' she said. 'I was just trying it for size when they came.'

Eva suddenly had the girl's-eye view from inside the chest. She shuddered.

'You'll be leaving tonight for Gothenburg,' she said, moving on to better things.

The girl smiled at the ceiling. The boy squeezed Eva's arm. There was a soft knock at the door. The boy crept back down the corridor and around the door. The girl was gone. Eva cleared her throat.

'Who's that?'

Another soft knock.

She opened the door. Two girls. One late teens, the other fourteen at the most. Yellow stars.

'Yes?' said Eva, looking down the stairwell behind them.

'Can you help us?' said the eldest girl. 'We've come from Herr Kaufman.'

'I can't,' she said, and heard the girls gasp as if they'd been stabbed. 'I'm being watched.'

'What can we do?'

'You'll have to go somewhere else.'

'Now?'

'It's too dangerous for you to stay here.'

'Where shall we go?'

She blinked. Why hadn't Kaufman said he was sending two more? She thumped her forehead with a closed fist and tried to think of somewhere nearby.

'Do you know Frau Hirschfeld?' she asked.

They shook their heads.

'Do you know Berlin?'

Again.

She wrote out the instructions for them. It wasn't such an easy place to get to after 8.00 p.m. without papers. She sent them on their way. She still had plenty of work to do with Hänsel and Gretel. She went into her office and unlocked and removed the second drawer. She took the contents out and turned it over. Taped on the underside were forged papers for Hänsel and Gretel in the names of Hans and Ingrid Kube.

Another soft knock on the door.

What now?

She put the drawer and the contents back into the desk.

Another soft knock.

Those girls. What was Herr Kaufman thinking of?

She strode across the living room and opened the door. The two girls were standing there in their coats, their

237

shoes planted together, good as gold. Behind them, with a hand on their shoulders, was Müller. Schmidt's colossal fist came into the light waving the instructions she'd just written – a moment's loss of concentration. The smaller girl began to cry.

'Frau Hirschfeld sends her regards,' said Schmidt, shoving Eva with the flat of his hand between her breasts so that she fell on her back and skidded across the room.

'How expensive did you say that chest was?' he asked, and slammed the door behind him. He took out the gun. Footsteps down the stairs. He eased off the safety catch.

'No,' said Eva.

'No? Why no?'

'I've found the key.'

'It's too late for keys. I haven't the time for keys.'

He pumped two bullets into the chest. There was a muffled cry. Eva launched herself at Schmidt's gun arm and he cracked her across the forehead with the barrel. She went down but not quite out. Schmidt pumped another bullet into the chest. Eva felt herself lifted, her cheek landing on the carved top of the chest. Schmidt rucked up her skirt and his hand grabbed her roughly between the legs, his fingers finding their way in.

There was a shout from the back of the house, an incoherent wail. Something fell, something big and heavy, like the wardrobe Eva hadn't been able to move out of there. The hand left her. There was a stupendous crack and then a small stroke of silence, before the back end of the whole apartment building collapsed with a noise that went on and on.

Eva slid off the chest: Schmidt was standing over her looking in the direction of the endless collapse, mouth open, unable to move, not knowing how much of the building was going to break up and whether they'd be consumed with it.

Eva no longer felt fear for the first time in two years. She felt relief that it was over. Relief, that was, until the house fell silent again and the floor was still there underneath her and Schmidt said:

'That really wasn't very safe at all, was it?'

1st October 1942, Largo do Rato, central Lisbon.

In the Largo do Rato Felsen had picked up a *táxi a gasogénio*, something introduced nearly a year ago when the fuel shortages began to bite. For some reason he felt less safe with a wood-burning stove mounted on the boot generating steam into a cylinder in the front than he did with petrol doing much the same thing. He couldn't wait to get out, which was what he did no more than seventy metres down Rua da Escola Politécnica, but not because he'd lost his nerve.

He thought he was mistaken but the likeness was so exact he had to get out to check. The girl turned right into Rua da Imprensa Nacional and he put in a limping sprint to catch up with her. He had not been mistaken. It was Laura van Lennep. He grabbed her by the wrist as she was taking another right turn and she spun round and tried to wrench herself away from him.

'Remember me?' he said, holding on.

She looked blank.

'Chave d'Ouro, Estoril Casino, Hotel Parque, March 1941. We fell in love,' he said, sarcastically.

She blinked and he looked at her more closely. There was something missing, something not quite right in her head that was making itself known in her face.

'I have to go to America,' she said, trying to twist her wrist away from him.

'Klaus Felsen,' he said, hanging on to her. 'You might remember . . . you stole my cufflinks. They were engraved

239

with my initials. KF. No? How much did you get for them? Not enough to get you to America by the looks of it?'

She backed away up the street, not out of fear but because she knew she had to get away from the pressure. The nasty pressure. She wanted to get to the place. The place where they were nice to you. The place where they looked after you. She turned. Felsen let go of her, hesitated and then followed. She went into the Travessa do Noronha where there was a soup kitchen and hospital set up by the *Commissão Portuguesa de Assistência aos Judeus Refugiados*. It was lunchtime. Other people were going into the building. He watched her queue up and receive her food. She didn't talk to anyone. She looked around occasionally, but furtively with her head dipped over her spoon. He approached a white-coated doctor who was waiting to be served. He pointed out the girl and asked after her.

'We don't know exactly what happened to her,' said the doctor, speaking in Portuguese but with a Viennese accent. 'We had another case very like hers in which we saw the same neurotic obsession with getting to America. This other case had been put on a train by her parents in Austria and told to get to America at all costs. She later found out that her entire family had been taken to the camps. This news induced a curious reaction, which was a deep need to obey her parents combined with an obsessive guilt which prevented her from achieving it.

'The only reason we think the same might be true of this Dutch girl is that we've seen in her passport that at one stage she had an American visa, and amongst her possessions we found a valid ticket for a sailing long gone. Sad . . . but look around you.'

The doctor rejoined the queue for his meal. Felsen looked around him without seeing what the doctor had meant. The girl wasn't at the table any more. He left the building, stood on the steps, lit a cigarette and flicked the match off into the street. He walked down through the Bairro Alto in the high autumn sunshine to the Largo do Carmo where he took the *elevador* down to the Rua d'Ouro.

He went up to the second floor of the building they'd leased for the Banco de Oceano e Rocha. The offices occupied the ground and first floors and there were two apartments on the floors above, the top floor being his and the second floor belonging to Abrantes and his family. Abrantes had asked him to be godfather to his second son. He'd called Felsen at the German legation that morning to say that Maria was being released from hospital and he should come and look at his new godchild.

The maid led Felsen through to the living room. Maria was lying on the chaise longue in a fur coat which wasn't necessary, given the weather. He could hardly bear to look at her. In less than a year the peasant girl had transformed herself into a travesty of a forties film star. She couldn't read but she'd flicked through the magazines, choosing whatever took her fancy, and Abrantes had indulged her. Felsen lit a cigarette to stop himself from sneering. Maria lit one too and blew smoke out in a practised stream.

Abrantes was staring down into the Rua do Ouro through windows criss-crossed with sticky tape against the bombing raids that the Portuguese were still expecting to move down from Europe like a bad weather front. Felsen had even heard air raid warnings and seen the soldiers sitting on sandbags behind their barbed wire barricades in the Praça do Comércio, wondering what the hell they were supposed to be doing.

Abrantes was dressed in a grey suit and now wore spectacles although he never pretended he could read. He smoked a *charuto*. His transformation from Beira peasant had gone better than Maria's. He had some stature and a sinister look that could command respect from the city-dwellers. He'd learnt things about behaviour and manners just as Felsen had done when he first came up from Swabia. He greeted Felsen flamboyantly, as a successful wartime businessman

241

should. He guided him to the edge of the cradle on which Maria rested a proprietorial hand.

'My second son,' he said. 'Your godson. We have called him Manuel. I would have liked to have called him after you but, Klaus . . . I'm sure you understand, a Portuguese boy can't bear the name Klaus. So we named him after my grandfather.'

Felsen nodded. The baby was sleeping, tightly wrapped in what seemed like far too many clothes. He looked like any other baby except a little less wrinkled than usual. Maria tickled the baby with her finger. Felsen was aware of her watching him. The baby struggled against the intruding finger. A bubble appeared at his pursed little mouth. His eyes suddenly opened, surprised and big for his face. Felsen frowned. Maria's face came into his vision.

'He looks like his mother this one,' said Abrantes, on his shoulder.

There was a lot of blue in those eyes and, maybe if you were the father, the faintest hint of Maria's green in them, but to Felsen they were blue eyes, his own eyes.

'A beautiful baby,' said Felsen, automatically, and Maria sat back on the chaise longue.

Abrantes dug the baby out of the cradle and held him high. He growled at him. The baby blinked at the big bad bear.

'My second son,' he said. 'No man could be happier than one with two sons.'

'What about a man with three sons?' asked Maria, cheeky, confident of her status.

'No, no,' said Abrantes, superstition rippling through him like wind through the broom in the Beira, 'out of three, one will always be bad.'

The baby gathered his small but impressive powers and let out a long piercing wail.

242

Chapter XIX

21st December 1942, SS-WHVA, 126–35 Unter den Eichen, Berlin-Lichterfelde.

'Stalingrad,' said Lehrer, who was sitting sideways to his desk, his elbow resting on a blotter, hand up in the air, poised, blade-like. 'Are they talking about Stalingrad in Lisbon? Are they drinking to Stalingrad in the goddamned Hotel Parque in Estoril?'

Felsen sat alone on the other side of the desk. He smoked but didn't answer. Nobody was talking about Stalingrad.

'Are they?' insisted Lehrer.

'Not at the dinner I was at last night.'

'Just cutlery clattering on the plates.'

'Not quite as bad as that.'

'And Poser? What did Poser look like?' asked Lehrer, shifting in his seat, his belt, longer than a pack mule's girth, creaking over the movement of his belly.

'Like Poser always does, but sicker.'

'Mmm,' murmured Lehrer seismically. 'Zeitzler, the Army Chief of Staff, went on Stalingrad rations for two weeks to show solidarity with his men at the front. He lost twelve kilos. What does that tell you?'

Felsen closed his eyes at another of Lehrer's endless test questions. He wanted to say that it told him that Zeitzler probably had more than twelve kilos to lose, but one look at Lehrer's creaking belt told him this would not lighten the tone.

'The Sixth Army is in big trouble,' Felsen trotted it out, Lehrer's best pupil.

'You know, I have my contacts in the East Prussian headquarters at Rastenberg, Herr Sturmbannführer. I am reliably informed that Field Marshal Paulus and his two hundred thousand men are finished,' said Lehrer, and his hand dropped, guillotining the Sixth Army off the Third Reich.

'Can't they break out, retreat, regroup?'

'The Führer won't allow it. He's obsessed with the disgrace of retreat, with the disgrace of losing all our heavy artillery. He doesn't appear to see Zeitzler's point that by leaving them there he will lose everything and not just Stalingrad . . . the whole Russian campaign.'

'Does Stalingrad have some vital strategic importance?'

Lehrer held up his hands, if not to God then the blackout blinds.

'It's mythical,' he said. 'You hold Stalingrad, you hold Stalin by his steel balls.'

They talked about wolfram. Lehrer was listless and disinterested. He couldn't even raise the flag for the latest smuggling operation where Felsen had loaded 200 tons into rail cars in Lisbon and seen them travel on papers as manganese all the way through the border without even the customs opening them up. The Allied agents had come close to a fist-fight with the customs *chefes* who cleared the cargo in Lisbon and Vilar Formoso. They hadn't grasped that these two public servants creamed five million escudos between them which made their thousand escudos per month salaries look like Felsen's bar bill.

Lehrer managed a few half-hearted questions about the bank, which hadn't been doing very much except lending money to buy mining concessions on the border.

It was early evening by the time Felsen finished his report, but before Lehrer released him, the Obergruppenführer suddenly staggered to his feet, hobbled around the desk and sat on the corner.

'We have a special understanding, you and I,' said Lehrer,

suddenly grave. 'I promised you when I took you away from your factory in Berlin that you would be properly rewarded for the work you have done. Next year, possibly, your job will be a different one. It is one in which you are experienced but whose nature is not the same. You must trust me. You must not be dismayed when I tell you that at this point we might have already reached the beginning of the end.'

'One thing Poser did say was that since Speer's promotion to Armaments Minister earlier this year there has been a massive improvement in our production capacity. I've felt it. The pressure for us to ship wolfram has been enormous . . .'

'This is true,' said Lehrer, batting him down gently, 'but my feet are telling me that this will only prolong the agony. And my feet are never wrong.'

Both men looked at Lehrer's boot-encased agony.

It was six o'clock and dark and freezing from a wind sent directly down from the eternal Finnish darkness. The car crawled forward like the half-blind creature it was. Felsen sat in the back confused. Did Lehrer know what he was talking about? He'd always billed himself as the visionary, but did the future of the Third Reich really come down to his being twenty kilos overweight, sitting behind a desk too much and atrocious chiropody? Could the great German army that had crashed through Europe, smashed through Russia all the way to the Caucasus, all the way to within twenty-five kilometres from Moscow, to the suburbs for God's sake, could it all be over for the loss of one city? Felsen smoked behind a cupped hand and looked at the destruction in the suburbs of Steglitz, Schönberg and Wilmersdorf and remembered Poser telling him something at the beginning of June he hadn't believed. On the night of the 30th May in just over an hour and a half, Allied bombers had dropped more than two thousand tons of bombs on the city. When Poser had told him this it was four days later and Berlin was still burning. He hadn't believed him and had tried to get past the demented Prussian and out of the room, but Poser had snagged his elbow with his prosthetic hand and said quietly in his ear, 'I've seen the damage estimation. The real one, not Goebbels' version. Now go and find your wolfram. We'll need every kilo you've got.'

As they came into the south of Berlin on the Potsdamerstrasse he asked the driver to carry on and take a left up the Kurfürstenstrasse. The street was unrecognizable with rubble piled in heaps on either side and destroyed and burnt-out buildings. Eva's apartment building appeared to be still standing. He took a torch from the driver and went down the cobbled side street and into the backyard of the building, through a gate which opened to a precise quarter circle of rubble and a narrow path to the door of the building, whose whole rear was down so that he could see into Eva's kitchen.

The place wasn't habitable and he started to back out when he heard a voice, thin as bone china, singing an absurdly robust children's song from his homeland:

Ich bin ein Musikant, ich komm vom Schwabenland,
Du bist ein Musikant, du kommst vom Schwabenland.
Ich kann aufspielen auf Meiner Geige,
Du kannst aufspielen auf Deiner Geige.
Dela schum, schum, schum,
Dela schum, schum, schum
Dela schum, schum, schum,
Dela schum.

Felsen went up the stairs, still solid and unbroken. The voice continued the manic refrain of the bow across a violin. The door to the apartment was open. The living room had been stripped to the floorboards and even some of those had been taken up at the far end. He followed the voice into Eva's study. Huddled in the corner in a wild mix of clothing – scarves, cardigans, skirts, even a man's waistcoat – was Traudl. She stopped singing.

'Did you bring me anything today?'

Her face had completely regressed to a child's. A child's with no fat in it. The white skin over her skull was thinner than the finest glove leather. Her temples were sunken. He knelt down to her.

'Oh,' she said, seeing he was a man, 'do you want to fuck me?'

'Where's Eva, Traudl?'

'All right then, let me sit with you, just let me sit with you.'

'You can sit with me, but tell me where Eva is too.'

'She's gone away.'

'Where did she go?'

The girl frowned but didn't answer. He tried to put his hand through her hair but it was too matted. She began singing her song again.

Footsteps up the stairs. Light wobbled in the living room. A woman appeared in the doorway.

'What are you doing?' she asked, aggressive until she saw the uniform.

'I'm trying to find Eva Brücke.'

'Frau Brücke was arrested by the Gestapo months ago.'

The girl stopped singing the grating song.

'What for?' asked Felsen.

'*Judenrein, judenrein, judenrein*,' chanted Traudl.

'Harbouring illegals,' said the woman. 'This one turned up some days after. She won't move, not even for air raids. I bring her something to eat now and again. But she'll have to move soon with this winter.'

Felsen took her to his apartment which had been requisitioned by the Organization Todt and filled with Speer's construction workers. He gave one of the women there all his ration cards and some money and left Traudl with her.

Felsen told the driver to take him to Wilhelmstrasse and booked himself into an absurdly luxurious room in the Hotel Adlon.

By 8.30 the next morning he was at No. 8 Prinz Albrechtstrasse sitting in the office of SS Sturmbannführer Otto Graf. They were waiting for the file to be delivered and Graf was enjoying one of Felsen's cigarettes and staring out into the still dark morning.

'What is your interest in this case, Herr Sturmbannführer?'

'I knew her.'

'Intimately?'

'She'd been running clubs and bars in Berlin for years. A lot of people knew her.'

'But you, what about you?'

'I knew her well enough to know that she wouldn't let herself be known.'

'Maybe . . . what she was doing, you have to be.'

'I knew her before the war. She was always like that.'

The file arrived. Graf looked at the photograph and remembered her. He flicked through the pages.

'Yes, yes, I know the type,' he said. 'She looks as if she'll snap like a pencil on the first morning and three weeks later she's told us nothing. Not that . . .'

'Three weeks?'

'It was a very serious matter. She was smuggling Jews out. Sending them in rail cars of furniture to Gothenburg.'

'And after the three weeks?'

'She was lucky. If the presiding judge had been Freisler she would have hanged. As it is she's been sent to Ravensbrück for life.'

Felsen offered another cigarette which was taken. They were American, Lucky Strikes he'd brought over from Lisbon. He gave Graf the packet and another one from

248

his pocket. He said he could arrange a carton, two cartons. Graf nodded.

'Come back at lunchtime, I'll have a visiting permit ready for you.'

It wasn't difficult to arrange a car, but it took all afternoon and another two cartons of cigarettes to get the petrol for it. He could have taken the train up to Fürstenberg but someone had told him the railway station was a long way from the camp and transport not always available.

In the evening he went to the back of the burnt-out Reichstag building and bought four bars of chocolate on the black market. He didn't sleep much that night but lay on his luxurious bed in the Hotel Adlon, drank far too much and swelled his chest with fantasies of rescue. He could see Eva and himself climbing the steps up to the aeroplane in Tempelhof airport and flying out of the bomb-shattered Berlin to the blue sea, the wide Tagus and a new life in Lisbon. It was the closest he'd come to crying, emotional crying, as a grown man.

The next morning was cloudless, the landscape on the sixty-kilometre drive north of Berlin was frozen still and dusted white with an iron-hard frost that the low winter sun would never burn off. Felsen's eyeballs felt hot and were cracked with red lines. His stomach was burning sour, but he still managed to feel some of the heroicism of the night before. He parked outside the camp and was admitted through the barbed-wire walls into a compound consisting of low wooden huts. He was taken into one of these and left alone with four lines of wooden benches. Time passed. Hours of it. No other visitors came in. He sat on the bench and moved with the sunlight coming in through the window to keep warm.

At lunchtime a female guard came into the room in a grey greatcoat and side cap. Felsen stood to complain but saw that she was followed by a figure in a striped prison uniform about three sizes too big with a green triangle on the breast pocket. The guard sent the shaven-headed prisoner down the benches towards Felsen. The prisoner marched like a soldier on drill.

'You have ten minutes,' said the guard.

Felsen was not prepared for this. The prisoner's appearance was so dislocated from the human beings beyond the barbed-wire periphery that he wasn't sure if his language would be the same. It took a full half-minute to find the vestiges of Eva Brücke, Berlin nightclub-owner, in the sunken, grey, papier-mâché skull. He had thought for a moment that this prisoner was going to take him to Eva – blonde, white-skinned and smoking somewhere else in the camp.

'You came,' she said, flatly, and sat down next to him.

He held out his massive hand. She folded her shrivelled, blackened monkey's paws in her lap. He broke off a piece of chocolate, she took it whole and swallowed it. The chocolate combusted inside her instantly.

'You know,' she said, 'I used to have dreams about my teeth falling out. Nightmares. People would tell me it was because I was worried about money. But I knew it wasn't that. I've never cared that much about money. Not like you. I knew that I was petrified of losing my teeth because I'd seen all those toothless women in villages, their faces fallen in, their beauty gone, their personality diminished. I have eight left, Klaus, I am still human.'

'What happened to your hands?'

'I make uniforms all day, every day. It's the dye.'

She looked at his hand still held out for hers and then at his face. She shook her head.

'I'm going to . . .'

'This is my lunch break, Klaus,' she cut in on him savagely. 'Give me some more chocolate, that's all I'm interested in. Not hope, not promises and certainly not sentimentality. Just chocolate.'

He broke off another piece and gave it to her.

'And I won't waste your time either,' she said. 'I presume you've come for an explanation. Well, you did see me that night in Bern. That pig Lehrer . . . he was such a bad loser. I warned you about him, didn't I?'

'Why Lehrer?'

'I knew him. I knew him before you, years before. He came to all my clubs. I was surprised you'd never met. He asked me one night if I knew anyone who could speak languages and was good at business, good at making things happen. And it all just fell into place. You, him and what I was doing. You should consider yourself lucky. If he hadn't sent you to Lisbon, you'd probably be in Dachau. It was a solution – Lehrer removed you from the scene and my involvement with him meant that people didn't look at me so closely.'

'But why didn't you tell me?'

He was angry. He looked into her ruined face, the prominent craters of her eye sockets, the remaining yellow teeth blackened by molten chocolate, the veins standing out on her shaved head, the scabs from shaving nicks in the down forming over her china-thin cranium. And she saw that he was angry.

'More chocolate,' she said, not bothering to answer the question from the man in an SS uniform, the man who had been a *Förderndes Mitglied* of the SS, the man who'd made couplings for the SS, for God's sake, the man who bought wolfram for the SS so that the Nazi war machine could thunder on. Why hadn't she told *him*?

He broke off another piece.

'Don't think I was being brave, Klaus. It all happened by accident . . . after what happened to those two Jewish girls, you remember that, I told you *everything* about that, didn't I, the ones I sent to Lehrer and his friend, that was a risk me telling you that . . . a risk I did not repeat when I saw . . .' she stopped, and controlled herself. 'So, I moved the other two Jewish girls I had out of Berlin and that was it, I

251

was involved. They kept coming to me and I couldn't turn them away. I'd become a link in the chain.'

'One more minute,' said the guard.

'When you saw what?' asked Felsen.

'Nothing.'

'Tell me.'

'When I saw that it didn't concern you,' she said quietly.

'I'll speak to Lehrer,' said Felsen in a rush, so that he didn't have to contemplate what she'd just said for too long.

'You don't get it do you, Klaus? It was Lehrer who put me in here. He got rid of me. I'd become an embarrassment to the Obergruppenführer. The only person who can get me out of here is the Reichsführer Himmler himself. So don't even think about it. More chocolate.'

He gave her the three bars in his pocket and they disappeared into her clothing. She got up and he rose with her. She stood to attention. He took the back of her baby's head in the palm of his hand. Her head jerked back in astonishment and she turned out of his hand and away from him.

'Visit terminated,' said the guard.

She marched to the door and, without looking back, straight out into the winter sunshine. It was the last he saw of her.

Chapter XX

24th July 1944, Hotel Riviera, Genoa, N. Italy.

Felsen lay in bed, the windows of his hotel room wide open, the sun streaming across the breakfast tray and his body. He was exhausted and drowsy as a dog in the village square. The hand that held the cigarette weighed twenty kilos, he had to drag it off his chest to his mouth. He felt himself floating like a barrage balloon, just a thin thread of cable tethering him to the earth.

He'd worked for sixteen months solidly, with only one break. The one break was to let him return to Berlin to view the total destruction of Neukölln Kupplungs Unternehmen in the bombing raid of 24th March 1944. Speer was not even going to attempt to revive it. It was flattened.

The only reason Felsen could think of, that Lehrer had brought him back for this miserable funeral, was to show him what had become of the capital of the Third Reich. From high up in the air it had looked like the same city apart from the various plumes of smoke. It was only as the aircraft dropped towards Tempelhof airport that he saw that where walls still stood the buildings were skeletal, windowless, gutted and roofless. They provided no accommodation. Everybody was living underground. The city had been turned upside-down – a honeycomb below, a catacomb above.

He'd walked through the rubble-strewn streets, past the fourteen-year-old firefighters still trying to control blazes started several nights earlier – the roads a pasta dish of hoses, torn-up tram tracks, overhead cabling, drainage and water pipes, their ends wedged shut by overturned buses and burnt-out trams. And walking had been the only option. No S-bahn, no U-bahn – all the stations were packed with people. No fuel. He'd walked to No. 8 Prinz Albrechtstrasse to ask Sturmbannführer Otto Graf one question which he didn't want to go down a telephone line. For a carton of Lucky Strikes, Graf had told him that Eva Brücke had died on the 19th January. When he flew out of Berlin that afternoon he could think of no reason for ever going back.

Lehrer had promised him that his job would change, but until the end of April 1943 he worked exclusively on smuggling wolfram out of Portugal. It was only at the beginning of May that he began hauling bullion. His first transport was to take four trucks containing more than 4000 kilos of gold from the Swiss border to Madrid, where it was deposited in the Spanish national bank. He repeated this twice in June. In early July he took his first convoy since the start of the wolfram campaign to Portugal and deposited 3400 kilos of gold in the vaults of Banco de Oceano e Rocha. Four hundred and eighty kilos were sold to the Banco de Portugal to buy escudos, the rest was shipped to the Banco Alemán Transatlántico in São Paulo, Brazil. Then came the Battle of the Kursk Salient and on 13th August 1943 he met Lehrer in Rome.

Lehrer had lost ten kilos in three months, his face was permanently red and not blasted by the sun. They went to a restaurant where Lehrer chased his food around the plate and consumed two and a half bottles of red wine before starting on the grappa. He winced and pushed his fingers into his stomach three or four times during the meal. He smoked all his own cigarettes and started on Felsen's.

'We lost Kursk,' he said.

'I heard,' said Felsen. 'There've been black days in Lisbon.'

'The war's finally got there has it?' said Lehrer, unpleasantly.

'Poser shot himself.'

'Not in the head I hope,' said Lehrer. 'That wouldn't have killed him.'

'What about wolfram?'

'Fuck wolfram. Don't you know what Kursk means?' Lehrer exploded, suddenly outraged, so that Felsen had to close his fist to keep himself calm. 'Kursk means we're not a tank-led army any more. *Blitzkrieg* is over. We can never replace the Panzers we lost at Kursk. The Soviets have opened a new factory at Chelyablinsk, ours are being destroyed daily by the Allied bombers. The Red Army is 1500 kilometres from Berlin. We don't need wolfram. We need a fucking miracle.'

'What about for solid-core ammunition?'

'Speer's using something called uranium from a special bomb project they've had to give up.'

'Is that the end of wolfram?'

'For you, yes. Abrantes can keep that running. Now your job is to take as much gold bullion out of Switzerland as possible and deposit it in Spain and Portugal. You'll receive instructions as to what to do with it.'

In the year since that Rome meeting Felsen had taken nearly two hundred and fifty trucks of bullion from the Swiss border to the Iberian Peninsula. From there the bullion was shipped out to banks in Argentina, Uruguay, Brazil, Peru and Chile. During this time Felsen became Lehrer's most trusted subordinate. He worked at it. As far as he was concerned it wasn't good enough just to be Lehrer's colleague, he had to be nothing short of the man's son. By the time Salazar proposed a total embargo of all wolfram on 1st June 1944 Felsen's success had been total. When Lehrer and he met now they didn't shake hands, they embraced. Lehrer even allowed himself to get emotional. They called each other Oswald and Klaus. For Lehrer, Felsen had become the only piece of solid ground in a Europe of chaos.

*   *   *

A knock on the door jerked Felsen off the bed. He stubbed out the cigarette and put on a dressing gown. He unlocked the door and Lehrer pushed in past him with a cloth-bound roll under his arm and a buff envelope in his hand.

'Is the truck loaded, Klaus?' he asked.

'The truck was lowered on to the deck of the SS *Juan Garcia* at six o'clock this morning.'

Lehrer leaned the roll up against the wall and put the envelope on the table. He helped himself to some of Felsen's breakfast. He'd put the weight back on and had got his ulcer under control in the last year.

'I'm worried,' he said, slurping at the top of the coffee. 'The Americans are going to hit us in the French Riviera any day now.'

'The ship's Spanish flag . . . and the Americans have got other things on their minds. What's in the roll?'

Lehrer's dark eyebrows jumped.

'A Rembrandt,' he said. 'Take a look in the envelope.'

Felsen emptied the envelope out on to the bed. There were photographs and details of Lehrer, Wolff, Fischer and Hanke.

'You know what to do,' he said. 'Papers, passports, visas for Brazil. I want you to take a property somewhere close to the border in Portugal. Not in the wolfram mining areas where you're known, further south perhaps. I've heard it's a desert down there.'

'The Alentejo. We've been down there buying cork. There are places on the border. You'd just have to get across the Guadiana river,' said Felsen. 'But getting there from Berlin . . .'

'There will be chaos, believe me.'

'And what about the Rembrandt?'

'It'll go with you on the truck. You'll keep it in the vaults of the Banco de Oceano e Rocha with the gold.'

Felsen looked down at the bed. The photographs, the personal details.

'So this is it, Oswald?'

'The last one.'

'Have you arranged an escort at Tarragona?'

'There's no escort. Nobody must know about this consignment. Not the Spanish and not the Portuguese either.'

'You want me to smuggle it into Portugal?'

'You must have smuggled over a thousand tons of wolfram over the years, why not two and a half tons of gold?'

'And then what?'

'You wait.'

'How long?'

'That I can't say. If the Führer capitulated it could be tomorrow but he won't. He can't.'

'Why not?'

'Did you read the documents for this gold consignment?'

'Read them? No. I don't read anything any more. I just signed them.'

'You didn't notice the origin of the three parcels?' asked Lehrer.

'No.'

'Lublin, Auschwitz and Majdanek.'

'Polish gold.'

'In a manner of speaking.'

'I don't follow.'

'My star pupil,' said Lehrer, shaking his head. 'There are no gold mines in those towns. Polish national gold was removed from Warsaw a long time ago.'

Felsen said nothing.

'Lisbon's been a long way from this war,' said Lehrer. 'Nobody's spoken to you about the Final Solution. It's not dinner-table conversation in Lapa. This gold has come from the Jews. Their watches, their spectacles, their jewellery, their teeth.'

257

'Their teeth?' said Felsen, moving his tongue over his own molars.

'The Führer will not capitulate because he knows, even in his madness, that the world will not accept his systematic annihilation of European Jewry. We will all have to go down fighting.'

On the 11th August 1944 Operation Dragoon began with a landing by American troops on the French Riviera. By that time 2714 kilos of Jewish dental and jewellery gold, and a rolled Rembrandt canvas were sitting in the vaults of the Banco de Oceano e Rocha in the Rua do Ouro in the Baixa in Lisbon. It would take Obergruppenführer Lehrer another nine months to come and claim them.

Chapter XXI

11th May 1945, Quinta das Figueiras, Alentejo, Portugal.

The farmhouse was huge and fifteen kilometres from the nearest village on a chassis-breaking track of dried mud and slate. Nobody came to this place except the odd wandering shepherd to get water from the well in the high summer. The house occupied the top of a small rise in a landscape of rolling hills flecked with cork oaks and olive trees. The east side of the house overlooked the confluence of the Lucefecit and Guadiana rivers and there was a large, terracotta tiled terrace surrounded by a low wall and seven fig trees. It was under these trees that people would sit in the perfect cool and watch the river beyond the walled orange grove disappear into a rocky gorge, heading south to the Atlantic.

It was hot. Not the brutal summer heat which came when someone left the Sahara's furnace door open, but hot enough that after midday the birds fell silent, the sheep lowered their heads and gathered under the wide spread of the cork oaks and the Guadiana slowed almost to a stop. A car could be heard arriving for an hour, and the local people would listen because they were rare in these parts.

Felsen and Abrantes were driving a three-ton truck through a field of blood-red poppies, mowing through the blooms, up to the rear of the *quinta*. They were carrying two weeks' supply of tinned food, forty litres of wine in five-litre flagons, a case of brandy, a case of port, four suitcases of clothes, a stack of bed linen and two Walther P48s which they'd stowed under the driver's seat. There was a briefcase between them containing identity papers and passports for four men, four densely packed blocks of 1000-escudo notes and a velvet bag with twenty-four uncut diamonds. Felsen was trying to smoke but the truck was bucking so violently over the ruts in the field that he couldn't get the cigarette to his mouth. It was 6.30 p.m.

They reached the beaten earth courtyard at the rear of the *quinta* and backed the truck up to the kitchen door. Felsen unlocked it and threw it open. The cool of the thick-walled house met him. They unloaded the supplies from the truck and drove it into the barn at the side of the house. Abrantes picked up two terracotta jars to fill from the well. Felsen took the bed linen further into the cool, dark house. He crossed the large dining room with its vaulted ceiling and opened up a set of double doors which led into a three-metre-wide corridor with eight bedrooms, four on either side.

The windows and shutters were closed in all the rooms with only cracks of intense light around the edges. The walls were half a metre thick here too, and all the ceilings vaulted. Felsen dropped linen into four rooms on the east side, and the last two rooms on the west side. At the end of the wide corridor was a crucifix which he straightened on the wall. He felt chill with the sweat of the drive still on him.

He opened a set of doors from the dining room to the terrace by removing a thick wooden pole inserted into holes within the walls on either side. He stood in the middle of the terrace and let the sun warm him through his damp shirt. He lit a cigarette and heard a distinct metallic click. He turned to find a man he didn't recognize, but whom he knew instantly was German, standing by the doors with a revolver in his left hand.

'Good evening,' he said. 'I am Felsen. We haven't met.'

The man was bigger than Felsen and brutal-looking with half-closed eyelids and a broken nose.

'Schmidt,' he said, and smiled.

Laughter came from under the fig trees and a familiar voice.

'Schmidt is very security conscious. We're glad to have him along, Klaus.'

Lehrer, Hanke and Fischer, all three of them dressed in collarless shirts, black waistcoats and trousers, came out from under the thick green fig leaves. Felsen embraced each of them.

'Where is Wolff?'

'He's here,' said Wolff who appeared alongside Schmidt with Abrantes in front of him on the end of a Mauser.

'I wasn't expecting you for some days,' said Felsen.

'We got away early,' said Lehrer, and the men laughed. 'We've spent two nights in the barn.'

'Has there been any news from Germany?' asked Hanke.

'Weidling surrendered Berlin on May 2nd. Jodl surrendered to Eisenhower on the seventh and Keitel to Zhukov the day after.'

'Wasn't one surrender enough?' said Hanke.

'And the Führer?' asked Wolff.

'They think he's dead but there has been some confusion,' said Felsen. 'They haven't found a body.'

'He will return,' said Wolff, and Lehrer looked at him sceptically.

'I've bought you new clothes if you would like to change for dinner,' said Felsen.

'No, no,' said Lehrer, 'we're quite happy as labourers after ten days as priests. Let's eat. We've been starving out here for two days living on unripe figs.'

After dinner they sat in candlelight around the table with the doors open on to the terrace. They were all drinking brandy or port, except for Schmidt who didn't drink but sat with his left hand resting on the revolver and the fingers of his right stroking the break in his nose.

261

Felsen had distributed the identity papers which they were inspecting in the weak light.

'Did Schmidt bring photographs?' asked Felsen, as if Schmidt was out of the room.

Schmidt removed a packet from his waistcoat and threw it down the table.

'That could take me a few weeks to organize,' said Felsen.

'We're in no hurry,' said Lehrer. 'We're enjoying the peace. You have no idea of the chaos we have had to endure.'

The five men nodded solemnly. Felsen poured more liquor and checked the men's faces to see how this endurance had worn them. Hanke's eyes had cratered deeper into his face, his eyebrows had greyed as had the heavy beard on his sunken cheeks. Fischer had added more ruches to the pouches under his eyes and there were more red tributaries on his raw cheeks which had lost some of their tightness. Wolff had lost his middle-aged youth, his blonde hair had thinned on top, his eyes had creased and he had two deep lines from his nostrils to the corners of his mouth. Lehrer's head was entirely white, the hair cut short and close to his head like a new recruit. He'd lost weight, a lot of it, and the unfilled skin hung off his face and below his jaw to his neck. Curiously his eyebrows were still dark. They were all tired but the food and drink had enlivened them so that they now looked like pensioners on a summer jaunt to the local spa.

They drank until midnight. They drank until Hanke, Fischer and Wolff staggered off, followed by the vigilant Schmidt. Abrantes, bored by the Germans' conversation, had turned in at ten o'clock. Lehrer and Felsen went out on to the terrace with a hurricane lamp and another bottle of brandy. They lit cigars, whose smoke lingered before dispersing into the night, now faintly perfumed by the vestiges of the orange blossom still on the trees in the walled garden.

'It's worked out,' said Lehrer, inspecting the coal on the

end of his cigar. 'It's worked out splendidly. Thank you, Klaus.'

'You of all people,' said Felsen, picking up on the sentimentality, 'have no need to thank me, Oswald.'

'It's important to thank people,' said Lehrer, swaying a little in his chair. 'You were always very good at showing your appreciation, way back in the Neukölln Kupplungs days. That's how I first heard your name. That's one of the reasons I chose you.'

'And this man Schmidt, why did you choose him?'

'Ah, yes. Schmidt was Gestapo and a very devout Catholic. His priest was very important to our plan. We came here from the Vatican.'

'His nerves might draw attention to you. He must learn to relax.'

'Ach, I know ... but it's good to have someone to be careful for you. It's in his nature. Gestapo men are always suspicious.'

Lehrer took a gulp of brandy, swilled it around his mouth and swallowed. He let his arms drop to his sides, dangling the glass and cigar, letting the stress pour off him. He breathed in the warm night, the crickets sawing through their longest shift and the frogs barking their chat like drunkards who never listen or give a damn.

'How long are you going to stay in Brazil?' asked Felsen.

'A couple of years,' said Lehrer, and then thought about it, rolling his cigar between his lips, 'maybe more.'

'It'll all blow over in a year,' said Felsen. 'People are desperate to get back to normal.'

Lehrer's head turned slowly in the leaping light from the lamp, his eyes black but not shiny, as if any health in them had gone for good.

'Nothing will be normal again after this war,' he said.

'They said the same after the last war. All those men dead for senseless stretches of mud.'

'Remember what I said to you about the origin of the

gold,' said Lehrer in a voice so tired and quiet he could have been on his deathbed. 'There are other names to be careful of . . . Treblinka, Sobibor, Belzec, Kulmhof, Chelmno . . .'

In this same quiet voice Lehrer gave Felsen his final lesson. He told him about the rail cars, the cattle trucks all joined together by couplings that used to be made in Neukölln Kupplungs Unternehmen. He told him about the selections, the shower rooms of Zyklon B, and the ovens. He told him numbers, the numbers of people in a single cattle truck, the numbers of rail cars, the numbers tattooed on forearms, the numbers that could fit in a shower room, the numbers they could put through a crematorium in a day. And he told him the names again just so that he would remember.

'I've told you these things,' said Lehrer, 'because this could take as long as five years for the world to forget and during that time any association with the SS will be very dangerous. If you are going to stay here . . . and there's no reason why you shouldn't . . . you must keep quiet about these things and when they are mentioned say nothing.'

Felsen did just that. He smoked his cigar and sipped his drink. Lehrer got to his feet and shook his history off his shoulders. He jammed his hands into his kidneys and stretched back his head to look up at the clear night sky.

'It's late,' he said. 'I've drunk too much and I must sleep.'

'Take the lamp, Oswald,' said Felsen. 'You'll need it to find your room.'

'I've slept well here,' said Lehrer. 'The peace has been magnificent.'

'Goodnight.'

'You'll go to bed too?'

'In a while. I'm not sleepy yet.'

Lehrer hobbled into the house, his feet still giving him trouble but not telling him anything any more. Felsen heard the faint click of the latch as he opened and closed his bedroom door. He sat for an hour in the darkness, his eyes gradually picking out the leaves of the fig trees, the line of the wall and the fields beyond. He tuned out the insect noise and listened to the rafters creaking in the cooling roof and to the rhythmic snoring from an open window.

He crouched under the branches of the fig trees and crawled over the low wall. He eased a piece of slate out of the dry-stone wall and took out a cloth package which contained a bowie knife and another, short-bladed, knife used for severing the spinal columns of animals. It was 2.30 a.m.

He went back into the house and opened the second bedroom door on the west side. Abrantes was waiting by the open window. He handed him the short brutal knife and crossed the corridor to the first bedroom. The room was full of Fischer's snoring. The man was lying on his back, his neck perfectly displayed. Felsen drove the blade unhesitatingly in and across the windpipe, feeling the tip connect with the vertebrae. Fischer's eyes snapped open, his mouth widened to draw in air. Felsen threw back the covers and jammed the blade up to the hilt under the man's ribs. He backed out of the room. Abrantes, who'd just delivered Hanke to a deeper sleep with a single stab to the cerebral cortex, was waiting for him. Felsen pointed him down to Schmidt's room at the end of the house.

Felsen pushed against Wolff's door and knew that something was wrong. The door would only open a crack. He rammed his shoulder into it which sent the bed in the room scraping across the floor. He squeezed himself through the one-foot space. Wolff came awake with his hand already enclosed around the butt of his Mauser. Felsen lashed out with his fist and caught him on the side of the neck. The blow smacked Wolff's head against the whitewashed wall but didn't stop him from loosing off a round which seemed to split the roof open with its colossal roar. Felsen grabbed the hand holding the Mauser and thumped the blade of the

265

bowie knife high into the man's rib cage. It went through but only punctured a lung. He yanked it out and punched the blade in once more and hit bone and the knife clattered to the floor. He tore the gun from Wolff's slackening grip. Wolff grabbed at him and hung on. He coughed a splatter of warm blackness into Felsen's neck and chest. Felsen fitted the gun barrel into the man's stomach and fired twice, the force of the bullets jerked the body but Wolff did not release him and they fell on to the bed, exhausted as lovers. Felsen pushed away from him and reeled out into the hall and down towards Lehrer's room.

'He's not there,' hissed Abrantes across the hall, pointing into Schmidt's empty room. 'The window was open and he wasn't there.'

'Before or after the shot?'

'He wasn't there,' said Abrantes, confused.

'Find him.'

'Where?'

'He's out there. Find him.'

Suddenly Abrantes' features crept out of the darkness and into the yellow oily light of a hurricane lamp. Lehrer stood in front of them in a vest and undershorts. He had a Walther PPK in his right hand.

'What's going on?' he asked, not groggy with sleep, but wide awake and full of his old authority.

'Hanke, Fischer and Wolff are dead. Schmidt is not in his room,' said Felsen without pausing to think.

'And him?' he asked, twitching his gun at Abrantes whose short brutal knife was dangling from his hand. 'And you? Your shirt.'

The front of Felsen's shirt was black with the blood from Wolff's haemorrhage. The two men looked at each other. Lehrer's eyes widened with horrific comprehension.

Lehrer's gun was pointed at neither man. Felsen hit it and a bullet ricocheted through Schmidt's open bedroom door. Felsen fired Wolff's Mauser low into Lehrer's body, just to get a round off, not bothering to bring the barrel up and get a killing shot in. Lehrer went down fast with a shout and his gun slithered across the floor. The hurricane lamp shattered and the paraffin burst into yellow flame.

Lehrer was foetal holding on to his bloody knee, roaring. He had flames attached to his ankles, shins and shorts. Felsen stepped over the body and picked up the gun. He carried on into Lehrer's room, tore the sheet off the bed and smothered the flames. Lehrer gritted his teeth and hissed in agony. Abrantes stood over him, the knife in his hand. Felsen gave him Lehrer's Walther PPK and told him to find Schmidt.

Felsen grabbed Lehrer under the armpit and hauled him up to the dining room, the man shouting out in pain all the way. He lit the candles on the table. He propped Lehrer up on a chair who collapsed across the table, gasping. One leg was badly burned, the flesh blistered and blackened. His other leg had a bullet below the kneecap. Felsen sat opposite him, the warm Mauser between them. He reached for the brandy and two used glasses. He filled them and slid one across to Lehrer.

'Drink it, Oswald. It'll get you through the next ten minutes.'

Lehrer's head came up, the sweat of pain and effort peeling down the side of his face, tears spreading across his cheeks. He drank. Felsen refilled.

'There's some morphine in my room.'

'Is there?'

'A small leather case by the window. There's a syringe and four ampoules.'

'What's that for?'

'Just in case, you know.'

Felsen didn't move. He lit a cigarette.

'I didn't think that with your deep understanding of it, you'd be afraid of pain.'

267

'By the window . . . a small leather case.'

Felsen sat back and smoked. Lehrer let out rhythmic grunts as if constipated.

'What was the worst thing, Oswald?'

'Get me the morphine, Klaus . . . please.'

'Tell me the worst thing.'

'I can't say.'

'What does that mean? There were too many or one was too awful?'

'I can't . . . I don't know what you mean.'

'I just want to know if there was one thing that made you suffer . . . I mean personally.'

'Just do me the kindness of shooting me, Klaus. I'm not going to play this . . .'

'Not until you've tried.'

Felsen lit another cigarette and handed it to Lehrer who took it and hid his face in the crook of his elbow, like a schoolboy faced with an ugly test.

'I'll start you off, Oswald,' said Felsen, taking a gulp of brandy. 'There was a woman who used to be a whore, who got some money together and opened a club. Not much more than a bordello with drinks and bad acts, but a popular place with the military, because the woman could always find something special for her clients . . . Your turn, Oswald.'

Lehrer's head came up, bewildered to find himself in such a place. He knocked the brandy glass over. Felsen righted it and refilled. Lehrer tried to get the cigarette into his mouth. Felsen pushed it in.

'One day she got a telephone call from a Gruppenführer in which she was asked to send two Jewish girls to an address on the Havel. They were taken into a beautiful high-ceilinged room with a view over the lake from tall windows. There were two officers in there. The Gruppenführer and his superior. The girls were told to strip naked and then to put their coats back on. The Gruppenführer's superior pinned a Star of David on each lapel. Do you remember this, Oswald?'

Lehrer said nothing. The cigarette smoked in his lips. The sweat continued.

'The girls were given a horsewhip each and told to administer a beating on the the bare buttocks of the superior officer. They were young girls and not very strong and the horsewhips were too short, so they were given canes instead. After they'd laid stripes across the officer's arse they were told to kneel down and, still with his trousers around his ankles, the SS officer shot them both in the head.'

'Is this true?' asked Lehrer, as if he'd dreamt it.

'You were there. You saw it. You told Eva. You had to tell her what had happened to her girls. That's why she started harbouring illegals. That's why the Gestapo called one day.'

'Hah!' said Lehrer, leaning into the candlelight. 'That's what this is all about. Eva Brücke. You're a sentimental one after all, aren't you, Klaus?'

'You had her arrested.'

'Schmidt told me what she was doing. I had no choice in the matter.'

'Is that true?' asked Felsen.

'You don't have to justify what you're doing,' said Lehrer. 'You don't have to try and ennoble your actions with some sentimental cause. Shoot me and take the gold, Klaus. You deserve it. You outplayed me. I chose too wisely and too well.'

They sat there for a few more minutes in silence. Felsen not quite satisfied, wanting to draw something more from the situation. Lehrer stared into the wavering light of the candle and smoked another cigarette. A shot broke open the night. The echo cracked over the terrace. Felsen picked up the Mauser and walked around the table. He bent over Lehrer like a solicitous waiter. He put an arm around him and lifted him up. Lehrer hooked an arm around Felsen's neck. They walked out into the cool night, across the terrace, past the thick, rough green leaves of the fig tree, through the break in the wall, across a rutted track and out into a field of grass and wild flowers which were closed up for the night. After barely fifty yards Lehrer's legs gave way and Felsen lowered him to the ground. He lay on his side, panting and blinking like a wounded animal which has retreated into itself. Felsen put the barrel to Lehrer's temple and fired once. The gun kicked back, the jolt ran through the body and there was a sharp cough as if there had been something inside that couldn't wait to get out.

Felsen walked back to the house with a pre-dawn freshness in his nostrils. Abrantes was waiting for him drinking brandy, his face dirty and sweating.

'You found Schmidt,' said Felsen.

Abrantes nodded.

'Where was he?'

'Down by the river.'

'You shot him.'

'He's in the river . . . I weighed him down with rocks.'

Felsen went out to the truck and came back with a mattock and a shovel. In the dining room he gave the mattock to Abrantes and drank brandy from the neck of the bottle. Abrantes spat on his hands. They walked out across the terrace with the first light turning the darkness.

Part Two

Chapter XXII

Saturday, 13th June 199–, Rua Actor Taborda, Estefânia, Lisbon.

It had been dark in the teacher's apartment. The evening had felt more advanced than it really was. I crossed the Largo Dona Estefânia, with Neptune riding his two dolphins to eternity in the fountain, and headed for Rua Almirante Reis and the Arroios Metro station. The streets were empty and there was no traffic. The tall trees were still in the evening heat, there wasn't a single child in the Arroios park, not even a couple of old boys playing cards, just pigeons. It was as if the population knew something I didn't and had skipped town.

I telephoned Carlos who wasn't there and left a message that I was going to the Alfama to speak to Jamie Gallacher.

I peeled my jacket off and walked the silent blue mosaicked corridor into the deserted Metro station and waited fifteen minutes in the strip-lit tunnel. Music was playing faintly on the sound system. I couldn't pick it up and it was broken anyway by the thunder and hiss of a train heading north. I thought about meeting Luísa Madrugada under different circumstances, but none of my conversations with her got very far, because the only thing I wanted to do was go back to the darkened room in her apartment with all its intimate possibilities. What would a different woman be like, after eighteen years? A different smell, shampoo, perfume, sweat?

Wind thumped in the tunnel, pushing out the smell of burnt brake linings. As I got into the empty compartment

273

the music became more distinct. It was Al Green and it was absurd, because he was singing 'I'm so tired of being alone'. Why do these things happen? I looked at my blurred reflection, two images, slightly different, laid over each other until the door shut leaving a single sharp outline of my new face.

I got off the Metro at Martim Moniz and took a number 12 tram full of Spanish tourists, all talking as if they were due to go on a Trappists' retreat for a month the next day. The tram groaned up the steep hill, bored to death. I got off early and walked to the Largo das Portas do Sol to catch the breeze and a beer perhaps, and to look out across the red roofs of the Alfama to the blue Tagus, wide as a sea at this point. The Spanish herd followed me, and sat down at the café that I'd wanted to and ordered fifty drinks between them. The barman soaked up the order without changing his expression.

I retraced my steps and followed the Rua das Escolas Gerais around the corner and dropped into the medina of alleyways that made up the Alfama. The old Arab quarter wasn't smelling so fresh after the night of Santo António, after a night when half a million sardines have been grilled and consumed. Jamie Gallacher lived just off the Beco do Vigário, above a barber's shop in which an old boy was having his weekly shave, lying down on an old black leather hydraulic chair. A crew-cut kid stood beside him taking an interest, and the old guy ran his hand down the boy's shirt, reminding himself what it felt like to be young.

I walked up a narrow staircase barely wide enough for my shoulders, and knocked on the only door at the top. It took some time for Jamie Gallacher to open it. He was unshaved with hair like an exploded mattress. He was wearing a wrinkled and faded Led Zeppelin T-shirt, and a pair of rucked-up boxer shorts gathered in a twist around his crotch. He had a joint, unlit, in his left hand.

'Yeah?' he said in English, with a very slight Scottish inflection, one eye gummed up. 'Who are you?'

'Police,' I said and showed him my ID.

He cupped the joint, ungummed his eye.

'You'd better come in,' he said, polite, apologetic. 'Sorry about the mess. Bit of a session last night.'

Every surface in the room was covered with empty bottles of wine and beer, plastic cups and glasses stuffed with cigarette butts, piled ashtrays, and empty packs of cigarettes. Pictures nose-dived down the walls. The carpet was freshly stained. A kitten nosed through the debris, looking for something non-alcoholic.

'I'll get dressed. Be with you in a sec.'

He scooped up the kitten and left the room. Voices started up further in the apartment. I followed him to a door in the corridor open three inches. A naked girl with a mass of frizzy hair was sitting cross-legged on a mattress on the floor. She was rolling a joint and looking unconcerned. Slowly a black foot appeared in her lap and the toe rubbed up against her pubic hair. She breathed in sharply.

'For fuck's sake,' said Jamie, and ripped open the door.

The owner of the black foot was slumped across the mattress, eyes half-closed. The girl stroked the black leg. Jamie slammed the door shut behind him.

'Fucking people.'

'Friends of yours?' I asked in English.

'Can't even sleep in my own bed without strangers fucking in there, all day and night.'

We went back into the living room. Jamie searched the ashtrays for a usable butt. He found one, lit up and pulled a face.

'Where did you sleep?' I asked.

'Where I fell.'

'Tell me what happened yesterday . . . after you left school.'

'I came back here about fiveish, had a few hours ziz.'

275

'On your own?'

'On my own, yes. I don't have a girlfriend at the moment.'

'When did you last have a girlfriend?'

He dragged on the butt, winced and stuck it into a half-glass of red wine with a hiss.

'I'd call that a pretty unusual question, Inspector Coelho,' he said, spitting out the smoke. 'Zé Coelho. Good name that, for a detective. Joe Rabbit. Did you ever think of that?'

'Tell me about the girlfriend.'

'Depends on what you call a girlfriend. I had sex with a girl last night, but she wasn't my girlfriend.'

'Where?'

'What?'

'Your bed was occupied . . . where did you have sex?'

He leaned against the wall, crossed his legs at the ankle and scratched his cheek with a nail.

'In the bathroom. She knelt on the toilet seat. I'm not proud of it, Inspector, but you have to know and there it is.'

'You were seen leaving the school with Catarina Sousa Oliveira yesterday afternoon, about four-thirty.'

A rhythmic grunting came from next door.

'Jesus Christ,' said Jamie, hammering on the wall. 'I bloody told them I've got the fu . . . the police in here 'n' all.'

'Come on, Mr Gallacher. Four-thirty, yesterday . . . what happened?'

'What the fuck's all this about? What do you want to know about Catarina for? What sort of police are you?'

'Answer the question, Mr Gallacher.'

'We were just talking, for Christ's sake.'

'What about?'

'I was trying to persuade her to come to the party.'

'To practise her English?'

He started poking in the ashtrays again. I gave him a

cigarette. He sat in the single available chair and hunched over his knees. The pressure next door seemed to be rising. Skin slapped against skin. Jamie looked over his shoulder and back down again. The girl was shouting out.

'I'm at the aftermath of your party, Jamie. I've got a pretty good idea of the scenario. So why don't you tell me about you and Catarina and what you had in mind?'

'I'd been seeing her.'

'Seeing her. Is that like knowing someone in the biblical sense?'

'Your English is pretty fucking good for a cop,' he said. 'All right, I was sleeping with her.'

'Did she ever stay the night?'

He took a deep breath.

'I'd been seeing her pretty regular for six months until a couple of weeks ago. And no, she didn't stay the night. Ever.'

'Did you ever give her money?'

He eyed me from the side of his head.

'When she asked to borrow some, yes.'

'And she gave it back?'

'No.'

'What happened a couple of weeks ago?'

The couple next door reached the end of the road – the man groaning and hissing as if he was being hosed down with cold water, the girl whimpering.

'I told her I was in love with her.'

'So there was more to it than sex as far as you were concerned?'

'It was great sex. We hit it off in bed.'

'But you talked as well.'

'Sure.'

'What about?'

'Music.'

'Anything personal?'

'Music is personal.'

'What about families, relationships, friends . . . feelings, emotions.'

He didn't reply.

'Did she talk about her parents?'

'Only to say she had to get back to them.'

'What did she say when you told her you were in love with her?'

'She didn't.'

'Nothing?'

'*Nada*.'

'Wasn't that disappointing?'

'Of course it was fucking disappointing.'

'Let's go back to Friday afternoon. You're outside the school talking. You've asked her to your party. What does she do?'

'She turned me down. She said she had to get back to Cascais. Her parents were expecting her. I told her to call them, tell them that she wanted to stay in town and go to the *festa de Santo António* in the Alfama. She wasn't interested. I told her I was in love with her again and she started to walk off. I grabbed her by the wrist. She twisted it out of my hand.'

'Where are you by now?'

'Just up from the school on Duque de Ávila.'

'On your own?'

'Yes. Most of the other kids had gone, or just hanging around on the corner.'

'And?'

He squeezed his forehead and took a fierce drag of one of my non-cigarettes.

'I hit her.'

'What with?'

'I slapped her face.'

'How did she take that?'

'Well . . . it was weird . . . because she just fucking smiled at me. She didn't put her hand to her face. She didn't say anything. She just smiled.'

'As if she was saying "That's how much you love me"?'

He nodded, without thinking that.

'I cracked. Said I was sorry. Asked her to forgive me. All that . . .'

'What did she do?'

'She turned on her heel and fucked off down the street. I slumped against a car. The alarm went off. She didn't turn round. At the end of the street, by the traffic lights, a car pulled up. She looked at it, stepped off the pavement, talked to the driver for a minute, the light changed, she got in and the car drove off.'

'Tell me about the car.'

'I don't know anything about cars.'

'You haven't got one?'

'I don't even drive.'

'Let's start at the simple end. Was the car big or small?'

'Big.'

'Dark or light?'

'Dark.'

'Any insignia?'

'It was way down the end of the street.'

'Do you think she knew the driver of the car?'

'I couldn't tell.'

'Exactly how long did they talk for?'

'Shit. Less than a minute. Forty seconds, something like that.'

'Where did the car come from?'

'Down the street somewhere, I don't know. The fucking car alarm was going and I was, you know, upset.'

'You're going to have to do better than that, Mr Gallacher.'

'I don't know whether I fucking can.'

'You're going to have to, and I'm going to make you,' I said. 'You're coming down to the *Polícia Judiciária* with me and write it all down.'

'Jesus. You're going to make me write a statement? What is all this?'

'Catarina's dead, Mr Gallacher. She was murdered yesterday afternoon about six o'clock and I want to find out whether you did it.'

He didn't look as if he'd done it. He looked as if a trapdoor had just opened up underneath him and he was on his way down into the abyss. When he stood his legs were shaking.

'What about those two in there?' he asked.

'They're leaving.'

I went into the corridor and threw open the door. The black guy was lying collapsed on his back, still breathing heavily, slick with sweat in the airless room. The girl lay face-down with her legs apart. I kicked their clothes at them. The girl twisted round, her cheeks flushed, her eyes unfocused.

'You two. Out!'

Chapter XXIII

15th April 1955, Abrantes' office, Banco de Oceano e Rocha, Rua do Ouro, Baixa, Lisbon.

'Absinthe eats the brain,' said Abrantes. Abrantes suddenly knowing everything about everything these days, full of his success in the Lisbon business fraternity. Felsen took another sip of the green liquid in his glass and watched the platoons of black umbrellas in the rain-lashed street below. It was ten o'clock in the morning and the second absinthe of the day. Felsen fingered his head wondering where the rot would start and why Abrantes had dragged him out of his apartment before lunch.

Felsen had been back from Africa for two weeks, having spent most of the last decade out there setting up branches of the bank in Luanda, Angola and Lourenço Marques in Mozambique. He was at a low point, as he always was whenever he set foot back in Europe and its unfolding history.

Berlin had been isolated by the Reds, the Iron Curtain was rusting into place across the middle of the continent and the whole of the Iberian Peninsula was as good as cut off and adrift out in the Atlantic with Salazar and Franco, madmen on the bridge, flying their old-fashioned fascist flags. The great empires were breaking up. The British lost India. The French lost Morocco, Tunisia and Indo-China culminating in the humiliation of Dien Bien Phu in May last year. World power transferred to the Americans while Europeans contemplated their own nations, bleakened by the expense of war, their nails torn and bloody from the last

281

desperate attempt to hold on to world domination.

To Felsen the whole place had the stink of death about it, the rotten odour of decline and to keep that stench out of his nostrils, during the second coffee of the morning, he'd let the absinthe trickle greenly into his glass.

After the war the Allies had moved into Portugal. The Americans had set up shop in the Nazi legation's old *palácio* in Lapa. But Felsen and Abrantes had been lucky. Their wolfram mines had been sealed, but wolfram had little value. Their stocks of cork, olive oil and canned sardines had been confiscated because they were perceived as future German goods. But the bank, with its curious management structure, had survived several attempts at having its assets frozen by the men in dark suits sent by the Allies. It was Abrantes' connections in the Salazar government that had saved them. As the war ended, construction boomed in Portugal and Abrantes was there, sitting at the table, knowing nothing about building but everything about graft. Officials in the Ministry of Public Works received plots of land and had houses built for them, their sons earned jobs they didn't deserve, planners and municipal architects in Lisbon town hall, the mayor, all suddenly began to find life more affordable. The Banco de Oceano e Rocha developed a property company, a construction arm, eased projects towards friends and earned protection from the highest offices in government.

And the gold was still there, ten metres below Felsen's feet, sitting in the underground vaults with the traffic on the Rua do Ouro thundering above it.

Abrantes sat over his third small half-cup of tar of the morning. He drank these until he moved his bowels which normally happened around number five or six. After a successful movement he'd take an *anis*, after a poor one, more coffee. He smoked cigars now. They too seemed to help loosen his guts, constipation a problem since he'd moved away from the Beira to worry at a desk, and eat too much meat.

'Haven't they finished that house of yours yet?' he asked Felsen, knowing they had.

'I suppose you need my apartment for one of your mistresses,' said Felsen, turning away from the window, quick to find the acid that morning.

Abrantes sucked on his cigar knowing something Felsen didn't. He stared up at the ceiling looking for inspiration. A stain was developing up there after the winter rains and these April showers. It was fat and broad at the corner where a crack ran through it like a river and tapered off to something like Argentina, and Tierra del Fuego close to the ceiling rose.

'Have you thought any more about Brazil?' asked Abrantes.

'You can have the apartment, Joaquim,' said Felsen. 'I'll move out, really. There's no problem.'

They grinned at each other.

'Brazil's a natural step,' said Abrantes. 'Maybe we should have gone there first. The Brazilians, they . . .'

'We didn't know anybody . . . we still don't.'

'Ah!' said Abrantes and took a flamboyant drag of his cigar, enjoying himself, grinding Felsen down. He blew the smoke out extravagantly.

'Tell me,' said Felsen, bored.

'You were always the German who spoke Portuguese with a Brazilian accent. That's how I first heard about you.'

'I told you about that, a Brazilian girl in Berlin taught me.'

'Susana Lopes,' said Abrantes, 'wasn't that her name?'

An image flashed in Felsen's brain – Susana hooking her legs over the back of his knees and pressing her pubis down on to him. He cleared his throat. His penis lumbered in his trousers.

'Did I tell you about her?' said Felsen.

Abrantes shook his head. We're getting to it now, thought Felsen.

'I don't think I told you her name even.'

'I had a phone call last night. Susana Lopes, looking for her old friend Klaus Felsen who she'd heard had become a director of the Banco de Oceano e Rocha.'

Felsen's heart leapt forward and he had to press himself back into the chair.

'Where is she?'

'A very charming woman,' said Abrantes, toying with his cigar clipper.

'She's here?' he said, possibilities suddenly opening up.

'We talked about Brazil.'

'Did I tell you how I met her?'

'No, she did,' said Abrantes.

'She was a girl in a club . . .' Felsen faltered as a huge chunk of complex history broke off the glacier of his memory and crashed into his mind.

'Those kind of girls know everybody,' said Abrantes.

'What?' said Felsen, still mid-avalanche.

'She seems to have done well over there. She owns a beachside club on an estate outside São Paulo . . . place called Guarujá.'

'You covered some ground,' said Felsen, cooling to him now.

'They're different to us, the Brazilians. They like to talk, have fun, they always look ahead. The Portuguese, well, you know the Portuguese,' he said, flapping his hand at the squally weather, the dark street, the stain blooming across the ceiling to the size of Russia.

Felsen sat back, not wanting to give Abrantes any more sport. His partner saw it was over.

'I said you'd meet her for lunch . . . in Estoril . . . Hotel Palácio.'

Felsen sat in the dining room of the Hotel Palácio. He was wearing a powder-blue suit and a yellow silk tie. The light outside darkened and brightened as clouds crashed across

284

the clearing sky, bringing showers which dashed through the gardens and wrestled with the palm trees in the square. He was feeling sick, then hungry, then sick again. His life came back to him in waves, in big, thumping Atlantic rollers. He gulped back another glass of white wine and reached for the bottle in the ice bucket, already three-quarters gone. He ordered another.

Felsen watched the diners arrive, watched all the women settle into their chairs until he found one who just kept coming and coming at him. She was taller than he remembered. Her youth had gone – the long black, shiny hair was cut short, the whippy slenderness of a girl in her late teens had filled out but had been replaced by what an American would have called 'class'. She wore a figure-hugging, crisp, white square-necked dress which looked as if it had some material in it, and her nyloned thighs swished like a mating call. Male heads strained to keep their eyes from drifting over to her.

Susana knew the effect she was having. She'd designed it. But there was only so much time she'd allow a man to get his slack jaw working.

'Well?' she said, and cutlery resumed on china.

Felsen got to his feet. The waiter appeared with another bottle of wine. They danced around each other, kissed, sat, manoeuvred closer.

'How long's it been?' asked Felsen, at a loss for a moment.

'Fifteen years . . .'

'No, no, sixteen, I think,' he said, and was annoyed at himself for being so German about it.

He held up his glass. They chinked and drank without taking their eyes off each other.

'My partner says you're a big success,' he said.

'That's only what I told him.'

'You *look* successful.'

'I've just been to Paris and bought some clothes.'

'That proves something.'

285

'I've been lucky,' she said. 'I've had good friends. Rich men who wanted somewhere to go . . .'

'. . . to get away from their wives?'

'I learnt a lot in Berlin,' she said. 'From Eva. Eva taught me everything I needed to know. Do you still see her?'

The name shot past him like a wild animal in the night, leaving him stunned, shaky. The dining room darkened. Rain raked the windows, turning heads in the room.

'She died in the war,' he said, blurting it a little, sinking his face into the wine. Susana shook her head.

'We heard about the bombing.'

'You got out just in time,' said Felsen.

The waiter laid a bread roll on her side plate with a pair of silver tongs.

'So what did you learn from Eva?'

'What men want,' she said, and left it at that, so that Felsen began to think that she'd learnt other things from Eva, like leaving things unsaid. It excited him.

The waiter gave them the menus. They ordered instantly.

'You lost your Brazilian accent,' said Susana.

'I've been in Africa.'

'Doing what?'

'The bank. Minerals. Logging.'

'You should come to Brazil. You're not in Brazil yet, are you?'

'We're thinking about it.'

'Well, I'll be there . . . if you need any help.'

'With your friends,' he said, and she smiled at him without volunteering what he wanted to know.

The soup arrived. A crab bisque. They sipped through it. The wind shuddered against the dining room windows and the rain thrashed the petals off the roses in the gardens.

'I wanted to ask you,' he said, 'if you ever came across someone called Lehrer, in Berlin? Oswald Lehrer.'

She put her glass down. The waiter removed the soup plates.

'I didn't like him,' she said, looking above his head. 'He had very unpleasant tastes.'

'He gave me a job down here in the war. He knew I spoke Portuguese.'

'That was Lehrer's way,' she said. 'He always liked to know everything.'

A piece of turbot in a white sauce appeared in front of her, a swordfish steak before Felsen. Felsen found himself wanting to smoke, drink, eat and everything else humanly possible. Susana opened up her fish. Felsen tore a roll apart. They'd touched on all their history. Each point with its pain and pleasure. He felt welded to her in spots.

'You're looking good, Susana,' he said, confirming his notion out loud.

'Even after two children,' she said, looking to see how he took it.

'A mother,' he said.

'But not a wife,' she said. 'And you?'

He laid down his cutlery and opened his hands.

'I didn't think so,' she said.

'And why not?'

'A powder-blue suit and a yellow tie doesn't say "Daddy" to me.'

He smiled. She laughed. The sun came up in the room like theatre lights zoomed to the maximum. They ordered more wine and talked about her two children who were with her mother in São Paulo. She didn't elaborate on the absent father.

They took coffee in another part of the hotel and Felsen smoked one of the slim tan-coloured cheroots which Susana preferred. They went wordlessly up to her room. She unlocked the door. They kissed. Her hand went to the front of his trousers, firm, expert, gripping.

Felsen stripped and was naked before she'd stepped out

287

of her underwear. He fell on her. Her suspendered thighs rasped on his. They made love with only marginally less urgency than they had done sixteen years ago. The only difference – after Felsen had come shuddering to a halt – she pushed his head down into her lap and drew him to her. He wasn't sure about it. He hadn't done that before. He didn't like it. But she held him there until he felt her trembling in his hands.

Susana had a week left of her stay. She'd wanted to go to Berlin but couldn't get a visa and that had left her with spare time in Lisbon. They spent most of the week together. Felsen moved into her room at the Hotel Palácio for the duration. They spent the time driving out to his house, the westernmost house on mainland Europe – only heather, gorse, the cliffs and the lighthouse at Cabo da Roca between it and the ocean. They walked through the empty rooms which still smelled of paint and the musty humidity of drying plaster. They bought two chairs and sat in the enclosed terrace on the roof and drank brandy and watched the storms out at sea, the deranged clouds and the blood-orange sunsets. They talked. They renamed the house – Casa ao Fim do Mundo – House at the End of the World. Together they furnished the house from the contents sale of an old *palácio* on the Serra da Sintra, Susana bidding wildly for a pair of old rose-coloured divans which they 'christened' the next afternoon and lay under rough blankets telling each other their own plans and then, eventually, making one together.

Felsen bought a ticket on the same plane to São Paulo. He spent an afternoon talking things through with Abrantes about the opening of the São Paulo branch, how Susana would introduce him to her friends, get the business started. The three of them had lunch the next day, Abrantes on one side of the table, impressed by Susana and nearly jealous of Felsen.

On the day of the flight Felsen woke with a teak-hard

erection and his head full of the future. He pressed himself against Susana and felt her stiffen. She rolled. He
grinned over the monolith. She flicked the tip. The menhir
toppled.

'I came on in the night,' she said. 'We're going to be
late.'

The luggage was enough to make the bellhop straighten
his cap. Felsen went down to pay the bill, which was enormous and came on several pages. He wrote a cheque with
his mind on other things.

They sent the luggage in one taxi and followed in another.
It was a bright, clear, blustery day and the sea, by the
Marginal, was deep blue and white-capped. They didn't
speak. Susana looked out of the window. Felsen drummed
the upholstery, still smarting slightly from the morning's
rejection.

At the airport Felsen organized a porter for the luggage.
Susana paced around in tight geometry, her heels nervous
on the pavement. They joined the queue at the check-in
desk. Susana gave Felsen her passport and went to find the
ladies' room. Felsen flicked through her passport, checked
her photo, one taken a few years ago, the hair longer,
the eyebrows denser, unplucked. He riffled the pages. A
paper fell out which he picked up. It was a ticket stub for
a return internal flight Frankfurt/Munich/Frankfurt dated
28th March 1955, just over three weeks earlier. Felsen
turned over the stub. There was a telephone number written on the back, not a local one.

He went back to the passport and found the German visa
and an entry stamp for the 24th March in Frankfurt. There
was an exit stamp from Lisbon next to it and below it the
stamps for the return dated 13th April. On another page
were the exit and entry stamps out of São Paulo and into
Lisbon dated 20th March. There were no other stamps.
There was no French visa. He looked at the telephone
number again, thinking quicker than he had done for a

month. He took out the hotel bill and noticed, this time, the colossal amount of the telephone bill. He turned the pages. Seven calls had been made to a number which matched the one on the ticket stub.

He went to one of the airline offices and asked to use the telephone. He called the operator and gave her the number and asked where it came from. She told him immediately that it was a Brazilian number and after a minute that it came from a town called Curítiba. His chest suddenly felt as a cold as a cathedral.

Susana appeared next to the luggage looking around for him. He crossed the highly polished floor on stiff legs, his thigh muscles feeling weak and cold. Susana asked if anything was the matter. He shook his head. They checked in. The flight was delayed until three in the afternoon. Susana fumed silently as she reclaimed her passport and boarding card. They went to the restaurant and sat opposite each other. The place was as crowded as Felsen's head. He ordered wine and looked out of the window as the four propeller engines of a cargo plane started up with a clatter followed by a long, unending howl.

The wine was poured into the palpable silence between them. Susana looked around, aware that the presence in front of her was not where she wanted her eyes to rest. Felsen relaxed his shoulders down from around his ears, leaned back.

'*Saúde!*' he said, raising his glass, forcing some lightness. She matched him.

'I never asked,' he said, lighting a cigarette, 'how you found me.'

'By accident,' she said. 'I was looking for the number of a friend of mine whose surname is Felizardo, yours was underneath. I didn't think it would be you but I called anyway. There was no answer. The next day I was in Lisbon I went to the address and found your apartment above the bank. My friend's father knew who you were. When I came back to Lisbon after my trip, with my extra week, I called again – this time the bank. They put me through to your partner.'

He nodded through the plausibility. The lengthy, well-thought-out, plausibility.

'But you didn't go to Paris, did you?'

'Is this . . .' she paused, '. . . an interrogation?'

He laid the ticket stub out in front of her.

'I was in Germany,' she said, coolly, eyes sliding to the right.

'That number on the back,' said Felsen, 'comes from Curítiba in Brazil. You've called that number every day since we've been in the Palácio. Whose is it? Your friends?'

'My family . . .'

'A different one to your mother and children in São Paulo?'

The waiter came and reared away from Felsen who'd shown him the back of his hand.

'Yes,' she said, defiant now, teeth gritted behind her lips.

'You never showed me any photographs of your children,' he said, and lunged at her purse.

She snatched it away from him.

'You didn't ask.'

'I'm asking now.'

She tore out two photographs and held them to his face for a fraction of a second. The boy was dark, Brazilian-looking, but the girl, although dark-skinned, had blonde hair and blue eyes. Susana's mouth was bent into a sneer.

'I've heard of Curítiba,' said Felsen. 'There's a very large German community there. I know what they'd have been doing . . . just three days ago, in fact. The 20th of April every year. The Führer's birthday. They raise the flag. Who sent you, Susana?'

She didn't answer.

'I can't think of anybody who would know about me, except perhaps ODESSA. They might have have had

291

the resources, the information. The *Organisation der SS-Angehörigen* . . . was it them, Susana?'

'The most important thing I learnt from Eva,' she said, sitting back, chin up, the contempt radiating out of her, 'was that Klaus Felsen only ever thinks with his big, stupid, Swabian cock.'

That cut him, right through, and he hit her for saying it. He slapped her across her face with his big open hand. It went off like a tyre blow-out and everybody looked out of the window. Susana wheeled out of her chair and came up with the mark of his hand on her cheek. Her eyes were fixed and dark, flashing with anger, an intensity of hate. She muttered something at him. He'd have liked to smack her again, so raw was his humiliation, but the eyes of the restaurant were on them now. He turned and went to retrieve his luggage.

1st July 1955, Abrantes' apartment, Rua do Ouro, Baixa, Lisbon, Portugal.

Maria Abrantes sat at the arm end of the chaise longue in a blue pencil skirt and a white blouse with the suit jacket open. She had a tight string of pearls at her throat which was red with anger, right up to her earlobes and had infected her cheeks too. She smoked and listened as she had been doing for the last three-quarters of an hour, crossing, uncrossing and recrossing her legs once every three or four minutes, waiting for what was going on in the next room to come to an end.

She'd thought that it was over three times already and had braced herself, tightened her mouth, and clenched her fist. But each time it had resumed and she'd breathe in a slow, deep breath through her nose and unlock her jaws. In the hand that wasn't smoking she held a card of the type distributed by tobacco kiosks for the last ten or fifteen years. She tapped the arm of the chaise longue with it. The card was a photograph of an actress who called herself Pica but whose real name was Arlinda Monteiro. Maria looked at the card for the hundredth time – Pica the dyed blonde with large glossed lips trying to look American. She straightened her own true blonde hair as if it conferred a higher status.

The bedroom door opened a crack and shut. Maria Abrantes' foot started nodding and stopped. The bedroom door was flung open with a laugh and Pica, with her head thrown back over her shoulder, came into the living room. Her high heels were strict with the wooden floor. She didn't see Maria at first but the bristling presence in the room slowed her heels' progress. When she did see her, the heels took four little steps back and her shoulder hit the closed half of the double doors to the bedroom. She glanced into the bedroom and lengthened her neck to muster some drama-class dignity. She tilted her jaw and resumed her passage across the bare wooden floor, swinging her white handbag from her left hand.

'*Puta*,' said Maria Abrantes, quietly.

The word thudded into the actress's back and turned her round. Her bosom inflated. Maria Abrantes was hoping for a spew of abuse but the hatchet she'd set her face into must have been too sharp. The actress only managed the kind of hiss she must have heard from the back stalls on a slow weekday night.

Joaquim Abrantes appeared at the bedroom door, sensing wildlife in his living room. He was in the grey trousers from a suit, a white shirt with cuffs already linked up, and a silk tie in his hands which Maria had never seen before.

'What are *you* doing here?' he asked.

Pica turned, her heels rapped the floorboards and the apartment door opened with a gust of wind and closed, gunshot loud. Abrantes slowly made up his tie and stretched his neck free of his collar. Everything Maria had rehearsed scrambled and fled from her mind, leaving neat spite and no words.

'I thought you said you were going to be in Estoril today,' said Joaquim Abrantes, who left the doorway, went into the bedroom and came back in a grey suit jacket.

'I was . . .' she started.

'What brought you back into the city?' he asked, performing as if Pica had never been in the apartment. 'Shopping?'

He took a seat in front of her and shot his cuffs. He opened a silver box on the table and removed a cigarette, which he tapped on the lid. He lit it and sat back, inhaling the smoke grossly into his snarling mouth. It maddened her.

'No, it wasn't shopping,' she said.

'Oh?'

'It was because I can't stand any more talk in Estoril about the whores you're entertaining down here.'

'They talk in Estoril about whores down here? I don't think so.'

'They do. They might not call them *putas*, they might call them . . . actresses, maybe, but they're paid in presents and dinners just as surely as the whores at the docks get cash.'

Abrantes wondered who'd helped her rehearse that. He didn't think those words were her own. In the cafés of Estoril they might see the Parisian cut of her suits, the American nylons, the millinery in from London, but *he* saw a girl from the Beira with an urn of water on her head.

'And you?' he asked, the imitation Lisboeta making him cruel.

'I'm your wife!' she shouted, and flung the kiosk card of Pica in his lap.

He picked up the card, checked it and snapped it down on the table next to him. He gave her a flat, level stare with dull black onyx eyes. She froze and corrected herself.

'I'm the mother of your children, your two sons,' she said, thinking this would weaken him, but this time it didn't.

'I've had some news,' he said. 'From the Beira. Two weeks ago.'

'Two weeks ago?' she repeated automatically, a strange darkness settling on her like the shadow on an X-rayed lung.

'My wife died.'

'Your wife?' she said, momentarily confused.

'Don't repeat everything I say. I know what I'm saying. My *wife* died. You remember her, don't you.'

She did. The old hag on the hill who'd been moved out for her. She nodded.

'She died,' said Abrantes. 'Do you understand?'

'I understand,' she said, the realization creeping up her like hemlock.

'I am going to marry again,' he said, getting to his feet and walking away from her. 'I'll be announcing my intention to marry *Senhora* Monteiro at the end of this week.'

She yelled something at him which was incoherent. It turned him. The large, slow head, blacker than a bull's inside.

'And me?' she shrieked. 'What about me?'

'You will continue to look after the boys in Estoril.'

'Like a nanny,' she said, leaping to her feet. 'Like an English nanny!'

'You're their mother,' he said, icily. 'They need you.'

'And you're their father,' she yelled, stamping her foot, 'and we . . .'

The words stopped. There were no more inside. Abrantes saw a flit of pure malevolence behind her eyes. She was puce, her fists clenched by her hips. He thought he might have to slap her to bring her out of this little fit and took two steps towards her for the purpose.

'You remember Christmas 1941?' she asked, and he stopped mid-stride.

'No,' he said, weighing his hand.

'You were out selling your wolfram across the border

when *Senhor* Felsen came back early and caught you.'

'How would you know this? You were still a child then.'

'You were trying to cheat him . . . I knew that much and so did he. I saw him waiting for you all day, furious,' she said, slowing down now to deliver. 'But he cheated you too.'

'Cheated me?'

'He raped me in our bed that night and the night after and it . . .'

She saw what it did to him. She saw that momentary self-pitying shallowness in his eyes and the muscles in his face slackening, punched silly by her words. She felt suddenly strong, too strong, because she was enjoying herself. She leaned her face out at him.

'Manuel is not your son,' she said quietly, and laughed, the emotion in the room too high for her. The giggle grated over her larynx like claws screeching down glass. Abrantes' head lowered, his eyes blinkered by his thick forehead. The big spaces in his head were suddenly filled and directed. His fist came up slowly and then snapped into her face. Her nose crunched. She felt the splintering of it in the bones of her face and cranium. Warm, thick blood spread in a fast gush over her lips, the metallic taste creeping into her mouth. She fell flat on her bottom, her head kicked back into the arm of the chaise longue, stunning her. A wide cravat of red opened down her blouse. She felt another blow coming and managed to get her hands up. Abrantes' fist slammed the back of her own hand into her mouth taking her two front teeth with it and shattering her knuckles. She fell sideways, choking, and saw the blood pool out and soak into the edge of the carpet.

'You're going back to the Beira and live with the pigs.'

Chapter XXIV

Saturday, 13th June 199–, Alfama, Lisbon.

I arranged for a car to pick us up. I let Jamie Gallacher buy cigarettes and he smoked all the way to the *Polícia Judiciária* and played with the door lock until the driver couldn't take it any longer. I hadn't let him wash or shave. He was still in the creased T-shirt and beer-stained jeans but with a brand-new pair of Nikes on his feet which might not be his for very much longer in the *tacos*, which is what I had in mind for him after he'd made his statement. It wasn't that I didn't believe him. It was that I didn't like him.

The big, dark car possibility coincided with the way my thoughts were leaning, that a creep had turned up after Valentim and Bruno, after Jamie Gallacher, and had sodomized her and killed her for being someone out there who knew the type of person he really was. It felt right, too, that the victim had had a spat and stormed off. It could happen to girls – they got emotional, became vulnerable and that was when a creep might pick them off and rape or kill them. I've seen them, not many of them, Lisbon's not a violent city. They're cruel these creeps. They offer comfort – a hug, a stroke, a little kiss, a small squeeze, an ugly grab and then mayhem.

It was possible that the driver of the big dark car knew her already. Maybe he'd been waiting outside the school, seen Gallacher hit her and moved in. My stomach was telling me things. The only problem was that it had been telling me things since I'd been in Luísa Madrugada's apartment.

Jamie Gallacher made his statement and I sent him

down. He protested, telling me he had to teach on Monday morning.

'You're under suspicion of murder, Mr Gallacher. You've admitted to a sexual relationship with an underage girl who was one of your pupils,' I told him. 'I can keep you in a police cell for a year without charge while I carry out my investigations. This is Portugal. It's our system of law. You're guilty until proven innocent. Have a nice weekend.'

Carlos had the search warrant. We drove out to Odivelas. It was getting late now but I had to see.

The tick opened the door and read the warrant through. He took it to Valentim's mother. She sat at the kitchen table, smoking, facing away from the television in the next room which showed fat people pretending to be rich and trying to be funny with no success. The tick sucked on a bottle of Sagres. She looked up, red-eyed, the sockets blackened by mascara, lipstick worn off. Her voice was thick with saliva, from drink and tears.

'Where do you want to start?' she asked.

'Just his room. Is it locked?'

She shrugged. The tick nodded.

'Key?'

The tick shook his head. The tick knew everything.

I turned the door handle down and leaned into it. It cracked open easily, the door too small for the frame. I started at one end of the room, Carlos at the other. He gave me a pair of surgical gloves and snapped into a pair himself. He was methodical, careful. I knew he would be. He went through every page of every book, treating each one as if it was his own. He did the same with the sheet music. I went through the bedside locker. There was nothing unusual in the drawer. The cupboard contained spiral-bound exercise books which were full of notes from academic books. I leafed through them. Carlos slid under the bed with a pen torch in his mouth. A few moments later he grunted and came out with a key with a plastic tag. It had '7D' written on it. We bagged it and left the room.

'Find what you want?' asked the mother.

I asked them if the key meant anything to them. The tick shook his head, but he knew. The woman looked down at the ashtray in front of her, the strap of her bra down her shoulder.

We sat in the car and held the key up to the street lighting.

'What do you think?' asked Carlos.

'Garage maybe.'

'The car?'

'Possibly. Or just somewhere to keep his things private.'

A face appeared at the window on Carlos' side. The tick out for more blood.

'You want to know which door that key opens?'

'You don't like him do you?' I said.

'Little piece of shit.'

'Get in.'

The tick took us on a short drive of less than two kilometres into a light industrial zone with small warehouses, workshops for panel-beating, car repairs, foam-rubber furniture-makers and other low capital businesses. Unit 7D was the size of a double garage with a large door for shipping and delivery and a small door for the office. It was a cheap place, if you weren't a student and this was how you made your money. I tried the key. It fitted and turned. I pulled it out.

'You're not going in?' asked the tick.

'Not without a search warrant.'

'*I'm* not going to tell.'

'I don't give a shit,' I said. 'If there's something in there I don't want to risk not being able to use it. And I don't know what your game is either. Maybe you'll change sides.'

We dropped the tick at a bar close to the apartment block. He went in there and hooked his buttock up on a stool and flicked his finger for a beer. We drove back to Saldanha and did the paperwork for the key. Carlos was sulking so I took him across the road and bought him a beer in the only place open, the city dead on its feet around here after a long week and the heat. We sat in silence under the glare of neon and sipped Super Bock with our jackets hooked over the chair backs. The barman was watching football. I asked him the score, not that interested.

'Zero-zero,' he said, barely listening.

'You can watch that stuff all year round now,' I said.

No answer. I turned back to Carlos who was weighing things in his head.

'You speak English like an Englishman,' said Carlos.

'I was there for four and half years, four and a quarter of them in the pub,' I said. 'I only spoke to my wife in English and I still use it with Olivia.'

'You didn't tell me why you were in England.'

I lit a cigarette and gave him a direct look.

'Aren't you tired?' I asked.

'Something's got to happen while I drink this beer.'

'You don't want to talk about football.'

'I don't know anything about football.'

'Shit!' said the barman.

We looked up in time to see the ball sailing into the stands.

'My father was in the army, you know that already. He was serving in Guinea fighting those good old colonial wars under General Spínola. Maybe you know this too . . .'

'Carry on.'

'They were unwinnable wars. Guys your age were getting killed every day for no very good reason other than that Salazar wanted to be an Emperor. General Spínola had a brilliant and unconventional idea. Rather than killing people in order to make them Portuguese citizens why not be nice to them. He decided to wage what was called a 'hearts and minds' war. He improved medical care, education, supplied books, that kind of thing and suddenly the Africans loved him and the rebels lost their cause. It meant that my father's men didn't get killed any more, and it also made him a big Spínola fan.'

Carlos sat back, a little resistance building already. It made me feel tired.

'So after the revolution, after the euphoria had worn off, when Portugal was a seething mass of dozens of different political parties and agendas, with the communists cornering a fair amount of the functionary power, my father decided that his old pal Spínola's solution to the problem of this chaos was the right one.'

'A second coup,' said Carlos.

'Exactly. And as you know, it was uncovered and my father had to get out fast. He had friends in London so we moved there. That's it.'

'He should have been shot,' said Carlos, into his beer.

'What was that?'

'I said . . . your father . . . he should have been shot.'

'That's what I thought you said.'

'There'd been a revolution. The democratic process was in hand, chaotically in hand, I agree, but that's the process. What it didn't need was another coup and the installation of a military dictatorship. I think, without absolutely any doubt at all, that your father and all the rest of them, should have been shot.'

It had been a long day and a hot one. I'd had a beer on an empty stomach. I'd spent a day having my new, exposed face read by people who didn't know me. There were all sorts of reasons why hearing this kid calmly condemning my father, my dead father, to death . . . well, it brought something out in me that hadn't been aired for some time. To use an English expression – I lost it. I'd never been sure what the 'it' had been until then. Now I know. It's the control that makes us human. I lashed out claws exposed for once.

I slammed my fists down on the table, the two beers jumped and hit the deck, the barman braced himself against the steel counter.

'Who the fuck do you think you are!?' I roared. 'Are you the prosecutor, jury and judge rolled into one? You weren't even out of your nappies when all this happened. You didn't even have your own teeth. You didn't know my father. And you have no fucking idea what it's like to live under a fascist dictatorship, to see men getting killed, to see them saved by the ideas of one man, to see your country dropped in the shit by a bunch of power-seeking, self-aggrandizing bastards. So who the fuck do you think you are condemning men to death? You're the whole bloody reason this kind of shit happens in the first place.'

Carlos tipped back on his chair and saved himself on the front window, beer down his shirt and trousers, but his face calm, impassive, not cowed.

'And you think that's part of the democratic process, do you? To get back into your tanks and drive down the Avenida da Liberdade. You think that's the proper way to address political differences in a modern world? Maybe they should have shot you as well.'

I went for him, crashed straight through the table, tripped over it, cut my hand on some broken glass, slipped on the beer, got back on to my feet, lunged at him and found myself connecting with the fat, porky shoulder of the barman, who must have seen this sort of thing happen before and had vaulted his hundred kilos over the bar faster than a Chinese gymnast. He grabbed my flailing arms.

'*Filho da puta!*' I roared.

'*Cabrão!*' Carlos shouted back.

I lunged at him again, taking the barman with me and we all went down in a pile by the glass door of the bar. God knows what anybody would have made of it from the outside looking in – another football argument that had got out of hand.

The barman got to his feet first. He kicked Carlos out into the night and hauled me away to the toilets at the back of the bar. I sat down shaking, blood streaming down my wrist, soaking into my shirt cuff. I washed the wound out in the sink. The barman gave me some napkins.

'Never in my life,' said the barman, 'have I seen you like that. Never.'

He went back behind his counter. I picked my jacket up and opened the door.

'Shit!' said the barman, back at the TV, 'how did it get to be 2–1?'

I crossed the road to the *Polícia Judiciária* building and did some first-aid on my hand. I drove home, my blood still fierce, rocketing around my system with bigger and better arguments ripping though my brain. I was approaching a choppy version of calm by the time I parked up in Paço de Arcos and walked to the house.

Olivia was out and the door locked. I searched my pockets for the keys.

'Inspector?' said a female voice behind me.

Teresa Oliveira, the lawyer's wife, was standing a couple of metres down the street, looking different, her hair tied back and wearing jeans and a red T-shirt with the word GUESS on the front. I tried to summon some gentleness from the corner of my brain where it was still cowering.

'Is this important, *Dona* Oliveira?' I asked. 'It's been a long day and I don't have any news for you I'm afraid.'

'It won't take long,' she said, but I thought it might.

We went into the kitchen. I drank some water. She upset herself over my bloody shirt. I changed and offered her a drink. She went for Coke.

'The medication, you understand,' she felt the need to explain.

I poured myself a glass of whisky from an old bottle of

303

William Lawson's that hadn't seen the light for the last six months.

'I've left my husband, Inspector,' she said, and I lit a cigarette.

'Was that wise?' I asked. 'They say it's better not to make traumatic changes immediately after a tragedy.'

'You might have realized that it's been coming for some time.'

I nodded without commenting. She fumbled in her bag for her own cigarettes and lighter. Between us we got one going for her.

'It never worked, right from the start it didn't work,' she said, referring to her marriage.

'How long ago was that?'

'Fifteen years.'

'That's a long time for a marriage not to be working,' I said, looking for angles here and seeing none.

'It suited us to keep it going.'

'And now you're leaving him,' I said, and shrugged. 'Was your daughter's death the catalyst?'

'No,' she said, flatly, the hand with the cigarette shaking so badly she had to hold it with the other. 'He was abusing her . . . sexually.'

Her Coke fizzed in its glass.

Now we're getting to it.

'That's a very serious allegation,' I said. 'If you're going to make a formal complaint I would suggest you get a lawyer on your side and establish some strong evidence. And, if it's true, it could also have an impact on my murder enquiry, but I am not the person you should be talking to.'

I laid it out for her so that she knew I knew.

'It *is* true,' she said, feeling stronger. 'The maid will corroborate it.'

'How long had this been going on for?'

'Five years, that I know of.'

'With you tolerating it?'

Her hand still shook as the cigarette went to her mouth.

'My husband has always been a powerful man, both publicly and privately. He extended that power into his relationships . . . with me and his children.'

'Was that the attraction in the first place?'

'I never went for men my own age,' she shrugged. 'My father died when I was young . . . maybe that was it.'

'You were twenty-one when . . .'

'I was only ever interested in established men,' she cut in. 'And he took an interest in me. He can be very charming. I was flattered.'

'How did you meet?'

'I worked for him. I was his secretary.'

'So you know everything there is to know about him?'

'I used to know,' she said, 'when I was his secretary. As you might know, wives are not so well informed.'

'So you don't know who these few clients are he's working for now?'

'Why do you ask?'

'I want to know who I'm up against.'

'I only know who he used to work for, fifteen, sixteen years ago.'

'Who were they?'

'Big people.'

'For example?'

'Química, Banco de Oceano e Rocha, Martins Construções Limitada.'

'Very big people,' I said. 'Do you think you, your maid and whatever lawyer you can find for the money are up to taking on this kind of person?'

'I don't know,' she said, her thumb flickering over the filter of her cigarette.

'Is that why you came here tonight?'

She looked up with charcoal-smudged eyes in deep sockets, her face not puffy as it had been in the morning, gravity taking over from fluid retention.

'I'm not sure what you mean by that?'

'I have my work cut out for me in this case already, *Dona* Oliveira,' I said, shying away from a small but unpleasant truth. 'Your daughter was very promiscuous.'

'Wouldn't you expect that from a girl who'd been abused?' she said, getting a handkerchief out and wiping her eyes.

'The behaviour's been noticed in girls who haven't been abused,' I said. 'But that's your point, not mine. As the day's gone on we've discovered that she's had sex with your ex-lover and she's had sex with two boys from the band in a group session in a *pensão* in Rua da Glória. The landlord of that rooms-by-the-hour *pensão* had seen her before on Friday lunchtimes with other men who he thinks were paying customers. And I've just finished interviewing one of her teachers, who had a six-month involvement with her. Catarina could have gone with anybody and I've got to the point in my investigation where I need some luck to move it on.'

'I know all that,' she said. 'I'm trying to help. I'm trying to show you that there were psychological . . .'

'I'm not on anybody's team, *Dona* Oliveira,' I said, quiet and firm.

She stood and chased the ashtray around the table, crushing her cigarette out. She shouldered her handbag. I followed her to the door with half a mind to ask my burning question. Was Catarina your daughter? But I was too exhausted for the reply. The front door clicked shut. I opened it again to call after her, but she was already halfway down the street, walking into the yellow glow of the municipal street lighting, having trouble with her heels on the cobbles.

Chapter XXV

23rd August 1961, Casa ao Fim do Mundo, Azóia, 40 km west of Lisbon.

Felsen looked down into the courtyard from the veranda on the roof of his house. It was full of people he didn't know, friends and business contacts of Abrantes. Some of them were standing, some sat at tables, some picked over the decimated buffet with the bald disappointment of vultures late at the kill.

The day was hot with hardly a breath of wind, which happened about once a year on this weather-blasted point of Cabo da Roca. The sea was in a flat calm, slow and viscous under the sun. Felsen smoked and sipped champagne from a shallow glass. The party was to celebrate his permanent return from Africa. He'd gone back there in the middle of June 1955 and spent almost the entire six years out there. But it was over now. Angola had exploded into war and business had collapsed.

Felsen looked across to the walled garden on the south side of the house. One of his current girlfriends, Patrícia, the only one he'd invited, was standing next to Joaquim Abrantes in a group consisting of Pedro, Abrantes' eldest son, Pica, Abrantes' wife, and the Monteiros, Pica's parents. Abrantes had one hand in the small of Patrícia's back and the other resting on his wife's waist. He was leaning forward listening to Pedro who, as usual, was charming everyone with one of his long, amusing stories which Felsen had probably heard before but never managed to grasp the humour.

He had no desire to be down there with them. He was used to Pedro's brilliance and, like good brandy, he didn't need too much of it. He looked around for Manuel, the second son, the one with his eyes. He found him there, in the walled garden, but four metres back from the group, standing on his own under the shade of a bougainvillea, perhaps hiding, merging into the shadows, ignored by all, invisible to them, waiting for something to happen of particular interest to him. Felsen had seen him in that position before at another party he'd thrown. Some of Pedro's friends had been standing near the bougainvillea, one a girl with blonde hair. Manuel's hand had stretched out from the shade, touched her on the head and half-frightened her to death.

Where Pedro was the tall, confident, light-haired, brown-eyed, football-playing eldest son, leader in his economics class at Lisbon University, the nineteen-year-old Manuel was shorter, fatter, and already losing his dark hair in a strange way that had left a straggling fuzz across his brown scalp. His jaw had merged into his neck, his breasts pouched in his shirt, and his trousers were inexorably drawn up the crack of his arse, however big he bought them. He had a magnificent moustache though. Compensating for what he was losing on top, it was thick, luxuriant, shining, as if all the energy in his head was drawn to it. And there were the eyes – long-lashed, blue with the faintest green in them from his mother. His best feature.

Manuel was a morose boy. He'd suffered from his mother's absence more than his brother had. School was torture. The reports on his academic ability were poor. He couldn't kick a football without sending a clod of turf after it, and the memory of his attempt at roller hockey still brought tears to people's eyes. He didn't even have the distinction of being very unpopular. He was just mildly so – not reviled, just overlooked.

If there was harsh treatment coming from his father's

hand, and there was plenty of it at school report time, it found its way to the back of his head or his backside and never to Pedro's. This didn't make him hate his brother. He liked him too much, as everybody else did, and his brother always stood up for him. He didn't hate his father either, but he became watchful and sly to avoid confrontation. It was women that he found difficult. He had no way of talking to them, couldn't find anything inside himself that might interest them and, as a result, they didn't like him. He wanted to learn about them and underwear drawers seemed as good a place as any to start.

These investigations developed, in Manuel, an adolescent passion for spying on people. He found it thrilling to observe without being seen, to soak up information that people would never know he knew. It empowered him against their unconcern and it taught him things about people, and about sex.

His sex education started with the next-door neighbour's maid and his father's chauffeur. He'd let himself in to the neighbour's house and was wandering about, rifling through drawers, poking about in cupboards, when he heard them come in. He hid in the laundry room, and waited for them to leave but they followed him in there. He wasn't sure what he was watching at first as the man and woman tussled gently, making strange scoffing noises. He was only twelve at the time. But as soon as he saw the girl's skirts go up, her bare legs and a coppery bush at their apex, his own excitement told him that this was a thrill in a totally different category to Pica's underwear drawer.

He was shocked by the chauffeur's behaviour, the man dropping his trousers as if he was going to do *caca* in front of the girl, who he'd picked up and placed on the table. It was repellent. But when he saw the man's equipment, the state of it, the size of it, where he put it, the way he rammed it up against the girl's shiny bush, her strange, fearful gratitude, the increased savagery of the chauffeur's thrusts, and the confusion followed by the man's semen spraying every-where – he realized he was on to something extraordinary. The state of his own pants told him so. His mind told him something different – part thrilled, part disgusted, with a strange overhanging calamity that this was what would be expected of him.

Part of the mystery was clarified two days later (the laundry room was now one of his permanent hideouts) when his father burst in with the same maid. Manuel realized that only lower-class people sprayed their semen everywhere, whereas proper people, more politely he thought, and less messy, left it all in the girl's bush.

It was a number of years later, and a succession of maids later, that he fully understood the situation and even then it took a visit to a prostitute around his eighteenth birthday to completely demystify the procedure. It was she who, with a well-positioned knee, demonstrated that the withdrawal technique was a cross-class practice in a Catholic society.

Felsen moved to get a better view of what was fascinating Manuel. Was it Pica's bottom? If so, it was a healthy sign as his own eyes had frequently drifted over that region. She'd kept her figure. She hadn't had any children. Abrantes had offered to take her up to see the *Senhora dos Santos* in the Beira and been met with a pitying silence. Instead he'd taken her to London several times and spent large amounts of money in Harley Street but she'd never even been pregnant, let alone miscarried. This was why her parents were excessively polite whenever they came to Abrantes' house or his parties. It made for dull conversation.

Felsen drifted back to Manuel who, in that instant, straightened as if he'd seen what he'd come for. His father's hand had slipped off Patrícia's back and was now definitely cupping a buttock while, with the other hand, he was playing with the suspender clip beneath the material of Pica's dress. The old dog, thought Felsen, as Pica turned and saw the white of Manuel's shirt beneath the bougainvillea.

310

She shrugged her husband's hand off her bottom. Abrantes' other hand shot off Patrícia's buttock quick as a lizard.

The afternoon progressed. People left as the food ran out. Abrantes joined Felsen on the veranda with two brandy glasses and a bottle of *aguardente* he'd brought down from the Beira. They sat on raffia-seated chairs with a wrought-iron table between them and drank and smoked cigarettes while Abrantes softly slapped the painted wooden rail.

'That's the Portuguese for you,' said Felsen, watching people leave, 'they can't do anything without food.'

Abrantes wasn't listening. He flicked ash over the rail not caring where it went.

'It's been a bad year,' he said, slipping into the role of very successful, but naturally pessimistic businessman.

'We got out of Africa without losing our shirts,' said Felsen.

'No, no, I'm not talking about business. Business was all right. It's what you say . . . it's the colonies. That African trouble is not going to go away.'

'Salazar will follow the British. They've given independence to Ghana and Nigeria. Kenya will follow. So will Salazar. In a couple of years we'll be back in Africa making money with new independent governments.'

'Ah,' said Abrantes, leaning forward, knees spread, ankles crossed, glad, for once, to be able to correct the German, 'if you think that, then you don't understand Salazar. You're forgetting what happened when the Australians landed on East Timor during the war. Salazar will never give up the colonies. They are Empire. They are Portugal. They are part of his *Estado Novo*.'

'Come on, Joaquim . . . the man's seventy-two years old now.'

'If you don't think he's got the stomach for it, you're wrong. It's a weakness of his. Everybody knows it. Why do you think he's having all this trouble at home?'

'Moniz trying to get him to resign?' Felsen sneered and

311

threw his hand up in the air as if he was chucking salt over his shoulder.

'And don't forget General Machedo. He's still out there.'

'In Brazil, a few thousand kilometres away.'

'*There's* a man with popular support,' said Abrantes, ignoring Felsen. 'There's a man who would do anything to get into power . . . and if he couldn't get the top military on his side he'd even talk to *those* people.'

'Those people?' asked Felsen.

Abrantes wound his hand round and round, slapping the rail each time to show there was more and more, the two businessmen acting at each other as if they were performing some brand of formal theatre.

'These people are drawing attention to themselves. They took that cruise liner, the *Santa Maria*. They hijacked that TAP aircraft. They . . .'

'Who are *they*? Who are those people or these people . . . which people?'

'The *communists*,' said Abrantes, his eyes widening in what Felsen assumed was mock fear, but was, in fact, astonishment. 'These are people to be feared. You, of all people, should know that. Look what they've done to Berlin.'

'The wall? That won't last.'

'It's a wall,' said Abrantes. 'You don't build a wall unless you expect it to last. Believe me. And they're gathering strength here too. I know.'

'How?'

'I have friends,' said Abrantes, '. . . in PIDE.'

'And PIDE talk like that about Salazar?'

'You don't understand, my friend. You've spent a lot of time out of the country. I am here in Lisbon all the time. The PIDE,' he said, stretching out an evangelical hand, 'the PIDE aren't just the police, they're a state within the New State. They see how things really are. They understand the dangers. They see the African wars. They see trouble at

312

home. They see dissent. They see communism. All these things are a threat to the stability of the . . . Do you know what communists do to banks?'

Felsen said nothing. He knew Abrantes as a lot of animals – the shrewd business partner, the ruthless practitioner of brutal labour relations, the cost-cutter, the deal-maker – but never, not to his knowledge, the political animal.

'They nationalize them,' said Abrantes, throwing his hand out as if there was a bible in it.

Felsen ran his hand over his grey fuzz. Abrantes was irritated by his apparent lack of concern.

'That means *we* own *nothing*,' he reiterated the horror.

'I know what nationalization is,' said Felsen. 'I know what communism is. I'm scared of it. I don't need any convincing. But what are you proposing? That we sell up and get out? *I'm* not going to Brazil.'

'Manuel is joining PIDE,' said Abrantes and Felsen bit back his instinct to shout with laughter – *that* was a solution?

'What about his university education?' he asked, automatically.

'He didn't get the grades,' said Abrantes, tapping his temple with his cigar end. 'I look at Pedro, I look at Manuel . . . I can't believe they have the same parents. But don't misunderstand me . . . I think Manuel will do very well in PIDE. I've made the introductions. They like him. The boy has a structure to his life now. And he doesn't like communists either. They won't have to teach him anything about that. You'll see. We will benefit. If there are communists working in our factories he'll root them out and run them up to Caxias prison. And they know what to do with communists in the Caxias prison.'

Felsen murmured, tired now, the man's fanaticism giving the *aguardente* a rough edge that it didn't have before. Abrantes sat back, plugged the cigar into his mouth, and straightened his tie over his belly.

313

Manuel's fuzzy head slipped back into the darkness of the enclosed terrace behind the veranda.

Abrantes left at dinnertime with his family and Patrícia, who claimed she wasn't feeling well, but it was because Felsen was powerfully drunk. Drunk to the point where it took several tentative stabs to get a cigarette between his lips.

He managed to put 'Jailhouse Rock' on the record player and somehow got himself up on to the veranda where he took extravagant nosefuls of the still slack sea air and looked out into the black night.

When the music finished, and he was left with static and the rhythmical click of the needle, he blundered downstairs and drank water until he was gasping.

A short aeon slipped by and he found himself miraculously in his bedroom, wrenching the windows open, tearing his shirt-tails out of his waistband and treading his dropped trousers into the floor. He felt hot and had a great need to be naked under cool sheets, unconscious.

He ripped the bedclothes off, jerked himself straight, and took two startled steps back.

In the middle of the bed was a huge lizard. A live lizard. It bobbed its head, braced itself against the white sheet. Felsen careered out of the room, grabbed tools and came back with a rolling pin and a hammer. His first strike was wildly off the mark and bounced the lizard on to the floor. They fought for ten minutes, wrecking the bedroom, until Felsen managed to stun the animal with the rolling pin, hurled in frustration. He beat the lizard with the hammer and only stopped when an incident on a hot, dusty road in the Beira leaked into his mind. He picked the lizard up by the tail. It was surprisingly heavy. He threw it into the courtyard.

In the morning he was woken up by his heart thumping into his chest wall. He was still drunk. He knew it because his head didn't hurt and he wasn't disturbed by the sight of blood across both pillows and the sheets. Weak grey light, and an open sea chill came through the windows. There was cloud in the room. It was ten o'clock in the morning. The house was buried in dense fog.

Felsen had an encrusted gash on his forehead. He cleaned it in the bathroom and showered some sense into his body. He went out to the car wearing a suit under a wool coat. He skirted the lizard, backing towards the garage, amazed at it, a huge thing, half a metre with its tail. He went back and rolled it with his foot. Not an indigenous beast, he thought.

He opened the garage and looked straight down at his feet as if instructed. At the back of the car on the floor below the bumper a pair of crossed rusty horseshoes had been arranged. He dropped to his haunches. Other horseshoes had been placed behind each rear wheel. He gathered them up and hurled them over the wall with exaggerated force. One bounced back at him and he gave it special treatment.

He was panting as he reversed out. When he went back to shut the garage he saw two other horseshoes which had been under the front wheels. He ran at them and launched them into the scrub outside with crazed strength. He drove down to Estoril with a pounding just beginning behind his eyes.

Less than a kilometre from the house he emerged into brilliant sunshine. He arrived in Estoril in sweat and took a coffee in the main square which seemed to damage the part of his brain controlling his breathing. His heart raced as if pumping ether instead of thick, strong blood. He left his coat in the car and walked up to Abrantes' house with his suit jacket over his shoulder. He arrived with his eyebrows full of sweat and dark African states on the front and back of his shirt. The maid nearly shut him out. She sat him in the living room with a glass of water but Felsen

315

was too agitated to sit and paced the room like a caged panther.

Joaquim Abrantes rolled in full of energy and purpose until he saw Felsen in his patched shirt, his head gashed and wearing his hangover on the outside.

'What happened?'

He told him.

'A lizard?' said Abrantes.

'I wouldn't mind knowing who put it there.'

Manuel was called, and the accusation of a practical joke levelled. It stunned the boy who was standing like a soldier at ease. He denied it vehemently and was dismissed.

'I wonder about that boy,' said Abrantes. 'He's always snooping around people's houses.'

Felsen told him about the horseshoes. Abrantes stood stock still, hunched, and Felsen caught a glimpse of the peasant from the Beira – superstitious, pagan, nose turned up to the smell of things not right.

'This is bad,' he said. 'This is very bad. Perhaps you've upset your neighbours.'

'I don't have any neighbours.'

'People from the village, maybe.'

'I don't know anybody from the village apart from the maid and she's happy to take my money.'

'You know what you have to do?'

'I'm hoping you're going to tell me. These are your people.'

'You must go to the *Senhora dos Santos*.'

'In the Beira?'

'No, no. A local one. Ask in the village. They'll know. This magic is not from the Beira.'

'*Magic?*'

Abrantes nodded gravely.

Felsen drove back up to Azóia which was still in fog, a

316

stationary, closed, muffled world and freezing after the August sunshine in Estoril. He went to the bar which contained four people, three in black and a barman. Nobody spoke. He asked his question, and a boy, Chico, was called.

Chico led the way into the narrow lanes of the village, the fog so thick that Felsen, in his state, would stop occasionally and rear back as if from a solid wall. The boy took him to a low house on the edge of the village. The moisture had collected on his black hair like morning dew.

A woman came to the door in a blue floral overall wiping her bloody hands on a rag – fresh from killing lunch or maybe an entrail inspection. She was round-faced with very small eyes which only opened to the tiniest slits. She looked at the boy who was her height but it was Felsen who spoke.

'I have a problem, I'd like you to come and see my house,' he said.

She shooed the boy away. Felsen gave him a coin. They went through to the yard at the back of her house where there was a large domed dovecote the size of a church's cupola. She reached in and the doves flapped and cooed. One came out on her hand, white with brown traces on its wings. She held it to her bosom and stroked it down. Felsen felt strangely calm.

They drove to the house in fog so thick that Felsen stuck his head out of the window to see if it would improve his vision.

The *Senhora dos Santos* inspected the dead lizard already seething with ants.

'You found it in your bed, you said.'

Felsen nodded, scepticism crouched on his shoulder.

'It would have been better if you hadn't killed it.'

'Why?'

'Let's look in the house.'

As soon as she entered the hallway her breathing became

laboured as if she was having a respiratory attack. She walked through the house, struggling with every step, her face reddening and, despite the oceanic cold, sweating. Felsen found himself close to laughing at the absurdity of the spectacle. He walked behind her, unmoved, as if on some vague barracks inspection.

The *Senhora dos Santos* looked at the bed, which was still bloodstained from his head injury, as if there was a thrice-stabbed body on it. She staggered from the room, down the stairs, and out into the courtyard pursued by Felsen, keen as a ghoulish schoolboy.

Her breathing recovered, her face went back to its natural colour. The dove was not so fortunate. It fell dead and already stiff from her hands. They looked at it, she sad, Felsen affronted by the woman's quackery. He was in no doubt she'd killed it herself.

'What do you make of it?' he asked.

The face that looked up at him was not encouraging. Her eyes were now fully open from the slits they had been before. They were black, all pupil, no iris.

'This is not our magic,' she said.

'But what does it all mean?' he asked. 'The lizard? The horseshoes?'

'You killed the lizard . . . in your own bed. It means you will destroy yourself.'

'Kill myself?'

'No, no. You will bring yourself down.'

He snorted.

'And the horseshoes?'

'They will stop you from going anywhere. They will . . .'

'I've just been somewhere. You and I have just *been* in the car.'

'Not the car, *Senhor* Felsen,' she said, and he wondered for a moment how she knew his name.

'What then?'

'Your life.'

'What is this . . . this . . .' he said, his hand revolving over and over looking for the word.

'This is *Macumba*.'

'*Macumba?*'

'Brazilian black magic.'

Chapter XXVI

Saturday, 13th June 199–, Paço de Arcos, Lisbon.

During those six hard months of controlled fat intake to get myself back into shape, I'd planned to celebrate the end by cooking something exquisitely drenched in fat for Olivia and myself. Somewhere in my body there was a high whining for something like *arroz de pato*, duck with rice – the fat soaked into the rice, studded with *chouriço*, the flesh of the chunks of duck falling apart, the skin crisp – and a deep, cutting, slatey red to wash it down. But the dish took hours to make, it was late, nearly midnight, Olivia wasn't home and there was nothing in the fridge. I tipped the whisky undrunk into the sink. I showered and changed.

I slapped around the kitchen in bare feet and thawed some turkey steaks I'd found in the freezer in warm water. I boiled up some rice, a tin of corn and opened a bottle of Esteva red.

By half-past-midnight I was sitting with a small coffee and an *aguardente*, smoking my penultimate cigarette. Olivia came in smelling of perfume and beer. She sat down and smoked my last cigarette for me. I complained. She hugged me around the head and kissed me loudly on the ear. I crushed her to me and resisted biting her like I used to when she was small. She squirmed away from me and asked what had happened to my hand.

'A little accident,' I said, not wanting to face that again.

'So,' she said, taking a sip of my coffee, speaking in English as we did from time to time.

'You look happy,' I said.

'I am.'

'You met somebody you liked?'

'Sort of,' she half-lied, automatic at any age. 'How was *your* day?'

'You heard anything?'

'The girl on the beach, Dad. Paço de Arcos hasn't been talking about anything else.'

'And Cascais?'

'Cascais, too.'

'You stopped talking about the Manic Street Preachers for two seconds.'

'Not that long.'

'Yes, well, she was dead on the beach. Hit on the head and strangled. Not nice. The only thing . . .'

'How old was she?'

'A bit younger than you.'

'What was "the only thing"?'

My sweet daughter, my little girl. I still saw that under the clothes, the hairstyle, the make-up and perfume. I used to disturb myself at night, because I'm a man and I know men, thinking about all those young guys who wouldn't see that, who saw . . . who saw what she wanted them to see. I suppose that's it. Girls don't want to be little girls for ever . . . not even for ten minutes these days.

'Maybe you knew this girl,' I said, deviating.

'Me?'

'Why not? She's the same age. Her parents live in Cascais. She goes to school in Lisbon – Liceu D. Dinis. Her name's Catarina Sousa Oliveira. Privileged kids get murdered too.'

'I don't know anyone at the Liceu D. Dinis. I don't know anyone called Catarina Sousa Oliveira. But that wasn't "the only thing". You changed your mind. I can tell. You don't . . .'

'I did. The thing was . . . she was under sixteen and for a kid that age she was getting up to a lot of tricks.'

'Tricks?'

321

'It's what prostitutes do . . . they turn tricks.'

'I know *that* . . . it's just a weird word for the work.'

'I bet your mother didn't teach you that.'

'Mum and I talked about everything.'

'Turning tricks?'

'It's called "Sex Education". She didn't get any herself so she gave me some.'

'Did she use those words?'

'That's what women do, Dad. When boys are kicking footballs in the park, we're talking about . . . everything.'

'Except football.'

'I bought you a present,' she said.

'What else did your mother tell you?'

'There,' she said, and laid out a razor, five blades and a can of shaving foam. I pulled her over and kissed her on the head.

'What are these for?' I asked.

'Don't be difficult.'

'Go on.'

'What?'

'We were talking about your mother.'

'You were being nosey about our conversations . . . and if Mum didn't talk to you about what she talked about with me, then she probably thought it was none of your business. Or, more likely Dad, you wouldn't have been interested.'

'Try me.'

She looked up into her head, smoked a bit and polished her teeth with her tongue.

'You first,' she said.

'Me?'

'Tell me something personal that you talked about with Mum to show me . . . good faith.'

'Like what?'

'Something personal,' she said, enjoying herself, 'like sex. Didn't you ever talk about sex?'

I looked into my *aguardente* glass for quite some time.

'She talked to me about what it was like having sex with you,' she said.

'Did she?' I said, astonished.

'She said, let me get this right: "It's a wonderful thing to have sex with a man you love. Once you've felt that tenderness, the deep intimacy of his total regard for you, the thrill of that mental connection, then there's no going back . . ." I think that was more or less it. She told me that after my first time when I complained that it wasn't all that it was cracked up to be.'

Olivia stopped. I was in trouble, unable to swallow, my eyeballs prickling, my stomach clenching. It was silent in the room. A single dog barked in the night, a long way off. My daughter put her hand on my back, rubbed me between the shoulders. I pulled back from the precipice. She put her forehead on to my arm. I stroked her soft, black hair. More time passed. She kissed my wrist. The traffic reasserted itself in the room.

'Your first time?' I said, coming round.

Olivia sat up.

'She didn't tell you, did she? I didn't think she would.'

'Why?'

'I asked her not to. I thought you'd probably have arrested him.'

'When was this?'

'A while ago.'

'I'm not sure how long a while is in English? Sometimes it's short, sometimes it's long.'

'About eighteen months ago.'

'When exactly. I want to remember that time.'

'February last year, Carnival time.'

'You were only just fifteen.'

'That's right.'

'What happened?'

She stretched and shivered with nerves, not used to talking to me like this. Neither of us were.

323

'You know,' she said.

'Tell me.'

'It was at a party, he was eighteen . . .'

You think of these things, and then you find they've happened without you knowing. Why hadn't I seen it? Don't women get that look in their eye when they've eaten the forbidden fruit? I know boys don't – they're nerds before and afterwards they're just happy nerds.

It happened again. I thought I was relaxed, but I was coiled tighter than a metal spring. Where was all this . . . this rage coming from? For the second time that night my fist came down on the table and I roared against the bastard stranger who'd deflowered my daughter. I harangued my dead wife. I railed against my reflection in the window for being so blind. I castigated Olivia who kicked back her chair and volleyed her entire love-life straight back in my face. Yelling at the top of her voice, so that ship's crews heading out into the Atlantic that night would have lined up on the rails to listen. It didn't stop until she hit me, tears streaming down her face, she thundered her fists into my chest and stormed out, the doors crashing behind her, heels cracking the stairs, a final door slam and I could see her thumping face-down on the bed.

Then quiet, apart from the blood thundering in my ears, and the tick of a woodworm eating its way up the table leg.

After half an hour of circular thinking I went upstairs. Olivia's light was out under her door. I continued up the stairs to my attic room and the weakness I'd been indulging for the past six months.

I had a desk set up in the dormer window with a simple raffia-seated wooden chair. In the desk I had a photograph of my wife, a head shot taken by me at night on the terrace of a house we were staying in near Lagos in the Algarve. In the shot her face is luminous. It was a colour shot, but only black and white and a yellow aura had come out in the flash. She never liked having her photo taken. I'd surprised her, but she wasn't wide-eyed and shocked. She was actually staring intently and with some intensity, at the moment just before evasive action would be taken.

I set the photograph up in a black frame on the desk facing the window. Her face came up in one of the panes of glass, as if she was outside looking in.

Also in the desk, in a locked drawer, was a bag of grass and a packet of Rizla+ papers. I used to smoke it as a kid in Africa. It was the poor man's booze and the gardeners used it all the time. I hadn't smoked since I left London, but when I had to stop drinking to lose the weight, I knew I wasn't going to get through the occasional hard, lonely moment without something to soften the edges.

I'd smoked maybe two or three joints a week for six months. When I smoked I talked to my wife in the window, and the strange part was, that after the dope had taken hold and I'd fallen into myself, she'd talk back.

I sat with the desk lamp on to give the reflection and smoked. It didn't take much. It was good stuff. Not local. I mean, I could have just walked out the front door and bought a deal in five minutes but that wouldn't do. My father's old driver from Guinea provided the gear for me. My black brother.

'It's been a day,' I said.

No answer, her gaze as steady as a ship's purpose through water.

'You like my new face?'

Her lips, slightly apart, dark against her white face, didn't move.

'I've lost my rag twice today. What does that mean? I've never lost control like that before, not even when I've been drinking. That stuff about my father . . . Carlos talking about my father like that. I couldn't stand it.'

'Maybe you feel guilty,' she said.

'What was that? I didn't catch that.'

'Maybe you feel guilty about your father.'

'Guilty?' I said. 'I was defending him.'

'But you were lefter than left when I first met you.'

'It was the way to rebel against the . . . against fascism.'

'Was it? Was it just that?'

Silence. I steeplechased a marathon around my head. I knew the answer to this, but how to get it out?

'You can just say it,' she said. 'It's only me and you.'

'It wasn't the right thing for him to have done,' I said.

'That's what you thought?'

'And I still think that now.'

'That's a hard thing for you to have to admit,' she said. 'I know how much you admired him.'

'But why did I go crazy like that? Banging my fists down on the table . . .'

'You always said that the Portuguese prefer to live in the past . . . perhaps you've decided to live in the present and the future,' she said. 'You're changing. You're lonely and you're changing. Maybe you don't want to be lonely any more.'

'I missed you tonight. Hearing Olivia say your words, I missed you.'

'You didn't mind me telling her that?'

'No, no. Not that.'

'What then?'

'I just had the thought that even when you were alive I was still a bit lonely.'

'Not lonely. A loner,' she said, correcting my English. 'It's what makes you the man you are, but it can break you, too.'

'In my job you mean?'

'You don't have to think of your job all the time, Zé.'

'You're right. I spent too much time thinking about that.'

'You were too inquisitive for the truth about everything and everybody. Nobody likes that. Not even policemen, and the ones closest to you don't always want to tell it or know it, either.'

'I don't get that.'

'Especially when you don't reveal your own little truths . . . when you hide.'

'Ah, yes, I knew we'd get to that. The beard.'

'The beard,' she snorted. 'The beard didn't matter.'

'Metaphorically, I meant.'

'OK, if you like,' she said. 'But remember, that's the first time you've told me about what you thought of your father's actions.'

'Why didn't you tell me about Olivia?' I said it in a rush.

'She trusted me not to.'

'I see.'

'She said she couldn't have borne your disappointment.'

'My *disappointment*?'

'She remembers all those times you used to take her off as a little girl. All those hours you spent with her telling her about things and about how wonderful she was and how much she meant to you. Were you disappointed?'

I took the joint down to the roach and stubbed it out in the tin seashell ashtray. I re-experienced that crushed feeling after a girl you've fallen for lets you down lightly.

'We're strange creatures,' I said.

'Love is a complicated business.'

I stared at my own reflection in the pane above my wife.

'I met someone today,' I said.

'Who was that?'

'A teacher.'

'He or she?'

'She.'

'What about her?' she asked, with a little edge.

'I'm . . . I like her.'

'Like? What's like?'

'I'm attracted to her.'

Silence.

327

'She's the first woman I've met that I'd like to . . .'

'You don't have to be explicit, Zé.'

'I didn't mean to . . .'

'Then don't.'

'It was just that . . .'

'Zé?'

Her image shuddered in the windowpane, a breeze smartening off the sea rattled the loose panes, whose putty had come out long ago. The lamp buzzed on the corner of the table. I leaned back and found myself crouching, braced against the edge of the desk. Tiles on the roof shifted against each other as the breeze freshened more. The jolt, when it came, seemed to come from behind my sternum. It thumped me forward into the desk, the photograph collapsed, the pane blackened, the lamp keeled over.

I lay on the floor in the dark, my hands folded on my stomach. I was half under the desk, unable to get enough air in my lungs. A doctor might have thought it was a heart attack and it was, of sorts. After a small aeon I crawled up the chair, just made it to the door and half-fell down the stairs.

I stripped vehemently, my clothes sticking to me like a crazed lover's. I lay on the bed with my hand in her dent of the mattress. Tears leaked down the side of my face, over my ears and wet the pillow.

Chapter XXVII

24th December 1961, Monte Estoril, near Lisbon.

Felsen sat on the edge of a wooden chest with his back to the black, rain-lashed window which in daylight would have shown the grey ocean and, off to the right, the Fort of Cascais, squat, robust, taking on the waves. He was watching Pica's family leave after a Christmas Eve dinner. Pedro, Joaquim's eldest son, was in amongst the guests, kissing and shaking hands. Manuel leaned against the wall, feet crossed at the ankle, hands in pockets, watching. Confident in his watching.

The party broke up, Pica went upstairs, Pedro and Manuel disappeared into the house. Abrantes and Felsen poured themselves some pre-war *Armagnac* and lit a Cuban cigar apiece. Abrantes sat down in his favourite piece of furniture, a high-backed leather armchair with an arched hood. He liked to gently and absentmindedly slap the arm of this chair, and there was a dark patch where the natural grease of his palm had been kneaded in.

'You don't look well,' said Abrantes. 'You're not eating properly.'

It was true Felsen hadn't had any appetite for some weeks. He felt as if there was a big moment pending, and to be ready for it he wanted to be sharp, hungry, concentrated. He looked out of the black window watching Abrantes' reflection.

'You put alcohol on an empty stomach, you'll ruin yourself,' said Abrantes, demonstrating his all-round expertise, as if his visits to Harley Street with Pica had been part of

329

his education, and allowed him to pontificate on all things medical. Felsen puffed on his cigar, the coal at the end sending Morse code back to him.

'Smoking's bad too . . . unless you eat,' added Abrantes, which tempted Felsen to announce a midnight swim to see if his partner would say that that would kill him too. 'Everything's all right as long as you eat properly.'

Felsen paced the length of the window looking out across the other houses to the ocean.

'You're nervous too,' said Abrantes. 'You can't sit still any more. You're not working. You're spending too much time with too many different women. You should calm down, marry . . .'

'Joaquim?'

'What?' he asked, looking up from his chair, innocent, put-upon. 'I'm just trying to help. You haven't been yourself since you came back from Africa. If you had a wife I wouldn't have to worry about you . . . that's what wives do.'

'I don't want to get married,' said Felsen, for the first time out loud.

'But you have to, you have to have children or . . . or . . .'

'Or what?'

'It all stops. You don't want to be the end of the line.'

'It's not as if I'm the last male Habsburg, Joaquim.'

Abrantes wasn't sure what a Habsburg was. It shut him up. They drank. Felsen refilled and went back to the window. He saw Abrantes reflected, craning his neck to see what was worth looking at.

'Manuel is doing very well in PIDE,' said Abrantes.

'You told me.'

'They say he has a natural ability for the work.'

'A suspicious mind, maybe?'

'An enquiring mind,' said Abrantes. 'They tell me he likes to know everything . . . they're going to make him an *agente de 1ª classe*.'

'Is that impressive?'

'After less than six months in the job? I think so.'

'What does he do?'

'You know ... he checks up on people. He talks to informers. He finds the worms in the apple.'

Felsen nodded, hardly listening. Abrantes writhed in his favourite chair unable to get comfortable.

'I meant to ask you this,' said Abrantes. 'I meant to ask you this months ago.'

'What?' said Felsen, turning away from the window, interested for the first time that night.

'Did you see the *Senhora dos Santos* about your problem in the summer?'

'Of course I did.'

Abrantes sat back, legs spread, relieved.

'I was worried,' he said. 'That you wouldn't take it seriously. It's a very serious business.'

'She didn't do anything,' said Felsen. 'She said it wasn't her type of magic.'

Abrantes came out of his chair as if a mechanism had thumped him in the back. He took Felsen by the elbow, squeezed it hard to impress upon him the gravity of the matter.

'Now I know,' he said, his eyes staring and wide. 'Now I know why you're behaving in this way. You must see someone. Immediately.'

Felsen eased his elbow out of the man's mechanical grip. He threw back the *Armagnac* remaining in his glass and left the house.

It was 10.30 p.m. He was drunk but not too drunk to drive himself back out to Cabo da Roca. He drove his Mercedes through the silent streets, black and glistening from the rain. He slowed past a couple of addresses in Cascais but each time moved on – not lacking in any physical appetite, just the talk necessary to get him to that point. He smoked the remains of the cigar and drummed his fingers on the

331

steering wheel and it occurred to him out there, in the blustery darkness on the Guincho road with the storms stacked up over the Atlantic waiting to come in, that in a fit of madness Maria might have told Abrantes that Manuel was not his child. Was that why she was back up in the Beira? Was that why Abrantes talked about continuing the line, and in the next breath mentioned Manuel and his success in PIDE? Abrantes had made a remark at that party in the summer too, about Manuel not having the same parents as Pedro. He shook his head at the indecisive windscreen wipers, at the rain gusting across the road, slashing and buffeting the car. His thoughts unnerved him. He began to feel uncomfortable between his shoulders and up the back of his neck, suspicious suddenly that the back seat of the car was not empty.

Drunk again, he sighed.

A car approached on a long straight section of the road. They dipped their headlights at each other. As the car drew nearer he took advantage of the light to check the back seat in the rear view. Nothing. He reached behind him and swept his hand across the seats. Stupid drunk.

Red lights receded into the blackness, quickly obliterated.

The road climbed up through the dense darkness of the pine trees, past Malveira da Serra, the road winding, cutting back on itself, the steering wheel shooting through his hands, a little sweat on his top lip from the drink oozing out of his system.

He turned off at the top and dropped down through the village of Azóia and out towards the lighthouse where his house, huddled in its own courtyard, shouldered the weather. He got out to open the gates. The wind inflated his lungs, the rain battered his hot ear. He drove the car up to the garage and went back to close the gates. He'd left a lamp on outside the house on the corner and in the light that shone off the hard wet mud in the courtyard, he saw footprints going to the side of the house.

He put his own foot down over one of the footprints. His were smaller. He squeezed his chin and swallowed. The GNR had warned him that bandits were operating on the roads around the Serra da Sintra. He drove the car into the garage. He opened the glove compartment and removed an old Walther P48 he'd kept from the war. He checked the magazine and tucked it into his waistband. His mind worried over ammunition corroded by the sea air, and he tried to remember when he'd last cleaned and oiled the damn thing. Still, having it in his hand was the important thing.

He stumbled into the house and saw his rubbery face in the hall mirror. Maybe, that was it. He was just drunk and they were the gardener's footprints. That must be it. He took off his coat, shook the rain off it and hung it up. The gardener was small, didn't even come up to his shoulder, had the feet of an elf. His ears strained for movement and returned to him the tinnitus that had developed since coming back from Africa.

He wiped his feet and moved down the corridor. His leather soles sounded loud against the wooden flooring. He turned on the kitchen light. Empty. He crossed to the living room. Flicked that light on. The Rembrandt looked down on him. He went to the sideboard and poured himself a shot of *aguardente* from an unmarked bottle. He sniffed it, the raw alcohol unstuffed his head, the paranoia backed off a notch. He lit a cigarette, took two fast drags and crushed it out. He removed the gun from his waistband and turned.

A man was standing by the door, grey hair swept back, blue raincoat, the wet shoulders glistening in the light. He had a gun in his hand.

'Schmidt,' said Felsen, surprisingly calm, given that the name had come into his head like a lobbed grenade.

Schmidt adjusted his grip on the .38 revolver, and the four-inch barrel performed a small circle. He was surprised that Felsen wasn't thrown against the wall in astonishment at the sight of him. He was surprised to see the Walther in the man's hand. How could he be armed and ready? Did he know things?

'You should put that down,' said Schmidt.

'You could do the same.'

Neither of them moved. Schmidt breathed loudly through his broken nose, his mouth sealed, the stress of the situation working his jaw muscles, his brain calculating as hard as a chess grandmaster's but without the clarity.

'Smoke?' said Felsen.

'I gave up,' he said. 'My lungs didn't like the tropics.'

'A drink then?'

'I had a brandy earlier.'

'I didn't think you drank.'

'I don't usually.'

'Have another then, see if you can get a taste for it.'

'Put the gun down.'

'I don't think so,' said Felsen, his heart pounding in the roof of his mouth. 'Why don't we both put our guns down over here on the sideboard.'

Schmidt moved through the furniture, his gun leading. As he came closer the greyness in his face became more apparent. He was a sick man and more dangerous for it. With a nod they laid their guns down simultaneously on the polished wood. Felsen poured drinks.

'I'm surprised,' said Felsen, not sounding it, a day's drinking and the burst of adrenalin having a curious effect on him. 'I was told you were lying in a river with your pockets full of rocks and a bullet in your head.'

Felsen handed him a glass of the *aguardente*. Schmidt sniffed it.

'Your partner. He never even came after me. I saw him. He stayed close to the house as if he was giving me time to get away, and when he thought I was well gone, he walked out into the poppy fields and let off a round into the air. Not a brave man, but not a stupid one either. I'd have killed him.'

'Why didn't you come into the house after us?'

'Like they do in the films,' said Schmidt, canting his head to one side, sardonic. 'I thought about it, but I decided it was too dangerous, and anyway, killing the two of you wasn't the point at that time.'

'Was that why you sent Eva after me?'

'Eva?'

'Susana. I meant Susana Lopes . . . from São Paulo.'

'Susana got close. She made a beginner's mistake, but then, that was what she was.'

'Are you working for someone, Schmidt?'

'This is a personal thing,' he said.

'Why don't we start with what you want,' Felsen said. 'Let's get that out into the open. You're not after the gold, are you?'

'Gold,' he said, not a question, not an answer.

'You're sick,' said Felsen, disturbed by the man's lack of direction. 'I can see that.'

'Fibrosis of the lungs,' said Schmidt.

'Where are you living now?'

'Back in Germany, Bayreuth,' he said, sipping his drink. 'I was from Dresden. Did you know that? You know what they did to Dresden. I haven't been back.'

'Did your family survive?'

'They're in Dortmund,' he said.

'Children?'

'Two boys and a girl. They're quite grown-up now.'

'I see,' said Felsen, feeling oddly like a bank manager. 'That's an American gun you have there.'

'A souvenir.'

'Does it fire the Stars and Stripes?'

Schmidt smiled. The stress eased. Felsen edged him away from the guns. He sat on the arm of a leather sofa with Schmidt on the arm of one of the chairs, their knees almost touching.

'That painting looks familiar,' said Schmidt.

'Another souvenir.'

'It doesn't look like a cheap print.'

'I bought it on the Bayswater Road in London.'

'Is it a copy of . . . ?' asked Schmidt, starting to get up.

Felsen rested his hand on the man's shoulder.

'It's a Rembrandt, Schmidt. Now tell me the purpose of your social call. I've had a long dinner and I'm tired.'

Schmidt's creased neck turned in its frayed collar. He had a patch of grey bristles visible under the jawline missed in the morning shave. A thicket of dark hair protruded from his ear.

'I'm not the only one with a sensitive past,' he said.

'Ah,' said Felsen, the angle revealed. 'Another of your American imports, Schmidt. I've heard blackmail's very popular over there now.'

Schmidt's eyes switched back to the guns on the sideboard, the old man in the Rembrandt watching.

'They're very interested in certain circles,' he said, his mind not on it.

'You don't think they've got their hands full with the Russians?'

'They've got plenty of hands when it comes to a multimillion-dollar corporation established with wartime SS funding.'

'There's a risk, of course, that it could all blow up in your face, Schmidt. You've got no evidence except your own colourful past.'

Schmidt threw himself at the sideboard. Felsen, who'd been half-waiting for this moment, found that the other half wasn't as alert as it should have been. He lashed out with his foot and caught Schmidt on the shin. Schmidt's arms flailed but his hands managed to come down on the sideboard. A gun clattered across the uncarpeted edge of the floor. Schmidt fell and twisted on to his back. Felsen found himself kneeling and looking down the barrel of his own gun held in Schmidt's hand.

'I thought we were talking, Schmidt.'

'We were, but I changed my mind,' he said. 'Blackmail's a complicated business . . . a lot of things can go wrong in it.'

'So is burglary and fencing an old master.'

'I was thinking about murder.'

'Murder?' asked Felsen. 'What do you get from murder? Your health's gone, you should be thinking about your children's future.'

'They don't know me. I've seen them . . . but they don't know me.'

'What is this?' asked Felsen. 'I don't know what this is about any more.'

'This is about loyalty,' he said.

Felsen gasped as Schmidt pulled the trigger. There was a dry click. Schmidt racked the slide. Felsen leapt towards the corner of the room, his hand reaching out for Schmidt's gun. There was a head-ringing explosion, far louder than a detonating bullet in a confined space, and Felsen's ear and arm burnt white hot. The next sound he heard was the horror sound from Prinz Albrechtstrasse, the sound of a man on the brink of orgasm. He picked up the gun and rolled over.

Schmidt was slumped against the sideboard, his legs out in front of him, his eyes wide and staring at the bloodied stump at the end of his right arm. Blood covered his chest and lap. His raincoat was torn open, his face and grey hair flecked with red. Schmidt wanted to scream but, like a man having a nightmare, his mind shuddered but his voice only whimpered.

The quantity of blood that had spurted from his severed brachial artery was creating a creeping stain through the carpet towards the leather furniture.

'I'm going,' he said in a strange polite voice, as if he'd got what he'd come for and he'd be running along now.

Felsen got to his feet. His reflection in the window showed dark streaks across his face. The mirror showed him that he'd lost half an ear. His left arm burned from shoulder to wrist. He eased the fingers of his right hand around there and they disappeared into a deep wound in his triceps. His knees went and he nearly fainted.

He stripped off his jacket in the bathroom and washed himself as best he could. He ran water over his arm. It made no difference. It felt as if he had a white hot lump of charcoal in there. He hung his head over the sink. Not only did he have Schmidt to move, but he also had furniture and a large antique Arraiolos carpet to shift. He wrapped a towel around his arm.

He went back to the living room. He reached over Schmidt and uncorked the *aguardente* bottle and drank heavily from it. He sat on the divan with the bottle in his crotch and with the most westerly telephone in Europe put a call through to Abrantes. The operator connected him.

The maid answered and refused to disturb Abrantes. Felsen worked on her for half a minute. He knew what Abrantes was doing. He drank again and found a new packet of cigarettes. Abrantes finally picked up the telephone.

'I need your help,' said Felsen.

'Can't it wait?' he said, irritated.

'I need help from your friends . . . the ones Manuel works for.'

Silence now. He had the man's attention. He gulped more spirit, blinked back the tears.

'There's been a development from that situation I had with Susana Lopes. There's a man dead up here.'

'That's enough,' said Abrantes. 'Shut up now. I'm sending somebody. Are you hurt?'

Felsen's face was burning from the alcohol. His lips, with the cigarette stuck to the bottom one, itched. Sweat sprang from the sandpaper of his moustache.

'My arm.'

'Leave the door open,' said Abrantes.

Felsen rattled the phone back. He made it to the front door and halfway back. He fell across the threshold to the living room, Schmidt's white face was his last image.

He was vaguely aware of people in the room. Shadows and light in his eyes, furniture scraping, voices remote and indistinct and the wind still driving into the house, rattling the windows. He was being moved. Something flashed in the dome of his cranium and he floated out again, his raft creaking under the heave of a big sea.

He woke up several times over a period he could not judge. Each time the heat inside him was tremendous as if his body was burning fossil fuels. On the last occasion there was a smell, a terrible smell, one that frightened him and left him as weak as the runt cub in a litter of twelve.

There was morning light when he came round. The very first inch of the day when the earliest grey seeps out of the black. His head was too heavy to lift off the pillow. Was he awake this time? Was he conscious? He waited to see where he was, to make sure that he wasn't still inside his own head. More light leaked into the room, a little white, the colour of bone. He felt cool. Not so much pain in his bad arm, a saline drip in the other. Not parched as before. He heard voices talking in the corridor about a coup attempt in Beja, the name of General Machedo, but it was too much effort to listen and he tuned out.

He lifted his right arm. It was secured to the bed frame by a pair of handcuffs. He lifted his left, gingerly, the pain still there. The arm came up easily. He looked down his chest at it, but it wasn't there. It felt there. But it wasn't. The hand was there but it wasn't. The wrist. The elbow. The biceps. All there, but not. He yelled loud enough to split the two sacs of his lungs.

Two guards, both with rifles, crashed into the room.

'What the hell's going on?' said the first and older one.

'My arm,' roared Felsen. 'My arm's gone.'

They looked at him dumbly from across the room.

'That's right,' said the younger one. 'They cut it off.'

The older guard nudged him with his elbow.

'What?' said the younger one.

'He's lost his arm, for God's sake.'

'He smells a lot better now than when they brought him in.'

The older guard gave him a dead-eyed look and went to get a doctor. The younger one paced the room.

'Why am I chained to the bed?' asked Felsen.

'You killed a guy,' said the guard. 'You were completely drunk and you killed a guy. As soon as you're fit to move we're taking you back to Caxias.'

'I don't remember the trial.'

'That'll come.'

Felsen dumped his head back on the pillow and did some blinking at the ceiling.

'Will you do something for me?'

'You don't look as if you've got much money on you.'

'If I give you a number will you call Joaquim Abrantes? He'll give you money.'

The guard shook his head. Not worth the bother.

Two weeks later Felsen was moved back to the Caxias prison. A week after that he was taken out of his cold damp cell to a room with a table, an empty sardine tin for an ashtray and two chairs. Abrantes was shown in by a prison officer. He and Felsen shook hands. Abrantes clapped him on the shoulder and tried to nod some encouragement into him. Felsen tried to keep the coldness out of his eyes – Abrantes the only man on the outside who could help him. They sat down. Abrantes produced some of Felsen's favourite Turkish cigarettes and a hip flask of brandy. They lit up and drank to each other.

340

'So what's happening?' asked Felsen.

'A very difficult and now, bureaucratic, situation.'

'I don't remember very much after I called you.'

'That was the first problem. You came through to an operator in Cascais. By the time I'd contacted my friends in PIDE another squad had already been advised by the telephone exchange that a death had occurred and that you weren't phoning the police to report it. Suspicious. Very suspicious.'

'He broke into my house. He was armed.'

'So were you. Your fingerprints were on the unregistered gun. A bullet from that was found in the dead man.'

'I don't . . .' Felsen drifted, and chewed on his remaining thumbnail.

'You see how complicated it has become.'

'That wasn't *my* gun. *He* had my gun. *My* gun blew up in *his* face.'

'What was he doing with your gun, what were you doing with his?'

Felsen closed his eyes and squeezed the bridge of his nose. He told Abrantes as best as he could remember what had happened. Abrantes listened, glancing at his watch and drinking more of the brandy than was his share. He nodded and murmured to keep Felsen going.

'You know,' said Abrantes, once he was sure the German was finished. 'I don't think you can say any of that in court.'

'In court?'

'There has to be a trial.'

'What about your PIDE friends?'

'As I mentioned . . . a very difficult and now, bureaucratic, situation. You're in the system. It's not so easy to get you out.'

'I don't remember being charged.'

'The charge, my friend, is murder.'

Felsen dabbed the sardine tin around the table with the end of his cigarette.

'You know who he was, don't you?'

'Who?'

'The dead man.'

'According to his papers he was a German tourist called Reinhardt Glaser.'

Felsen shook his head, his eyes so intense, they grabbed Abrantes around the throat.

'You owe me,' he said.

'I owe you?'

'The dead man was Schmidt . . . you remember him?'

'Schmidt?'

'The one you told me you shot that night in the Alentejo. You said you put him in the river . . .'

'No, no, no, no.'

'Yes, Joaquim,' said Felsen, easing the hip flask from Abrantes' grip. 'It was him. You lied to me. He said you didn't come after him. He said you fired a shot out in the poppy fields. He saw you. Schmidt saw you.'

'No, no, no . . . his name was Reinhardt Glaser. You made a mistake.'

'I didn't make a mistake. You know I didn't.'

'Me? How? I never saw him.'

It was quiet enough to hear the tobacco crackling in their cigarettes.

'You owe me for that, Joaquim.'

'Look,' he said, 'you lost your arm, I'm sorry for that. You've had a bad experience. You're still in a state of shock. Your memory is playing tricks with you. This is what I'm going to do for you. I'm getting one of the best criminal lawyers to help you out of this mess. If he can't get you an acquittal nobody can. Now drink. I have to be going. Pica is waiting for me in the Chiado. The later I am, the more she spends. *Força, amigo meu.*'

That was the last Felsen saw of Abrantes. The lawyer never appeared. His old partner didn't attend the trial nine months later, and he wasn't present to see Felsen sentenced to twenty years' imprisonment for the murder of the German tourist, known from his passport details as Reinhardt Glaser.

As Felsen began two decades of imprisonment in Caxias he had a short, vivid dream. It featured four horseshoes which gradually straightened out into a lattice of metal strips, and behind the strips was a live lizard with its head mashed to a bloody pulp, front legs braced, bobbing. He woke with a jerk and into his head came the memory of a dark stretch of road out to Guincho on a squally Christmas Eve night. He knew then, that even in his drunken state, his instinct had been right – Maria had told Abrantes that Manuel was not his son. He replayed that last meeting with Abrantes. The man seemed to have come with drink and cigarettes and the possibility of hope, but Felsen now realized that he was there to enjoy his satisfaction, to rub his hands over the warm fire of completed vengeance.

Two weeks after the trial on November 18th 1962 Joaquim Abrantes sat down with his new lawyer, Dr Aquilino Dias Oliveira, and rewrote the statutes of the Banco de Oceano e Rocha. Amongst the shareholders and directors there was no mention of the convicted murderer, Klaus Felsen.

Chapter XXVIII

Sunday, 14th June 199–, Paço de Arcos, near Lisbon.

Olivia was still sleeping when I looked in on her in the morning, face-down under her black hair. I went downstairs and ate fruit, drank coffee, and talked to the cat, who'd stretched herself out into the longest cat in Paço de Arcos. The time snipped round to 9.00 a.m. and I went to look at the telephone. The telephone had been mildly interesting years ago when we had a large Bakelite affair that was heavy enough to curtail young girls' conversations. Now we had a sleek graphite-grey push-button apparatus that looked absurd in the room's decaying décor, and was light enough for Olivia to tuck it behind her ear and cut a suit of clothes whilst talking about boys. I straightened the telephone on its table, checked the flex. Olivia came in wearing a T-shirt down to her knees, her eyes still puzzled by sleep.

'What are you doing?' she asked.

'I'm looking at the phone.'

She did, too.

'Is it due to perform?'

'I was thinking of making a call.'

The cat came in and sat beside her, paws neat, sensing a moment of possible interest. She yawned widely.

'Who are you going to call?'

I gripped my chin and looked up at her, suddenly feeling in need of something and not just a beard. My head was suddenly crowded – I was going to call a possible witness in a murder trial to ask her out to lunch, I was going to have to tell my daughter about her, I had to explain last night's madness.

The door bell rang.

'I wanted to talk to you about what happened last night,' I said, shifting on to my back foot.

The door bell rang again. She left the room, fast. Glad to be out of there. The cat looked around to see if there was anything worth nicking and left too. I lunged at the telephone and dialled Luísa Madrugada's number. She picked it up before it had even rung.

'This is Inspector Zé Coelho,' I said, the words sprinting out, panic-struck. 'Would you like your work interrupted?'

'I always want my work interrupted, Inspector, we talked about that yesterday. It's by what and whom . . . that's the question.'

'Lunch,' I said. 'Would lunch . . . ?'

'Inspector?' she asked, suddenly grave and chill. 'Is this business?'

Something cold ran through me. I felt sick with regret.

'Absolutely not,' I said, changing my original idea, forcing the words out.

She laughed and told me to come to her apartment at one o'clock.

Olivia came back into the room followed by Carlos with a newspaper under his arm and the cat still looking for the cocktail party.

'Progress,' said Olivia, still unimpressed.

I refitted the handset, reliving the rollercoaster moments of the start of something new – hope, despair, joy – all in ten seconds. I'd forgotten the stamina it took.

Carlos approached and held out his hand. I took it. He held on and, with his head bowed, uttered an extensive apology that must have kept him up all night. I looked at Olivia, who was transfixed until something more important occurred to her and she left the room.

I put my hand on Carlos' shoulder. He was suffering and

345

still couldn't look me in the eye. My chest felt as big as a cathedral roof. If I'd opened my mouth there'd have been a chord from an organ with all the stops pulled out. I put an arm around his shoulders.

'You're a good man,' I said. 'Apologizing's never easy, especially when it wasn't entirely your fault.'

'I should never have said that about your father. It was unforgivable. It's my problem. I say things when they come into my head. I don't think about other people. I've tried to get my thoughts into some kind of holding pattern, but I can't. That's why they move me around. I upset people. You know that by now.'

'It's a sensitive subject . . . the revolution,' I said. 'We shouldn't have been talking about it after a day like that.'

'That's what my father said. He said it's not even a generation old. It's still raw.'

'And you . . . your generation can be objective about it. I'm still . . . I was . . . involved,' I said. 'What about your father?'

'He was a communist, a union activist in one of the shipyards. He did nearly four years in Caxias.'

We stood there nodding. The seriousness too big and awkward to be commented on. I felt like a man who'd joined hands with someone around the trunk of a massive tree. I steered him into the kitchen and sat him down with some coffee. He put the well-read newspaper down on the table.

'Anything interesting in that?' I asked.

'Catarina Oliveira's in there.'

'Is she?'

'You wouldn't have thought . . .'

I read the article. It was the facts of the case – where her body was found and when, the time of death, the school she went to, her Friday routine after school, the way she was killed, and most surprising of all, I got a mention.

'What do you make of it?' asked Carlos.

346

I shrugged. I didn't know. It was very unusual. If I was of a suspicious mind I might think it was Dr Aquilino Oliveira telling his friends to be careful who they talked to. I began to sense a higher profile to the case, a public face.

'It might throw up something we can use,' I said. 'What else?'

'There's a long article about this gold business.'

'I wasn't aware there was any gold business?'

'We're setting up a commission to look into it. There's been a lot of pressure from the United States, the European Community and Jewish organizations and we've been trying to squirm away from it but now, finally, we've got to do something about it.'

'We? Who? What?' I said. 'You sound like a Portuguese reporter, they say everything except the nugget you want to hear.'

'The government has set up a commission to look into Portuguese complicity in accepting looted Nazi gold in exchange for raw materials during the Second World War and, towards the end of the war, laundering the gold out to South America.'

'The government?'

'Actually no,' he said spreading out the newspaper, 'it's the governors of the Banco de Portugal. They've appointed a guy to look into their archives.'

'Who?'

'Some professor.'

'That's going to be a carefully managed exercise,' I said. 'Who's making us wash our linen in public?'

'The Americans. One of their senators says he has proof of Portuguese involvement . . . listen . . . our gold reserves in 1939 were nearly fifteen hundred million escudos, by 1946 they were nearly eleven thousand million. How about that?'

'So we sold a lot of raw materials in the war. That's not laundering. Where did all this gold come from?'

347

'Switz . . .' he started and stopped.

I followed his eyes. Olivia had come into the kitchen and sat down sideways on a chair at the table. She was in her shortest mini-skirt and a pair of her mother's strappy high heels. Her legs were long and honey-coloured already from a day on the beach. She crossed them and poured herself a cup of coffee. Her hair was brushed to a glossy blue blackness. Her lips were chilli-red. Her young breasts strained against a midnight-blue top which ended two inches above the waistband of the skirt showing the taut, brown skin of her belly.

'Going somewhere?' I asked.

She tossed her hair over her shoulder as if she'd been practising.

'Out,' she said. 'Later.'

'This is my new partner, Carlos Pinto.'

Her head turned as if there was a very expensive mechanism in her neck for smoothing things out. Her tongue was attached to her top lip.

'We met at the door.'

Carlos cleared his throat. We looked at him. He hadn't intended to draw attention to himself but he had to say something now. Remember the holding pattern.

'I had a fight with your father last night,' he said.

Never mind.

'Brawling in pubs,' she said in her fanciest English accent, 'I thought you were the police,' she finished in Portuguese.

'It was just the two of us,' he said.

'What about the barman?' I said. 'Don't forget the barman.'

'My father was fighting with everybody last night. You, me, my dead mother, the barman . . . did I miss anybody?'

'It was my fault,' said Carlos.

'What were you fighting about?' she asked.

'Nothing,' I said quickly.

'What about you?' asked Carlos.

'Me?' she said, and somehow stopped a blush from creeping along her jawline. 'Nothing too.'

'It was important at the time,' I said.

'And what was all that noise up in the attic last night?' she turned on me.

Carlos frowned. The cat loped in.

'I fell over in the dark,' I said. 'Where did you say you were going . . . later?'

'I've been invited to lunch by Sofia's parents.'

'Sofia?'

'The banker's daughter. The guy who gave you all that money for your beard.'

'You see a lot of them . . . the Rodrigues?'

'Sofia's in my class. She's . . .' Olivia hesitated, looked across at Carlos, whose eyes hadn't left her face. 'She's adopted. The past year we've been getting on. You know how it is.'

Carlos seemed to.

'I'll be in Lisbon this afternoon,' I said.

'I'll be going home,' said Carlos.

'If you're going to the station,' said Olivia, with a grab in her voice, forgetting that 'later' hadn't quite arrived. 'You could walk me up there.'

Olivia kissed me on the cheek and rubbed the lipstick in, something she liked doing, something she saw as grown-up.

'Don't forget to shave,' she said, rubbing her fingers together.

They left. I shaved and went down to the café and drank a *bica* with António Borrego. I felt relaxed after Olivia's performance. If a sixteen-year-old can manipulate two grown men then I might as well deliver myself into the hands of Luísa Madrugada and let her make a monkey or a man out of me.

*   *   *

I drove into Lisbon wrestling with my octopodial conscience. Should I really be taking a possible witness out to lunch when I didn't know her level of importance to the case? It was an ugly argument. That word *possible* became very important, and for once I let the impetuous personal beat the responsible professional into the ground.

I spent twenty minutes in Rua Actor Taborda sitting in my car waiting for the time to get less embarrassingly early. I was watching the entrance to a porno cinema, faintly interested in the type of people who would have the strength for *sessões contínuas* on a Sunday lunchtime. Apparently no one.

I rang the bell at 1.00 p.m. and to my slight disappointment Luísa came down to meet me. I didn't know what my subconscious had been hoping, but my stomach was telling me it wasn't to miss lunch. I wanted her to grab my arm, as Olivia would, and march down the street, which finally made me rein in on hope and instigate some equanimity. We went to a *cervejaria* on Avenida Almirante Reis, one in a chain well-known for their seafood. I wanted to stand at the bar because I liked to eat seafood in an informal way, but the bar area felt cheap and sleazy even with the magnified tanks of puzzled crayfish and lobster.

The waiter sat us in the window of the restaurant. There were two other couples and the rest of the cavernous interior was empty. We ordered a plate of large prawns and a couple of dressed crab and two beers.

'I have to admit you surprised me,' she said.

'By calling you up? I surprised myself, too.'

'Well, yes, that . . . but I meant you surprised me by being a policeman.'

'I don't look like one?'

'The ones you see are taken over by their jackboots and sunglasses. The ones you don't, people like you in the *Polícia Judiciária*, I don't know. I imagined them to be stern, hard men . . . weary too.'

350

'I was weary.'

'Weary of life . . . weary of the worst aspects of life. You were tired.'

The beers arrived. I offered her a cigarette and she sneered at the Ultralights and took out a pack of full-strength Marlboro. She lit the cigarettes with a petrol Zippo, which she buffed on the tablecloth as she looked into the tree-lined street outside. She rested her chin on the heel of her hand and smoked and thought about something that made her eyes greener.

'I've always thought,' she said, 'that if you want to be sad, Lisbon is the place to do it.'

'And you're sad?'

'I meant melancholy.'

'That's better, but . . .'

'I'm sad too, sitting up there in front of my computer on the first beautiful Sunday afternoon of summer.'

'But you're not . . . any more.'

'You're right,' she said and shook her head to get rid of it. Her strange and large earrings bounced off her cheeks.

'The earrings?' I asked.

'I have a friend who makes jewellery out of restaurant detritus. These were made out of the gold netting from a wine bottle.'

'I saw the spoons yesterday.'

'The spoons,' she said, her mind still elsewhere . . . on the beach with somebody else maybe. She went back to the window.

'You know why Lisbon's a sad place,' I said. 'It's never recovered from its history. Something terrible happened here which marked the place for ever. All those shaded, narrow alleyways, the dark gardens, the cypresses around the cemeteries, the steep cobbled streets, the black and white *calçada* in the squares, the views out over the red roofs to the slow river and the ocean . . . they've never shrugged off the fact that almost the entire population of the city was wiped out in an earthquake that happened nearly 250 years ago.'

Silence. Her chin pivoted on the heel of her hand. She blinked at me twice. What had I done?

'Poetic police,' she said.

'The Igreja do Carmo. Can you think of anywhere else in the world where they've left the skeleton of a cathedral in the heart of the city as a monument to all those that died?'

'No,' she said after a moment's thought.

'Hiroshima,' I said. 'That was the scale of it. Do you think Hiroshima will ever be a happy place?'

'Pensive police,' she said, and this time not joking.

'I can do pitiless police as well,' I said, thinking Hiroshima was not date talk.

'All right.'

I gave her my dead-eyed look reserved for lying mother-murderers. She shuddered.

'How many other police have you got in there?'

'Pleasant police,' I said, giving her my born-again-Christian smile.

'I don't believe pleasant police.'

I slumped in my chair, head on chest.

'And that?'

'The police that everybody wants to see . . . posthumous police.'

'You've got a diseased brain.'

'It helps with the job.'

The waiter put the prawns and crab down. We ordered two more beers. We ate the prawns. I liked her. She sucked the heads out, ladylike or not, she didn't give a damn.

'You don't look like a schoolteacher,' I said.

'Because I'm not. I'm the worst teacher I know. I love kids but I have no patience. I'm too aggressive. Two more weeks and I'm out.'

'Into what?'

She sized me up for a second to see if I was worth telling what she had to say, whether she wanted to go that far yet.

'I've been resisting it for some time, but now I'm going to do it. I'm going to run one of my father's businesses.'

She sucked hard on a prawn head, smacked her lips, wiped them and drank three-fifths of her beer down in three gulps.

'Just one of them?' I asked, and she stopped wiping her hands to check me for irony.

'I'm ambitious,' she said, tossing her napkin to one side.

The waiter lowered two more beers in front of us.

'For what?'

'For a life in which most, if not all, the decisions are my own.'

'Is this a recent development?'

She smiled and looked down at the shattered prawn shells on her plate.

'Was that perceptive police?'

I finished my first beer and started on the second.

'Have you been in business before?'

'I worked for my father for four years after university. We had a fight. We're the same type. I left and went to do a doctorate.'

'On what?'

'Was that deaf police? I told you yesterday, remember?'

'I was concentrating on other things.'

'I know,' she said, and suddenly quantum mechanics came back into my life. I was aware of every photon between us.

'Your turn to be perceptive,' I said.

'The Economics of Salazar,' she said, slowly. 'The Portuguese Economy from 1928–1968.'

'We don't have to discuss it now, do we?'

'Not unless you can do it on your own.'

'Which of your father's businesses are you going to run?'

'He owns a publishing company.'

'What does it publish?'

'Too many male writers. Not enough fiction. No genre fiction, like crime or romance. No children's books. I want to change all that. I want to get people who don't read to read. Get them hooked, grow them.'

'The Portuguese take literature like their food – seriously.'

'You're a policeman and you've never read a crime novel?'

'I'm worried it's going to be as boring as the real thing, and if it isn't it won't ring true.'

'You're missing the point. A thirteen-year-old will never read José Saramago but give him a crime novel and by the time he's seventeen he will.'

'And then what'll happen to our great footballing nation?'

'They'll be well-read footballers,' she said and laughed a deep, dirty laugh that probably came from smoking Marlboro but what the hell, it made my chest boom, my spine prickle. We ate the crabs, drank more beer and talked about books, films, actors, celebrities, drugs, fame, success and I ordered a lobster split and grilled and Luísa said she'd pay for a *vinho verde* Soalheiro Alvarinho 96 which had more spunk to it than any *vinho verde* I've ever tasted. So we ordered a second bottle and drank that down in flashing gulps and two and a half hours after we'd arrived we fell out of the air conditioning and into the hot empty street with no traffic, no people and the trees still in the siesta silence.

We walked arm in arm. At the door of her apartment building she grabbed hold of my wrist and half-pulled me up the stairs. She only let go to get her keys out and then we were in the dark corridor, kissing, and she kicked the door shut with a bang so loud, glasses tinkled in the kitchen cupboards.

She led me through the living room, walking out of her sandals into her bedroom where she turned and yanked the shirt out of my trousers and ran her hands up my chest. She shrugged and the straps fell off her shoulders and the dress to the floor. She tore my jeans down my thighs. I wrestled out of my shirt. She gripped me through my undershorts and looked up with eyes that dared me. She pulled the shorts out and over and stripped down her own panties. I pulled her to me and she jumped and wrapped her legs around my waist, crooked an arm around my neck. She lowered herself slowly, her pubic hair scratching my belly, impossibly hot, heat beyond human tolerance, until we connected and she held herself there until we were both trembling, shuddering. She straightened her arms and leaned back smiling at me, smiling at my agony and, as we fell on to the bed, I felt like the surfer who feels the big wave hump underneath him, tons of ocean drawn up, the surge, the roll, the terrific speed and monumental collapse.

The traffic woke us. The Lisboans coming home at dusk. Wordlessly, we crawled into each other and made love again. The mirror looked darkly on. A red light passed across the scrap of velvet sky visible from the open window, followed by the sound of thumping helicopter blades. The room smelled of sex – sweat, perfume and something sweet like berry juice smeared on skin. Life felt suddenly rich, the city ripe, the room wine-dark and full of easy, complex possibilities.

I don't know how I got myself out of her apartment. There was a brief leaden moment and I was in the car, heading out of the city through the darkening Monsanto park, with her body smell still on me and something unfurling in my chest like the sails of a flotilla setting out.

The earth felt solid under my feet in Paço de Arcos. As I let myself into the house I had that feeling of money in the bank and a fridge full of food, neither of which was true.

It was 10.00 p.m. There was a light on in the kitchen and voices. Olivia was tucked tight under the kitchen table listening to Faustinho, a local fisherman, who was sprawled on a chair well back from the table barely within reach of his beer. He was working himself up into a lather about the government, the European Union's fishing quotas and Benfica in ascending order.

He struggled to his feet when I came in. Olivia looked relieved, tired. We kissed.

'You smell different,' she said and went to bed.

Faustinho, grey as a wolf, tossed his beer back and put an arm around my shoulder.

'Come,' he said, 'you have to see this boy. He saw something the other night. It'll help with your investigation. You must talk to him. Have you got any money?'

We walked to the gardens and through the underpass to the car park on the other side of the Marginal. Faustinho strode ahead, looking under boats, in the sheds. I lagged behind, enjoying some purposelessness.

'What's the rush?' I shouted after him.

'It's been an hour already,' he said.

'I thought you said he was bedding down for the night.'

'He's a street kid, anything could have happened. Maybe he got scared.'

'You didn't tell him I was the police.'

'No, no, but I've been gone an hour and maybe he starts thinking.'

'You know this kid?'

'I've seen him before. Skinny little bugger. He's got some black in him too. Wears a jacket two sizes too big for him.'

We searched the boatyard and car park. Nothing. I sat on the keel of a boat and smoked and looked out to sea, feeling useful. We went back to *A Bandeira Vermelha* and drank *aguardente* distilled from *vinho verde* that António had brought down from the Minho in five-litre flagons.

Faustinho gave another longer description of the kid, having persuaded himself that I didn't believe him. António and I leaned into each other on either side of the bar and looked impassively on as Faustinho measured the kid up with the aid of his own shoulder.

I strolled home in the warm night. I hovered at the bottom of the attic stair, tempted. I went into the bedroom, stripped and got between the sheets naked, still with her smell on me.

Chapter XXIX

16th July 1964, Pensão Isadora, Praça da Alegria, Lisbon.

Manuel Abrantes woke up with a jerk, staring at the threadbare central panel of the bedside carpet. His moustache was full of sweat, his head confused by alcohol gone bad in his brain. He didn't know the room until the smell of cheap perfume made it through his dense nasal hair and a light snoring at his back reminded him some more. He looked over his shoulder trying to remember a face or a name. Neither came to him. She was young and a little fat. She was lying on her back, the sheet down around her waist. Her breasts were widely spaced and had slipped down her ribs under her armpits. She had a light moustache. Her Alentejano accent came back to him.

He got up, wiped the sweat out of his moustache and was repelled by the smell of the girl still on him. He found a towel and went down the corridor to the bathroom. He showered under a trickle of tepid water standing up in a cast-iron bath. A small headache had emerged which didn't bother him, and a sore penis which did. They always tell you they're clean, but . . .

He dressed. His shirt was in a ghastly state. Yesterday the weather had been torrid and he'd drunk too much and that had made him sweat doubly. He'd have to go to work via the family house in Lapa and pick up a fresh shirt. A suit, too. This one was trampled to death. He looked like a broken salesman rather than an *agente de 1° classe* in the *Polícia Internacional e de Defesa do Estado* (PIDE) and still not even twenty-two years old.

He clicked a coin down on the bedside table and left. He looked for his car in the Praça da Alegria, until he remembered he'd left it up in the Bairro Alto. He walked down Rua da Glória and caught the funicular up the hill and found his car parked on Rua Dom Pedro V. He drove to Lapa. The house was silent. The rest of the family were in the Estoril villa for the summer. He shaved, showered, moved his bowels massively and changed into fresh clothes which felt cool around his chafed penis.

He straightened himself up in the mirror, pulled his shirt loose over his gut and then tucked it back in again, undecided which looked better. He had wanted to be at his best for this day's work and it had all started badly, but he hoped he'd pulled himself back on track now.

He drove out on to the Marginal and noticed for the first time on the outskirts of the city that the air was fresher and purer. After five days of brutal swelter, the sea was blue again, the sky clear and the twin steel towers of the Ponte Salazar, the new suspension bridge being built across the Tagus, were pin-sharp in the flat calm of the estuary. The workmen were already out on the massive concrete ramp, preparing to string the first cable across the river.

He stopped off in Belém to take a coffee and a *pastel de nata* in the Antiga Confeitaria. He ate three and smoked a cigarette. Now that his body was clean and his stomach sweetened he began to relish his work. He'd been with the PIDE for two and a half years and hadn't regretted a moment. He'd spent his first year in the PIDE headquarters in Rua António Maria Cardoso in the Chiado district of Lisbon, where he'd demonstrated to his superiors a natural talent for the work. They didn't even have to tell him how to recruit informers. He knew. He found out people's weaknesses, he implied PIDE interest in their activities, and then saved them from arrest and the dreaded Caxias prison by bringing them into his network. It surprised him that his most significant weapon was charm. He'd thought he

359

was devoid of it, but he'd learnt more than he'd thought from his elder brother, Pedro, and now that he was in a new world, where he had no history, he could use what previously he'd only observed. It was so facile. Charm was just a question of demeanour. If he smiled people liked him. The smiling made his long-lashed, blue-green eyes shine, which attracted their attention, while his moustache made him appear genial, and his thinning hair gave him an air of vulnerability so that, overall, people trusted him. He never made the mistake of despising people for this because he was so glad to be liked. He just made sure that his superiors knew that this carefully crafted exterior concealed a ruthless persistence, an unflinching severity, and an unswerving relish for following through.

Manuel asked the barman at the Antiga Confeitaria to make up a packet of six *pastéis de nata*. He crushed out his cigarette, paid and drove to the Caxias prison.

In his first year at the PIDE headquarters he'd been particularly successful at rooting out dissent in the university. It had been easier than he'd expected. His brother was at the university. He was very popular. His friends were constantly in the house. Manuel listened. He took down names and fed them into his network. He did more recruiting. He cajoled, threatened and manipulated until by the end of 1963 he had compiled dossiers on two professors, who would never work again, and eight students whose futures were over before they'd even begun. His superiors were impressed. His father wanted him to root out all the union men and communists from his factories, and was annoyed to find that he didn't have the influence over this institution that he'd come to expect elsewhere. Manuel was moved to the interrogation centre in the Caxias prison where the *Estado Novo* detained their more serious, more politically active dissidents. These people needed more persuasive methods to encourage them to help PIDE uncover the network of communist cells threatening not just the

the stability of the government, but the country's whole way of life.

The first months in Caxias were spent honing his interrogation skills, partly through practice but initially by watching more experienced men through a recently installed two-way mirror. The new mirror excited Manuel. It brought back memories of childhood. He liked to sit close to it, almost with his nose touching, and sometimes with the prisoner's face pressed right up against it on the other side. The pleasure was exquisite, almost sexual for him, to openly observe, without being seen, a man's shattered face as he was brought to the limits of his endurance.

This was another part of the training – the breaking-down of the prisoner. The preferred method was a combination of sleep deprivation and random beatings. They had installed sound equipment which, with little supervision, could keep a prisoner awake for days. They still used the old method, the statue, where the prisoner was made to lean against a wall, his bodyweight supported by his fingertips, but it was time-consuming and required regular beatings and therefore manpower.

Manuel parked up outside the fort. He put his jacket on, picked up his briefcase and the cakes and remembered with a thrill the reason why he'd bought the girl the night before, and why he'd particularly wanted one with an Alentejana accent. He showed his pass, which the guard ignored. He walked across the inner courtyard to the interrogation centre. Waiting for him in his office was Jorge Raposo, an overweight twenty-one-year-old from Caldas da Rainha who was an *agente de 2° classe*. He was talking to another *agente* about an English pop group called the Beatles and their new single called 'Can't Buy Me Love'. Jorge was translating the title into Portuguese but he shut up when Manuel came in and the other agent slipped out after a hurried *bom dia*.

'What's his problem?' asked Manuel, laying his briefcase down and the packet of cakes. Jorge shrugged and eyed the cakes. 'We haven't got to the stage where we're reporting each other for listening to pop music.'

Jorge shrugged again, lit a cigarette and turned the box of matches over and over on his desk.

'So, you like the Beatles,' said Manuel.

'Sure,' said Jorge, sitting back and blowing smoke at the ceiling.

'She loves me yeah, yeah, yeah,' said Manuel in English, to show he was groovy, too.

'She loves you . . .' said Jorge.

'What?'

'She loves *you* yeah, yeah, yeah. Not "me".'

Manuel grunted and sat at his desk and laid his hands down flat. Jorge regretted correcting him now. He thought it might have an impact on the cake situation.

'What have we got today?' asked Manuel.

Jorge stuck his cigarette back into the corner of his mouth and looked down at his papers wondering how he could remedy the situation. The name sprang off the page.

'There's always that Maria Antónia Medinas girl,' said Jorge, who saw immediately that he'd hit the right button.

'Ah, yes,' said Manuel, frowning as if he'd forgotten her, 'the girl from Reguengos.'

'The one with the blonde hair . . . the blue eyes . . .'

'And I thought they were all Arabs out there,' said Manuel. 'You know . . . dusky . . . Moorish.'

'*She* certainly isn't,' said Jorge, licking his lips.

'Shut up, Jorge, and have a cake,' said Manuel quickly.

Jorge opened up the packet and took two.

'God, they're good,' he said. 'We should bring some cinnamon to the office.'

'Get them to bring up the Medinas girl,' said Manuel.

Jorge reached for the internal phone.

'Do you want to talk to her or . . . ?'

'No, no, I'll watch this time,' said Manuel.

*   *   *

The girl stood in the interrogation room. Jorge moved her up close to the mirror. Manuel looked into her face, haggard now from lack of sleep. The blue eyes were dark and sunken. She blinked frequently in the harsh strip-lit room. Her hair was beginning to grease up. She was scared but keeping it to herself. Manuel felt pity and admiration. She stood with her shoulders square in a tight-fitting grey top with four buttons that started between her jutting breasts and finished at her neck. She wore a grey calf-length skirt and a pair of black pumps. She was neat and still looked clean, apart from her hair.

Jorge began with the same litany of questions. He wanted to know about the copies of the communist rag *Avante* which had been found in her possession as she'd tried to board a ferry in Cais do Sodré. Her answers were the same. She didn't know anything. She'd picked up the packet by mistake. They weren't given to her. She didn't know about any clandestine printing operations. She didn't know any names. She didn't know any addresses of safe houses.

. Jorge grilled her for two hours. She stuck rigidly to her story. When Jorge's questions flagged and she began to drift into sleep he'd slap her awake and make her stand in the crucifix position and do knee-bends until she was sobbing. After the third hour Jorge had her sent back down to the cells.

The political side of the prison was overcrowded and they'd had to put the sleep deprivation equipment in one of the cells in the long-term block for criminals. The guard took her down, strapped her on to the hard wooden bench and clamped the earphones over her head. Felsen watched through a crack in the grille of his cell door, such comings and goings were interesting to a man to whom nothing had happened for two years. And to see a woman, too.

Jorge and Manuel went out to lunch. They ate fish, drank a bottle of white wine and two *bagaços* each. In the afternoon they interrogated a further four prisoners. At five o'clock Jorge went home. Manuel went down to the sound room. He took the keys from the guard and let himself in to the narrow cell. Maria Antónia Medinas lay on the board, convulsing under the straps. The noise pounding through her head was faintly audible from the door. Manuel turned the machine off. Her body stilled. He leaned over her, hands clasped behind his back. The good doctor. She looked wild, confused and frightened, like a car-crash survivor staring up through a shattered windscreen. Muscles twitched. Her breasts heaved.

Manuel lifted off the earphones. She swallowed hard. He brushed the hank of hair off her forehead, which was clammy cold with sweat. He wiped his soft, dry palms together slowly and sat on the edge of the bed. He smiled without showing his teeth. The good father. The sick child.

'It's been hard,' he said, in the softest, most calming voice he could find. 'I know how it's been. But it's over now. You can go to sleep. A long deep sleep. Then we'll have a little talk and, you'll see, after that everything will be all right.'

He patted her cheek. Her lids dropped. Her mouth crinkled oddly and a tear crept down her cheek. He wiped it away with his thumb. Her eyes opened. He could see her gratitude.

'Don't say anything yet,' he said. 'You sleep first. We'll have time, plenty of time, later.'

Her eyes closed and her mouth slackened in her face. He replaced the silent headphones over her ears. He left her and instructed the guard that nobody was to go into the cell.

Manuel drove west to Estoril. He felt good. He felt happy. For once he wanted the company of family. They ate dinner together, his father, Pica and Pedro. There was a festive mood in the house with everybody finding their appetite again after the days of brutal swelter. They all agreed to go up to the cool of the mountains in the Beira for holidays in August.

Manuel slept until his alarm at 2.00 a.m. He woke up with a leap in his heart, a strangling excitement. He dressed and made a cheese sandwich with the best *Queijo da Serra* and drove back to the Caxias prison.

The guard was playing cards on a different floor and it took some time for Manuel to find him and get the keys. He let himself into the cell and relocked the door. He heard her rhythmical breathing. He undid the straps on the bed. The girl rolled on her side and curled up. He sat and rested his hand on her hip. He shook her shoulder. She whimpered. He kept at it, jiggling her small shoulderbone between his thumb and forefinger. She came awake with a desperate sigh. She rolled and her eyes snapped open, straight into fear.

'Don't be scared,' he said, holding up his hands, showing no weapons, no intent.

She pushed herself up the bed and sat with her back to the wall, her knees tucked up under her chin. One of her shoes was missing. He retrieved it from the floor. He put it next to her bare foot. She slipped into it. She remembered this man. The kind one. The one to watch.

'I have something for you,' he said, and gave her the cheese sandwich wrapped in a paper napkin.

'Water,' she said, hoarsely.

He found the guard's clay pitcher full of cool water. She drank heavily, the spout of the pitcher not once touching her lips. Water spilled over her lip and dripped down her chin darkening a patch on the top of her left breast. She checked the inside of the sandwich and ate it. Then she drank again, not knowing when the kindness was going to stop.

Manuel offered her a cigarette. She didn't smoke. He lit one himself and paced the room. He gave her the last *pastel de nata* he'd bought that morning. She wolfed it.

She rested the back of her head against the wall. He's strange this one, she thought, but they're all the same underneath. Manuel suddenly sat down, close to her, so that she inched back her feet. He crushed out the cigarette with his foot. He looked at her throat.

'What do you do in Reguengos?' he asked.

'I'm a loom operator. I make *mantas*.' Blankets.

'Is the factory closed for the summer?'

'No. They gave me time off to come and see my uncle.'

She tried to take it back once it was out. She'd never spoken about the uncle before. Manuel noted it, but ignored the obvious. It would all come out in the end. She clasped her fingers together around her knees as if that would stop other things leaking out. You have to watch this one.

'There's a big fair for *mantas* down south somewhere, isn't there?' asked Manuel.

'Castro Verde.'

'I've never been.'

'There's not much call for *mantas* from Lisboans,' she said, and he felt a little stupid.

'It's true, it's true,' he said. 'I'm from the Beira myself.'

'I know.'

'How's that?'

'The cheese in the sandwich,' she said, to show him she was sharp again.

'My father has it brought down, and all the *chouriços, morcelas* and *presuntos*. The best in Portugal, without a doubt.'

'There's nothing wrong with a good *paio Alentejano*.'

'The heat. The heat's not good for it. It sharpens the meat.'

'We have ways of keeping things cool.'

'Of course, the cork.'

'And the cork oak produces acorns, which feed the pigs, which makes . . .'

'You could be right,' he said, enjoying himself talking like this with a woman. 'We only think of the heat when we talk of the Alentejo.'

366

And communists, she thought.

'And the wine,' she said.

'Yes, excellent *tinto*, but I prefer Dão.'

'You would, coming from up there.'

'When this is all over you should let me show you . . .' he let the sentence drift.

She stiffened inside and looked intensely at the man's ear. He was staring across the room, smiling. He turned. Their eyes connected.

'When what's all over?' she asked.

'This resistance.'

'Whose resistance . . . to what?'

'Your resistance,' he said and looked down.

He ran a finger and thumb around her slim ankle and then drew them down her foot to the rim of her shoe. The touch shot panic up to her throat. She wanted to squeal. She pressed her head back into the wall, closed her eyes for a moment to gather herself. He smiled at her. When she reopened her eyes he was closer, his soft face moving closer, his full, red lips under the moustache, parted.

'*Filho da puta*,' she said, under her breath, but they were so close her breath mingled with his, and he reared back as if she'd slapped him.

Things happened in the man's face. The softness went. The jaw bunched. The eyes closed a fraction and walled over. His large soft hand reached over her knees and grabbed a twist of her blonde greasy hair. He yanked her head round so sharply her body was forced to follow.

She was kneeling on the edge of the bed, her neck stretched back. He pushed her face into the corner, his thick fist bunched in the back of her head. A hand reached round and wrenched the skirt out from under her knees. Her voice left her. Nothing would come up over her voice box. Her cheekbones hurt where he forced her face into the corner. She felt her skirt come up over her thighs. She lashed out with her fist behind her. He pulled her

367

head back and thudded her face into the wall. Her skirt was around her waist. He tore at her underwear like a feral animal. It had gone green inside her head and she couldn't get things straight any more. There was only one moment when she managed the faintest cry of the smallest child in the night. Pain flashed between her legs. Her body jolted. Her forehead thumped into the wall.

It was over in less than a minute. She slid off the bed on to the floor. Her face cold against the rough concrete floor. She vomited the cheese sandwich and water. He tried to pull her up but she was a dead weight. He kicked her in the stomach, harder than he'd intended. Something like an organ seemed to break inside her. He grabbed hold of her leg and hair and pushed a knee into her belly and heaved her up on to the bed. The pain reached right up to the top of the inside of her head.

He rolled her over, strapped her down, replaced the earphones. Breathing heavily, he pinched his nose with thumb and forefinger and flicked a hank of sweat and snot on to the floor. He turned on the sound machine. Her body strained. He zipped up his fly with a short, sharp jerk. He picked up the pitcher and left the cell.

As he relocked the door the flesh at the back of his neck began to crawl. He heard his name whispered softly over and over. Manuel. Manuel. Manuel. The cell corridor was empty. He shuddered, picked up the pitcher and nearly ran back to the guard's empty chair.

He drove back to the house in Lapa needing to be quiet and alone. He drank heavily, *aguardente* directly from the bottle. He slept deeply and horribly until late. He was woken by the sun streaming through the undrawn curtains, the clap of the palm trees in a nearby garden, the noise of children playing. His face was hot, swollen and sweaty. His insides felt black.

He showered and soaped himself until his body squeaked, but he couldn't get shot of the blackness in his gut. He drove to Belém and had a coffee but couldn't get a *pastel de nata* down his constricted throat. He was an hour and a half late getting to work. Jorge Raposo was waiting for him.

'We've got a problem,' he said, and Manuel's black guts ran cave-cold.

'Do we?'

'The Medinas girl. She's dead.'

'Dead?!' he said, the blood vacating his head so that he had to sit down.

'The guard found her this morning. Blood everywhere,' he said, waving a hand distastefully around the genital area.

'Has the doctor seen her?'

'That's how we know she's dead. She miscarried. Died of internal and, by the looks of it, external bleeding.'

'Miscarried? Did we know she was pregnant?'

'No, we didn't, and by the way, the boss wants to see you.'

'Narciso?'

Jorge shrugged and looked at Manuel's hands.

'No cakes today?'

Major Virgilio Duarte Narciso eased the phone back on to its cradle and smoked the last inch of his cigarette as if each drag was lacerating his lungs. Manuel had been trying to cross his legs but he was in such a sweat that the material stuck to every inch of his lower limbs and he just couldn't get one over the other. His boss, the major, rubbed the end of his large, brown nose, as thick as the thumb of a boxing glove with every pore visible, as if they'd been pricked there.

'You're being transferred,' he said.

'But . . .'

'In this matter there is no argument. The orders have come down from the Director himself. You are to head a team responsible for bringing that charlatan General

369

Machedo to justice. We've had an intelligence report that he is over in Spain preparing another coup attempt. You are being promoted to *chefe de brigada* with immediate effect and you will be briefed by the Director himself this afternoon in Lisbon. There. What do you think of that? You don't look very happy, *agente* Abrantes.'

Manuel still found himself staring into the cold crevasse of his own thoughts.

'I'm honoured,' he stammered. 'I thought I was too young for such a promotion.'

The major closed an eye and looked at him shrewdly.

'Caxias is no place for a man of your ability.'

'I thought you wanted to see me about the Medinas girl.'

'Who's she?'

'She died in her cell last night. Miscarried. Internal bleeding.'

The beat of silence was broken by the phone ringing. It jolted them both and the major yanked it to his ear. His secretary informed him that his son, Jaime, had been taken to hospital with a broken wrist after falling out of a tree. Major Narciso hung up, mesmerized by the space between himself and Manuel until he refocused once more. Manuel tried and failed to swallow.

'Ah,' said Narciso, finally crushing out the cigarette, whose end was stinging his nail, 'one less communist for us to worry about.'

On February 19th 1965 Manuel Abrantes was having dinner in a small restaurant in Badajoz in Spain, no more than two kilometres from the Portuguese border. His two fellow-diners were enjoying themselves and Manuel himself was a mask of geniality. In two hours' time he and his two companions would be taking a short walk to a dark place for a meeting with a Portuguese army officer from the barracks in Estremoz, who would outline the strategy which could be the beginning of a new life for eight million Portuguese. Manuel's two dinner companions were General Machedo and his secretary, Paulo Abreu.

This meeting had taken six months to bring off, not to mention the four previous years PIDE had spent infiltrating the top echelons of General Machedo's entourage. Manuel had arrived at the best possible time. He'd brought fresh ideas to a man who'd spent the best part of a decade in exile. He'd cured the melancholia that surrounded the General and had infected him with a new optimism. Around Manuel, the General had begun to believe in a future.

The February night was cold and the heating in the restaurant inadequate. They sat in their coats and drank brandy to quell the shivers. At 11.00 p.m. a man came in and drank a coffee at their table. Fifteen minutes later they put on their hats and made the short two-hundred-metre walk to the churchyard, where the meeting was supposed to take place. There was a half-moon in a freezing clear sky and they had no trouble seeing their way. The man who'd come to their table walked a few metres ahead of them. The men didn't speak. The General's shoulders were hunched against the cold.

Inside the churchyard the man told them to wait in a narrow passage between some marble mausoleums. The General looked through the window of one and remarked on the smallness of the coffins.

'They must have been children,' said his secretary, which were his last words. A hammer struck him on the back of the head and his forehead broke the glass in the mausoleum door. The General stepped back, shocked, and found two men on his shoulders. His hands were lifted out of his pockets and held behind him. He watched in horror as his secretary was strangled in front of him. Even in his unconscious state Paulo Abreu struggled to hold on, his legs straightening and straightening until they were still and the feet slack.

The General was forced to his knees. The man who'd come to the restaurant removed a handgun from one pocket and a silencer from the other. He screwed them together and handed the piece to *chefe de brigada*, Manuel Abrantes, who looked down at the General whose hat had fallen off in front of him. The face, the whole body of the old man was suddenly completely exhausted. The General shook his head but his neck couldn't support it and it sank on to his chest.

'*We* must have been children,' he said, bitterly.

Manuel Abrantes placed the muzzle of the silencer on the back of the General's head and squeezed the trigger. There was a dull thud and the man shot forward with such force that his arms were torn from the grip of the two PIDE men.

Manuel handed the gun back to the *agente*. He reached down to the General and felt for a neck pulse. There was nothing.

'Where are the graves?' he asked.

The man with the gun walked down the corridor of mausoleums and turned left to a corner of the churchyard. The holes were barely a foot deep.

'What the hell is this?' said Manuel.

'The ground was too hard.'

'Bloody idiots.'

Chapter XXX

Monday, 15th June 199–, Avenida Duque de Ávila, Saldanha, Lisbon.

By 7.00 a.m. I was washed, inexpertly shaved, suited and standing outside the Liceu D. Dinis on the corner of Duque de Ávila and República, enjoying the early cool of the day. I'd woken up at 5.00 a.m. wanting it to be my summer holiday, with nothing to think about other than book choice, beach position and lunch. The photos in my pocket of Catarina Oliveira jolted me back on to the rails. I was going to work on the streets around the school to see if there was anything in Jamie Gallacher's car pick-up story.

I had a *bica* in the Pastelaria Sequeira on the corner opposite the art nouveau school building and asked myself if I felt lucky. I had to after a weekend like that and immediately I drew a blank from the staff of the *pastelaria*. I went up to the café Bella Italia whose barman had seen Catarina come in for a coffee after the session in the Pensão Nuno. It wasn't the same barman as on Saturday, but he pointed me to an old woman who sat in the window.

'It's her first shift,' he said. 'Morning, lunchtime, end of the afternoon. Nothing happens on that stretch of pavement that she doesn't know about.'

I spoke to her. The skin of her face was like crêpe paper. She wore white gloves with a single button at the wrist, a heavily pleated blue dress and hefty white, leather low-heeled shoes. She nodded at the photo of the girl. She'd seen her with a man that fitted Jamie Gallacher's description.

'They were not happy,' she said, and returned the photo.

Fifty metres down the street from the Bella Italia was the traffic light where Avenida 5° de Outubro crossed Duque de Ávila. This was the point where Jamie Gallacher said Catarina got into the car. The crossroads was surrounded by apartment and office buildings. This was a place of work. At that time of the afternoon there must have been plenty of people on the street heading for their weekend. I went to the bus stop opposite the Bella Italia. As the time approached 8.00 a.m. more people arrived. If Gallacher had hit the girl there must have been someone on this side of the street who'd been at the bus stop and seen it.

Marshalling Portuguese people is not an easy thing to do, even when they're from the same family and heading for lunch, but when they're getting off a bus on the way to work they become a thunderous herd. But I was lucky that day, and so was Jamie Gallacher. I found a twenty-five-year-old marketing executive who worked for an international computer company on 5° de Outubro. She'd seen the man hit the girl and walk away down Duque de Ávila. She saw three cars pull up at the traffic light. The first was small and silver, the second one was large and dark, the third white. The driver of the second car, dimly visible behind tinted glass, had leaned across the seat and shouted out of the window. The girl had come off the pavement. They'd talked briefly. The lights had changed, the silver car took off and the girl got into the passenger seat. The car had crossed Avenida 5° de Outubro and headed in the direction of the Gulbenkian Museum and the Museum of Modern Art complex.

'Did you see what make of car it was?'

'I was looking at the girl most of the time,' she said. 'I'd seen him slap her face and if he'd gone after her I'd have done something, but he didn't, he fell back on a car and its alarm went off.'

'The car the girl got into, did it look expensive?'

'It was new. The windows were tinted . . . that's all I can tell you. You can talk to my work colleague who was with me. He's a guy, he'll know about the car.'

The woman's work colleague remembered the car. Without a doubt, he said, it was a black Mercedes.

'If I send you some Mercedes brochures do you think you could give me a series type and a model number?'

He shrugged his eyebrows.

I took down their telephone numbers and walked back to the *Polícia Judiciária* building. I took a slight detour so that I could walk the length of Rua Actor Taborda and look up at Luísa's attic window. I knew she wasn't there but I wanted to enjoy feeling young and foolish. I succeeded on one count only.

I went to the personnel department in the PJ building to follow up Jorge's lead on the private detective who'd been sniffing around after Catarina in the Pensão Nuno. I asked one of the older guys if he knew of any retired policemen who were currently engaged in private work. He gave me a list of six names.

'Do you know any of these guys to look at?'

'Most of them. If I haven't seen them in the flesh I've seen their photographs.'

'Short, stocky, grey hair, no facial hair, brown eyes . . . wears a black, brimmed hat which he never takes off.'

'Lourenço Gonçalves. He was bald and had a red birthmark on the back of his head which was why he never took the hat off.'

'Have you got a number for him?'

He told me to try the phone book and gave me the full name.

I went up to my office. Carlos had the search warrant for Valentim's garage unit. I sent him out to get the Mercedes brochures and take them round to the computer company. I had Jamie Gallacher brought up from the *tacos*. I

375

called Lourenço Gonçalves' apartment in Benfica. There was no reply.

I pumped Gallacher for more information on the car. He was in poor shape, but relieved and keen to help. When I saw invention begin to play behind his eyes I sent him back to the cells.

I sat down and, in an hour and a half, wrote a six-page report on the investigation. Carlos came back towards the end of that time and said that the car had been identified as a C series. I rounded off the report, collected the statements together and sent them up to Narciso. I tried Gonçalves again. Still no reply. He must have a place of business. I dropped it for the moment.

By 11.30 a.m. I was sitting in front of Narciso, watching him smoke his SG Gigantes and fingering my report as if it might be worth something. He went to the window. He was a small man in his mid-forties who took such care over his appearance that you'd have thought he was due on television at any moment. Even in high humidity he could always get his shirts to puff out at the back and the creases down his arms were never anything less than blade-sharp. He looked more powerful and cooler than any policeman in the building.

'How's it going with *agente* Pinto?' he asked, something I'd forgotten about already.

'There's nothing wrong with *agente* Pinto, he'll make a good detective.'

'Answer the question will you, Inspector.'

'Nobody likes him, I know.'

'And you do?'

'I have no problem with him.'

'I heard there was a fight across the street on Saturday night. Your hand, you cut your hand.'

'And that fight wasn't his first?'

'I'm surprised to hear you like him, that's all.'

'He has a difficult personality but it doesn't bother me.'

Narciso turned his smooth handsome face on me. It had darkened a few shades over the sunny weekend but it hadn't warmed him up – he was still and chill as always.

'The one concern I have about your report is this spurious allegation from *Senhora* Oliveira about child abuse.'

'I presume she didn't make a formal complaint.'

'No, she didn't,' he said. 'She died yesterday.'

Silence. The air conditioning reached my bone marrow.

'You make that sound like natural causes.'

He shook his head.

'Overdose,' he said. 'She was found in her car parked on a street in São João do Estoril, about three hundred metres from a friend's house where she'd spent the night.'

'A considerate woman,' I said, more guilt humped up on to my shoulders.

'We're looking into it now.'

'Who is?'

'Inspector Abílio Gomes.'

'Ask him to make sure that Dr Aquilino Dias Oliveira can account for every minute of his Saturday night.'

'Which brings us back to your report.'

'The allegation, you mean.'

'An allegation made to the wrong person on an informal basis with no supporting evidence by an unstable woman with a history of barbiturate dependency.'

'Has the maid said anything?'

'Not that I know of.'

'You don't think it warrants inclusion in the report?'

'That was a good day's work, Inspector. Let's see what Valentim Almeida's garage unit produces. I want to see your report on that and the interview with him afterwards.'

I grabbed Carlos, signed out a car from the pool and headed north to Odivelas. We sat in a traffic jam on Campo Grande for half an hour. I told him about Teresa Oliveira which silenced us for several minutes. Horns blared, indifferently. Techno music thumped loudly from behind tinted windows adjacent.

'You're right about Olivia,' he said, seeing as we were following a van with that name on the back.

'Are we talking about my daughter now?'

'She's different.'

'Half-Portuguese, three-quarters English,' I said. 'What did she talk to you about?'

'She told me about a kid at her school who has his own Range Rover.'

'That doesn't sound like her to be impressed.'

'She wasn't. That's what I meant. She's different. She asked me what I thought a seventeen-year-old kid with a Range Rover could aspire to.'

'A test question – what did you say?'

'I said it could leave him free to aspire to greater things than more material wealth.'

'Did she buy that?'

'No,' he said. 'She thought he'd already been corrupted. It was good. I found I was arguing against myself for once.'

'She likes that,' I said, looking across at his face staring resolutely out of the windscreen. 'Ideas. Arguing. Intellectual aggression . . . it's something she rarely sees in girls her own age. What would you call her . . . ?'

I got his attention.

'A chicken with giblets?' I asked.

The traffic jam unlocked. The vertebrae of metal snake stretched. The techno music behind the tinted glass took off. Other things were playing on Carlos' mind.

'You were in there a long time,' he said.

'What are we talking about now?'

'With Narciso,' he said. 'Was that all you talked about . . . *Senhora* Oliveira's suicide?'

'And her allegation against her husband.'

378

'Anything else about the investigation in general?' he hedged.

'He asked how we were getting on, too.'

Carlos' hand tightened around the ceiling grip.

'I suppose he knew about the fight,' he said.

'Not your first by all accounts.'

'I had one with Fernandes in Vice.'

'I don't know Fernandes,' I said. 'What happened?'

'Fernandes is a pig,' he said, jutting his face at the windscreen. 'He had something going with some pimps and their girls. He wanted to initiate me into his little score. I refused. He asked me if little boys was more my thing and I hit him.'

'You've got to try and lengthen that fuse of yours, you know.'

'I overdid it, too. I punched him in the gut and he didn't get off the floor for fifteen minutes. I was transferred away from him the next day.'

'I'm glad we didn't get that far.'

'I'd never have hit you. You had every right to be angry. When I told my father what I'd said to you, he damn nearly beat me up himself.'

'He sounds a good man.'

'He's a hard, proud Alentejano who still eats pig's tail and ears at Christmas.'

'Boiled or what?'

'No, no, grilled.'

'He must be a hard man.'

It was lunchtime when we arrived at the garage units and most of the others were closed. Only a tyre shop was doing any business. We let ourselves in through the small door and walked into a black partition wall and the smell of death.

The lights didn't work. We took out pen torches. Carlos squeezed past a wooden staircase and went through a black curtain underneath. I went up the stairs. Carlos gagged at the smell getting stronger. I came out on to a platform in the roof gable. I still couldn't find the fuse box for the unit. There was an expensive piece of computer equipment, a video camera and a television. Along the wall were seven polystyrene heads with wigs. All the eyes had been burnt out with cigarette ends.

'*Porra!*' said Carlos. Fucking hell.

'What?'

'This stink. I've found it. There's some dead chicks down here.'

'Chicks?'

'That's what I said . . . and a snake. A very unhappy snake.'

'I don't like snakes. Is it in a cage?'

'Do you think I'd be talking like this if it wasn't?'

'I'm coming down.'

I joined him in a three-walled stage set. At the back of the set there were seven pairs of stilettos, three rubber dresses, a bed, a chest, a moped, a spare can of petrol and a tool board.

'Have you seen what's missing from the tool board?' asked Carlos.

From the outline, a short-handled heavy lump hammer was missing.

'Let's find the electrics.'

'There's a box over there by the moped, near the floor.'

'Turn it on and let's take a look at Valentim's *oeuvre*.'

Carlos stepped over the chest and opened up the box. He flicked the main switch and dropped four others. There was a loud crack and four powerful halogen lights came on overhead.

'Shit!' yelled Carlos. 'This is . . . Out! Get out!'

The studio lights suddenly went out, sucking us back into a more intense darkness, except the darkness wasn't total. Around the electrics box were yellow flames. Carlos crashed over the moped. I ran at the black partition and dropped my shoulder into it. It collapsed and I tore it away from the wall. Carlos was at my back when I heard the low thump of the spare can of petrol catching alight and I ripped the door open. We fell out into the parking area followed by smoke and flames. I got into the car and reversed it away from the unit. Carlos called the fire brigade. I sat on the car bonnet in the shade of the units opposite and watched 7D burn. Carlos was wild, sweating, still scared and pacing up and down in front of the car.

'He booby-trapped it.'

'Are you sure?'

'No, I'm not sure. I didn't have enough time to check the fucking wiring diagram . . .'

'*Calma pá, calma.*'

'You saw what happened.'

'I'm asking you.'

'I threw the switches. The thing started fizzing. Sparks everywhere. There seemed to be petrol, the smell of petrol.'

'From the moped or a booby-trap?'

'Why don't we go and ask him.'

At 3.00 p.m. we were sitting in an interview room with Valentim playing the air guitar, his eyes closed in simulated ecstasy. I introduced the cast to the tape recorder and asked Valentim to give his full name and address. He complied without stopping his guitar practice.

'Do you like film?' I asked.

'Movies?'

'Making them with film . . . or do you prefer video?'

'I like film.'

'I didn't see any in your studio . . . just video. I suppose it's cheap, but it gives an ugly effect. You have to light everything or you lose it, that's the problem. Film's more subtle. Even 16 millimetre.'

381

'But it's expensive.'

'There are other problems too, aren't there?'

Valentim stopped playing his guitar. He tapped a single finger on the table, keeping time in his head. Waiting.

'What other problems?'

'You have to develop the film. Edit it. Make a master print. Teleciné that on to a videotape and then make your copies.'

'Like I said, it's expensive,' he nodded.

'And not private, either.'

'That's true.'

'But if you go the video way, there's a heavy initial investment. You have to come up with what? Thirty million escudos?'

'You don't know anything about computer equipment, do you, Inspector?'

'Tell me.'

'That edit suite was a million escudos,' he said. 'Cheap, isn't it?'

'You'd be a long time working in McDonald's to put that sort of money together.'

'If you thought that was the best way of raising it.'

'How did you?'

'Like normal people. I went to the bank.'

'And they don't mind lending to a student.'

'I'm not a policeman, Inspector Coelho. It's not a compulsion of mine to be totally honest about who I am and what I do. Banks want to lend money. They've got a lot of it. Interest rates are going to come down when we join the Euro. I'll make the repayments. What do they care?'

'How many movies did you make of Catarina?' asked Carlos.

Silence.

'Don't make us go through your whole collection.'

'You wouldn't enjoy it.'

'How do you know?'

'You don't seem to have a very artistic temperament.'

'Just tell us how many films.'

'Three. They were silent movies. Not pornography. Sorry, *agente* Pinto, to disappoint you.'

'We're talking art, are we . . . with baby chicks, a snake, rubber dresses?'

'Take a look. I'd be interested in your opinion.'

'What were the three films of?'

'Her face . . . looking into camera.'

'That sounds interesting.'

'She had a very special look.'

'Which was?'

'That's why it was special,' said Valentim, staring at me.

'What did this look say to you?'

'This seems to have gone from interrogation to therapy now.'

Carlos snapped.

'I'm going to bust you, you piece of shit,' he said, quietly. 'I'm going to bust you for murder.'

'Then you've got a job on your hands, *agente* Pinto, because *I* did not kill her.'

'Where's the hammer?'

'The hammer?'

'From your tool board. It was missing.'

'It should be in there somewhere. Take another look.'

Silence, while Valentim played a drum solo on the table.

'Where were you on Friday afternoon?' asked Carlos, desperation creeping in.

'I told you.'

'Tell us again.'

'I went to the Biblioteca Nacional. I stayed there until closing time which is seven-thirty. Go and ask the librarian. We had an argument. She wouldn't let me use the computer after seven o'clock.'

'Do you know anybody with a C series black Mercedes?'

Valentim laughed and frowned.

'I didn't borrow that much money from the bank.'

'How do you make your repayments?'

'I work. I sell my videos. I make money.'

'Pornography?'

'Like I said . . . you don't have a very artistic temperament. Perhaps it's something to do with your work. It must be quite boring . . .'

Carlos' fist was already closed.

'I should stop the tape recorder if I were you, Inspector Coelho. *Agente* Pinto wants to resort to more conventional police methods.'

I terminated the interview at a few minutes before 16.00. Carlos and I walked to Duque de Ávila.

'He's involved,' said Carlos, still furious. 'I know he's involved. We should have asked him if he booby-trapped the switchbox . . . just to see his face.'

'I think he'd humiliated us enough by then. We'll let the fire department give us that bit of information.'

By 4.25 p.m. we were working the bus queues on either side of Duque de Ávila showing photographs of Catarina. It was an advertisement for not committing crime because there's always somebody out there who's seen you. Four people saw Catarina get into the black Mercedes. One guy remembered it like it was one of the best scenes from his favourite movie. The car in front was a metallic grey Fiat Punto. The black Mercedes was a C200 series, petrol engine with the letters NT in the registration. The car behind it was an old white Renault 12 with a rusted rear wheel-arch. And the car that Jamie Gallacher fell against was . . . I told him that he'd given us more than we needed and took his name. I sent Carlos back to the *Polícia Judiciária* and told him to give the information to Traffic. I also gave him Lourenço Gonçalves' name and told him to find a business address and phone number. And I did what I'd wanted to do all day – I went to my favourite apartment in Rua Actor Taborda.

Chapter XXXI

24th April 1974, Rua do Ouro, Baixa, Lisbon.

Joaquim Abrantes stood in the dark in front of the open window, it was late, close to midnight. His wife, Pica, lay on the chaise longue playing with the dial of the radio, trying to find some entertainment that didn't drive her husband into a frenzy. She'd almost lost the radio to the street below once already when she'd come across some foreign station and picked up the Rolling Stones singing 'Angie' at a sudden full volume.

'Turn it off!' he'd yelled. 'I hear music like that . . . and I think it's the end of the world.'

'What are we doing here, anyway?' she'd asked, annoyed. 'Why don't we go home and relax in Lapa. You're always like this when you're on top of your work.'

'I'm worried,' he'd said, but didn't take it any further.

She settled for a local station called Rádio Renascença. She recognized the voice of José Vasconcelos whom she'd met several times when she'd been in the business. Abrantes grumbled again. He didn't like music. It offended his inner workings. He smoked from one of four cigarettes he had going in various ashtrays around the room.

'And now,' introduced the quiet voice on the radio, 'Zeca Afonso sings *Grândola, vila morena* . . .'

'I don't know what you have to worry about.'

'I'm worried,' said Abrantes, crushing a butt out into another ashtray and picking up a lit cigarette from it, 'because something is happening.'

'Something's happening?' said Pica, with mock astonishment. 'Nothing's happening. Nothing ever happens.'

'Manuel told me he thought something was going to happen.'

'What does he know?' said Pica, who'd never liked Manuel.

'He's an Inspector with PIDE. If he doesn't know, nobody knows. I'm going to call him.'

'It's after midnight, Joaquim.'

'Turn that radio off,' said Abrantes, hearing the lyrics now. 'That Zeca Afonso is a communist.'

He dialled Manuel's number. Pica toyed with the volume, turning it lower.

'He's a communist,' said Abrantes, to the ceiling, 'and I won't have him in the house. Now turn it off.'

He listened on the phone. It rang continuously. Pica turned the radio off.

'He's in bed and that's where I'm going,' she said.

Abrantes ignored her. He walked to the window with the phone in his hand. He disconnected and dialled another number but couldn't get a line.

Four men sat in a car just off the Eduardo VII Park in the centre of Lisbon. They were a major, two captains and a lieutenant. The captain in the front seat had a radio on his knees which they all stared at, hardly hearing it. The major leaned back in his seat to look at his watch in the street lighting. The lieutenant yawned with nerves.

'And now,' said the quiet voice of José Vasconcelos from the radio, 'Zeca Afonso sings *Grândola, vila morena* . . .'

The four men held their breath for a moment until Zeca Afonso began to sing. The captain turned in his seat to face the major.

'It's started, sir,' he said, and the major nodded.

They drove two blocks to a four-storey building and parked up. The four men got out and each took a pistol from his pocket. They walked into the building which had a small plaque outside: Rádio Clube Português.

Manuel Abrantes was sleeping at the wheel of his Peugeot
504 saloon. The front right-hand tyre thumped into a
pothole and he came awake to find grass scudding under
the front of the car. He threw the wheel to the left and the
car latched back on to the tarmac. He stopped and breathed
in quick, short breaths until the scare subsided. He wound
down the window and sucked in the chill air. He felt for
the passenger seat and found his briefcase. He unclipped
it and pulled out a file, his own personnel file from the
PIDE/DGS headquarters on Rua António Maria Cardoso.
He fed it back in. Everything was as it should be. The little
anxiety dream he'd just had at the wheel was only that. He
loosened his trousers which were cutting into his belly and
startled himself with a loud, uncalled-for fart. His stomach
still upset. He put the car in gear and started moving again,
calmer now.

'Where am I?' he asked, out loud as if a passenger in the
back might lean forward and tell him.

A sign loomed at the end of a long straight piece of road.
He gripped the steering wheel and blinked the sleep away.
Madrid 120 km.

An eighteen-year-old Zé Coelho was drinking cheap *bagaço*
in a white-tiled *tasca* in the middle of the Bairro Alto with
three of his schoolfriends when the owner came thundering
down the stairs from his apartment above.

'Something's happening,' he said, breathless and shocked.
'I was listening to the radio . . . some army officers busted
in on the programme. Now they're just playing music
continuously.'

'If you want to go to bed,' said Zé, 'you don't have to
invent a coup.'

'I'm serious.'

The seven people in the bar looked at the man for several seconds until they'd all seen his seriousness. They

got up as one and went out into the street. Zé Coelho flicked his shoulder-length hair over the wolfskin collar of his floor-length woollen *capote Alentejano* and they started running down the narrow cobbled alleyway towards the square below.

They were not alone. A crowd was gathering in the Praça de Luis de Camões and the words 'coup' and 'revolution' ricocheted off the statue in the middle of the square. After fifteen minutes the crescendo of excitement hit its top note with a shout to march on the PIDE/DGS headquarters in Rua António Maria Cardoso. They entered the street from the Largo do Chiado and found another gang of people coming up from Rua Vitor Cordon.

Behind the arched gateway and high walls the doors to the building were shut and the front dark, but the faint glimmer in the windows told the crowd that there were lights on in the building somewhere. They hammered on the gates yelling incoherently. Zé stood in the middle of the street, punching the air with his fist and shouting 'Revolution!' and, inclined to go one step too far, 'Off with their heads.'

Windows opened at the top of the building and dark figures leaned out over the street. Four shots shattered the night air. The crowd split both ways down the street with screams and shouts. More shots followed them. Their boots thundered on the cobbles. Zé ran back up the hill and fell in a confusion of legs around him. He rolled over on the cobbles and, further down the street from in front of the PIDE building, he heard terrible noises coming from a man's throat. He checked the top of the building again but could see nothing. He crouched and ran back down the street, grabbed the man by his coat collar and hauled him up the hill. When he was safe he fell back and reached down to the choking man. His fingers found the slippery warmth of a neck wound.

* * *

388

Joaquim Abrantes had slept very badly. He woke up at six o'clock feeling groggy and bad-tempered, as if he'd spent the day before drinking. He tried to call his sons, but still couldn't get a line. He opened the window and looked out into the empty street. Something was wrong. The street should not have been empty. He sniffed the air, it was different, like the first whiff of spring after a long winter except that they were in the middle of spring already. A wild-eyed young man burst into the street from the direction of the *elevador* up to the Chiado. He raised his fist in the air and shouted to the empty street:

'IT'S OVER!'

He ran up the street towards the Rossio.

There were horns blaring and a faint seethe of chatter and singing. Abrantes leaned further out of the window. He wasn't wrong. People were singing in the street.

'This is bad,' he said to himself, and strode back to the telephone.

'What's bad?' asked Pica, standing by the bedroom door in her red silk dressing gown.

'I don't know yet, but it sounds bad. People are singing in the street.'

'Singing?' said Pica, both charmed and mystified that something really was happening. 'Ah, well, even if there has been a coup . . .'

'COUP!' roared Abrantes. 'You don't understand, do you? This isn't a coup. This is a revolution. The communists have arrived.'

'So what?' she said, shrugging herself off the door jamb. 'What are you worried about? Half your money's in Zurich. The other half's in São Paulo. Even the gold's out of the country . . .'

'Don't mention the gold,' growled Abrantes, wagging his finger. 'Don't even say the word "gold". That gold does not exist. It never existed. There never was any gold. Do you understand?!'

'Perfectly,' she said, and went back into the bedroom, slamming the door.

Abrantes pulled on his coat and went out into the street and walked towards the Terreiro do Paço and the river. The Praça do Comércio was full of troops, but they were all laughing and joking with each other. Abrantes moved amongst them, stunned.

At a little before 8.00 a.m. a column of tanks appeared from the barracks of the 7th Cavalry. Abrantes positioned himself in the arcade at the north of the square.

'Now we shall see,' he said to a soldier, who looked him up and down as if he was Neanderthal.

The column of tanks drew to a halt. The turret of the lead tank opened. A captain on the ground stepped forward. The lieutenant in the tank shouted down to him. His voice was clear in the fresh early morning and the total silence in the square.

'I have orders to open fire on you,' said the lieutenant, and the soldiers in the square shifted, 'but all I really want to do is laugh.'

The shifting stopped and a murmur ran around the square.

'Go ahead then,' said the captain.

The troops in the square cheered. The lieutenant held up his hand, splayed his fingers and pointed back to the column. The captain sent a platoon to the fifth tank and four of them clambered up on to its shoulders. The turret opened and an explosive colonel put his head out and found himself looking up at four rifles' barrels.

On the River Tagus the navy ship *Almirante Gago Coutinho* cruised to a halt in front of the Praça do Comércio, its guns pointing into the heart of the city. The troops and tanks in the square watched in silence, preparing for the first volley. Several minutes passed. No sound came from the ship. The guns didn't move. There was no signal until slowly one by one the ship's guns turned away from the city and faced the south bank of the Tagus. To the gunners it looked like a flock of pigeons had taken off as a thousand caps were flung into the air on the back of a tumultuous roar in the Praça do Comércio. Joaquim Abrantes turned and walked back up the Rua do Ouro.

Zé Coelho didn't get home until 10.00 a.m. He and his friends had taken the wounded man to the hospital and the nurses in the *Urgência*, on seeing his bloodstained clothes, had singled him out and refused to let him leave until a doctor had examined him which took some time. They'd washed him as best they could but the wolf collar was still badly and irrevocably stained from the man's neck wound. His mother opened the door and screamed which brought his father out of the bedroom. His sister took Zé's coat and went to run a bath for him. The telephone rang. His father took the call. Zé and his mother watched in silence as the colonel spoke quietly and seriously, looking at the floor refusing to catch anyone's eye. He replaced the heavy Bakelite handset. Zé's sister appeared in the doorway.

'General Spínola,' he said, summoning a grave and quiet voice to communicate the full weight of the occasion, 'has asked me to go to the Largo do Carmo barracks. Prime Minister Caetano is there with his cabinet and I have been asked to persuade them to allow General Spínola to accept the unconditional surrender of the government.'

'Did you know about this?' asked his wife, her voice quavering with fear and shock at the terrifying implications for her and the children, had the coup turned out differently and badly.

'No, and neither did the General. Apparently the coup was organized by the junior officers, but the General knows that Caetano won't surrender to them. The Prime Minister won't want power to fall into the hands of the mob.'

'He means the communists,' said Zé.

'And what have you been doing?' asked the colonel, giving his bloodstained son his eagle look.

'I was outside the PIDE headquarters when they opened fire on us. Some people were hit and we took one of them to hospital.'

Zé's mother had to sit down.

'The General said there'd been no casualties.'

'Well, you can tell him from me when you see him that more than one went down in Rua António Maria Cardoso.'

'Did they bring anybody else into the hospital while you were there?'

'They locked me up in a room to prevent me from leaving.'

The colonel nodded, his forehead creased, but smiling at his son.

'You stay here now and look after your mother,' he said, pulling his daughter to him, kissing her on the head. 'Nobody leaves this apartment until I say it's safe.'

'You'll see,' said Zé, teasing his father now, 'they're dancing in the streets out there.'

'My son . . . the communist,' said the colonel, shaking his head.

At 12.30 p.m. the guard came in to Felsen's cell in the Caxias prison with a tray of food. He put it on the bed. The noise from the rest of the prison, which had been going on all morning, had not abated. The politicals were into their fiftieth rendition of the anti-fascist song *Venham mais cinco* and the guards had given up trying to quieten them long ago.

'Anything I should know about?' asked Felsen.

'Nothing that will affect you,' said the guard.

'I was just commenting on the different atmosphere in the prison today.'

'Some of our friends might be leaving soon.'

'Oh yes? Why's that?'

'Just a small revolution . . . like I said, nothing that will affect you.'

'Thank you,' said Felsen.

'*Nada*,' said the guard.

Dr Aquilino Oliveira should have been happy following the nurse down the corridor of the maternity wing of the São José hospital. He'd been told that his fourth child was a boy, weighing 3.7 kilos and was completely healthy. The nurse was gabbling at him over her shoulder as she batted her way through the swing doors. She didn't seem to need any response from him to keep herself going.

'. . . four dead and three wounded. That's what they said down in the *Urgência*, only four. They can't believe it. I can't believe it. There are tanks in the Terreiro do Paço and the Largo do Carmo but they're not doing anything. They're just there. The soldiers have rounded up the PIDE agents but not to punish them . . . you know . . . just for their own protection. The soldiers. I haven't seen it . . . but they say the soldiers have put red carnations down their rifles so that the people will know, you see . . . they'll know that they're not there to shoot anyone. They're there to liberate them. Only four people dead on a night like this with tanks in the streets and battleships in the Tagus. Don't you think that's just incredible, *Senhor Doutor*? I think that's incredible. You know, *Senhor Doutor*, I never thought I'd be able to say this in my lifetime but I'm proud. I'm proud to be Portuguese.'

She flung open the door to the maternity ward and led the lawyer in. His wife was screened off in the corner of the room with six other women in it. His shoes skidded on the highly polished floor and he had to grab a bed to save himself from falling.

'Watch yourself,' said the nurse, whose rubber soles squeaked on the floor.

He went behind the screen. His wife was sitting up, concerned.

'Are you all right?' she asked.

'He nearly slipped over on the floor,' said the nurse. 'I've told them before not to polish it so much. It's all right for us, but anybody coming in here with leather soles . . . they're in trouble. Do you know what you're going to call him?'

'Not yet.'

'Well, you won't have much trouble remembering his birthday.'

Ana Rosa Pinto sat with her mother in the kitchen. They were holding hands and crying, looking down at the three-year-old Carlos, who was playing on the floor. She'd started off the day annoyed because they wouldn't let her board the ferry to cross the river to get to her doctor's appointment for Carlos in Lisbon. Then they'd pointed out the *Almirante Gago Coutinho* with her guns up and she'd gone home scared but excited to wait for news.

In the late morning her father had gone down to the first open meeting of the *Partido Comunista Português* on the docks in Cacilhas on the south bank of the Tagus. Ana Rosa and her mother were hoping he'd bring back news of the release of political prisoners from the Caxias prison.

Little Carlos had never seen his father. His mother had been six months pregnant when the GNR had broken up a union meeting at the shipyard and his father had been taken across the river for questioning. Just two weeks before Carlos was born Ana Rosa had heard that her husband had been taken to Caxias to serve a five-year prison sentence for illegal political activities.

They waited all day, until dusk had just changed to night, when there was a knock at the door of the apartment. Ana Rosa eased her hand out of her mother's and answered it. A boy handed her a message and ran off without waiting. She read it and the tears which had gradually dried through the day sprang back.

'What is it?' asked her mother.

'They've taken the boat across. There's a crowd gathering in the Rossio. They're going to march on Caxias prison tonight.'

At 3.00 a.m. on 26th April the door to António Borrego's cell in the Caxias prison was unlocked. The guard didn't say anything, he didn't even open the door, he just moved on to the next cell and opened that one. António looked out down the dimly-lit corridor. Other men were doing the same. There was cheering and embracing. António squeezed past them and trotted down the three flights of stairs into the courtyard. There were another fifty-odd men down there all looking expectantly at the gates to the prison. He jogged across the courtyard to the hospital block and ran up the stairs two at a time. He had to catch his breath at the top, more out of condition than he'd thought.

There were three men in the ward. Two of them were sleeping and the third, Alexandre Saraiva, was sitting on the edge of his bed, trying to get his socks on but only managing to cough. António took the socks and fitted them on his friend's feet. He found the man's boots and pushed Alex's feet into them and tied them up. Alex spat into the metal dish on the bedside and inspected the phlegm.

'Still bloody,' he said, to no one in particular. 'Have you come to take me home?'

'I have,' said António.

'Who's paying the cab fare?'

'We're walking.'

'I don't know whether I'll make it. It's damned nearly killed me to get dressed.'

'You'll make it.'

António wrapped Alex's arm over the back of his neck.

They stood. António hooked his thumb into the waistband of Alex's trousers. They went down the stairs into the courtyard. There were more than a hundred people now. The sound of a crowd clamouring on the other side of the gates reached them. Names were shouted out and lost in the noise. António leaned Alex up against the wall and held him there lightly with a hand on his chest.

The gates opened to pandemonium from the huge crowd, who'd come up from Lisbon on free train rides. The prisoners came out blinking into the flashlights of cameras, searching for faces that meant something to them.

António waited for the courtyard to empty before he moved Alex out into a freedom neither of them had known for nine years. They skirted the euphoria and walked down the hill into Caxias. They didn't have to go far. They got a free ride to Paço de Arcos from a tearful cab driver.

The cab dropped them off at Alex's bar next to the public gardens. The tiled sign set into the wall was still there. It showed a blue line-drawing of the Búgio lighthouse and underneath *O Farol*. Alex tapped the lighted window of the house next door. A woman sounding old and tired answered.

'It's me, *Dona* Emília,' said Alex.

The toothless woman, dressed in black, opened the door and peered out into the night, her eyes not so good any more. She saw Alex and grabbed his face with bent and twisted fingers and kissed him on both cheeks, harder and harder as if she was kissing him back into existence. She produced the key to the bar from her front apron as if she'd been prepared nine years for this moment. She brought them candles from her kitchen.

Alex unlocked the bar door and António sat him down on a metal chair next to a wooden table in the dark. They lit the candles.

'There should be something behind the bar,' said Alex. 'Nice and mature by now.'

396

António found a bottle of *aguardente* and a couple of dusty glasses which he blew into. He poured out the pale yellow liquid. They drank to freedom and the alcohol set off a coughing fit in Alex.

'We'll go to the notary tomorrow,' said Alex.

'What for?'

'I want to make sure that when I go, this place is yours.'

'Eh, *homem*, don't talk like that.'

'There's one condition.'

'Look, forget it, you're . . .'

'Pour another drink and listen to me,' said Alex.

'I'm listening.'

'You have to change the name of the bar to *A Bandeira Vermelha*. That way nobody will forget.'

On 2nd May 1974 Joaquim Abrantes, Pedro, Manuel and Pica had lunch in a small restaurant in the centre of Madrid. It was agreed that Manuel would fly to São Paulo in Brazil and open a branch of the Banco de Oceano e Rocha. Joaquim and Pedro would go to Lausanne and track the political situation in Portugal from there. Pica wanted to know why they couldn't do it from Paris, but nobody paid any attention to her.

On the 3rd May 1974 just as Manuel Abrantes' flight from Madrid to Buenos Aires was leaving the West African coast, thirty-six ex-PIDE/DGS *agentes* made themselves available to the new regime for traffic control and vehicle registration.

Chapter XXXII

Tuesday, 16th June 199–, Polícia Judiciária, Saldanha, Lisbon.

There was a rush on at the office that morning which did not include me. Narciso's secretary was waiting for me in the corridor and led me straight up to see him but, of course, he wasn't ready and the five minutes that his secretary had promised turned into twenty. She wouldn't let me leave.

At 08.30 I was standing in front of Narciso on the other side of his desk. He was standing too, with his chair pushed back to the wall, his hands spread wide apart gripping the edge of his desk as if he was going to tip it over me. Emotions made rare appearances in his face but that morning there was one – anger. Not the eruptive, volcanic type, more the penetrating, gelid variety.

'I haven't seen your revised report yet.'

'I haven't had the opportunity to get behind my desk this morning.'

'I also haven't seen the report on what happened yesterday.'

'For the same reason, *Senhor Engenheiro*.'

'But I *have* already heard things,' he said, 'about you and *agente* Pinto putting yourselves at risk and the destruction of all evidence in a fire.'

'That was unfortunate.'

'What have you learnt from the fire department?'

'I haven't . . .'

'I've heard a taped interview with the suspect of such glaring incompetence that I can't believe the two of you have got your minds properly on the job.'

398

'Our minds are very firmly on the job, *Senhor Engenheiro*.'

'What time did you leave this building yesterday?'

'Something like quarter-past-four, we were working the bus queues on Avenida Duque de Ávila, which was where the girl was last seen, getting into . . .'

'And you didn't come back to the office.'

'I sent *agente* Pinto . . .'

'And where did you go?'

'I had nothing further . . .'

'You were seen going into an apartment building just up the road here in Rua Actor Taborda.'

'The victim's teacher lives there.'

'How long did you spend with her?'

Silence.

'I can't hear you, Inspector.'

'Four hours.'

'Four hours! And what did you have to discuss over four hours?'

'I'm seeing her privately, sir.'

Narciso hardly missed a beat. He'd planned this through to the end.

'Do you have any idea of the pressure I'm under?' he asked.

'I'm sure it's considerable.'

'You asked me to make sure that Inspector Abílio Gomes found out where Dr Aquilino Oliveira was at the time of his wife's death.'

'It was just a thought.'

'He was having dinner in the private residence of the Minister of Internal Administration.'

I shut up. The situation was not calling for my observations on the friendship between the lawyer and the minister. Narciso dropped his head and stared into his desk top.

'I'm taking you off the case,' he said, quietly. 'Abílio Gomes will handle it from now on. I want you to go down to Alcântara and investigate a body that's been found in a rubbish bin at the back of the Wharf One club.'

'But *Senhor Engenheiro* Narciso, you haven't . . .'

'You are in no position to defend your professionalism on the Catarina Sousa Oliveira case. "Investigating officer has affair with witness",' he said, stretching his hand out into the possible banner headline in the *Correio da Manhã*. 'Now take *agente* Pinto and go down to Alcântara.'

I sat in my office chewing various nails. Carlos had left a note with Lourenço Gonçalves' telephone number and a business address on Avenida Almirante Reis. I tried the number wondering why Narciso had praised me yesterday morning for looking in the wrong direction, and frozen me out twenty-four hours later just when I was getting somewhere. There was no reply. Carlos came in and sat across the desk. I put the phone down.

'We've got a problem,' he said.

'I know.'

'Traffic won't give me the information.'

'We're off the case.'

'Do *they* know that?' he asked, slumping back in his chair.

'Maybe,' I said, and picked up the phone.

I called one of my friends in Traffic who would do favours for me. He put me on hold. Five minutes later he told me the computer had crashed. I hung up.

'We have an internal problem here,' I said.

Carlos looked suddenly bewildered, cold, like a kid on the beach who'd lost his parents. I gave him a résumé of Narciso's conversation.

'What does it mean?'

'It means that whereas before we were swimming close to the beach, now the tide has suddenly swept us out over the continental shelf and we've got ten fathoms of dark, cold water underneath us.'

Carlos leaned closer, serious as a headstone.

'What are you talking about?'

'I don't know any more.'

*   *   *

It was hot and humid down in the Alcântara docks complex and the body in the rubbish bin was already high enough for people to be holding handkerchiefs to their faces. The photographer had been and gone, and the pathologist, a woman I didn't know, was struggling into a pair of surgical gloves. I took a quick look at the body which was of a male, about eighteen years old, dark-skinned, with black, wavy hair, no fat on him and only wearing a pair of brief burgundy underpants with a smiley face over the genital area. I felt his feet. Soft. The killer had stolen his shoes or somebody else had come along afterwards. The pathologist joined me.

'A couple of the staff were finishing cleaning up the nightclub,' she said. 'They emptied the rubbish at five o'clock and by seven when they closed up to leave out the back there, the body was in place. They also told me he's a known male prostitute. Can I move the body?'

I nodded her on. She was fast and thorough. I briefed Carlos on what he had to do and we waited for the pathologist's initial report.

'Right. Cause of death,' she said. 'Severe cerebral haemorrhage caused by savage and multiple blows to the top, back and side of the head. The killer wanted this one unambiguously dead. I'll run an HIV test on the blood, that could be a possible motive. I had a quick look in his rectum and he'd been working. I'll be fuller once I've seen him in my lab.'

I left Carlos with his notebook and dark intelligence and walked to the Alcântara train station. I telephoned my friend in Traffic again while waiting for the train.

'Is your computer still down?'

'Sorry, Zé,' he said.

'Does that mean that it's always going to be down when I call?'

'I can't say.'

I telephoned the lawyer's house and the maid answered.

I said I wanted to speak to her. She said she was alone in the house.

I boarded the Cascais train and by 10.00 a.m. I was walking up to the lawyer's house through the old village. I rang the bell. The maid opened the door but Dr Aquilino Oliveira was walking down the corridor behind her.

'Thank you, Mariana,' he said, and ordered her to bring us some coffee. He stood at his desk in his study. I remained standing too.

'I wasn't expecting you, Inspector,' he said. 'I called your office and they told me you were off the case. I was put through to Inspector Abílio Gomes. Not the same calibre as yourself, of course, but no doubt competent. What can I do for you?'

'I came to offer you my condolences. Your wife. It's hard to believe what you've had to go through in the last forty-eight hours.'

He lowered himself slowly into his chair. His eyes didn't leave my face.

'Thank you, Inspector Coelho,' he said. 'I didn't think policemen could afford to care.'

'One of my weaknesses . . . but possibly a strength, too.'

'Is that what drives you, Inspector?'

'Yes,' I said, 'that . . . and I still have a belief in the sanctity of the truth.'

'You must be a lonely man, Inspector,' he said, which shook me.

'There's the mystery, too,' I said, papering over my unease. 'Humans need mystery.'

'Speak for yourself.'

'Yes, perhaps lawyers and mystery don't go together.'

'Well, we love to mystify . . . so I've been told by my clients.'

Mariana brought the coffee in. She poured. We waited. She left.

'Your wife came to see me the night before she died, *Senhor Doutor*. Were you aware of that?'

His eyes came up from his coffee, blinking but galvanized, searching the inside of my head.

'She'd tried to kill herself before, Inspector. Did *you* know that?'

'How many times?'

'Check at the local hospital. They've stomach-pumped her there twice before. The first time Mariana found her just in time. That was about five years ago. The second time I did. Last summer.'

'What did you put these attempts down to?'

'I'm not a psychiatrist. I don't know how neuroses work on the human brain. I don't understand chemical imbalances, that kind of thing.'

'A neurosis usually results from an original trauma which the victim is trying to suppress.'

'That sounds about right, Inspector. How do you know such things?'

'My late wife was interested in the works of Carl Jung,' I said. 'Were you aware of anything that could have . . .'

'Did my . . . ? What did my wife say to you that night?'

'She said your marriage hadn't worked from the beginning. I thought fifteen years was a long time for a relationship not to be working. She seemed to be scared of you and dependent on you. Your small exercise in humiliation at the beginning of the investigation confirmed that.'

'And you don't think *I* was humiliated by her having an affair with a boy ten years her junior, Inspector?' he said, fast and fierce, almost hissing it.

'When did you find out about the lover?'

'I don't remember.'

'Last summer possibly?'

'Yes, yes . . . it was last summer.'

'How?'

'I found a receipt for a shirt from a shop I don't use.'

403

'Did you confront her with it?'

'I watched and waited. The shirt could have been for her brother, after all. I knew it wasn't, but my profession demands that I am certain.'

'So how did you confront her with it?'

The question knocked him back. He tried to cover his reaction by an elaborate alteration of position. It snapped him out of the cosiness of our dialogue. His finger had brushed the truth and found it razor-sharp. His surface temperature dropped quickly to sub-zero.

'None of this is relevant to the investigation of my daughter's death, Inspector. More especially now that you are no longer working on the case.'

'I thought we were just talking.'

He leaned forward and sipped his coffee. He removed a small cigar from a box on his desk. He offered me one. I declined and lit a cigarette of my own. He smoked and uncreased himself. My question burned inside me.

'You were telling me what my wife said to you that night,' he said.

'She said things, very important things, without explaining them and I was very tired after a long day. She said your marriage had never worked but not why. She said you were a powerful man and that you extended that power into your intimate relationships but she didn't say how. She made a very serious allegation but offered no evidence to back it up. It was not . . .'

'. . . a conversation with somebody of sound mind,' he finished.

'There were traces of the truth, I thought.'

'What was the serious allegation?'

'She said you were abusing Catarina sexually.'

'Do you believe that?'

'She offered no evidence . . .'

'But do you believe it?'

'I'm a homicide detective, *Senhor Doutor*. People lie to me, not just occasionally, they lie to me *all* the time. I listen. I cross-reference. I probe further. I examine evidence. I find witnesses. And if I'm lucky I can put together enough *facts* to make a case. But one thing I can assure you of, *Senhor Doutor*, if somebody tells me something, I don't automatically believe them. If I did, we could empty our prisons of all those innocents and refurbish them into *pousadas*.'

'What did you say to her?'

My insides winced at that. A nagging memory. A prickling responsibility.

'I told her to proceed with extreme caution . . . to get a lawyer and some evidence would help.'

He sucked on his cigar, the lawyer observing the weak point.

'Sound advice,' he said. 'Did you tell her you were not the right person to be speaking to, that if . . .'

'I did.'

'So why do you think she came to you, Inspector?'

I didn't answer.

'Do you think she was trying to influence you perhaps . . . your attitude to me, for instance?'

Still I didn't answer and the lawyer came across the desk at me.

'Perhaps she offered as evidence our daughter's promiscuity, her complete disdain for any sexual morality brought about by what . . . ? A confusion. The man, in whose unconditional love she completely trusted, took advantage of her innocence . . . Yes. I imagine that would do it. That would qualify as a trauma and the promiscuity as a neurosis. Am I right? Was that my wife's thinking?'

The pressure of the man's intelligence, its rapacity, had the boiling intensity of a piranha shoal stripping a body down to its skeleton. Why did you marry her? I thought. Why did she marry you? Why did you stay with each other?

'I'm right,' he said, slumping back. 'I know I'm right.'

He crushed out his cigar with venom, until he felt himself observed. I stood, annoyed and confused, my initiative gone. I opened the door to leave, my question still unanswered, the weight not with me to ask it yet.

'There are two forms of child abuse, *Senhor Doutor*,' I said. 'The one you read about is sexual abuse. It's more shocking. But the other type can be just as brutal.'

'What's that?'

'Withholding love.'

I went into the corridor, closed the door and then reopened it.

'I forgot to ask, *Senhor Doutor*. Do you have another car apart from the Morgan? I imagine that's your fun car and you have something more formal as well.'

'A Mercedes.'

'Was that the car your wife was driving on Sunday night?'

'Yes it was.'

I sat in the public gardens outside the lawyer's house and waited for Mariana, the maid, to come out, which she did at lunchtime. I followed her. She was a small, thick-set woman not much more than a metre and a half tall. She had dark shiny hair curled tight around her head. She was the type of person you take one look at and trust completely, the kind of woman, perhaps, that Dr Oliveira didn't deserve to have working for him. I caught up with her on a steep cobbled street, startling her.

'Can we talk for a few minutes?' I asked.

She didn't want to.

'Let's walk,' I said, and stepped into the road to let her have the narrow shaded pavement. 'You're upset.'

She nodded.

'*Dona* Oliveira was a good person?'

406

'She was,' she said. 'An unhappy woman, but a good person.'

'Will you carry on working for Dr Oliveira?'

She didn't answer. Her low heels clattered on the cobbles.

'Was Catarina a good person, Mariana?'

'I've worked for Dr Oliveira for nine years. That's how long I've known Catarina, every weekend and every summer for nine years, Inspector . . . and no, she was not a good person, but it wasn't her fault.'

'Even when she was six years old?'

'I have an understanding of unhappiness, Inspector. That of the rich, is not much different to that of the poor. My husband is a drinker. It changes him and he makes my children unhappy. But at least when he is sober he still loves his children.'

'And Dr Oliveira doesn't?'

She didn't answer. She couldn't bring herself to say such a thing.

'*Dona* Oliveira tried to give that child all the love she had, but Catarina didn't want it. She hated her mother and, you know, the strangest thing . . . she'd do anything for her father.'

'*Dona* Oliveira came to see me the night before she died.'

Mariana crossed herself rapidly.

'She told me that Dr Oliveira had been abusing Catarina sexually.'

Mariana slipped on the cobbles. I grabbed her. She backed into a wall and stood there appalled.

'*Dona* Oliveira said that you would corroborate this accusation,' I said. 'Is that true, Mariana?'

She swallowed hard and shook her head. The street was hot, bright and empty. The sky was a deep blue against the sunblasted whitewashed walls. The smell of lunch was on the sea breeze. Mariana was looking at me as if I was a man with a knife. She brushed a graze of whitewash off her shoulder.

'I wouldn't have been able to stay in that house,' she said.

I wanted to leave it at that, but I couldn't resist asking the question that I hadn't been able to ask either of the Oliveiras.

'Whose daughter is she, Mariana?'

'Who?' she asked, bewildered now.

'Catarina.'

'I don't understand.'

I stopped it there. A car rumbled up the street, tyres battering the cobbles. I fell in behind Mariana and followed her down to the main street and the cool of the trees. At the door to the supermarket I said goodbye, but with one last easy question. Mariana was relieved to tell me Teresa Oliveira's friend was an Englishwoman called Lucy Marques and gave me an address in São João do Estoril.

I caught the train back down the *Linha* to São João and walked away from the sea and station for a nearly a kilometer until I found myself in front of a traditionally-styled, but recently-built house with gates, a circular drive and wide steps leading up to a portico. It said money to me, but not enough for the real thing. I introduced myself to an intercom and video camera at the gate which opened electronically. There was a large white satellite dish on the roof of the house.

A heavy-set Cape Verdian maid took me across tiled white marble floors towards a living room from which came the sounds of an English soap opera. Lucy Marques was sitting with her feet up on the sofa cradling a remote and a large tumbler of what proved to be a gin and tonic with plenty of backbone. There was a stack of *Hello!* magazines on the floor beside her. She clicked off the television.

408

'I'm not speaking any more bloody Portuguese,' she said, fanning me away, 'so if you don't speak gin and tonic you can get lost right now.'

'My gin and tonic's pretty good,' I said.

'Is it? Pass me a nail then.'

'A what?'

'Fallen at the first, Inspector. A coffin nail. A cancer stick. A bloody fag, for God's sake . . . in the box there on the table.'

She took two cigarettes from the box and put one behind her ear. I lit the one in her mouth.

'Help yourself,' she said. 'Have a drink. Do the necessary. You look a bit sharper than Gumbo Gomes. What a depressing character he was.'

'Abílio . . .'

'Able was I ere I saw Abílio,' she said and cackled at her own madness.

I put Lucy Marques in her mid-fifties from the back of her hands but her face and body age seemed to have been arrested at around thirty-eight, an achievement given her regime. She wore white jeans and a T-shirt with some nautical appliqué.

'Can we talk about Teresa Oliveira?'

'Only if you join me with a drink. Gin and tonic. That was the agreed language.'

I poured myself a weak one and lit a cigarette.

'Teresa, Teresa, Teresa,' she sighed, and gulped her drink. 'What a mess.'

'I was investigating her daughter's death.'

'You were?'

'I was taken off it. Internal politics. Gumbo Gomes is working it now.'

'Gumbo Gomes. He's just the kind of Portuguese I detest. So serious. So gra-a-a-ave. You couldn't brighten him up if you offered him a Molotov cocktail and a light.'

'Mrs Marques. I'm sorry, can we . . .'

'Of course, gin makes me gabble. Teresa. No. Catarina. Yes, well, I'm not surprised she came to a sticky end. She was what we call a little minx that one. Do you know what a minx is, Inspector?'

'I can guess.'

'A flirty, dirty little schemer,' she said, and wriggled herself into the sofa preparing to deliver the dirt. 'You know Teresa had a lover last year.'

'Paulo Branco.'

'Right.'

'And she caught Catarina in bed with him.'

'It was a little more graphic than finding them under the covers, Inspector Coelho. Pumping buttocks. Ankles round the ears. The works, I can tell you. Teresa felt faint for weeks after whenever she thought about it.'

'I understood that Catarina called her to the house so that she would catch them at it.'

'You are well-informed. You must like to gossip, Inspector.'

'I was married to an Englishwoman.'

'Naughty, naughty now.'

'You had a crack at the Portuguese.'

'One all,' she said licking a finger and scoring the air.

'The lover, Mrs Marques?'

'Ah, yes. Teresa was convinced that he put her up to it.'

'Who?'

'Aquilino put Catarina up to it. Finding out about the lover and then taking him to bed.'

'My God,' I said, 'how did she get to think that?'

'Well, I said to her: "You're paranoid, dear." But she told me she'd cornered Catarina one day and confronted her with it, and Catarina's reply? "You shouldn't be having sex with other men." Nice family, eh?'

'Why didn't Teresa leave him?'

'You Portuguese and your marriage contracts,' said Lucy

Marques, shaking her head. 'Aquilino and Teresa's agreement was . . . how do you call that arrangement when everything from both sides is thrown in the pot?'

'*Communhão total de bens*.'

'That's it. Teresa came to him with hardly an escudo to her name. She worked for him, remember. It was all Aquilino's. He wasn't going to divorce her and let her have half his cake, which was what she'd have had to take . . .'

'But . . .'

'Exactly. He was crazy about her. He left his first wife for her and *she* was loaded . . . money and name.'

'So what happened?'

'Something right at the beginning and I don't know what. Teresa never talked about it. And believe me, I tried,' she said, tapping her *Hello!* magazines. 'This lot would have paid money for that, I can tell you.'

Suddenly I wasn't sure how much I liked Lucy Marques.

'Teresa came here on Saturday night.'

'She slept here, Inspector.'

'She came to see me first. She told me that Aquilino had abused Catarina sexually.'

'She was always telling me he was impotent, and I don't know how she knew that because she also told me that they didn't have sex again after Catarina was born. So, make of that what you will, Inspector.'

'What did she do on Sunday?'

'She must have taken a rhino-sized sleeping pill because she didn't get up 'til midday. I was worried about her, and checked on her breathing several times in the morning. She left here at one o'clock, saying she was going out to lunch and I didn't see her again.'

'She had a Mercedes, what colour was that?'

'Black.'

'Model, series number?'

'Haven't a clue.'

'Registration number?'

'I might look like a sad old lush to you, Inspector Coelho, but I've got better things to do with my time than remember my friends' registration numbers. Anyway, Gumbo Gomes has the car . . . ask him.'

I took the train back to Lisbon wondering if it had come to that. The mother killing her own daughter. I couldn't see it. I couldn't feel it. I stared out to sea, mesmerized by the waves breaking over the hump of a sand bank in the middle of the estuary and thought about the Oliveiras, their hopes foundered, the family broken up and dead . . . because of what? Because it had all gone wrong from the beginning.

I didn't get off at Alcântara. I could see from the train that the scene at the back of the Wharf One was now empty. It was lunchtime by the time I got to Cais do Sodré. I started to cross the tram rails on Avenida 24 de Julho to get to a restaurant near the market. One of the new trams, a humming electronic slug of effervescing 7Up, approached. The crowd of people around me waiting to cross seemed to contract and pop open. Somebody thumped me in the back. I fell off the pavement, my ankle went, my knee connected with the tarmac. My fingers slid into the silver strips of track scintillating to the approach of the tram. Life slowed. Sound crunched. Faces slipped across my retina. A dark, curly-haired girl, wire-hanger thin, reached out a hand, not to help but to point. A thick-set man, with vast belly and wrestler's forearms stepped forward and reared back. The woman's face next to his had pencilled-in eyebrows which disappeared into the creases of her forehead, her mouth opened and a strange and distant ululation came out. The strip of film in my head jumped out of its sprockets. Light and dark colour ripped through the gate. My muscles unfroze. I rolled. Metal squealed. Hydraulics hissed. My fingers slipped out of the silver rail. A steel wheel screeched through.

I was looking up at the sky, through the criss-cross cables overhead, and everything beyond seemed suddenly simple after life's complexities. Faces canopied over me. Someone held my hand, which was cold, and rubbed it warm. I must have been smiling like an idiot because everybody was smiling back. Today had not been the day. I sat up. People helped me to my feet. A woman brushed me down. Someone told me I'd been lucky. I said I knew it and laughed and they all laughed with me, as if they'd escaped it too. I found myself swept into a restaurant with three or four people and they sat down with me at a long table and told all the other lunch people that I'd nearly been the slice of lemon under the 7Up tram.

After lunch, still dazed, I decided that underground travel was safer. I stood well back from the tracks in the Cais do Sodré Metro. The train travelled as far as Anjos and I climbed the stairs on to Avenida Almirante Reis. It was there that I discovered that the day had edged up to 35°. It was there that I felt strange and cold inside. It was there that I threw up my lunch and that I realized that I wasn't as safe as I had been before.

Chapter XXXIII

20th April 1975, Banco de Oceano e Rocha, São Paulo, Brazil.

The rain had stopped for the afternoon. The lights flickered back on. Manuel Abrantes stroked his bald head and tried the phone. It was working again. He pressed a button for an outside line and dialled a number. He sat back and loosened his tie another inch and shouted for his secretary.

'The air conditioning's not working,' he said to the twenty-five-year-old university graduate.

'It was . . .'

'But it isn't now because when the power goes off . . . Wait,' he said into the telephone.

'I'll get the *técnico*.'

'It's the one thing that never comes back on.'

'I'll get the *técnico*.'

'Good,' he said and waved her away. 'Roberto?'

'Yes, *Senhor* Manuel,' said the voice.

'What have you got for me?'

Silence.

'Are you still there, Roberto?'

'Yes, but *Senhor* Manuel, you didn't like what I sent you the last time?'

'She was fine.'

'Then I'll send you the same.'

A knock on the door.

'Wait. I'm busy. There's an engineer coming to see me. Come in! Hold the line.'

The *técnico* came in. Manuel pointed him to the air conditioner.

'Just hold the line for a moment,' he said, and turned to the *técnico*. 'It never comes back on after a power cut. Do you think it's . . . ?'

'It's the fuse,' said the *técnico*, impassive, unimpressionable. 'When the power comes back on it surges and blows the fuse.'

The *técnico* put in a new fuse and left. The condenser kicked in and cold air blasted down Manuel's back.

'Roberto?'

'I'll send her again.'

'Don't you have anyone who owns a business suit?'

'A man?' asked Roberto, confused.

'A woman, you idiot. Women have suits, too. I don't want any more of these girls in bright orange and lime green mini-skirts with their backsides hanging out . . . I'm running a serious business here.'

'Oh, OK.'

'Buy her a suit. I'll give her the money.'

'You want her to come up now?'

'I'm just getting the room to cool down after the power cut.'

'So, when?'

'Twenty minutes.'

Manuel put the phone down. It rang immediately.

'Your brother, Pedro, on line two,' said his secretary.

He pressed the button . . . loving the technology.

'Are you all right?' asked Pedro.

'Just busy, that's all. The power failures don't help.'

'Father's sick again.'

'What's the matter this time?'

'You know they took that piece of his bowel out.'

'The tumour?'

'The tumour. They think he's got an infection now and that it . . . you know, the cancer has gone into the lymph.'

'What does that mean?'

'I think you should come back.'

415

Silence, as Manuel took cold sweat off his forehead.

'Is it that serious?'

'I wouldn't have said that you should come back.'

'You know my problem.'

'You'll be flying to Switzerland.'

'But it's Europe . . . you know what it's like.'

'What do you mean?'

'Even if Franco died tomorrow I wouldn't be happy flying into Spain.'

'You're not a Nazi war . . .'

'Be careful what you say. You know whose birthday they still celebrate out here. And we read about what's going on over your side all the time.'

'What are you talking about now?'

'Hitler's birthday.'

'But what's going on over my side?'

'The communists.'

Silence, just a hiss from Lausanne.

'They nationalized the banks in Portugal,' said Pedro.

'You see,' said Manuel. 'That's the end of us.'

'So, you're not coming.'

'I don't want to risk it yet. Can I speak to him?'

'He's on a ventilator.'

'You didn't tell me that. You said it was his bowel and the lymph. He can't breathe now?'

'I didn't want to worry you. His breathing packed up.'

'How long has he got?'

'It could be any time. The doctors won't say.'

'I'll try and get a flight now.'

He put the phone down and it rang again instantly. He shook his head and rolled his eyes. 'Busy, busy,' he said to himself.

'There's a *Senhora* Xuxa Mendes here to see you,' said his secretary, and without backing off on the derision, 'she says it's business.'

A tarted-up mulatto in a cheap light blue suit came in.

She was carrying a plastic briefcase which looked even cheaper than her face. Her unmanageable bottom was already splitting the seam down the middle of the short skirt.

'*Senhora* Mendes,' he said, taking the girl's hand and closing the door on the graduate. 'What's in the briefcase?'

The girl was confused but opened it up, took out the wad of newspaper and handed it to him. He pushed his chair back and told her to come round. He stood, hitched his trousers and ordered her to bend over the desk.

Chapter XXXIV

Tuesday, 16th June 199–, Avenida Almirante Reis, outside Anjos Metro, Lisbon.

I fell into a café close to the Metro station. If it had a name it didn't snag in my brain. If there were people in it, they were faceless. I went to the toilets at the back and washed my face. I asked for a glass of water and swilled my mouth out. I ordered a cup of tea with two tea bags. Catherine of Bragança might have introduced tea to the British but her legacy in Portugal is Lipton's. I sugared the tea heavily and drank it. I ordered something stronger and sat down, sweating again, the breathing not going well, unsynchronized. The barman kept an eye on me. The TV was encouraging us all to go to Madeira.

A large presence came from the rear of the bar, stood over me and blocked out some of the neon in the room.

'Is this where all the old detectives come to cure their troubles?' he said, sitting himself down at my table.

I knew him. I knew that big nose, those seedy eyes. I knew that smooth, black moustache sharpened at the tips.

'I just had an accident,' I said. 'Nearly fell under a tram. I feel a bit shaky that's all. Had to sit down.'

'In a city of trams like this one, it's amazing how few people disappear under them.'

'I don't remember your name . . . but I know I know you.'

'You're Zé Coelho,' he said. 'I nearly didn't recognize you. You used to have a beard. João José Silva . . . they called me JoJó. You remember now?'

418

I didn't.

'I was "retired" three years ago, you know . . . eased out.'

'You weren't on Homicide, were you?'

'Vice.'

'Did you just say that old detectives come in here for the cure?'

'They used to . . . until three days ago.'

'What happened then?'

'You remember a guy called Lourenço Gonçalves?'

This name is following me around.

'No I don't, but I've heard of him,' I said.

'He was in Vice too.'

'Were you partners?'

'More or less,' he said, evasive. 'He used to come in here . . . until three days ago.'

'I heard he set himself up in business.'

'He calls himself a security consultant now. A fancy name for private detective work. Following rich guy's wives around the place, seeing if they're doing something more than the shopping on a Wednesday afternoon. You'd be surprised.'

'Would I?'

'He was . . . so were the husbands, which meant he didn't always get paid.'

'So why doesn't he come in here any more?'

He shrugged.

'We used to have a drink and go and play cards in the park in summer.'

'Was he married?'

'He was. His wife went back up to Porto. Couldn't stand us southerners down here. Thought we were all Moors. Took the kids with her.'

I finished my drink. The man was depressing me. I didn't know why. The seediness of those eyes maybe.

'I've got to go,' I said. 'I don't want to get retired early.'

'You're not interested in what's happened to Lourenço?'

'You mean, after three days, he's missing or what?'

'He used to come in here every day.'

'Have you been to his office?'

'Course I have, it's right across the street, second floor. No answer.'

'Maybe he went away.'

'He didn't have the money to go away.'

'Call me if he shows up,' I said, giving him a card. 'And call me if he doesn't show up by the end of the week.'

I didn't wait for his reply. I had to get out of there before the neon split my head open. I walked up to Luísa's apartment. She was out. I went to the *Polícia Judiciária* building. No Carlos. I took some aspirin and began to feel stronger. Abílio Gomes put his head in and told me I looked like death. I watched him disappear down the corridor. I went into his office and opened up the Teresa Oliveira file on his desk. It was nearly the first detail on the front page. She was found dead in a black Mercedes E series 250 diesel, registration 14 08 PR. I closed the file.

I walked down to the Avenida da Liberdade to get some air in my lungs. It wasn't a pleasant walk. The traffic was heavy and the pollution high in the afternoon heat. I carried on down to the Pensão Nuno and up the same strip of lino, which must have been a mid-seventies vintage, up the same dark flights of stairs, which must have been eighteenth-century, to the one-metre bar of neon over the reception, the most modern thing in the place. Jorge Raposo was still there, smoking over a different newspaper. I put my hand on the counter.

'Looking for Nuno?' he asked, without looking up.

'I've heard that one before.'

'Inspector,' he said, not pleased to see me. 'It's you.'

'Your memory for faces is coming back.'

He sucked his teeth and considered that.

'Only the ones I *have* to remember. Troublemakers for instance.'

420

'Those three kids who were in here Friday lunchtime.'

'You see what I mean, Inspector,' he sighed, his eyelids closing and only returning halfway.

'Did anybody come out after them?'

'Like three went up and four came down,' he said, his shoulders beginning to shake with fake mirth. 'It takes a little longer than that, so I understand.'

I gave him a long look. He held it, untroubled.

'How many times a year do you get hit, Jorge?'

'In the last quarter of a century? Not once.'

'And before that?'

'The police force was the same, just the uniforms were different and the methods. You know – not so sensitive.'

I nipped round the back of the counter and drove my knee into the side of his thigh. He went down hard on the strip of dead carpet he had behind there. The cigarette left his fingers. I picked it up and stubbed it out.

'A bit of nostalgia for you, Jorge,' I said. 'Now when you wake up every morning you're going to say "Shit, Inspector Coelho might come and see me today. I'd better start remembering how it happened with that young girl who came in here on Friday lunchtime, walked out and got herself killed four hours later." Your memory'll have an open line to pain and just when you think you've got over it and you can walk up the stairs one at a time, I'll be back and do the other one.'

I went up to the room and looked around. The bed had been moved back to the wall. That was the only change. I sat on it and smoked, but nothing came to me. I checked myself in the mirror. Still not good.

Jorge was lying where he'd fallen behind his counter grunting. He looked up at me from the corner of his face. He squeezed his eyes shut.

'Keep trying, Jorge,' I said and left.

I called Luísa. She was in. I called Olivia to tell her I'd be late. I took a bus up to Saldanha and walked down to

Luísa's apartment. The stairs felt long and hard. She let me in and sat me down with a glass of ice tea. I told her about the accident. She sat on the chair with her knees up holding on to her ankles, unblinking.

'I had a little note,' she said, when I'd finished. 'It was under the windscreen wiper on my car.'

She reached over to the table and handed it to me. It was a sheet of A4 paper. Written in red felt-tip pen was the word *PUTA*.

'How daring,' I said, unimpressed.

I told her about my conversation with Narciso that morning and how he'd moved me off the case.

'They *know* about me?'

'They saw me going into this building and they know your car now, don't they?'

'But you're not sure who "they" are?'

'I wouldn't say it's a concerted effort,' I said. 'If it was, I'd probably have been suspended by now. I think we're just talking about certain elements in the police force who have been told that influential people are not happy about how my investigation has developed.'

'All this because of Catarina?'

'She had a full sexual history. There are plenty of people out there who want to have sex with young girls. Some are persuasive, others offer money and there are a few who just take it. Catarina had been sodomized. Even in this permissive age, sodomizing a young girl is a shameful act. The thought of appearing in court on that kind of charge could have been enough for her assailant to kill her. There are some big men circling in this case. Her father, you know. And he's connected to the Minister of Internal Administration. Dr Oliveira was having a drink with him when his daughter was killed and having dinner with him when his wife committed suicide.'

'Teresa Oliveira committed suicide?'

'Sunday night . . . the loneliest time.'

It upset her and she had to get up and pace the apartment floors. I smoked and sipped ice tea, no closer, after talking it through with Luísa, to knowing who was applying pressure from where. Did it emanate from Narciso or was he just a channel? She kissed me to give some reassurance. I kissed her back because it tasted good. She thumped into the chair again.

'And I had some good news today, too.'

'You don't have to do your doctorate any more?'

'Not *that* good,' she said. 'My father's offered to let me launch this magazine he's had on the blocks for the last two months.'

'I thought you wanted to publish books.'

'I do, but this lets me burst on to the Lisbon publishing scene, which will be good for the book-publishing business. There's always more interest in a new magazine and I'll get a lot of attention . . .'

'But . . . ?'

'I have to come up with the launch idea. What's going to make this magazine stand out from the rest.'

'And your father couldn't find the answer?'

'So he's made it sound like a present in that I get all this free publicity, but there's just this little Gordian knot I have to untie.'

'You need a good old-fashioned sex scandal. People caught with their trousers down.'

'Something a little more serious than that, Zé. It's a business magazine for the Iberian Peninsula not a tabloid rag for the hairdresser's.'

'You didn't say. Had I known . . .'

'What?'

'I'd have suggested a businessman with his trousers down.'

'Nobody's going to have their trousers down in any magazine I publish.'

'Then you might have circulation problems because that,

423

as far as I know, is all people are interested in these days.'

'You're depressing me.'

'Then let's drink to the rise of frivolity.'

It was close to 9.00 p.m. and still light, with the days getting longer and the time shorter, as I walked down through the blocks of flats from Paço de Arcos station. A siren was blaring and men were running to the *Bombeiros Voluntários* building. Moments later two fire engines blasted out into the street, leaving me with the impression that nothing ever stops. There are no blank spaces any more to colour in at your leisure.

I hovered at the street corner, contemplating a beer with António Borrego. I was earlier than expected. I'd felt too tired to have dinner with Luísa, but I'd come alive on the journey back. I needed a shower first. Inside the house I knew I wasn't alone. The cat was sitting on a chair in the darkening kitchen, paws and tail neatly tucked away. She closed her yellow eyes at me and I left her to contemplate her night's killing.

I went up the stairs and stood at the top and thought I heard the faintest sound of someone in pain. There were no lights on. I walked the strip of carpet to Olivia's room and opened the door straight into her wide-open eyes and mouth just beginning to gape with horror. I shook my head and stepped back but the image kept coming at me. She was lying on her back, her bare legs wrapped around Carlos' rib cage, her ankles crossed and resting on his buttocks. He loomed over her, naked, board-straight on outstretched arms. His head snapped round. I slammed the door shut and reeled back two small steps as if I'd been hit in the face.

And then, like someone who *has* been hit in the face, I was furious. Mad enough that my eyeballs pulsated. I reached for the door handle, the blood thumped in my forearm, as a tremendous hammering started on the front door. I gripped the door handle and felt it gripped from the other side. The hammering at the front door didn't stop. I thought of the fire brigade, my mind going for an odd link.

I ran down the stairs. The cat had vacated the kitchen chair. I ripped open the front door. There was a man I knew, but not in this context, standing with six men behind him and a van behind them.

'Inácio?' I said, my mind in pieces now, holding out my hand.

'I'm sorry, Inspector,' he said, ignoring the hand. 'But this is business.'

'Narcotics business? Here?' I said, hearing movements up the stairs behind me.

'That's right,' he said. 'I'm still with Narcotics.'

'But you said this was business. I don't . . .'

'We've come to search the house,' he said, holding out a warrant, which I didn't read. 'You know a local fisherman called Faustinho Trindade?'

'I know Faustinho,' I said, looking through the warrant now. 'He was . . .'

'He's a well-known drug-smuggler. He was seen going into this house. You were seen leaving with him and going down to the boat club.'

'Search the house, Inácio. Search the house. Take your time,' I said.

Inácio stepped into the hall and gave the men their instructions. Two went back to the van and returned with large tool boxes. Olivia and Carlos met them on their way down the stairs. Inácio directed us into the kitchen. The three of us sat around the table with an *agente* standing over us while the rest thundered around the house. Olivia engaged me in some direct eye contact.

'Who are these guys?' she asked in English.

'Narcotics agents. They're searching the house. If you've got any in your room you'd better tell me now.'

425

'No, I haven't,' she said, unblinking.

'Are you sure?'

'*I'm* sure.'

Only then did I become aware of each blood cell, every platelet in my veins. My stomach went into free fall. The bag of grass in the attic room.

Carlos looked like a dog who'd regretted eating some green meat from the bin. There was a loud cracking noise from above. I asked the *agente* what was going on.

'Floorboards, I imagine,' he said. 'Empty your pockets on the table.'

We emptied our pockets. Carlos', I noted, contained 4000 escudos, some change, four condoms, which I was glad about, a pen, his ID card and his *Polícia Judiciária* card.

'I didn't know you were a cop,' said the *agente* looking at Carlos' card. 'Are you boyfriend and girlfriend?'

Nobody said anything. The *agente* shrugged. He picked up Olivia's card and measured the birthdate against Carlos'.

'Maybe not,' he said.

They were in the house for forty minutes. They found nothing. Inácio apologized and this time shook my hand which was running with sweat. The men left. I stood in the darkened hallway and looked into the lit kitchen. Olivia and Carlos were standing together like some movie couple who'd survived a hurricane. I pointed a finger at Carlos.

'You can leave now,' I said. 'Go on! Get out! Fuck off out of here!'

He came towards me and slipped out of the door. I had nothing to say to my little girl. Nothing to say to my daughter. I went up the stairs one at a time all the way to the attic room. I turned on the table lamp. I sat at the desk. I opened the drawer. No bag of grass. No papers. I took out my late wife's photograph which was face-up and not how I'd left her. I closed the drawer. I put her photograph on the desk facing me. I felt betrayed,

426

defiled, rifled, my world shaken up so that I was reduced to the one constant – the unflagging image of my dead wife.

Half an hour passed and three ships in the night.

Olivia appeared, reflected in the dark panes of the window.

'Your bag of grass is outside in the bougainvillea . . . and the papers.'

'You've been in here before?' I said, tired, not angry any more.

'After school . . . just to look at Mummy,' she said. 'But I don't talk to her like you do.'

'You think a year is a long time, but it isn't,' I said.

'I sat here the other day and wondered what it would be like to have her back . . . whether I would want to have her back.'

'Wouldn't you?'

'I've never stopped thinking "Mum would be interested in that, I'll tell her when I get home",' she said. 'And then I get home, and there's nobody here and there's never going to be anybody here. Absolutely never. And that's when I miss her. I want to have her back, but it would have to be as it was before. This gap. This one year without her has changed everything.'

I nodded, slightly exaggerated, like a drunkard. I lit a cigarette, Olivia took it. I lit another and played with the tin seashell ashtray.

'Loss is like a shrapnel wound,' I said, 'where the piece of metal's got stuck in a place where the surgeons daren't go, so they decide to leave it. It's painful at first, horribly painful, so that you wonder whether you can live with it. But then the body grows around it, until it doesn't hurt any more. Not like it used to. But every now and again there are these twinges when you're not ready for them, and you realize it's still there and it's always going to be there. It's a part of you. A still, hard point inside.'

She kissed the top of my head. I put an arm around her hips. I put the photograph back in the drawer.

'I've met somebody,' I said.

'I know.'

'Do you?'

'That business with the telephone on Sunday. The way you smelt when you came back and . . . you might not know it, but you're happier.'

'I'm not sure how to do it . . . this getting to know someone again.'

'What's she like?'

'I couldn't tell you yet,' I said. 'It's been a rocket ride so far. She's different to your mother, but she's like her too in the important ways. She's a good person, a real person. Someone you can trust.'

She stroked my head.

'Like Carlos,' she said.

I resisted a reply, but I didn't deny it.

'I'm angry with him. I'm not going to tell you otherwise. If Inácio hadn't turned up . . .'

'Why?'

'He knows what he's doing. He knows your vulnerability. He knows he's ten years older than you. He even knows it's against the law. He met you on a Sunday morning and by Tuesday evening he's in bed with you . . . he abused . . .'

'He *didn't* know what he was doing. I've already talked to him about Mum. What's ten years? The law's stupid. And so what? Mum told me that you two were in bed with each other inside a week and I knew I wanted him more than anything else in my life. And that's what I did. He did *not* seduce me. He didn't abuse anything. He's . . . he's got something. He's got something that all those fancy kids I go to school with haven't.'

'What? What's he got . . . ?' I said and stopped the second half of that sentence just in time . . . that I haven't.

428

'That's the point, Dad,' she said, running a hand through my hair.

'What is? You're being as cryptic as your mother used to be.'

'I don't know . . . but I want to. The thrill of that mental connection, remember.'

Chapter XXXV

23rd October 1980, Banco de Oceano e Rocha, São Paulo, Brazil.

Manuel Abrantes' secretary came in to his office with a padded package which had been delivered by courier.

'He needs you to sign for it,' she said.

Manuel beckoned the guy in and signed. His eyes fell automatically on the two inches of his secretary's legs between the desk and her skirt hem. He wondered if her underwear was as sensible as the girl. The courier backed out. He told his secretary to straighten the magazines on the table and peered around his desk. She dropped down on to her haunches to do the work. After six years working for him, she knew Manuel Abrantes' sly tricks.

He waved her out of the room, annoyed. Maybe he should take her out to dinner before he left, get her back to his apartment, show her a thing or two. He opened the package. Inside was a passport, an ID card, an envelope of cheques, a cheque wallet from a Portuguese bank, a Visa card, and an Amex card. There was also a photograph of a thirty-two-year-old woman called Lurdes Salvador Santos. She looked good-natured, despite a severe hairstyle and a faint moustache. A four-page letter from Pedro explained the documents and photograph.

He checked the ID card and passport. The latter was well-used, broken in with plenty of stamps. He opened the packet of cheques. He removed three and put the rest in the cheque wallet. He made up three fictitious amounts and wrote them in the account movements booklet within the wallet. He read the letter four times and memorized every detail. He burnt it with the three blank cheques.

He took one thousand US dollars from his top drawer and left the office. He walked six blocks in the staggering afternoon humidity to a rubber stamp maker, who'd already prepared a Brazilian entry stamp for him. He went to a travel agent and booked a flight from São Paulo to Buenos Aires and on to Madrid. He went to the Argentine embassy with his tickets and they gave him a visa while he waited. He went back to his office.

He took all his old documents out of his pockets and desk and passed them through the shredder. He emptied the shredder and burnt the contents in the waste bin.

He went out past his secretary, paused and came back to her. They looked at each other. Too complicated, he thought. He nodded to her and left. She gave him the finger to his departing back.

At 2.00 p.m. the following day his passport received an exit stamp as he went through to the departure lounge in São Paulo airport. The Immigration officer had no thoughts or opinions as to why a Portuguese national, Miguel da Costa Rodrigues, should be leaving Brazil for Argentina and he didn't ask him any questions.

By the 25th October, after two flights and a car journey, Miguel da Costa Rodrigues was sitting in the office of Pedro Abrantes, Director of the newly privatized Banco de Oceano e Rocha, still in their old offices on Rua do Ouro in the Baixa.

'I can't believe what's happened to Portugal,' said Miguel, looking up from the latest photograph of his brother's wife, Isabel, and their three children.

'The government's determined that we are going to join the EEC at the same time as Spain. We have to make progress,' said Pedro.

'No, no. I mean I can't believe the sex. There's sex

431

everywhere on the advertisements, the film posters. Have you seen that kiosk in the Rossio? The nudity. I mean it's incredible. It would never have been possible . . .'

'Yes, well, *salazarismo* was very Catholic and respectful of women,' said Pedro, frowning. 'There were censors. You, of all people, should know that.'

'Me, of all people?' asked Miguel, alarmed by his brother's casual slip.

'Sorry, *Senhor* Rodrigues, I forgot,' said Pedro. 'You'll see . . . we've put all that behind us.'

'The Portuguese never put anything behind them except a chair to eat lunch. We live with our history as if it's still all happening around us. There are people in this country who think the Hidden King Sebastião is going to come back after four hundred years, to lead them on to greater things. For all I know there could be people waiting for me.'

Pedro didn't say anything. He loved his brother, but he thought he was exaggerating his importance in the *ancien régime*. His brother had never told him about General Machedo. His brother thought that Pedro was an innocent – an intelligent man, a charming and gifted banker, a much-respected and well-liked person, but an innocent.

'I sold the gold,' said Pedro to get off the old subject, back on to something he felt confident with and the future.

'Seeing as we're talking about history, you mean?' said Miguel.

'I used it to capitalize the bank.'

'Who bought it?'

'A Swiss-based Colombian.'

'What did you get for it?'

'It seemed the right time to sell. This US budget deficit scare is nothing. It's just a . . .'

'How much?'

'Six hundred dollars an ounce.'

'Didn't it go as high as eight hundred?'

'It did, but he was the right buyer in the right climate. Not inquisitive, if you understand my meaning.'

'Doesn't this US budget deficit bring into question the real value of the dollar?' asked Miguel, trying to sound knowledgeable, spouting stuff he didn't fully understand, from reading *Time* on the aeroplane.

'That's why I've moved into property.'

'If the US goes bust it won't matter what you've moved it into.'

Pedro stood up and spun the dial on a wall safe behind him. Miguel saw the small kid in him, the excited one at Christmas.

'The US won't go bust, but if it does . . .' he said, and opened the safe door.

Inside were two gold bars. Miguel joined him on his side of the desk and rubbed his thumb over the eagle and swastika stamp of the old German Reichsbank.

'I'm hoping their value will be purely sentimental,' said Pedro.

'Tell me about the job,' said Miguel, sitting back down, sweating a little, not sure, in his slightly paranoid state, whether it was such a good idea to have kept those souvenirs.

'We've bought some property just off the Largo Dona Estefânia. Old apartments, falling to pieces. We're expanding. We don't fit in this old building any more. So we're going to demolish those old apartments and build ourselves a new office building. We'll take the top three floors and rent out the rest. I want you to manage the project. The architect's on my back and I haven't got the time for him.'

'When do you want me to start?' asked Miguel, unnerved at the immediate possibility of heavy responsibilities.

'As soon as you're comfortable. There's an office ready for you upstairs. We've had to convert the apartments to fit ourselves in here.'

Miguel stood and shook himself out.

'I need some time to get used to being back in Portugal. I want to go back to the Beira and smell the air again. I want to eat some fish on Guincho beach, you know, that sort of thing.'

Pedro, suddenly moved to have his brother back in the country, went round his desk to him and embraced him.

'Before you do any of these things we have to go to the notary tomorrow,' he said. 'Now that you're Miguel da Costa Rodrigues there are a few small problems. The first, and most important, is that I have to make you guardian to my children in case anything should happen to me and Isabel. Dr Aquilino Oliveira has arranged everything.'

'Of course,' said Miguel, nearly emotional.

They clapped each other's shoulders and Miguel made for the door.

'There's one other thing,' said Pedro. 'Klaus Felsen was released from prison last month.'

'Isn't that a year early?'

'Don't ask me why. You just have to know and you also have to remember that it was one of our father's dying wishes that we have nothing to do with him.'

Miguel was surprised to see his brother cross himself.

'Has *Senhor* Felsen called?'

'He's tried.'

'Well, he won't have much interest in Miguel da Costa Rodrigues.'

'I'm just telling you because . . . he has every reason to be angry. Not with us, maybe, but . . .'

'You should make him an offer.'

'Father made me promise . . . on his deathbed. I can't.'

Miguel shrugged. It felt good to have a heavy suit on his shoulders again, to not be sitting in the chill of air conditioning.

Pedro straightened the photograph on his desk and watched his brother's wide back fit through the doorway.

He hadn't told him about his father's other dying wish, which was that his younger brother should inherit nothing from the Banco de Oceano e Rocha or any of its associated companies. It was the only thing he hadn't understood and his father hadn't explained but now, strangely, he'd been relieved of the problem – Manuel Abrantes no longer existed and Miguel da Costa Rodrigues would have to be on the board.

Miguel da Costa Rodrigues was a different man to Manuel Abrantes. The old Manuel wasn't just a shredded passport or an old skin left in a São Paulo apartment. He was a dead man. Miguel da Costa Rodrigues proved to be more than just an identity change. He wasn't someone who'd tortured, raped, murdered and summarily executed anybody. He was a graduate from an American university, with an MBA and seven years' work-experience in Brazilian banking. He was charming and affable with a long line in bad after-dinner jokes. He liked children and children liked him. He was popular at work, respected for his unique relationship with the owner of the bank and his instinctive ability to manage people, to know their weaknesses and strengths.

For the second time in his life he became a success.

On January 19th 1981 he married the woman his brother had found for him – Lurdes Salvador Santos. Not even the name bothered him. That huge build-up of sainthood would have had him sweating in the dark ten years ago. Now he basked, if not in her beauty, then in her sweet nature and, of course, in her total dedication to him. Their only unhappiness was over two miscarriages in quick succession, and the doctor's advice not to try again.

That last miscarriage had come at a time when he believed that nothing could go wrong. In June he had delivered the planning permission for a twenty-storey high-rise on the Largo Dona Estefânia site. A week later construction had begun and he became known to the Lisbon business community as the *Director Geral de Oceano e Rocha Propriedades*

Lda with a seat on the full board of the bank and a major shareholding.

His wife's news disappointed him and he unconsciously turned more of his attention to his work. He bought property around Saldanha for future development. He bought old factory sites on the outskirts of Lisbon for development into light industrial units and small businesses. He bought sites on the edge of Cascais, near Boca do Inferno, to build tourist apartments. He bought an apartment block in the Graça area of Lisbon, with a panoramic view of the city. He converted the top two floors into his Lisbon residence. He refurbished his wife's house in the old part of Cascais. He became fatter, and even more genial.

It was New Year's Day 1982 and Miguel and Lurdes Rodrigues had invited Pedro and Isabel Abrantes with their three children over to Cascais for lunch. The sun had shone all day but it was cold and when, in the late afternoon, the sun went down, the temperature hovered around freezing point.

Pedro's wife was seven and a half months pregnant with their fourth child. She was enormous which had surprised her, because with the first three she'd hardly altered shape. It meant that on the way back to Lisbon she sat in the back seat with the two girls, while the young Joaquim travelled up front with his father.

They were just driving out of São Pedro do Estoril in their six-month-old Mercedes estate in the fast lane of the Marginal when three things happened at once. Little Joaquim stood on the seat, a car coming the other way swerved briefly over the double white line into the oncoming fast lane, and a BMW overtook Pedro on the inside. Pedro put his hand across to pull Joaquim back into his seat. He yanked the steering wheel across to his right but hadn't seen the BMW which hit him in the rear wing. The Mercedes span twice, turned over the roadside kerb,

436

rolled on to its roof and back on to two wheels on a high bank which dropped down to some rocks by the sea. The Mercedes rolled, twisted, and slid down the bank. The front end crunched into the rocks shattering the windscreen. The three children spilled out. The car somersaulted over them and finished roof-down in the freezing Atlantic.

The *Bombeiros Voluntários* were there within ten minutes. People were already weeping at the crushed bodies of the three children on the rocks. The firemen quickly ascertained that Pedro had not survived but that Isabel was still breathing and crushed between the front and rear seats. It took an hour to cut her out and they rushed her straight into Lisbon with a police escort. The foetus, a baby girl weighing 2.7 kilos, was delivered by Caesarean section and placed in an incubator. Her mother's heart, weakened by the shock of the accident, did not survive the operation.

The funerals took place twenty-four hours later at the Mosteiro dos Jerónimos in Belém. The coffins were all closed, the spirit of the congregation broken by the size of the smallest three. The Abrantes family were placed in a family mausoleum in the Cemitério dos Prazeres in Lisbon, which already contained Joaquim Abrantes senior whose body had been brought back from Lausanne in 1979.

Miguel da Costa Rodrigues didn't get out of dark glasses for weeks and when he did his eyes were bruised and ruched. His brother's death blackened him in a way that had only happened once before. He derived small consolation at the delivery from the incubator of the child they named Sofia which had been her intended name.

It was from early January 1982 that Miguel da Costa Rodrigues began to get visits from Manuel Abrantes. The Banco de Oceano e Rocha moved from the Baixa into larger temporary offices on the Avenida da Liberdade while the construction of the Largo Dona Estefânia building was completed. Miguel decided to maintain his brother's office in the Rua do Ouro. He began trawling the streets around the Praça da Alegria for girls.

On the 26th March 1982 he found himself climbing the stairs of an old eighteenth-century building on the Rua da Glória followed by a twenty-three-year-old prostitute from Sines. The top floors belonged to the Pensão Nuno, which rented rooms by the hour. He dinged the bell and heard a newspaper fold in a nearby room. Into the light of the neon strip above the reception came Jorge Raposo, his old colleague from the Caxias prison days.

Miguel da Costa Rodrigues no longer had to walk the streets of the Rua da Glória. Jorge Raposo arranged for the girls to visit him in his office on the Rua do Ouro.

From the beginning of April, Friday lunchtimes and afternoons were spent in the Rua do Ouro office. Any papers that needed to be signed were brought to him by secretaries from the main office who knew where to leave them.

On May 4th 1982 a secretary from the bank's law firm needed a signature which couldn't wait until Monday. There were no bank secretaries available to take the papers so she went down to the Rua do Ouro office herself.

Chapter XXXVI

Wednesday, 17th June 199–, Lisbon.

I caught the train in early to Cais do Sodré. I walked along the river, buffeted by purposeful people arriving for work from the ferries. It was another hot day and I had my jacket off and over my shoulder. I looked out across the river and saw the massive Lisnave gantry crane rising up out of the early morning haze. I thought about Carlos Pinto. I thought about seeing him again, working with him, accepting him.

You think you know yourself until things start happening, until you lose the insulation of normality. I would have called myself 'aware' before I lost my wife. People would look at me, Narciso for instance, and think there goes Zé Coelho, a man who knows himself. But I'm like anybody else. I hide. My wife was right. I'm inquisitive for the truth but I hide from my own. The stuff I've carried with me and ignored.

My father – a good man who thought he was doing the right thing for his country. He died of a heart attack without ever talking to me. Maybe a three-line conversation would have been enough, and we could have unburdened ourselves.

My daughter, unable to bear my disappointment . . . like an unfaithful lover. An horrific concept. The sight of her and Carlos in the graphic act . . .

An image flashed in my mind, Lucy Marques' description of what Teresa Oliveira had seen. Her daughter. Her lover. Pumping buttocks. Ankles around the ears. What an absurd act, but what a crucial one. An unrecoverable situation.

I saw it then looking out over the water of the Tagus, the dazzling, shimmering river. I saw that I could pick up another bag of rocks, hump another sack of guilt or history and carry that through the rest of my days. Or I could accept, trust, accommodate . . . give myself a break.

But if I was going to do that there was something I had to see first.

I turned away from the river, walked up through the Baixa to the Largo Martim Moniz and caught the Metro north.

Carlos and I were called straight into Narciso's office without a word being exchanged.

'I sent you down to Alcântara yesterday,' said Narciso, his mood unchanged in twenty-four hours.

'That's where we went, *Senhor Engenheiro*,' I said.

'You went there but you didn't stay, *Senhor* Inspector. A PSP officer saw you leave the crime scene and board a train in the direction of Cascais. I want to know where you were going on police time?'

'I went to see Dr Oliveira . . .' I said, and Narciso's tanned face purpled, '. . . to offer my condolences.'

'As part of the Inspector Zé Coelho service?'

I didn't answer. Narciso looked between Carlos and me.

'And what can you tell me about the murder of this eighteen-year-old down in Alcântara, *Senhor* Inspector? The *maricão* in the bin . . . what's his name?'

'He doesn't have a name, *Senhor Engenheiro*,' said Carlos. 'He's known as Xeta.'

'*Cheta?* As in *não tenho cheta*?' I haven't got a penny.

'It's Brazilian for "kiss", *Senhor Engenheiro*.'

'These people. My God. Just tell me what's been going on.'

'The investigation . . .' started Carlos.

'I want the investigating officer's report,' Narciso cut in.

'The boy was a known prostitute. We've conducted . . .' I started.

'Don't give me any more bullshit, Inspector. You don't know anything. You haven't done anything. You're heading for suspension, you know that, suspension without pay. And, *agente* Pinto . . .'

'Yes, *Senhor Engenheiro?*'

'The Narcotics agents who'd mounted a surveillance on the Inspector's property noted that you went in there at six-thirty p.m. What the hell were you doing in Paço de Arcos?'

'I wanted to brief the Inspector on developments.'

'There haven't been any.'

'To discuss alternative approaches.'

'With the Inspector's daughter?'

'She let me into the house, yes. I had to wait some time before the Inspector turned up.'

'You're at the end of the road now, *agente* Pinto. If you don't make your assignment with Inspector Coelho work, you're finished. You're out. You'll be looking for a job in the PSP. Do you understand me?'

'Perfectly, *Senhor Engenheiro.*'

'Get out, both of you.'

Carlos made it out of the door first. Narciso called me back. I clicked the door shut. He stuck a finger in his collar and pulled it out, too much blood stuck up in his head and the collar not letting it back down.

'Your tie, Senhor Inspector,' he said. 'Where did you buy it?'

'My tie?' I said, marking time, looking for the angle.

'What you have around your neck, *Senhor* Inspector?'

'My daughter made it for me.'

'I see . . .' he said, embarrassed by that. 'Would she make one for me?'

'You'd have to ask her, Senhor *Engenheiro* . . . she'd have to see your face, you know, to work out what would suit.'

He wiped his face with his hand and waved me away. I left his office with his aftershave in my nostrils and went back down to my own. Carlos was staring out of the window at the crowds of people in the photo booths in Rua Gomes Freire. I collapsed into my chair and lit an SG Ultralight and drew on it fiercely, desperate for a proper hit of nicotine.

'Who's going to get coffee?'

Carlos left without a word and came back with two mini plastic cups with an inch of coffee in each.

'Are we going to talk?' he asked, putting my *bica* down.

'Have you spoken to your father?'

'What about?'

'About what happened last night.'

'No.'

'No. I didn't think you would. You wouldn't have made it into work with two broken legs after he'd thrown you off his balcony.'

He looked off out of the half-open door with his hands clasped between his knees.

'So, you want to talk,' I said. 'Let's talk. Let's talk about how *agente* Carlos Pinto has gone through my life in a pair of jackboots, trampling everything underfoot.'

He ran a hand over his cropped hair and rubbed his nose vigorously with his finger and thumb.

'She's sixteen. You're twenty-seven. Shit. I'm beginning to sound like that bloody lawyer now. We have laws about sex, *agente* Pinto. Do they cover that in the police academy these days?'

'They do have laws, yes, and they cover them, but as you know Inspector, you can be an old hand at fourteen or an innocent at twenty-four. That's a ten-year grey area.'

'Twenty-four?' I said, engaging his eyes.

He stuck his chin out . . . daring me.

'That's right, Inspector, I live with my parents. It's not so easy.'

Olivia had said he didn't know what he was doing.

He grinned, his nerves getting to him.

'You're lucky, *agente* Pinto. You're lucky Narcotics turned up. You're lucky I talked to Olivia. You're lucky I was married to an Englishwoman for nearly half my life. You're lucky . . .'

'To have met her,' he said, fixing me with a look. 'I'm lucky to have met your daughter . . . and you for that matter.'

'That's what she told me,' I said, riding that wave, struggling with all sorts of things now.

'I'm in love with her,' he said, the statement of fact, no frills.

'I'm not sure if she's been around long enough to know the difference between someone who's in love with her and someone who's just looking for an easy lay.'

The anger flared in him, quick and bright as a magnesium flash. It was what I'd wanted to see.

'At least I'm not black,' he said, which I probably deserved.

I pointed a finger at him, my longest, most penetrating one and jabbed it at him.

'I trust you, Carlos Pinto,' I said, 'and that was the last reason why you were lucky.'

He sat back, blinking. The anger gone now and something like pain in his face. He nodded at me. I put the finger down and nodded back. I pulled the drawer open in my desk and put my feet up on it and stared at the ceiling and sipped my coffee for five minutes, wincing.

'What now?' asked Carlos, still nervous.

'I'm thinking that this tooth here under my new bridgework hurts when I drink something hot.'

I called my dentist who said she'd fit me in some time during the afternoon.

'What about Xeta?' asked Carlos.

'Narciso knows that's a hopeless case.'

'The lab report from the pathologist said he had three

types of semen in his rectum, two different types in his stomach and he was HIV positive.'

I threw up my hands.

'I don't like not giving my full attention to a case, but you have to recognize when it's unwinnable. Narciso knows. He's put us out to grass.'

'So . . .' he said, weighing things up, 'we have lunch in Alcântara?'

'You're learning,' I said. 'You're learning too fast.'

We sat outside the Navigator restaurant, two establishments up from the Wharf One nightclub, with a large platter of sardines, boiled potatoes, grilled peppers and a salad. We shared a carafe of white wine. The sardines were perfect, not too large and fresh off the boat. We dismantled them without speaking. The waiter came and took our plates away. We ordered coffee.

'Let's think about what we've got,' I said.

Carlos took out his notebook and flicked through the sheets. He began a résumé.

'We've got a sexually loose girl, called Catarina Oliveira, who was last seen getting into a black C series Mercedes 200, petrol, with tinted windows and the letters NT in the registration. This happened about an hour before she was murdered and took place about a hundred metres from her school on Avenida Duque de Ávila.

'It seems this girl would do anything for her father to get his attention, but despised her mother to the point where she would collude with the father in her humiliation, probably in a desperate attempt to strengthen her relationship with her father.

'We don't think that the lawyer is the real father,' he concluded.

'Have you checked that in the hospital records?' I asked.

'Yes, *Dona* Oliveira was definitely the mother. There's no doubt about that.'

'I'm impressed.'

'You don't have to tell me to do everything,' he said. 'I even checked the librarian at the Biblioteca Nacional and all the other alibis.'

'I'm not used to initiative,' I said. 'Carry on.'

'The victim is associated with Valentim Almeida, the guitarist in the band who we suspect is a pornographer and who had sufficient hold over her to persuade her to indulge in an unusual sexual act in the Pensão Nuno, during the lunchtime before she was killed.'

Carlos flicked backwards and forwards through his notebook.

'There's no evidence so far that the killer followed her from the *pensão* to the school . . . or rather the café near the school.'

'Go back to the notes you took from the people we interviewed at the bus stops. Four of them saw her get into the car. Did any of them say where the car came from?'

'We didn't ask that question. We just wanted to know about the car she got into.'

'You've got all the telephone numbers of those people at the bus stop. Call them and ask that question,' I said. 'If he was a passing motorist that's one thing, but if he was waiting for her to come out of the school then he'd already tracked her down.'

'The barman in the Bella Italia said she was alone when she drank the *bica*.'

'I tried to talk to him the other day but he was off,' I said. 'I'll try again after I've been to the dentist.'

'And then there's Valentim,' said Carlos. 'He's still got something to tell us. I don't know what, but . . . something.'

'I wouldn't mind establishing a link between him and Dr Oliveira.'

'There's one already. The lawyer gave us his telephone number.'

445

'I mean a relationship of some sort.'

'A financial one . . . the video equipment?'

'Maybe. That's an interesting possibility. He won't tell us anything but maybe we can surprise it out of him. Is he still being held in the *tacos*?'

'I'll check.'

I left Carlos making calls and told him to carry on working the Xeta case in Alcântara while I went to my dentist on Campo Grande. I took the 38 bus all the way from the docks. It took for ever.

I sat in the waiting room flicking through *Caras* magazine, looking at all the half-celebrities, thinking about Luísa and her dismay at the idea of sex scandal in a serious business magazine. I dropped *Caras* and picked up *VIP*, another in the genre. Flicking from the back I came across a bunch of photographs of charity functions. There was one at the Ritz and the photograph showed Miguel da Costa Rodrigues and his wife in a line-up of people who mattered. *Senhor* Rodrigues was wearing one of Olivia's ties, the same one he'd been wearing that Friday night in Paço de Arcos. His wife was wearing a suit that I'd seen Olivia working on for the past month. I tore the picture out and folded it into my wallet to show Olivia later.

The dentist patched up a small gap between the bridge-work and my tooth. It took her thirty seconds and she told me I'd have to come back for a filling. The repair work cost 8000 esc. and the filling would be another 12,000 esc. It sounded like easy money to me if you could bear looking in rotten mouths all day.

I came out of Campo Grande and tested my repaired bridgework with a coffee. I found myself looking at a building, which I realized was the Biblioteca Nacional. I wandered in and around the stacks of books until I got to the psychology section. I saw him from the back first, with that swag of brown ringlets. He was out of the *tacos*. That hadn't taken long, I thought. I sat down next to him. He glanced over and I had his full attention.

'Are you interested in books, Inspector?'

'I like José Saramago.'

'Really? You surprise me.'

'He has the same attitude to punctuation that I do.'

'You don't need it.'

'Or maybe he's no good at it,' I said, thinking. 'It's a solution, isn't it?'

He nearly smiled. I nodded in the direction of the door and we left the building. We sat outside the café on white plastic chairs. He ordered a *bica*. I had a glass of water this time. He took one of my cigarettes. I let him.

'How's it going, Inspector?'

'I'm off the case.'

'Is this a social visit?'

'I've been through a lot these past few days.'

'How many of them did *you* spend in the *tacos*?'

'I didn't say yours had been a beach party.'

'It hasn't.'

'I had my house turned over.'

'It wasn't me.'

'By some Narcotics agents.'

'Sharks'll eat anything, even each other, you know that.'

'Who do you think organized it?'

'You're the detective.'

'Why did you end up three or four nights in the *tacos*?'

'Because you put me there.'

'And who gave me your phone number?'

He bounced against the back of his white plastic chair.

'You're cleverer than you look, Inspector.'

'That's why I used to have a beard, so that people wouldn't see the stupidity.'

'And now it's all out in the open.'

'Can you think of any reason why Dr Oliveira should give a damn about you?'

'It would be curious if he started now,' he said, 'because we've never met.'

'Before your studio went up I had time to leaf through your bank statements,' I lied.

'Well that's the kind of interesting person you are, Inspector.'

'I didn't find a loan account and not one repayment detail in your current account.'

'So what are you saying now, Inspector? That Dr Oliveira bought the equipment for me? If you are, you're off your head.'

'Am I?' I said, and left him with a small bill for a *bica* and a bottle of water.

I called Carlos who'd contacted all the people from the bus queues.

'Two women saw the car parked outside the school with the engine running for maybe five to ten minutes.'

'Waiting for the kids to come out of school.'

'Looks like it.'

'I'm going to talk to the barman at the Bella Italia now. Did you get anywhere with Xeta?'

'Nothing,' said Carlos. 'I spoke to the sergeant about Valentim . . .'

'I've just been talking to him.'

'Right. The sergeant said that a guy called João José Silva has been looking for you.'

'At the *Polícia Judiciária*?'

'That's what he said.'

'Did he say anything?'

'He said he still hasn't heard from Lourenço Gonçalves. What does that mean?'

'I don't know if it means anything. It's just one of those names that keeps showing up.'

Chapter XXXVII

Friday, 12th June 199–, Pensão Nuno, Rua da Glória, Lisbon.

How come girls do this now? How come this girl is doing this now? How has it come this far? 'My God,' said Miguel, finally and out loud, but not so loud that who he was watching in the next room, through the back of the mirror, through the rough hole in the plaster, through the ragged edges of the lath, would hear the thick, blood-clotted lechery in his voice.

It had been a long slow slide to this latest little vice. He'd done with whoring now. It was surprising how boring it got and how quickly. Pornography was no more than biology. Whoring no more than practical dissection. He hadn't liked it. It hadn't been the point.

The pressure of names had finally got to him, too. All the Teresas, the Fátimas, the Marias. All those little saints, the *santinhas* he called them, with their eyes staring up at him. He didn't need it. He got enough of that at church on Sundays.

No more whores. No more *santinhas*. He thought he might be cured, except that he found himself still reaching for something, like an artist who's painted the same scene again and again, trying to find what it was he had to say.

He'd told Jorge not to send him any more girls and that had been that. But Jorge . . . Jorge had kept something back. He had something special, but Miguel would have to come to the *pensão* to see it.

He'd come on a Friday lunchtime. When was that? Years

ago now or not? Jorge had taken him up to the room, told him about the two-way mirror and left. A familiar constriction had come into his throat and he'd pinched the skin around it with his thumb and finger. He lifted the mirror away on his side of the wall and there, framed raggedly, was a leading Lisbon architect he knew by name for God's sake, with a girl, a young girl, her legs splayed, heels braced against the sink.

As he was watching he had a sudden jagged fear that this wasn't a mirror but a window. Then he realized the heavily made-up eyes of the girl were focused elsewhere. Of course they were. There'd have been uproar if they'd seen his bald head ducked into the alcove. He waved at them to test their reactions. They toiled on, oblivious. He sat back on the bed unblinking for the minutes it took the architect to finish his business.

He watched, fascinated, as they fell back on to the bed and the man tipped the girl off his lap into the pillows. He shuddered slightly as the man came to the mirror and inspected his face for telling defects and then set about some frantic washing of his peeled-prawn penis, jaw clenched, teeth bared. He found himself enclosed by the drama of this private screening. The architect dressing, tearing at his shirt, desperate to be clothed again. The throwing of money, too much, on to the bed, the girl still not moving. He found his heart thumping in his chest as the door closed and he heard the clattering feet on the wooden stairs. He ran his hands over his pate and into the hairline of his neatly clipped, brilliantined head to the fat of his neck and shoulders which he gripped.

The girl remained face-down in the pillows. She stretched a small hand behind her. He was touched to see a cheap puzzle ring on her third finger. She reached in between her legs with thumb and forefinger and, as if she was pulling a splinter, yanked out the used condom. The fat man sank to his knees with a low groan. This had satisfied something

450

in him, turned some grey beaten crust of earth and found dark rich soil underneath.

Miguel admired history. He liked its weight, its huge, glacial, unstoppable movement onwards. He would have liked to have fashioned it. He had in a way. But not enough. He supposed that this was why he enjoyed this little scene so much – a shot of a man's secret history. His real story. The one that would never get published but would be known . . . had *been* observed.

Then he saw *this* girl.

Jorge had been right. She was different. She was 'something special'. Jorge remembered things that worried him.

She was naked now and looking across the room to the mirror. He liked to see her face. He liked to see her front-on facing the mirror across the bed. She never closed her eyes. Her big blue eyes stared out with terrible innocence and this is what joined him to her. In all these things she did she was looking for something. Like him. Turning things over and over. Reworking things over and over. Never quite getting to the source, not knowing what the source was.

He'd already made up his mind. He had to speak to her. He already knew where she went to school. He'd followed her. Today would be the day.

He sat on the edge of the bed and held his belly in both hands. Black hairs burst through a hole in his shirt where a button had come undone. He opened up his shirt and stood in front of the mirror. He sucked in his gut. Fatter than an acorn-fed black pig's arse. He rebuttoned the shirt, flicked the collar up and fed the tie round, the tie made for him by Sofia's friend, the Inspector's daughter. He humped on his jacket and from a pig's arse made a patrician banker.

He looked around the room as if for the last time. The cracked cornice, the concentric stains on the ceiling, the seasick floor, patched with shagged and pileless rugs, covering holes in the biscuit-brittle lino, the wardrobe with its door hanging open, permanently stupid. He put his hands in his pockets and buffed his leg with his credit cards. He left the room, down the weakly-lit wooden staircase with its strip of blue lino, past the neon-lit reception with no Jorge, down more stairs, and more stairs to the huge wooden front doors and into the dark and shade of the sunstroked street and the distant applause of traffic. He breathed. That was the last time. That was definitely the last time.

He sat outside the school on Avenida Duque de Ávila, in his wife's Mercedes with the engine running. She'd be coming out soon. There was something sharp sticking into him from his pocket. He put his hand in and . . . what was this? A tube of lubricant. How did that get in there? He didn't want to do that. And condoms. This was not what he had intended. He threw them in the glove compartment.

It's her. Who's she with? Who's she talking to? He's after her. The look in his eyes. He's been there. Anybody can tell. She's walking away now. This is not how it should be. Look at her walk. One foot in front of the other, just like the models do. He's not letting her get away. He's after her. He's grabbed her wrist now and she's turned and twisted it away from him. She doesn't want this. My God. He's hit her. That look on her face. What does *that* say?

Miguel swallowed hard. Everything happening quicker than he'd expected. More things happening than he'd expected. All these people in the street. He pulled out. She was on the move again . . . down the catwalk.

He pulled up at the traffic lights and buzzed the passenger window down.

'Excuse me,' he shouted.

She's turned to him. Those eyes are on him now. Can he get the words out?

'How do I get to the Monsanto park from here?' he said.

She's come off the pavement. She's rested an elbow on the window ledge. She's glanced into the back of the car.

Why? What does she want suddenly? Her fingernails are bitten down to nothing.

'Monsanto park . . . from here. That's a bit complicated,' she said.

The sweat came up into his palms.

'Am I going in the right direction?'

'More or less. It's just . . . it can get complicated after the Parque de Palhavã.'

'You're not going in that direction are you?'

'I'm getting the train to Cascais.'

'I'm going to Cascais. I just don't want to go out on one of the main routes at this time of day on a Friday. I want to cut through Monsanto and join the Cascais motorway that way. I'll give you a lift . . . to your door. How's that?'

She looked at Miguel. Those blue eyes looked into his. And what did they see? The vulnerability of the old fat guy. Nothing to worry about.

'Unless . . .' he said, inspired by the stress of the moment. 'You haven't got to go back to your office first or anything, have you?'

The psychology was right. He remembered things.

She got in. The lights changed. Miguel's foot came off the clutch a little too quick and the car shot forward with a squeak from the tyres. He eased himself back into his seat. Calmed down. They were together now. He'd done it. He'd made contact.

She had a small bag. She threw it between her feet. She didn't put on the seat belt. He buzzed the window up. They were comfortable in the air conditioning.

'Keep going straight,' she said, and rocked very slightly backwards and forwards.

Sadness flapped inside his chest like a flag at half-mast.

He changed gear. His knuckle made contact with her brown thigh. She didn't move it away. He rested his hand on the gear stick.

'What's your name?' he asked.

'Catarina,' she said.

He smiled behind his moustache. She didn't ask him his. Kids don't.

He talked about his daughter, Sofia. His brother's daughter, but he didn't say that. He tried to shut out the second voice in his head, which told him that it knew what he was doing. He was being nice. He was good at being nice and it was working already. She kicked off one of her clumpy shoes and brought her leg up, rested the heel on the edge of the seat.

'Go right here, and take the first left,' she said.

'Do you like music?' he asked, wondering instantly if that sounded stupid.

'Sure,' she said, and shrugged a small shoulder at him.

'What sort of music?'

'Maybe not your sort of music.'

'Try me. I know them all. My daughter plays them all the time.'

'The Smashing Pumpkins.'

He nodded and engaged her in a game to translate the band's name into Portuguese, but there were too many names for different types of pumpkin and they couldn't decide. That was when she told him that she was a singer in a band, and they missed the turning to Monsanto. They headed north and wandered the streets of Sete Rios around the zoo, and then back down towards the gigantic Águas Livres aqueduct striding out into the hot afternoon, and then on to the right road which underpassed the railway line and into the park.

As they talked, as she fielded his questions, she'd gather her blonde hair behind her in a fist and, gnawing a non-existent nail, would study the windscreen looking for a reply in her head. It made him feel how young she was again. How sometimes she was fifteen, and other times twenty-five. How sometimes she was a schoolgirl, and other times she could be having sex in a *pensão* with . . . forget that. Strike it from the text.

They climbed up into the park through the pines, the stone pines threaded with empty tarmacked tracks, some leading up to the military installation and the Forte de Monsanto, others cutting through to the motorway and still others heading deeper into the park.

'What time is it?' she said and leaned over to look at the dashboard.

He smelt her hair.

'Just gone five o'clock.'

She sat back and slipped her shoe back on again and stretched her legs out into the footwell.

'There's a place up here with a great view of Lisbon, shall we take a look?' he asked, wanting it to be just an outing.

'OK,' she shrugged.

He pulled into the empty car park of the restaurant at the Alto da Serafina and drew up at the low wall. They got out and stood on the wall. The city stretched out before them. The squat, colossal dark glass towers of the Amoreiras dominated the skyline.

'Those towers . . .' she said.

'That whole area used to be mulberry trees for the Lisbon silk industry,' he said, talking to her like he talked to his own daughter, his brother's daughter.

'They're alien those towers . . . they look like they're going to kill the city. Suck up all its energy.'

It surprised him. He didn't say anything.

'Do I know you?' she asked, doing her catwalk away from him down the low wall.

He tensed in his shirt and looked at her legs.

'I don't think so.'

'I keep thinking I've seen you.'

'Let's get back in the car,' he said. 'I don't want to be late.'

She got off the wall, flashing the gusset of her knickers.

He pulled out of the car park and carried on through the pines, the endless umbrella pines. He took a wrong turning. Out of the sun. She didn't notice. He stopped the car.

'This isn't right,' he said, his heart pounding in his throat.

He backed into the trees.

'What are you doing?' she asked.

'I'm just turning round.'

He moved deeper into the trees and into a clearing. Out of sight of the road now. The engine stalled. The sun shone into the car. The tinted windows darkened. She looked down at his hand on the gear stick.

'What's the matter?' she said.

'I don't know.'

'I did see you before,' she said. 'I remember now. You came into the café near the school. You were standing behind me.'

'The café? What school?'

'The Bella Italia near the school.'

'Not me. I didn't know you were at school.'

'I'm sure it was you. That tie. In the mirror.'

'In the mirror?' he asked, something travelling through his veins now like electricity gone bad.

He saw everything pin-sharp, right down to the tiniest blonde two-millimetre-long hairs on her leg. She moved into the corner of her seat and brought her feet up on to it, not slipping out of her shoes this time.

'I've seen you before,' he said, and she brought her fists up under her chin. 'In the Pensão Nuno at lunchtime with your two boyfriends. Were they the ones from your band?'

The information mesmerized her.

How had it happened? How had it gone wrong? It should not have been like this. He swallowed again looking at her but not. Looking at her reflection in the windscreen.

'What do you want?' she asked, her voice quavering.

There was still time to stop this. He could stop it now, go back to the talk, go back to the Smashing Pumpkins. He didn't have to . . .

He stretched out a hand. A hand thick with hair. Hair that went up the fingers nearly to the top joint. Animal hands. He circled her ankle with his thumb and forefinger.

She flicked her foot out and the rhinestone-studded heel of her shoe thumped into him just above his heart. He gripped the ankle and held on. She grabbed his tie. He crushed her wrist in his hand and she yelped and let go. He twisted her arm. She lashed out with her other foot and caught him high on the chest this time. He twisted her arm more and she turned. She had to turn. He pressed forward with his weight over her. He pushed her face into the corner of the seat and the door.

'Don't hurt me,' she said. 'Please don't hurt me.'

He grunted. Her noise coming to him muffled. He pushed up her skirt and yanked her pants down, under her knees, right off, over her stupid shoes. She felt her back cracking under his weight. Heard him fumbling in the glove compartment not far from her head. She wrenched her other arm out from underneath her and tried to lash out. He drew her head back.

'No,' she said. 'No, please. Don't hurt me. Do what you want, but don't hurt me.'

Chapter XXXVIII

15.30 Wednesday, 17th June 199–, Bella Italia, Av. Duque de Ávila, Lisbon.

The Bella Italia was empty at this hour except for the old woman at her table with her view of the street, and the young barman who'd served Catarina her last coffee.

'Do you remember me?' I asked the old woman, who was wearing a pink silk dress of some class and antiquity.

'You're the Inspector,' she said, looking up from under lids more heavily pleated than her silk dress.

'The day that girl got slapped out there on the street, do you remember a car, a black Mercedes outside the school around the time it happened?'

'Like an old taxi, except it didn't have a green roof.'

'Yes,' I said. 'I liked those old taxis, black with a green roof.'

'They were Lisbon,' she said. 'These beige things . . . I keep thinking I'm getting into someone's private car by mistake. Still, that's Europe for you. When we joined in 1984 my husband said by the year 2000 we wouldn't be speaking Portuguese.'

'So far it's only the taxis.'

'And McDonald's. My grandchildren won't eat *pastéis de bacalhau*.'

'McDonald's are American.'

'It's the same thing,' she said. 'We eat them and they eat away at us.'

I went to the bar and ordered another water, too much caffeine in my system already – life coming at me too bright and sharp for comfort.

'Do *you* remember me?' I asked the barman. 'And the girl. You remember the girl.'

He nodded.

'You said she was on her own when she came in here.'

'And I'm still saying that now.'

'And nobody came in after her?'

'No.'

'The place was completely empty.'

'Apart from her,' he said, indicating the old lady. 'She was just getting up to leave.'

'What's her name?'

'*Dona* Jacinta,' replied the old lady, still hearing pretty well.

'She's got her hearing aid turned up,' whispered the barman.

'Yes, I have,' she said. 'And the girl came in on her own and nobody came in after her on that particular Friday . . . last Friday.'

'What does that mean, *Dona* Jacinta?'

'That's what happened last Friday. The previous Friday was different. I was here. That couple who are always arguing about their dog were sitting in the corner. You were here, Marco, weren't you?'

'I was here,' he said, a little bored.

'The girl came in. And a man stood outside on the pavement for a few moments before coming in after her.'

'That's right. *Dona* Jacinta,' said Marco, suddenly revitalized, 'and he sat down on that chair right behind her. He was looking at her legs . . . so you see I'm not the only one, Inspector.'

'Did he do anything?'

'He ordered a coffee over her shoulder. I think they looked at each other in the mirror.'

'He was big and fat,' said *Dona* Jacinta, 'and bald with a moustache and an expensive suit.'

'And his tie,' said Marco. 'His tie . . .'

459

'What about his tie?'

'He bought his tie in the same shop that you bought yours,' said *Dona* Jacinta.

'My daughter made it for me,' I said automatically.

'Then your daughter also made this man's tie,' she said.

I sat down slowly on the edge of a chair.

'Drink your water,' said Marco, holding it out to me.

'You saw the tie as well?' I asked.

'I saw it.'

I opened my wallet and took out the picture I'd just torn from *VIP* magazine. I smoothed it out on to the bar and tapped the face of Miguel da Costa Rodrigues.

'Shit,' said Marco. 'That's him. Show it to *Dona* Jacinta. That's him.'

I drank the water and went to the door. *Dona* Jacinta had her glasses out. She took the picture and nodded.

'That's the same tie, too,' she said.

I folded the picture back into my wallet.

'Nobody says anything about this. Not one word.'

A man in dark glasses came into the bar. He looked at the three of us and backed out.

I ran down to Saldanha. I was sweating in seconds. I picked up a taxi and told him to go to the Rua da Glória and he gave me a knowing look. I sat in the back, astride the drive shaft of a despised beige taxi, and sweated, supporting myself on two hands. The traffic was heavy heading down to the Praça Marquês de Pombal and the driver cut down the back streets around the hospitals of Miguel Bombarda and Santa Marta.

I sprinted up the blue lino to the Pensão Nuno reception. No Jorge. I slapped and hammered on the counter. Dinged the bell. Jorge came down the stairs, his flip-flops slapping the heels of his feet, taking the steps one at a time leaning on the bannister.

'That leg doesn't look too good, Jorge.'

'It isn't,' he said, with instant aggression. 'What do you want?'

'I've come to balance you out.'

He stopped on the stairs.

'Look,' he said, 'I told you I'd been sick . . .'

'Are you going to answer my questions?'

'Ask them first. I'll see.'

'Catarina,' I said, 'the girl who was killed. You said she'd been in here before . . . Friday lunchtimes.'

'I did.'

'What about the Friday lunchtime before last?'

'She was here.'

'Where?'

He hesitated, sensing I knew something more this time. I came up the stairs at him.

'You can stay down there,' he said. 'I just need to think.'

'Show me the room.'

'It was the same one as last time.'

'Show it to me.'

He turned and shuffled round on the step, aged twenty years in as many hours. I followed his flip-flops, his feet blue at the ankle.

'Who was she with, Jorge?'

He didn't answer, his breathing laboured. At the top of the stairs he leaned over the bannister rail. There were noises coming from the room, wild ecstatic noises of the sort a working girl learns with her first customer.

'Who was she with, Jorge?'

'Could have been a tap salesman from Braga for all I know.'

'Let's take a look in the room next to it, see if that'll jog that memory of yours.'

'She wasn't in that room.'

'I don't feel like interrupting, so we'll go in this room.'

'It's occupied.'

'It's very quiet in there for a room that's occupied.'

'I told you.'

'Open the door.'

461

'It's locked.'

'Get it open.'

He knocked on the door as if he didn't want to wake a princess.

'You can do better than that, Jorge.'

But the door opened. A small man in a cheap suit with a neat little pot belly stood in the darkened room.

I nodded him out and he shot down the stairs quicker than a pickpocket. I turned the weak light on. The room was empty. No girl. I checked the cupboard, its door already hanging open from the slope of the floor.

'Interesting, Jorge.'

I checked the unrumpled bed. There was a single dent close to the foot of the bed, opposite the mirror. I sat on it. It was uncomfortably warm. There were two thumbprints on the mirror. I lifted the mirror off the hooks. There was a view into the next room of a guy doing his very best with a girl handcuffed to the bedstead.

'Who was in here last Friday lunchtime, Jorge?' I shouted. 'And the Friday before that and all the other Fridays, for all I know!'

The guy in the next room stopped and looked over.

'Come on, Jorge!'

The guy eased himself off the girl and came over to the mirror. The girl followed him with her eyes. I tapped on the back of the mirror and the guy leapt back as if he'd seen his wife at the window, and started ripping into his clothes, didn't even take the condom off. I took out the picture of Miguel Rodrigues and held it up to Jorge.

'Was this the guy who was in this room last Friday lunchtime?'

He nodded.

'Out loud, Jorge.'

'It was him.'

The guy from the next room appeared in the doorway, looking murderous.

'If you want to help with a police investigation leave your address at reception,' I said.

He thundered down the stairs without a word. The girl, framed in the hole left by the mirror, looked from one chained wrist to the other.

'How long have you known him, Jorge?' I asked. 'You must be old pals by now.'

'Thirty-five years or so.'

'Thirty-five years or so,' I said. 'Early sixties. A very old pal.'

I looked him up and down – this tired, ruined man.

'I think I need a cigarette, Inspector. Mine are downstairs.'

I gave him one and lit it for him, his hands trembling now. He lowered himself on to the end of the bed.

'You and Miguel,' I said, 'it looks like your trains got separated, went off on different tracks.'

'He had some advantages that I didn't.'

'Family?'

The room was stuffy, airless. Jorge sucked on the cigarette, pulled his shirt off the rolls of empty skin around his belly. His face, already grey and broken-down, began to take on a green tinge in the weak forty-watt light. His eyes, unshifting, stared into a deep waterless hole, silted with bitterness.

'His father owned a bank.'

'Banco de Oceano e Rocha?' I asked, and he nodded. 'Is that where you met?'

'No, no. We met in Caxias . . . in Caxias prison.'

I looked at the torn-out picture of the sleek Miguel da Costa Rodrigues at his charity function at the Ritz.

'You don't look like communists,' I said. 'I mean he doesn't.'

Jorge shook his head.

'Were you crooks?' I asked. 'That'd be more like it.'

'We were with the PIDE,' said Jorge brushing some ash

from his fly. 'We worked in the interrogation centre . . .'

'Wait a second here, Jorge,' I said. 'His father owned the bank? Fifteen years ago. I remember it. It was a big thing. It got into the newspapers all over the world. The owner of the bank was killed in a car crash on the Marginal. The whole family was killed. I don't remember the name but it wasn't Rodrigues.'

'It was Abrantes. His name is Manuel Abrantes.'

'Why did he change his name?'

Jorge dumped his cigarette in the sink. It hissed and stuck.

'You've come this far, Jorge.'

'He did some things, Inspector. We all did some things. Manuel Abrantes did some bigger things than most. He was an *Inspector de Polícia*, how about that?'

'What sort of things are we talking about?'

'He killed a woman in Caxias prison. It was an accident, I think. She miscarried. I don't know. Maybe he kicked her . . . anyway, after that he was promoted to *chefe de brigada*.'

'That sounds like pretty regular stuff for PIDE. I'm sure there are a lot worse . . .'

'He was the leader of the squad that shot General Machedo in Spain.'

A drop of sweat travelled the length of my spine.

'Now you see,' said Jorge, 'how you have to be careful.'

I lit myself a cigarette this time and the hand was not so steady.

'I'm finished with him now. I've protected him over this thing. This girl. And now I'm done with him. Look at me, Inspector,' he said, and I turned my eyes away from the floor, not really wanting to look at him. 'Do I look like someone who's ever eaten at Manuel Abrantes' table?'

I started out of the room and looked back at him from the door. A collapsed human being, he stared into the niche above the sink without seeing further than his own head.

'Don't rush it, Inspector,' he said. 'It's not over by a long way.'

'Don't worry, Jorge. I'm not ready yet . . . but if anything happens to me, I'll know where to come looking.'

'You don't have to worry about me.'

'Where does he live? Abrantes.'

'Somewhere in Lapa. Where else? He took over his brother's old house. I don't know the address.'

There was a faint cry for help from next-door. Jorge's eyes suddenly registered what he was looking at. He shook his head and hauled himself to his feet.

I ran down the stairs two at a time. It was after five o'clock now. I called Olivia and asked for Miguel da Costa Rodrigues' address in Lapa. I called Carlos.

At a quarter-to-six we were standing outside a house in Rua Prior, leaning up against an old wall on the other side of the street.

At 6.15 p.m. an old guy opened up the gates to the house. One of two garage doors opened electronically and a black Mercedes C200 backed out into the street. I could smell the petrol engine and the registration number was 18 43 NT, but it did not have tinted windows. Lurdes Rodrigues was clearly visible through the glass. She parked up in the sunny street and got out. She went back into the house and returned with an envelope. In those few minutes the windows turned to black.

Chapter XXXIX

20.30 Wednesday, 17th June 199–, Luísa's apartment, Rua Actor Taborda, Lisbon.

We were lying on the bed. She was at right-angles to me, with her head on my stomach. We were both naked, not even a sheet over us. The windows were open and the faintest cool breeze and late light were coming into the room. We smoked and shared a heavy glass ashtray which sat in one quarter of the bed and a glass of whisky which lay in another. We stared at the ceiling. I'd spent the last forty minutes telling Luísa Madrugada everything I knew about the murder of Catarina Oliveira. We hadn't exchanged a word for the last quarter of an hour. I fingered a small pool of whisky spilt between her breasts and put it in my mouth.

'I've been interested in the Banco de Oceano e Rocha for the past couple of months,' she said.

'Don't open an account there.'

'I've been trying to find a link between them and Nazi gold.'

'Leave your money under the mattress like a good peasant.'

'Listen to me.'

'I am listening,' I said, fingering more whisky into my mouth. 'Why are you looking at Nazi gold?'

'Because it's a hot topic. All these commissions are forcing banks to open up their archives all over the world. It'll look good in my thesis if I can pull something off here in Portugal. And anyway, a study of Salazar's economy without looking at wartime gold transactions would be a serious omission.'

'Carlos read a piece out to me on Sunday about our reserves going up sevenfold during the war.'

'On the back of sales of wolfram, tin, sardines, olive oil, blankets, hides . . . you name it, we sold it. To both sides.'

'Some people see a problem in that, or are surprised by it,' I said. 'To me, it's just the way business works. There's no morality in money.'

'My theory is that all Salazar's public building works – the motorways, the roads, the 25th April bridge, the national stadium, all the urbanization in and around Lisbon – I think it was funded, not just by his successful playing of the market during the Second World War, but also by his acquiescence towards the end of the war in allowing the Nazis to move their loot out of Europe. And somewhere in all that is the Banco de Oceano e Rocha.'

'That could be a dangerous conclusion,' I said. 'Maybe you should tell me how you got there.'

'Just on the other side of the Banco de Oceano e Rocha building, near the Anjos Metro, in Rua Francisco Ribeiro, is a very ugly building belonging to the Banco de Portugal. In there they have all the bank and company information, all the statutes from all the companies registered in Portugal since the nineteenth century. If you're a really boring, sad person you can go in there and leaf through the all the statutes of the Banco de Oceano e Rocha and you'll find that the three original directors of the bank were Joaquim Abrantes, Oswald Lehrer and Klaus Felsen.'

'When was this?'

'During the war,' she said, taking another sip of whisky. 'By 1946 there were only two directors – Joaquim Abrantes and Klaus Felsen with a fifty-one/forty-nine split in the shareholding.'

'I thought they confiscated all German assets in Portugal after the war.'

'They did. But Joaquim Abrantes' share was fifty-one percent. He was the owner. It was a Portuguese bank,' she said. 'Another interesting thing is that I've been looking through an old archive which belonged to a Belgian businessman. I'm a friend of the granddaughter. Guess whose name turns up there?'

'Klaus Felsen.'

'He was a wolfram exporter.'

'So you think you've nearly got something,' I said. 'What happened to Klaus Felsen after the war?'

'He's there in the company statutes right up to 1962 when he disappeared for good . . . never to rise again. So I asked my father if he'd ever heard of the name, and he said it was a bit of a scandal in the Lisbon business community. Christmas Eve 1961, Klaus Felsen shot dead a German tourist in his home and he spent nearly twenty years in the Caxias prison for murder.'

'Interesting.'

'And do you know who the company lawyer was?'

'I think I do,' I said. 'Dr Aquilino Oliveira.'

'He completely rewrote the statutes of the bank . . . excluding our friend Klaus Felsen.'

'How long was he their lawyer for?'

'Until 1983.'

'And then what?'

'He stopped being their lawyer. These things don't go on for ever, but maybe it had something to do with the fact that Pedro Abrantes, who'd taken over from his dead father, died in a car accident.'

'Even I remember that. Those children.'

'And Miguel da Costa Rodrigues became the new Director and major shareholder of the bank. Things change when that happens. Lawyers for one.'

'There's something, but I'm not really seeing a connection here. I'm not seeing a motive for killing Catarina. I don't see how this can . . .'

'You want to question Miguel da Costa Rodrigues?'

'I want to hit him hard and fast so that he doesn't have time to hide behind his big friends, so that he has to come down to the *Polícia Judiciária* and face me and a tape recorder.'

'Then you have to get public opinion behind you.'

'Through the media,' I said. 'But I haven't got a story. You should see this guy Jorge Raposo, he's ex-PIDE and the most pathetic, seedy human being in Lisbon.'

'But what about Klaus Felsen?'

'The guy's got to be a hundred and ten years old.'

'Eighty-eight in fact.'

'He's still going?'

'And there was an address in the old company statutes. So I did the easiest thing first. I looked in the phone book to see if he still lives in the same place. Klaus Felsen, Casa ao Fim do Mundo, Azóia, and you see that piece of paper on the bedside table? That's his phone number.'

'Have you called him?'

'I didn't really know what I wanted to ask him about. I thought I'd have to do a lot more work to be able to have a decent conversation with him.'

'And now?'

'I think we should both see what he's got to say.'

'Ah,' I said. 'Now I've got it.'

'What?'

'This is your launch story isn't it?'

'Could be.'

'No, no, no.'

'Why not?'

'You said, let me get this right, "Nobody's going to have their trousers down in any magazine I publish." I think that was it, wasn't it?'

'That's your end of the story, my end is that one of Portugal's largest international banks was funded directly by Nazi gold,' she said. 'You can do the trousers-down stuff . . . I'll let you tag that on the end.'

'You think Klaus Felsen's going to tell you everything . . . all on your first date?'

'See if he's alive first,' she said, nodding at the piece of paper.

I picked up the telephone and dialled the number. A woman answered speaking in German. I asked for Klaus Felsen.

'He's sleeping,' she said.

'What's the best time to speak to him?'

'What is it concerning?'

'The Banco de Oceano e Rocha.'

Silence.

'And who are you?'

'I'm a detective with the *Polícia Judiciária* in Lisbon. I'm investigating the murder of a young girl. I think *Senhor* Felsen might be able to help us with our enquiries.'

'I'll talk to him. But you know he doesn't keep regular hours. Sometimes he wakes up in the middle of the night, other times in the late morning, sometimes he sleeps all the way through. If he agrees to speak to you, you must come when I say.'

I gave her Luísa's telephone number and put the phone down. I paced the room naked, chewing my thumbnail. Luísa smoked at the ceiling. I called Olivia on her mobile and told her I'd be late, and possibly wouldn't come home at all, and that she should get a meal at my sister's.

'Don't worry about me,' she said.

'Are you in a car?' I asked, the signal breaking into static.

'I'm with Sofia and her mother. We're going back to Cascais. They're going to take me out to dinner and I'll stay the night. OK?'

'No.'

'What? I can't hear you.'

470

'No, that wouldn't be OK,' I said.

'Why . . . can . . . please . . . bloody thing . . . ga . . .'

'I want you back at home.'

'But you just said you wouldn't be there.'

'I know what I just said.'

'Then don't be unreasonable. Why should I go back to . . .'

'Because . . .'

'I can't hear you.'

'Olivia.'

'The line's breaking up . . . bye.'

The line went dead.

'Trouble?' asked Luísa.

The telephone, still in my hand, rang. I yanked it to my ear.

'Olivia.'

'Inspector Coelho?' asked a German-inflected voice.

'This is me,' I said.

'Herr Felsen is available now. He will speak to you. Do you know the house?'

'No.'

'It's the last house in Portugal. Just before the light-house.'

'It could take us up to an hour to get there.'

'Come as quickly as you can.'

We got into the shower together and dressed. I tried Olivia's mobile again but she'd turned it off. Luísa told me not to worry about it, that nothing was going to happen tonight, but the tension crept into me and stiffened a ridge across my shoulders. My daughter could be spending the night with a murderer, a murderer of young girls.

Luísa drove and talked me down on the way out of Lisbon. I sat with her laptop and camera on my knees and kept the lid on my panic. What could we do? Trawl through every restaurant in Cascais? I didn't even know where the Rodrigues' weekend house was in Cascais, and

471

when I checked the phonebook there was nothing under his name – the property was probably his wife's and the phone still in her maiden name.

We came off the end of the motorway and headed west, through Aldeia de Juzo and Malveira. We climbed the twisting road, the end of the day dying now behind the high chapel of Peninha. The lights of isolated houses suspended in the black velvet of the heather. The ships on the dark Atlantic heading for the last blue-grey moment. We turned off left to Azóia at the highest point of the road, past old windmills transformed into bars, through the village of barking dogs and out again into the heather and gorse, the blades of light from the lighthouse slashing through the now complete darkness.

We came off the tarmac on to a length of beaten track, which took us up to a low walled house, with an enclosed roof terrace on the top in which a little light was burning.

A woman bent into our headlights, opening the gate. A chained German shepherd was barking madly in the courtyard. When he saw us, he took long, pelting runs right to the limit of his chain.

'I am Frau Junge,' she said, in a sweet voice on the brink of a yodel. She shushed the dog, who liked the voice and sat down with his head cocked to one side.

Frau Junge took us up the outside steps to the enclosed roof terrace. By the little light was a huddle in a wheelchair, head down near his chest – not a lively-looking person. One of the blades from the lighthouse swept above the roof of the house.

Frau Junge spoke into the ear of the heavily-blanketed man in the wheelchair. His head came up. Frau Junge dragged two chairs across from the wall and placed them near the wheelchair. A single hand came out from under the blankets and beckoned one of the chairs closer. She sighed as if he was a pesky child and moved the chair closer.

'He wants the girl to sit next to him, that's all. Watch his hand. It's the only one he's got and it can be fast and . . . intrusive,' she said and left us in the room.

Luísa had the look of a woman who wished she'd worn a longer skirt.

'I suffer from the cold now,' said Felsen in a cracked-china voice, small shards missing.

The bones of his skull, the plates of his cranium, seemed painfully obvious under the thin stretched skin, under which veins operated close to the surface. His eyelids were gathered in swags close to the lashes so that the corners slid down towards the cheekbones, making him look inconsolable. His nose was sharp, pointed and scraped raw.

We introduced ourselves and he hung on to Luísa's hand.

'Do you know why we're here?' asked Luísa.

'You can smoke if you like. I don't mind people smoking near me.'

'Frau Junge told you why we're here.'

'Yes, yes,' he said, 'but please smoke. I like the smell.'

I lit a cigarette. Luísa lit one of her own.

'I'm half the man I was. I'm shrinking and they keep cutting bits off me. I lost an arm in prison and half an ear. When I came out they cut off my right leg up to the knee. I don't remember why. Too much lying down in prison . . . or was it the smoking? That might have been it.'

Luísa stubbed out her cigarette and scratched her calf.

'Of course they don't take the bad one,' he said. 'I've had a limp since I was a child. No, that's the one that stays. They take the good one. I told the surgeon, I said: "This hospital is eating me alive." What does he care?'

He laughed which strained his voice to shattering point.

'The bank,' he said, 'that's why you're here, you want to talk about the bank. I've been waiting fifteen years to talk about the bank, but you're the first people who want to listen. Nobody looks back any more. Nobody knows where

473

they come from. They only want to know where they're going.'

'I need my hands to write while you're talking,' said Luísa, withdrawing her hand and arranging her laptop.

'I'll rest it on your shoulder?' he said.

Klaus Felsen told his story in two parts. The first part, with breaks, took nearly four hours. He faltered twice. The first when he recounted the ambush on the car of the British agent. He seemed to stop short. He fell silent for some minutes and I thought he'd run out of steam again and needed to rest. But when he restarted, his tone of voice had changed. It was confessional. He described how savagery had got off the leash and he'd killed the driver and then in more chilling terms what he'd done to the English agent, Edward Burton. Luísa stopped typing.

The second time he faltered was over his last meeting with Eva Brücke. He gave two versions. The first was a noble one of love torn asunder by war and he quickly dried up when Luísa's hands stopped moving over the keys of the laptop. We waited. He gathered himself and he told the real version.

The killing of Obergruppenführer Lehrer seemed to take something out of him. His head dropped and he fell asleep. We waited for a few minutes, twenty or thirty turns of the lighthouse. Luísa eased herself out from under his hand and we went downstairs.

Frau Junge was still awake watching satellite television, eating apple pie and drinking camomile tea. She told us to wait, that he would probably come round again in an hour. She offered us some apple pie. We wolfed it down.

'Normally it's me listening to his endless stories,' she said. 'Ach, the war, it's all such a long time ago. My parents . . . they never talked about it. Never. This one . . . he talks about it all the time, as if it was yesterday. Has that hand of his been behaving properly?'

474

'The hand's been fine,' said Luísa, still dazed from the work and the horror of it.

'If he takes *your* hand, be firm. Don't let him put it where he wants.'

I tried Olivia again on her mobile which was still turned off. Luísa called her father, spoke to him briefly and plugged the computer into the telephone jack and squeezed the first half of the story down the line. Thirty minutes later he called back and Luísa gave him more background about my murder investigation. She hung up.

'He wants some supporting documents. He's not prepared to publish unless it's backed up with some kind of documentary proof.'

I looked at Frau Junge who sipped her tea and shrugged.

'I have photographs, but documents . . . you'll have to ask him.'

A red light flashed on the wall by her head with a faint buzzing sound.

'He's awake,' said Frau Junge.

The second half of the story was shorter, but took longer to tell. He needed more breaks. His mind drifted and resettled on details we'd already heard. He kept coming back to a woman called Maria Antónia Medinas, who he was convinced had been killed by Manuel Abrantes. I told him it fitted in with what Jorge Raposo had told me, but we couldn't get him to tell us what she was to him. Was she a fellow-prisoner, a criminal or a political? Had he known her before?

He held things back, whether on purpose or because his brain slid over things we couldn't tell. It was close to the end before he stunned us with the revelation that he'd been set up by Joaquim Abrantes' PIDE friends, who'd put him inside for twenty years, and that Manuel Abrantes was his son. We asked who the mother was and he couldn't remember her name, but he thought she might be still alive, up in the Beira somewhere.

Dawn came up unspectacularly. The lighthouse stopped flashing and became a foghorn, as a dense sea mist rolled in over the cliffs and submerged the house, so that the gate on the other side of the courtyard was only occasionally visible.

'We have days like this,' said Felsen. 'It wouldn't be so bad if you knew the whole country was like it, but I know that a hundred metres around the corner the sun is shining.'

'There's one last thing,' said Luísa. 'We need some documents if this story is going to mean anything. Have you got documentary proof that the gold existed?'

His hand disappeared under the blankets and came back with a warm key.

'Everything you need is in the metal filing cabinet in the study. Frau Junge will show you.'

We stood up. His hand went out for Luísa's, which she gave him and he pressed it to his lips which made her shudder.

'You've had an extraordinary life, *Senhor* Felsen,' she said, to cover herself.

'We all had big lives then,' he said, looking out at the fog-filled morning. 'Even an *SS-Schütze* could have a big life then, but it might not have been the one he wanted. The twenty years I spent thinking about this in Caxias I wouldn't have minded a smaller life. I wouldn't mind some of my regrets being smaller.'

'And what is your biggest?' asked Luísa.

'Perhaps you are the romantic type. You might think . . .' he said, and hesitated for a response which Luísa didn't give him. 'Perhaps, after all I've told you, you can tell me what my biggest regret should be?'

She didn't respond. He seemed to deflate.

'It wasn't Eva. It was regrettable that she despised me in the end, but that came about by my own inaction,' he said, and struggled in his blankets for a moment, like a baby.

476

'The *action* I most regret was what I did to the English agent, Edward Burton. I don't know why it happened. Over the years I blamed Abrantes for it, I blamed the drink, I've even blamed the Dutch girl for stealing my cufflinks. But after twenty years in Caxias with nothing much else to think about I still couldn't find any reason for it and I've had to come to the conclusion that I had a visit from pure evil.

'I am not, *Senhora* Madrugada,' he said, finally, 'a man with prospects.'

His head went down and we left. In the filing cabinet we found copies of the documents showing the gold's origination. There were also photographs showing Felsen and Joaquim Abrantes and other members of the Abrantes family, including the young Manuel.

Luísa dropped me off in Paço de Arcos. She continued to Lisbon. I had breakfast with António Borrego in his bar, which was empty apart from the two of us.

'You look tired, Zé,' he said, laying out the coffee and buttered toast.

'I had a long night.'

'You didn't eat properly.'

'No.'

'Maybe I should cook something for you.'

'No, this is fine.'

'What was keeping you up all night?'

'Work . . . as usual.'

'I heard they raided your house and they've arrested Faustinho.'

I sank my teeth into the toast, sipped some coffee.

'You fell under a tram, too,' he said.

'Fell?'

'I was being diplomatic.'

I wiped molten butter from my chin.

'Is she a girlfriend, the woman who dropped you off just now?'

477

'The whole world passes before you in here, doesn't it, António?' I said. 'You don't have to go outside. It all comes to you.'

'It's the nature of running a bar,' he said. 'I wouldn't do it if it was just a question of serving drinks.'

I poured more coffee, added milk.

'You were in Caxias, weren't you, at the end there, in 1974?' I asked.

'That was when I used to go out and do things and look what happened.'

'Did you ever hear the name Felsen? Klaus Felsen.'

'We heard about him. He was in for murder. The politicals and the regulars didn't have much to do with each other. They kept us apart.'

'What about a woman called Maria Antónia Medinas?'

Silence. I looked up from my toast. He was pinching the bridge of his nose with his eyes closed.

'I was just thinking,' he said. 'Was she a regular?'

'I don't know. I don't know anything about her. Just the name.'

'She wasn't on the political side . . . that I know of.'

'Have you still got friends you could ask?'

'Friends?'

'Well, comrades then,' I said, and he laughed.

I went back to the house and found Olivia in the bathroom, brushing her teeth.

'What happened to you?' I asked, in English.

'I did what my Daddy told me to do,' she said and looked back at the sink, annoyed.

'You spent the night here?'

'That's what you told me to do,' she said. 'Have I been a good *girl*?'

'How did you get back?'

'*Senhor* Rodrigues brought me back after dinner.'

'On your own?' I said, my hands suddenly ice-cold.

478

'The others didn't want to come,' she said. 'I felt a complete idiot.'

'What did you talk about with *Senhor* Rodrigues?'

'I don't know. Nothing much.'

'Try and remember,' I said. 'It would help.'

She spat the toothpaste out and swilled her mouth.

'Oh yes, he was asking me about the Smashing Pumpkins.'

'Smashing Pumpkins?'

'They're a band, Dad,' she said, saddened by my lack of cool. 'A popular singing group I think you used to call them in your day.'

Then I told her, without telling her why, she shouldn't spend any more time with the Rodrigues family.

Chapter XL

I was lying in bed unable to sleep, listening to the traffic, smoking cigarettes, reading Fernanda Ramalho's pathology report for the hundredth time. I was two hours away from a media storm that would change my life and now I didn't want it. I wanted the old life back.

It had been a terrible week. I'd assumed when Luísa had said her father, Vitor Madrugada, had a magazine on the blocks that everything was ready and all he had to do was press a button. But he didn't even have a printer and it cost him some very big money to get one, because printers' presses don't hang around doing nothing waiting for a job – they're running all the time. It took a week. It meant he had time to think.

He'd wanted a big story to launch his new business magazine, and had ended up with something monumental that would stand for as long as the Marquês de Pombal had stood in his *Praça*. He had to be reassured. I had to make a presentation to him, his board of directors including Luísa, and his editor. I had to lay out my entire case against Miguel da Costa Rodrigues and my reasons for attacking him in this fashion.

The editor was nervous. He was an intelligent man, but one who'd come from an age when the media still had respect for public figures, a hangover, perhaps, from the days when journalists were told what to write. To him the *Director-Geral* of the Banco de Oceano e Rocha was a very important man with influential friends and a wife, also from

480

an excellent family, and a very religious woman, whereas Catarina Oliveira . . .

'I'm not convicting him in this article,' I'd replied. 'I'm just making sure that Miguel Rodrigues also known as Manuel Abrantes comes down to the *Polícia Judiciária* to answer my questions. He's done everything he can to block this investigation. He's used his friends to make sure that I don't get the information I need about his car. He's had me removed from the case. He's had me pushed under a tram. I've had my home invaded by Narcotics agents and your boss's daughter has had hate messages plastered over her car. We do have some justification.'

The editor had looked at Luísa's father.

'I hope you're right,' Vitor Madrugada had said to me. 'This is a big story – important families, a dynasty based on Nazi gold, a PIDE murderer, sex, drugs and the killing of an innocent, or rather, a young girl who did not deserve to die. This is a story that will go through Portugal like a forest fire in summer.'

'And you don't want to be perceived as an arsonist.'

'No,' he'd said, 'I don't. And I don't think I am one.'

He'd pressed the button.

I'd left the meeting with elation and dread on either shoulder. I drifted around for a few days. JoJó Silva called me about Lourenço Gonçalves who still hadn't turned up. I told him to file a missing-persons report and I'd make sure it was handled. Carlos and I worked in a desultory fashion on the Xeta murder case with little success.

At 7.00 a.m. I made some coffee and already there was a murmur in the street. In less than ten minutes the *calçada* outside the house was full of journalists and cameramen. I called the PSP station and asked them to send down some men and a car.

At 7.30 a.m. I stepped out into the street and met a barrage of questions and flashlights. I said nothing and set off at a brisk pace to where the PSP were waiting with a car. I led a motorcade into Lisbon to the *Polícia Judiciária* building, where more newsmen were waiting. The PSP car dropped me round the back and I went straight up to Narciso's office. This time I didn't have to wait and it was a very different *Engenheiro* Jaime Leal Narciso on the other side of the door.

He asked me to sit down. He sat on the same side of the desk as me. We smoked. The secretary brought in some coffee. He quietly reinstated Carlos and me as the investigating officers in the case and gave me full permission to bring in Miguel da Costa Rodrigues for questioning.

'I'll want to search his property as well,' I said.

'There's a search warrant already prepared,' he said.

At 07.45 there was a phone call in Narciso's office from Miguel da Costa Rodrigues' lawyer, volunteering to bring his client down for questioning in the *Polícia Judiciária* building.

At 08.15 Miguel da Costa Rodrigues was in the building. His lawyer went out front and delivered an opening statement to the journalists. He denounced the *Polícia Judiciária*'s methods of trial by media and clarified the voluntary nature of his client's appearance in the building. He didn't respond to any of the questions that came back at him.

At 08.25 Narciso clapped me on the back and showed me a reassuring fist with which he would help me smash Miguel da Costa Rodrigues. He put on his jacket and went out to the front of the building. He beat the lawyer's statement to a pulp and took eighty-five percent of the credit for the investigation so far, leaving me with fifteen and Carlos with none. He was doing what he was paid for. He was doing what he did best.

At 08.30 Miguel Rodrigues was shown into interrogation room three which had the largest observation window. Some of the men gathering at that window I'd never seen in the building before. It was like a cocktail party in there.

At 08.32 I made the necessary introductions to the tape recorder. Miguel da Costa Rodrigues showed no sign that we'd ever met. He looked like a man who'd prepared a story in his head and it was going to take an earth-mover to get him to deviate from it. He was a PIDE man. He would know about interrogation. My only advantage was that he might not have been on the end of many interrogations himself.

He glanced at the reflective panel set in the wall. His lawyer sat next to him, like a trained hawk, with only the tips of his fingers on the edge of the table. I started by asking *Senhor* Rodrigues to clarify his identity and he calmly revealed that he was Manuel Abrantes and that he'd changed his identity in order to reduce the possibility that his previous employment might reflect against the bank. I didn't ask him to elaborate on that. I didn't want to blur the focus of my opening interview with him.

'*Senhor* Rodrigues,' I started, 'where were you at lunchtime, at around 13.00 on Friday June 12th?'

'I was in the Pensão Nuno.'

'What were you doing there?'

'I was watching three people engaged in a sexual act.'

'How?'

'I was in an adjacent room, watching them through a two-way mirror set in the wall.'

'Did you know any of these people?'

'No.'

'Had you seen any of them before?'

He conferred with his lawyer.

'I'd seen the girl before.'

'Where?'

'In the same *pensão*.'

'When?'

'Exactly a week before.'

'Engaged in a sexual act?'

483

'Yes.'

'How many times have you seen this girl?'

'A few times.'

'Can you be more specific, *Senhor* Rodrigues? You should know that *Senhor* Jorge Raposo the manager of the *pensão* is cooperating with the *Polícia Judiciária*.'

'I can't be certain. It could have been as many as twelve times.'

'And always in the Pensão Nuno?'

'And always engaged in sexual acts with other men, although last Friday was the first time I'd seen her with two men at the same time.'

'After any of these occasions did you make any attempt to follow her?'

He leaned over to his lawyer again.

'Two weeks ago on Friday I followed her from the Pensão Nuno to the school she was attending, on Avenida Duque de Ávila.'

'That's not quite correct, *Senhor* Rodrigues.'

'I'm sorry, no. She went to a café near the school first.'

'Did you go in there?'

'Yes.'

'Do you remember its name?'

'No.'

'How did you know she was attending the Liceu D. Dinis?'

'I followed her out of the café and saw her go into the building.'

'So when you were observing her in the Pensão Nuno last Friday you already knew she was a schoolgirl.'

'Yes.'

'The sexual act you were watching last Friday, can you describe it please?'

'The girl was kneeling between two young men, one of the men had his penis in her mouth, the other was sodomizing her.'

484

'Sodomizing her?' I asked, beginning to see his strategy now.

'Yes.'

'How did you know that he was sodomizing her?'

'I could see from where I was sitting.'

'How was that possible?'

'They had moved the bed in front of the mirror and I could see very clearly what was happening.'

'Would you say that she was enjoying what she was doing?'

'There was nothing in her face to indicate to me that she was not.'

'Did you follow her on that occasion?'

'No.'

'But you were in a car waiting for her outside the school later that Friday afternoon, at around four-thirty.'

'Yes.'

'Can you describe the car you were in?'

'It was a black Mercedes C200, petrol, registration 18 43 NT.'

'Is that *your* car?'

'The car is in my wife's name.'

'So you were waiting for the girl?'

'Yes.'

'What were your intentions?'

'To talk to her.'

'Talk to her? About what?'

'The possibility of having sex with her.'

'And what happened?'

'She came out of the school. She was talking to someone, an older man, perhaps one of her teachers. I don't know. They were talking or rather they were arguing, because at one point he hit her, slapped her face. She walked away from him up the street in the direction of Avenida 5° de Outubro. When I saw that, I pulled away from the kerb, stopped at the traffic light next to her, asked her if she was all right and whether I could give her a lift anywhere.'

'What did she say?'

'She got in the car.'

'She didn't say anything?'

'Not that I recall.'

'We have witnesses who say you talked for nearly a minute, until the lights changed.'

'That's correct. I remember now. I asked her the way somewhere. She started to explain and then said it was easier to show me.'

'What did you discuss in the car?'

'Music. We talked about music.'

'Is that it?'

'Yes.'

'Where did you go?'

'I wanted to go back to Cascais. I decided to cut through the Monsanto park to get to the motorway.'

'I thought you wanted to have sex with her.'

'Yes.'

'When was that discussed?'

'When we were in the Monsanto park.'

'Was she surprised?'

'How do you mean?'

'Originally you'd asked her the way somewhere. Where exactly?'

'I don't recall.'

'She seemed to think it was complicated.'

'Monsanto. I asked her the way to Monsanto. It *is* complicated to get to Monsanto from there,' he said, the flustering just starting.

'But having guided you to Monsanto I wouldn't think she'd want to be dropped there in the middle of nowhere.'

'As we began talking she told me that she was going back to Cascais and I said I'd give her a lift there. I was . . .'

'But you weren't. You were only going as far as Paço

486

de Arcos that evening,' I said, using a recognized tactic for confusing a scripted story – concentrate on a small detail and tease out the half-lies.

'Look, Inspector,' he said, frustrated now, 'I asked her the way somewhere. She said she was going to Cascais by train. I said I was going there by car. She seemed happy to get a lift. She got in the car. I did not force her to come with me. She got in there voluntarily. If your witnesses are saying I dragged her in . . .'

'They're not. I just want to know exactly how it was, *Senhor* Rodrigues. In order to get her in the car you'd told her you were going back to Cascais.'

He wasn't happy but he needed to get away from it.

'She got in the car. I drove. We started talking,' he said, firmly.

'About music and going to Cascais . . . so how did sex come up?'

It wasn't hot in the interrogation room, but *Senhor* Rodrigues was finding it uncomfortable. His collar was tight around his neck and sweat was beginning to pimple on his forehead. He changed position in his chair several times and wrapped an arm around the back of his lawyer's.

'I told her I'd seen her in the *pensão*.'

'That must have surprised her.'

'Why?'

'She thinks that she's got into a car at random. She thinks she's showing somebody the way to Monsanto. She thinks she's being given a lift to Cascais. You're talking about music . . . what sort of music were you talking about, by the way?'

'She said she liked the Smashing Pumpkins.'

That chilled me down to my liver.

'So you're talking about the Smashing Pumpkins, driving through Monsanto and then . . . you change it. Suddenly you're a punter, suddenly you're the one who's been watching her through a two-way mirror in the *pensão*. Suddenly, *Senhor* Rodrigues, you are not a nice guy giving a girl a lift. You're another creep.'

'You don't have to use that kind of abusive language to my client,' said the lawyer.

We both looked at him.

'*Senhor* Rodrigues?' I said.

'What was the question. I'm not sure . . .'

'What was her reaction when you told her that you'd seen her before, performing sex acts in the Pensão Nuno?'

'She was a prostitute, for God's sake.'

'She did not get into your car as a prostitute. She got into your car as a schoolgirl, who'd had a spat with a man, and who was going to show you the way to Monsanto so that you could take her on to Cascais. Think about it again, *Senhor* Rodrigues, and tell me how you changed it and what her reaction was.'

'Changed it? I haven't changed anything. Changed what?'

'How you changed the situation, *Senhor* Rodrigues.'

Silence. The lawyer looked at his client, unclear as to what the problem was, and already noticing that the truth was not coming out in a continuous milky flow.

'Did you perhaps make an assumption, *Senhor* Rodrigues?'

'An assumption? I don't follow you.'

'Did you assume that if you touched her in a sexual way that she would understand . . . or maybe, because you were being a nice guy, she would just like you. And when she didn't understand, you had to tell her that you'd seen her, and how you'd seen her, and that you knew that really she was a prostitute. If that was the case I don't think she would have liked it, *Senhor* Rodrigues.'

'Why not? That's what she was.'

'Because it was all going so well, *Senhor* Rodrigues, you were being a nice guy and then in one small sentence, perhaps one small action you've shown yourself as something else. A creep.'

488

'Inspector, please,' said the lawyer, exasperated by my disrespect.

'Did she put up a fight, *Senhor* Rodrigues? Did she lash out? Give you a little kick perhaps . . . so that you had to be firm?'

'No, no, and no,' he said, seeing his story off the leash and galloping away from him.

'We're stuck here, *Senhor* Rodrigues. You have to help this interview along.'

'I pulled over into the pine trees in the Monsanto park. I asked her if she was willing to have sex with me. She was, you're right, Inspector, she was a little surprised. I told her I'd seen her in the *pensão* but I didn't tell her that I'd seen her performing sex acts. I just offered her ten thousand escudos.'

'For what?'

'To have sex with me,' he said, annoyed.

'This isn't your first time with a prostitute is it, *Senhor* Rodrigues?'

'No, it isn't.'

'I understand it's common practice to state exactly what you want for the price.'

'I offered her ten thousand escudos to have straight sex with me.'

'And how did this straight sex take place?'

He took a deep breath.

'She knelt on the seat and pulled down her underwear.'

'Did she completely remove her underwear?'

'No, I don't think so.'

'And what did you do, *Senhor* Rodrigues?'

'I undid my trousers and knelt on the seat. She knelt with her legs across the handbrake.'

'Was that on or off?'

'Off.'

'You were on flat ground?'

489

'Yes.'

'Carry on.'

'I knelt behind her and . . .'

'You'd given her the money by now?'

He faltered.

'Yes.'

'So she must have been very angry.'

'Angry? Why?'

'When you sodomized her, *Senhor* Rodrigues. That wasn't in the deal.'

'I did *not* sodomize her, Inspector,' he said quietly. 'That was one of the boys in the *pensão*.'

'He says he didn't.'

'He's lying.'

'In this situation, *Senhor* Rodrigues, I have an advantage over you because I've read the pathologist's report a hundred times over and I've listened very carefully to what you've been saying. So . . .'

'I did not sodomize her,' he said quietly, placing his hand flat on the table as if there was a bible there.

'I've just warned you that it's not a question of your word against the boy's in the *pensão*, *Senhor* Rodrigues. I'm giving you an opportunity to tell the truth.'

He checked me over thoroughly. He thought I was bluffing. His eyes sneered at me.

'I did not sodomize her, Inspector.'

'The medical examination conducted by Dr Fernanda Ramalho indicates that Catarina Oliveira had been sodomized. A condom was used and a water-based lubricant. Dr Ramalho's examination of the victim's sphincteral muscle shows that it was torn indicating that the victim was not accustomed to this kind of sexual activity. What do you think that means, *Senhor* Rodrigues?'

'I don't . . . I did not . . .'

'It means that it would be extremely painful, *Senhor* Rodrigues. Did she shout out?'

490

'*I* did not sodomize her.'

'I'm sorry, my mistake, *Senhor* Rodrigues, she didn't shout out because, and I quote, "There was nothing in her face to indicate that she was not" . . . enjoying what she was doing. Catarina Oliveira did not shout out in the Pensão Nuno that Friday lunchtime did she *Senhor* Rodrigues?'

Silence.

'Did she, *Senhor* Rodrigues?'

'My client has nothing further to add,' said the lawyer.

'We'd like to search *Senhor* Rodrigues' two houses and his wife's car. Will you agree to that?'

'With a search warrant,' said the lawyer.

The rest of the interview was a series of denials. *Senhor* Rodrigues admitted that he had sex with the girl. He said that afterwards she'd left the car and that he'd driven at a leisurely pace to arrive in Paço de Arcos to present his cheque to the mayor at the *festa*. He denied hitting her on the back of the head, he denied stripping her, he denied putting her in the boot of his car and he denied dumping her naked body on the beach in Paço de Arcos later that night. I terminated the interview and took a team of men down to the house in Lapa.

Senhor Rodrigues and his lawyer met us in Lapa. The lawyer inspected the search warrant and then sat with his client in the living room. The lawyer was already avoiding looking at his client, in the way that humans do when they've been let down by someone they've trusted. I gave the house a quick inspection and announced to the team that I personally wanted to search the suspect's wardrobe and study. I left four men to work the rest of the house, the double garage and the garden. Carlos and I started on the Mercedes.

It had been valeted, seriously valeted. It was like a new car inside, with that new car smell. I told Carlos to get the name of the valet company and to go down there and talk, not to the manager, but to the actual cleaners of the car. I started with the front seats. Tucked under the front passenger seat was a pair of white knickers, neatly folded. The brand name was Sloggi. I bagged them. As Carlos came out of the house I told him to bring the person who'd found the knickers back here. I found nothing else of interest in the car.

I took *Senhor* Rodrigues up to his wardrobe and asked him to pick out the clothes he had been wearing on the afternoon of Friday 12th June. He pointed to a blazer, a pair of grey slacks and the tie Olivia had made for him. The blazer and the slacks had been dry-cleaned. The tie hadn't. There was a small red brown stain on the back of it. I bagged that and had it sent down to the lab.

In the study, behind an old eighteenth-century chest, we found a cupboard recessed into the wall. There were fifteen video tapes in there, two wine boxes containing pornographic magazines and, at the back neatly folded, a white T-shirt and a light blue with yellow check mini-skirt which were lying on top of a pair of clumpy shoes studded with rhinestones. The clothes and shoes were bagged. The contents of the cupboard were taken down to the *Polícia Judiciária*.

The man from the valet company who'd found the knickers said he'd been in two minds about what to do. He'd found them stuffed down the side of the seat. At first he thought they belonged to *Senhor* Rodrigues' daughter and he was just going to leave them on the seat. But then, because it was *Senhor* Rodrigues who'd brought the car in to be cleaned on the Monday morning, he thought this might be embarrassing, so he put them under the seat and decided to mind his own business.

Miguel da Costa Rodrigues was formally charged with the murder of Catarina Oliveira at 13.30. When he was asked to remove his clothing two large bruises were revealed on his chest. Photographs were taken and he was issued with standard prison clothing and taken to the cells.

492

Chapter XLI

Monday, 23rd November 199–, Palácio da Justiça, Rua Marquês da Fronteira, Lisbon.

I've never wanted fame. If I'd wanted to be famous I wouldn't have been a policeman. Fame has always struck me as a perverse form of prostitution. You perform, or just appear, and in return receive enormous attention, an uncomplicated love. Nobody knows the famous and the famous know nobody and yet the intensity of emotion, the wholesale adoration is bigger, more impressive than any individual's love. For me the greatest invasion of privacy was to have to accept the fame. An inability to accept it would have meant that fame had changed me and for the worse. It was the compulsory enjoyment that I couldn't stand.

I became famous. I was a hero. I was the little man from down the *Linha*, the one who'd shaved his beard off for charity (see how the smallest thing was changed for my benefit), took on the establishment and brought them to justice. The media loved me, but would they have loved me as much with a beard, no new bridgework and fifteen extra kilos? I learnt the value of a good suit and a permanent smile.

The feeding frenzy was ferocious. The River Tagus boiled pink with the blood of the past. Miguel da Costa Rodrigues' real identity of Manuel Abrantes, the much feared *Inspector da Polícia* in PIDE, who ran a network of hundreds of *bufos*, informers, who permeated the lives of thousands of ordinary people, and who was directly responsible for the suffering of many of the unfortunates in the Caxias prison, convulsed the nation. Current-affairs programmes and talk shows bloomed for weeks as people aired their memories of oppression, persecution and torture – the frying pans of Tarrafal on Cape Verde, the bull pens of Aljube, the flooding dungeons of the Fort of Caxias. But this angle was short-lived and, when the programmers saw the soaps reasserting themselves at the top of the league, they realized their mistake – people didn't want history. They wanted personal history.

They quickly found Jorge Raposo in his house of joy, and in a half-hour special he reassembled the PIDE infiltration of General Machedo's entourage, the trap set in the Badajoz churchyard, the killing of the General's secretary and the summary execution of the General by Manuel Abrantes. It was spell-binding television. I couldn't take my eyes off him. I got up close to see if I could find the familiar old ruined Jorge that I'd known, but his studio make-up was impenetrable, his new double-breasted suit as smooth and hermetic as armour plate. I could only imagine his crusty heels encased in their brand-new loafers. As a result of the programme the Spanish government announced an investigation into the affair as it had taken place on Spanish soil.

They found me. The heroic widower fighting against odds that I didn't recognize. They found Luísa, the committed teacher who'd become the fearless publisher and the hero's lover. They found Olivia, the hero's daughter who'd cut the tie that had given the investigation its biggest break, the new fashion designer who might have been backed, personally, by Miguel da Costa Rodrigues.

Finally, and perhaps the most damaging development for my privacy, was that, with the publication of the supporting documents for the origination of the gold, there was an immediate freeze of all the Banco de Oceano e Rocha's assets. This was followed by a raid on their offices, including the old offices on the Rua do Ouro in the Baixa, where two of the original bars of gold were found in an old wall safe. The *Polícia Judiciária* leapt at the chance of a publicity coup and my face appeared on the front of all the newspapers, flanked by the two bars of Nazi gold. In at least one publication appeared the legend *Inspector Dourado* – the Golden Inspector. This was followed by the announcement of a full government investigation into the origins, funding and affairs of the bank since its inception.

At this point I thought I was going to lose control of my life completely, but my luck turned. There were further revelations about the financial scandal that had plagued the companies which had built Expo 98 and the developers of the upmarket residential area around the site. The spotlight shifted. The media reloaded. But the *Zeitgeist* was the same – fat cats, acting with impunity.

By the end of June I'd been promoted. I didn't get a new job because one didn't exist at the time. I got a pay rise, which I didn't need because for weeks I wasn't allowed to buy a drink or pay for a meal. All bills were settled by others. More uncomplicated love.

I was given a secretary, temporarily, to handle all my calls which meant I hardly spoke to anyone who wasn't a journalist or a TV producer. I had little time. I did no work. The PJ rode high on the success of the investigation. I was envied and despised by my colleagues and welcomed into the brotherhood of my superiors.

It was a relief, after intense government pressure, when the trial finally took place, in record time in the middle of November. The prosecution took it seriously. I was endlessly coached and rehearsed. The defence built their case on Catarina's history: that although she was a schoolgirl from a respectable family, she was nothing more than a common prostitute and drug-user. They concentrated on her voluntarily getting into the car and her willingness to have straight sex (there was no apparent violence against her), the fact that no murder weapon was found, the lack of motive for the killing, there being no witnesses who saw the defendant hitting the girl, stripping her, loading her into the boot of the car or dumping her on the beach at Paço de Arcos. They puffed Miguel Rodrigues' good character, his charity work and that of his wife and the impeccable upbringing of his brother's daughter.

The prosecution's case hinged on whether the defendant had sodomized the girl or not. That was his motive for murder. Through my testimony, the initial interview with Miguel Rodrigues and the photographs of his bruised chest, they not only cast doubt on the veracity of anything that the defendant might have said, but also proved beyond reasonable doubt that he had sodomized Catarina Oliveira. That broke the back of the case. There was no murder weapon because the murderer had killed with his own hands, by strangling the girl. He wasn't seen stripping her, but ultimately the girl's clothes had been found in his possession. He wasn't seen dumping the girl, but it was clearly established that he was in Paço de Arcos, had left there at night and would therefore have had the opportunity. They scythed his good reputation to the ground.

On Monday 23rd November at 16.00 the judge handed down his verdict. Miguel da Costa Rodrigues, also known as Manuel Abrantes, was found guilty of murder and sentenced to life imprisonment.

I was invited by the Minister of Internal Administration to the Jockey Club, to celebrate with some editors, journalists, TV producers, presenters and high-ranking police officers. When I declined they sent Narciso after me. It was then that I realized why he was my boss. This was his territory. I was a stray cat. A photograph was taken of Luísa and me at the champagne reception and after half an hour Narciso let me know that I could leave.

We drove out to Paço de Arcos. Olivia had already eaten and was watching television at my sister's house. I took Luísa to *A Bandeira Vermelha* and a cheerful António Borrego served us his dish of the day. It was one of his favourite Alentejano concoctions – *ensopado de borrego* – a large tureen of lamb broth with neck chops and breast stewed until the meat has all but parted from the bone. Nobody cooked it like him. He opened a bottle of red Borba Reserva '94 and left us to it.

I sipped the wine and ate some cheese and olives. I didn't feel like talking even. Luísa was annoyed with me for dragging her away from the party. To her it was an opportunity to network in her new role as fearless publisher, and she would have preferred to stay.

'Eventually you'll tell me what the problem is,' she said, lighting a cigarette in time for the arrival of the main course.

'I'm depressed.'

'Is that a post-trial policeman thing, like post-natal depression is for women?'

'I don't think so.'

'Maybe you've got post-event blues . . . now you've got to get back to real life.'

'I *want* to get back to real life.'

'I don't have to tell you all the reasons why you shouldn't be depressed. Promotion. Pay rise. Pinnacle of your career. A bad man put away for life.'

'None of that matters. What matters is being here, eating António's *ensopado de borrego*, drinking red wine with you. I was not built for drinking champagne with arseholes. This is the best thing . . .'

'The best thing?'

'All right, we've . . .'

'Relax, Zé. I'm teasing.'

I sucked some more lamb bones, drank more red wine. We finished the meal. António cleared everything away and brought two glasses of *aguardente* and two *bicas*. We smoked. Luísa refused to coax me out of my mood. The bar emptied. António loaded the dishwasher. Tyres ripped along the Marginal. A bitter wind moved through the trees of the park.

'He didn't do it,' I said.

'What are we talking about now?' asked Luísa.

'The reason why I'm depressed,' I said, 'is that Miguel Rodrigues or Manuel Abrantes did not murder Catarina Oliveira.'

'How long have you been thinking this?'

'Do you want the truth or the media version?'

'Don't be a *chato*, Zé.'

'No, you're right. I'm being a *chato* to the last person I should be a *chato* to. I thought he didn't do it, from the moment I found the girl's clothes in his study.'

'Which was amongst the most damning pieces of evidence in the whole trial.'

'Exactly ... with those clothes in his possession he became the stripper of the body and therefore the most likely murderer.'

'And you think somebody else put the clothes there?'

'Two things. Miguel Rodrigues was supposedly harassing me on and off the case. I wasn't getting the information on the car from Traffic. I was taken off the job. I was invaded by Narcotics. I was pushed under a tram. If he was feeling the heat that much, why didn't he get rid of one of the most damaging pieces of evidence against him? And the second thing. Why weren't the girl's knickers with the ...'

It was at this point that the parasites got out of control, and the most virulent and debilitating of the diseases of the famous ran through me like a bad case of malaria. I got a large, ugly dose of paranoia.

Nobody knows the famous, the famous know nobody.

'With the what?' asked Luísa, who'd reared back at the same time. 'Why are you looking at me like that?'

'How am I looking at you? I don't mean to ...'

'You're looking at me as if you're looking into me, as if you're looking into the back of my head.'

'It's nothing. I don't know what I'm thinking any more.'

It wasn't true. I did know what I'd been thinking. I'd been thinking that I'd got a lot of harassment, right up to the moment when I landed Miguel Rodrigues, and having landed him under those difficult circumstances, I had to find a way of getting public opinion on my side. And what happened? My girlfriend of one week is an expert on the Salazar Economy, she's already been looking at the Banco de Oceano e Rocha, she produces the name Klaus Felsen, she has a father in magazine publishing, who's looking for a big story for a launch issue that's ready to go. And when the story broke it was all so easy. Narciso was suddenly as dreamy as a *pastel de nata* from the Antiga Confeitaria in Belém. And I was desperately hanging on to the mane of a bare-back media stallion, galloping across the open plains.

It is the nature of paranoia that things which had seemed so right at the time suddenly become inflamed with suspicion. And once I'd started thinking like that, other thoughts began to assert themselves. Who had given me Luísa Madrugada's number? Dr Aquilino Oliveira.

Like pure quinine for a bad malaria attack, there's only one cure for paranoia – the absolute, undiluted truth. The arranged truth, even though there is some justice in it, will never be good enough, will never absolve the most important people.

I was sick and I had to have the one and only cure.

If, then, I could have thought beyond the tight circles in my head, I would have realized that, in reaching for the pure truth, I was going to disrupt the arranged one. If it had been arranged, then it had been arranged by somebody. Somebody powerful and somebody vindictive, who would not take kindly to the disruption.

I looked at Luísa again, trying not to dig under the surface. António Borrego, the only man still letting me pay for my food and drink, put the bill down between us.

Chapter XLII

Tuesday, 24th November 199–, Polícia Judiciária building, Rua Gomes Freire, Lisbon.

I sat at my desk and booted up the computer. I accessed the missing-persons file and put in a search for Lourenço Gonçalves to see if he'd reappeared or been found. There was no record of a missing-persons report being logged. I looked out of the window at the brilliant sunshine and shivered.

I found Carlos and took him for a walk down to Avenida Almirante Reis. It was cold, very dry, and the wind was a lacerating northerly. There'd been no rain this year. The last three years it had rained the whole of November until I felt as depressed as an Englishman. This year it had been eerie. No rain. Day after day of brilliant sunshine, cloudless skies. And rather than joy, it brought with it the chilling notion that the planet had been irrevocably damaged.

The small, narrow bar between the Anjos and Arroios Metro stations where I'd first met JoJó Silva was packed with mid-morning coffee-drinkers. We went straight to the back of the café. JoJó Silva was sitting at a table staring into an empty coffee cup as if the grounds were going to tell him this week's lottery numbers. I blocked out his light. He looked up.

'Do they let you take your own calls yet, Inspector?' he asked.

'I stopped being a demi-god as from yesterday.'

'Welcome back to mortality.'

'What's going on, JoJó?'

'Nothing . . . as usual.'

'You didn't file a missing-persons report on your friend.'

'Lourenço Gonçalves?' he said. 'I did, Inspector. Oh yes, I did that. It was the least I could do for him. Why do you think I've been calling you and been told you're not available for the last three months? I even tried you yesterday.'

'Yesterday?' I said, knowing his name hadn't appeared on the message list.

'You want to know why I called you yesterday . . . of all the days?' he asked. 'The rent is up on Lourenço's office. He's not in a position to renew the lease, so the landlord is going to clear the place and rent it out to someone who exists. And once that's happened, Inspector . . . he really is lost. Wiped clean.'

The three of us crossed Avenida Almirante Reis to a 1960s featureless office building. Carlos and I went up to the second floor, while JoJó found the landlord and the key. It took him some time.

'Are you doing anything tonight?' I asked, leaning up against the wall outside the unnamed office, looking for something to take my mind off the monster that was forming in my head.

'Just taking Olivia to the movies.'

'To see what?'

'*City of Angels*.'

'*Again?*'

'She likes it,' he shrugged.

'It's a romantic movie.'

'It's not the romance she's interested in,' he said. 'She likes the idea that there's something bigger than all of us out there, acting in a unpredictable way. Not always good, not always bad. She says it makes her feel secure.'

'Maybe you have to be young to have that kind of faith in things.'

'Bad night, last night, was it?'

'I just have the feeling that there's something big on the other side of that door.'

'Why?'

'Lourenço Gonçalves ... that name ... whenever I've thought about it I've felt a need to do something but I've never cracked it. And now ... somebody's thought it's important enough to delete the name from the missing-persons file. That never happens, not even if he's found.'

The landlord opened the door and left us to it. JoJó sat in his missing friend's chair. The office wasn't crowded out with furniture. There was a desk, another chair and a filing cabinet. There were four files in the filing cabinet and three empty drawers. The files were old. All dating to work the previous year. Carlos began taking the desk to pieces. JoJó didn't move.

'Was he working when you last saw him?' I asked.

'He always said he was working,' said JoJó. 'He just grumbled about not getting paid.'

'None of this work is current.'

'The desk is empty,' said Carlos.

I moved the filing cabinet away from the wall. There was nothing behind it. I tipped it on its back. Carlos went to the door. I fiddled with the surround of the cabinet.

'Something big on the other side of the door,' said Carlos, tapping it.

There was a large poster covering most of the door. It was a movie poster of a massive Kodiak bear in mortal combat with a man.

'He was obsessed with that movie,' said JoJó. 'It gave him his catchphrase.'

'What was the line?' asked Carlos.

'I'm going to kill the bear.'

We laughed.

'He had a sense of humour, Lourenço,' said JoJó.

'Tap that door again, Carlos,' I said.

It was hollow-sounding at the edges and solid in the

middle. It was one of those cheap doors made by slapping two pieces of veneer on to a frame, and those sort of doors normally sound hollow from top to bottom.

'Take the poster off.'

Behind the poster was a panel. Carlos unscrewed it with a penknife. Set into the door was a thick file bound up with rubber bands.

'You know what that looks like,' said JoJó. 'Insurance.'

'You'd better leave now,' I said to him. He didn't want to. 'I'm telling you for your own safety.'

'If that's the bear you've found,' he said, making for the door, 'kill it.'

On the front of the file Gonçalves had written Oliveira/ Rodrigues. It was the only work in hand, and we saw why when we opened up the files. It appeared that Dr Aquilino Oliveira was the client and Miguel da Costa Rodrigues the job. In the file there were three thick dossiers containing every movement Miguel Rodrigues had ever made between August 30th of last year and June 9th of this year. Nine months' solid surveillance. In the last five months he'd only missed three Friday lunchtimes in the Pensão Nuno.

'What have you got there?' I asked.

'Photographs. Shots of girls in the street, dates on the back. Presumably girls that Rodrigues had bought. Look at them.'

'They're all blondes.'

'An obsession.'

'And that last one?'

'Catarina Oliveira.'

I shivered badly, shuddered the length of my body, as if I'd just had a trickle of liquid slime down my spine. Carlos raised his eyebrows at me.

'I was just wondering,' I said, 'what sort of a person Dr Oliveira is, to use his own daughter as bait in a murder set-up.'

'Not his *own* daughter.'

I planted the heels of my hands into my eye sockets and didn't move or speak for five long minutes. When I took my hands away the room was strangely dimmed, as if autumn had moved quickly into winter.

'Do I get to know?' asked Carlos, sitting across from me, looking young and unconcerned.

I had been thinking that I could stop this now, that I could shred the files and walk away. We could accept the original and believed version of events and move on. But I couldn't, I had to satisfy myself, I had to be sure that Luísa Madrugada had not been involved. And if I didn't do that . . . I could see myself lying in bed watching her sleep, one of those guys like a million others, wondering why I couldn't make that ultimate commitment, but knowing too.

'What are we going to do?' asked Carlos, sensing the decision crisis.

'Did you keep all your handwritten notes on Catarina's case?'

'They're somewhere, but it's all in the reports.'

'You might think it's all there, but you and I know it's not. Not absolutely everything and that's what I have to have now. I want every single thing on Catarina's case and I'm going to read it all from beginning to end ten times over. And tomorrow we're going to Caxias Prison to see Miguel da Costa Rodrigues.'

'What's he going to tell us?'

'Amongst other things, why he would think that somebody would spend nine months on his tail.'

I left the office early with the file and Carlos' notebooks and took them back home. I read everything through several times until it was late and dark and I was hungry. I had a quick steak in *A Bandeira Vermelha* and drank two coffees. I went back home and moved pieces of paper around again. Olivia came in about 11.00 p.m. and went straight to bed. I opened another packet of cigarettes.

By midnight I had the beginnings of three ideas. The first was to do with dates and times, but I didn't have all the information. The second was much more interesting, but I needed a photograph that wasn't in Catarina's case files. The third needed the help of *Senhora* Lurdes Rodrigues and another photograph I didn't have. I went to bed and didn't sleep.

Carlos was already in the office when I arrived. I'd finished the night with an hour of deep sleep between six and seven and had woken up feeling as if I'd been broken on the wheel. I sent him off to find the marriage date of Dr and *Senhora* Oliveira while I went to the personnel department and asked for Lourenço Gonçalves' old PJ file. I hoped he hadn't grizzled up too much because the latest photograph of him was during his last weeks as an officer with the PJ and was ten years out of date.

Carlos came back with the date of 12th May 1982 for the Oliveiras' marriage. I sent him down to the files to find a usable photograph of Xeta, the murdered male prostitute who'd been found in Alcântara and another of Teresa Oliveira looking as young as possible. I arranged with the prison in Caxias to see prisoner number 178493 at 11.30 a.m. I phoned Inácio in Narcotics and asked him whether he was still holding the fisherman, Faustinho Trindade. He wasn't.

We went first to the Rodrigues house in Lapa. The maid answered the door and left us on the step. Lurdes Rodrigues took her time coming to see us. She didn't want us in the house. Her face was unambiguously hostile.

'And now, Inspector?' she said.

'A question, *Senhora* Rodrigues. Did anybody you didn't know come into this house between Saturday 13th June and Friday 19th June?'

'What a question, Inspector. Do you really think I'd be able . . .'

'I'm talking about tradesmen, delivery men, repair men, electricity meter readers.'

'You'll have to ask the maid,' she said, backing into the house. 'She wouldn't even bother to tell me that sort of thing.'

The maid came back on her own. I asked the question again. She thought about it for some time until her eyes widened with memory.

'The only one I didn't know was the telephone man, but they're always different.'

'How come you remember him after all this time?'

'He wore a hat, and wouldn't take it off even when he came into the house, even when I glared at him.'

'What did he say the problem was with the phone?'

'People in the area had been complaining about static. He wanted to check all our lines.'

'Was he carrying anything?'

'A suitcase of tools and one of those phones they use for testing.'

'Did you see inside the case?'

'He opened it, but I wasn't much interested.'

'Where were you?'

'There are three lines,' she said. 'One in the living room and two in *Senhor* Rodrigues' study. One is a fax line.'

'Did you leave him alone?'

'Of course I did. I'm not going to watch a repair man for half an hour.'

'Half an hour?'

'Maybe less.'

'Did you see his van?'

'No. He didn't have a van.'

'You left him in the study for half an hour.'

'No. Fifteen minutes in the study.'

I took out the photograph of Lourenço Gonçalves.

'Is that the man you saw?'

She glanced over the photograph, with no hint of surprise in her face.

'He was greyer,' she said, 'but that was him.'

506

We continued down the Marginal to Caxias. The prison, high up on the hill, must have given some of the prisoners one of the most expensive sea views in the area. We parked up outside, watched with casual interest by some T-shirted inmates behind the chainlink.

We sat in an empty interview room while the staff brought the prisoner up from the cells. Miguel Rodrigues' body wasn't looking too bad on the prison regime. He'd lost maybe fifteen kilos. His face, however, was grey with depression, his eyes dull. He'd lost his manicured sleekness, his billion-escudo glow.

'If this is about that General Machedo business,' he said, without sitting down, 'I'm not talking without my lawyer present.'

'That's Spanish business,' I said. 'I just need some help on some dates.'

'I don't have much use for dates any more,' he replied.

'This might help you.'

'Or not,' he said.

'Did you know you were being followed for nine months before your arrest?'

'By the police?'

'Privately.'

'By whom?'

'We'll come back to that.'

'To answer your question,' he said, deliberately, 'no, Inspector, I did not know that I was being followed.'

'You had two offices. One on the top floor of the Banco de Oceano e Rocha building on the Largo Dona Estefânia and the other in the Rua do Ouro.'

'That's right.'

'Until five months ago you used to spend Friday lunchtimes and afternoons in the Baixa office. Was there any reason for that?'

'I liked my privacy at the end of the week.'

507

'Does that mean you used to entertain women down there?'

'I thought you were going to ask me about dates.'

'We're getting there.'

'Jorge Raposo used to send girls down to those offices.'

'And what happened to make you start going to the Pensão Nuno?'

'Boredom,' he said. 'Jorge revealed another service.'

'You only ever entertained women in the Rua do Ouro offices?'

'It was private. There were no secretaries. If papers needed to be signed my secretary would have them brought down to me. It was my Friday office.'

'Was it always that way?'

Silence for some long moments.

'Since my brother died,' he said. 'That was his office. I didn't want to get rid of it. I made it my own and . . .'

'When was this?'

'He died New Year's Day 1982,' he said, desperation and sadness leaking into his already grey face, as if this had been a watershed moment. 'Then soon after that it started.'

'What?'

'Seeing girls. That didn't happen when Pedro was alive.'

'Who was the company lawyer at the time?'

'The lawyer?' he said, sounding surprised. 'The lawyer was Dr Aquilino Oliveira. He was my father's lawyer, too, before the revolution.'

'And what happened to him?'

Miguel Rodrigues blinked, his brain trying to make a connection that would help him see why he'd ended up in prison for killing his ex-lawyer's daughter.

'I don't know. I'm not sure what you mean.'

'He's not the lawyer any more is he?'

'No, no, he retired years ago.'

'Retired?'

'I mean he stopped working for us. It was a very confused period in the company. I remember I wanted him to stay. I wanted the continuity, but he was adamant. He said he had a new wife and he didn't want to spend too much of his later years working at high pressure. That was it. I had to accept that.'

'Did you meet his wife?'

'No, never.'

'You didn't go to the wedding.'

'It wasn't that sort of relationship.'

'Did you ever see the wife?'

'If I did, I don't remember.'

'So from early 1982 you started seeing girls in your office in the Rua do Ouro. In those first few months did any of those girls stand out particularly?'

'I was a jaded man, Inspector. It's probably some kind of disease. I couldn't help myself. I used to feel very excited at the prospect, but afterwards it was nothing. My mind blanked the experience out. If a girl came back three or four times, maybe I'd remember her.'

'Were all these girls blonde?'

He sat with his wrists crossed between his legs and frowned, but not as if he was having to think about it, more as if he was examining new information.

'At that time, yes, they were pretty well all blondes,' he said finally. 'I've never thought of it like that. I never asked for blondes, but that seems to have been the case.'

'In those first few months of 1982 when you started seeing girls do you remember a time when you had to get rough with a particular girl . . . some time in April perhaps?'

'Rough?'

I took out the photograph of Teresa Oliveira. She was lying down, her dyed blonde hair all around her. She looked relaxed, asleep, not that young, certainly not as fresh as she would have been at twenty-one. I pushed the

509

photograph across to Miguel Rodrigues. He looked down at it without picking it up.

'There's no trick to this,' I said. 'You won't be charged with anything. This woman has since died quite recently. Can you remember whether this woman ever came to your offices in the Baixa and whether you had to get rough with her, in order to have sex.'

'I don't remember,' he said. 'I really don't. It was a very difficult time for me. I'd lost my brother, his whole family, it was an awful time.'

'Your secretary at the bank. Is she still there?'

He shrugged, a little aggressively.

'Was she the same one as in 1982?'

'Yes. But look, Inspector, who is this woman?' he asked, tapping the photograph.

'You tell me,' I said.

We left Miguel Rodrigues in a state of anguish, still shouting questions to us as he was taken back down to his cell. He had less idea than we did why he'd been followed for nine months. We went back into Lisbon and straight to the Banco de Oceano e Rocha tower. We took one of the glass bubble lifts up the full height of the atrium and on to the top floor.

The top floor of the bank felt empty. Most of the staff had already been laid off. The people who remained were the key workers, being interviewed daily by the government investigators. We had to wait half an hour to talk to Miguel Rodrigues' secretary. She was in her late forties, wore spectacles and looked efficient, and slightly fierce from some recent stress lines that had appeared around her mouth. She was the kind of woman who'd know everything there was to know about the company she worked for. She recognized me from the newspapers. It tightened up her mouth.

After a look through the diaries she recalled that period

in the bank's history. Early 1982 had been hell. They'd been in temporary offices in Avenida da Liberdade which were bigger than the Baixa ones but not much.

'Do you remember a Friday in late April or May,' I asked, 'a young woman from the lawyer's office coming in to get some papers signed? Probably urgent papers and probably a lunchtime.'

'I normally sent one our own girls down . . .'

'She was a blonde girl, no more than twenty-one years old.'

'Yes, I do remember her,' she said. 'She got married to our lawyer, Dr Oliveira. She was his secretary. I thought about her just the other day. I used to see her in *VIP*. She died you know.'

'Did she ever go down to *Senhor* Rodrigues' office around April, May 1982 . . . on her own.'

The secretary blinked behind her gold-framed glasses.

'Yes, she did. It was the week before she got married. And she didn't come up here any more after that. Yes, there was nobody available to take the papers down to *Senhor* Rodrigues and she said she'd do it herself.'

I showed her the photograph of Teresa Oliveira and she nodded slowly.

'She doesn't look so well in this photograph,' she said.

Chapter XLIII

Tuesday, 24th November 199–, Banco de Oceano e Rocha, Estefânia, Lisbon.

We went for a late lunch in a small seafood restaurant on Avenida Almirante Reis. I had grilled squid, Carlos went for the cuttlefish in its own ink, which my wife had always referred to as the tarry gym shoe. We drank a half-bottle of white and finished with coffee.

'Maybe you should have told Miguel Rodrigues who the woman in the photograph was,' said Carlos, meaning Teresa Oliveira.

'I'd have had to spell it out for him,' I said, 'and prison is a lonely place full of nothing but the smell of men cooped up together and empty time. Miguel Rodrigues is serving a minimum of twenty years for a crime he did not commit. I don't like him. I don't think he's a good man. He's possibly a sick man. But I am not going to be the one to inflict on his mind the fact that he sodomized his own daughter.'

There was a prolonged silence while Carlos stirred his coffee up to the required syrup.

'If he raped her, why didn't she report it?' he asked.

'She was a young woman on the brink of a brand-new life. A week away from getting married. And that's quite apart from it being 1982. The feminist movement hadn't exactly built up a head of steam in Portugal by then. You'd have had a job to find women anywhere, even in England, prepared to report rape in those days. Think about it. It would have had an impact on her marriage, it would have destroyed a large chunk of her husband's business, there

512

would have been a long, intrusive investigation, perhaps with a trial at the end of it. No . . . she just hoped it would go away and maybe it would have done, if she hadn't got pregnant. When that baby was born with those blue eyes . . . that must have been a hard day.'

We paid the bill and walked back up over dry, dead leaves to where we'd left the car. The kids had come out in the Arroios park to run screaming through the pigeons which swooped over the old boys playing cards in their woollen hats.

'So, we have a motive now,' said Carlos.

'I don't think we've got all of it yet. This was just the obsession of the man – he was going to bring Miguel Rodrigues down. But I think there's something else in this.'

'And the killer?'

'We'll find the killer.'

'You don't think Dr Oliveira paid someone to kill her.'

'Like Lourenço Gonçalves?'

'Possibly.'

'I don't think so. I think his obsession was a little more refined.'

We stopped under a shop's awning while a blast of freeze-dried air shot through the Largo Dona Estefânia.

'And what now?' asked Carlos.

'We go to Paço de Arcos and find Faustinho Trindade.'

'You don't sound happy about this.'

'I'm not.'

'If you think some justice has been done, why don't you leave it?'

'Don't you want to nail Dr Oliveira?' I asked, hating myself for asking it.

'We'll be interfering, won't we?'

'We will.'

'They've achieved some kind of result.'

'Are you including the Minister of Internal Administration in "they"?'

'I think I might be.'

'And all those big men who came to watch my first interview with Miguel Rodrigues . . . those spectators at the coliseum, who enjoy the smell of blood as long as it's not their own?'

He swallowed hard, disgusted by it. I put my arm around his shoulder.

'Let's go to Paço de Arcos,' I said. 'And take it from there.'

The traffic was terrible in Lisbon and out on the Marginal there'd been a four-car smash, the blood fresh and bright on the tarmac under the setting sun. It was early evening by the time we arrived in Paço de Arcos, the sea already dark, but choppy in the wind with white caps still visible in the failing light. The horizon was just a crack of light with two long, grey melancholic streaks of cloud. I did a small circuit through the town and came back on to the Marginal heading for Lisbon. We pulled into the car park by the boatyard of the Clube Nautico.

There were a couple of anglers out on the stone quay. I didn't know what they were expecting to catch in this weather but then fishing doesn't always seem to be about catching fish. The lighthouse on Búgio was already flashing. Three ships sat off the Costa do Estoril, their cabin areas lit. Faustinho was in his work shed, wearing a pair of blue overalls and a heavy jacket, working with very little light on a stripped-down outboard motor. His hands were dry and scaly with the cold. His dog got up and sniffed us over.

'When did you get out, Faustinho?' I asked.

'Just under a week ago and I'm not talking about it, Zé. I'm sorry if I caused trouble for you, but I'm not going to say anything. It's finished.'

'You should find a workshop to do this,' I said.

'It's too expensive.'

'You remember that kid . . .'

514

'Look, Zé . . . I told you,' he stopped. 'The kid . . . what kid?'

'You remember that kid you told me about, who saw something that night before the girl's body was found on the beach?'

'I never saw him again,' he said. 'He used to spend quite a lot of the summer out here . . . but this year . . .'

'Is this the one?'

Carlos handed him the photograph of Xeta.

'That's him,' he said, taking it down to the light, looking at it more closely. 'He's dead, isn't he? This is a photograph of a dead person.'

I nodded. Carlos took the photograph back.

'What does that mean?' he asked.

I looked across the Marginal, the town dark behind the trees in the park.

'It means that maybe we're going to have to look closer to home,' I said.

We went through the underpass and up into the public gardens. They were empty. The wind buffeted the trees. The paths were covered in their dry, scratching detritus. I wiped a bench off and we sat down. António's bar was shut, no lights on, and we could have used a drink.

'Remember what I said to you that first morning,' said Carlos, 'about the significance of the body being here, and you living nearby?'

'We've come full circle,' I said. 'We lost sight of that. I lost sight of it.'

A white car pulled up outside *A Bandeira Vermelha*. António Borrego got out and opened the boot. He lifted out a box of fruit, vegetables and a separate one of meat. He put them back in, opened the door to the bar and turned the light on. He went back to the boot.

'It's nice to see one of those still running,' said Carlos.

'And now, finally, you start talking about cars,' I said.

'*That*,' said Carlos, 'is a Renault 12. Car of the Year back

515

in the 1980s some time. My father had one . . . but his was a pile of shit. I spent a lot of my youth working on one of those.'

The two ventricles of my heart iced up. Suddenly the blood was only going through in thin spurts and the oxygen in my breathing hard to find.

'Come with me,' I said.

We walked out of the gardens towards where the old faded pink cinema had been, which was now the beginnings of an office block. We turned left and left again and came up behind António's car.

'You remember your handwritten notes. What did the guy say? The one who saw *Senhor* Rodrigues' Mercedes. What else did he see?'

'I don't remember.'

'What he saw in front of the Mercedes was a brand-new metallic grey Fiat Punto and behind . . .'

'Was a white Renault 12 with a rusted wheel-arch.'

'Rear wheel-arch.'

In the poor street lighting and with the light coming from the open bar the corroded edges of the rear wheel-arch were visible. António came out to pick up whatever else he had in his boot. He saw us. I waved.

'How is it?' he asked.

'It's fine,' I said.

'You want something to eat? I've got some beautiful spare ribs already marinated.'

'Sounds good.'

António picked up another box and went into the bar.

'When Faustinho took me to meet Xeta and he wasn't there,' I said, almost talking to myself now, 'we went back to *A Bandeira Vermelha* and Faustinho described the kid in detail in front of me and António.'

Carlos' head didn't move, his eyes stayed fixed on the light coming from the bar. I told him to go in there and talk to António about anything except the obvious while

I phoned the local PSP. If he'd already killed Catarina and Xeta, there was no reason why he shouldn't go down fighting. I went round the corner to make the call. It took me a couple of minutes to explain the situation to them, how I didn't want them sprinting in there and provoking him into an attack. By the time I walked back to the bar I was feeling sick, cold and tired, not ready for this, not wanting this.

I walked into the wedge of light coming from the door. Lying face-down on the bar floor, in a pool of blood that I couldn't imagine having got to that size in the short few moments I'd been away, was Carlos. The collar of his shirt showed red above his jacket and coat. The back of his head looked all wrong, his hand twitched, the thumb splashing in his own blood. António was standing between Carlos' feet with the hammer raised above his head. It was the hammer he kept behind the bar, next to the sickle. His relics. His workers' tools. His weapons.

I stepped into the doorway. He turned to me.

'What have you done, António? What the hell have you done?'

His eyes had gone. There was still the tiniest light in them, but it was a pinprick at the end of a four-mile tunnel, as if I was seeing straight through to some nicks of bone on the inside of his cranium.

'Let me call an ambulance,' I said.

He turned to me with his hammer raised and took one step forwards.

'What did he say to you, António? What did he say to make you hit him?'

'Maria António Medinas,' he said, each name separate.

'Is that what this is all about? Is that why you killed the girl?'

'He murdered her. That PIDE bastard . . . he murdered her.'

'And what was Maria António Medinas to you?'

517

'She was my *wife*,' he said, viciously. 'And he killed her and he killed our child inside her.'

'Let me call the ambulance, António. It can still be all right, if you let me call the ambulance.'

I moved. He tensed the hammer in his hand.

'Are you a girl-killer, António? Is that what you do? How did they get you to kill the girl?'

'She was his.'

'Did *she* kill Maria Antónia Medinas?'

'She was his.'

'She was an innocent.'

'She was his.'

'Just let me call the ambulance.'

He ran at me, the hammer raised, his teeth bared, the eyes now dead, black, lightless. I shut the door on him. His hammer smashed through the glass. Blood ran down his wrist. He wrenched the door open. I fell back into the street, half at a run, half staggering. He swerved away from me and ran to his car.

He pulled away in the rusting Renault, the boot still open. He crashed across the public gardens, through the flower beds, over the grass and directly on to the Marginal. The oncoming traffic screeched and squirmed. The Renault slashed straight across two lines of cars into the Lisbon lane. The PSP came running. I told them to call for an ambulance and to get a hospital prepared to receive a policeman with a serious head injury. I ran across the gardens, through the underpass and got into my car. I ran every red light on the way into the city.

I saw the Renault's boot flapping up and down as it went over humps in the tarmac around Caxias. I pulled in tight behind him and flashed my lights. He put his foot down.

Our two ancient cars roared through Belém and thundered under the whining 25th April bridge. He swung to the left, up towards the Largo de Alcântara where there was a sliproad to the bridge, but not accessible from our

518

direction. António crashed through the lights which had just changed to red and swerved across the two cars and a truck which had just taken off. The two cars missed him and slewed to a halt, but the truck clipped him on his rear wing and the car was jolted sideways a full metre. I stormed over the crossroads after him with my forearm on the horn and one hand raised out of the window. People were already out of their cars. We hit the ramp up to the bridge. António crunched through the gears and found one low enough to get him up the steep turn. I stuck on his tail. We were going slower and slower.

The Renault hit the main road to cross the bridge. We couldn't have been going more than fifty kilometres per hour and I saw the problem. His back tyre was flat, and the stoved-in rear wing was derinding the rubber, until the tyre was entirely stripped off and he was running on his wheel rim, sparks showering off it into the night. He stopped and got out, the hammer still in his fist. He started running.

The cars howled over the expandable metal lanes in the centre of the bridge and horns blared behind us. The ice wind, even stronger up here, blustered from the west and whistled at a high-pitched scream through the support cables. I ran after him. He turned occasionally, his face lit up – white with two black eye sockets – by the lights of the oncoming traffic. Suddenly he got up on to the bridge's rail and jumped over the edge as if it was nothing, as if he had no statement to make. I bellowed after him but my voice went nowhere over the hellish noise.

I got to the point where he'd jumped and saw him pacing about on a small platform a few metres below. What did I want from him? Did I want to catch him, bring him in? Was that what I wanted? And I realized that it hadn't been police work making me run. I had to talk to him. I had to tell him. I had to make him believe. He was part of the cycle. We were all part of the damaging cycle.

I swung my leg over the rail, my foot searched for the first rung. The platform was all that remained of the bridge works. It was for the men painting the new rail link. There was a lift that ran on a box rail down one of the concrete support columns to the docks below. The lift wasn't operating. António was contemplating climbing down the box rail. I shuddered as trucks crashed past, their weight undulating the road like a sea swell, the wind booming against their sheer sides. It was high enough up there that I could feel myself flying and, with that strong, knifing wind, I felt I could be at any moment. I screamed his name at him.

He responded by climbing over the rail of the platform and fitting his foot into the box rail. He dropped down a few rungs. I jumped down on to the platform. The wooden sheets bounced me and I fell to my knees. I crawled towards the lift and pushed my face over the edge. António was three metres down the rail. To the west the lights along the Marginal stretched out into the blackness. We were as good as night gliding.

'António!'

I yelled at him to come back up, but the wind whipped my voice away and shuttled it through the girders of the new rail link.

António looked up at me with the terrible religious eyes of a suffering saint, or a tortured sinner on his way down to the next circle of hell. His face seemed to be broken up into pieces now, just shards of pottery miraculously floating together in a deep purple light. He looked over his shoulder and saw what I'd seen. The lights curving away over the black planet. The sea and the sky dense and empty and only the dark, cold wind calling.

The hammer went first, a silver speck into the night. His other hand disengaged from the rail and he fell backwards. The wind caught him to begin with and shored him back up, but then quickly let him have his weight. He stretched his arms out and shouted something that the wind tore off him. His foot caught in the rung of the rail, the ankle snapped and then he was on his way, dropping through the howling dark, gravity making an ant of him in seconds, and then nothing of him in a few more.

The sirens came. Steel light revolved in the night. I rolled away from the edge and felt like a man who'd momentarily had everything – friends, family, love and then just as quickly lost them all.

Chapter XLIV

05.30 Wednesday, 25th November 199–, Hospital Egas Moniz, Santo Amaro, Lisbon.

Carlos was in Intensive Care, his head and neck supported by some strange contraption that would keep it totally rigid and the back of his head free from any contact. Everything was functioning normally, all his organs, even his brain showed normal activity, but he hadn't regained consciousness, and there wasn't a neurosurgeon in Lisbon who would tell us when he would come out of his coma.

We watched him. His mother joined on to his father, who was set in stone, staring his will into his son. Olivia in shock over Carlos' state, but also in tears because she'd known António Borrego all her life. And me, tarred and feathered with guilt. If Carlos didn't make it, if he didn't make a full recovery, it would be the end of all possibilities. I would be, as Klaus Felsen had said, a man with no prospects.

They'd taken him off the ventilator after a few hours, once they were sure he was breathing properly. Now he was wired and tubed up and, with the blood transfusion over, he had only a saline drip in his arm. He was silent and still. The monitoring machines made noises for him. His muscles didn't twitch. His closed eyes didn't flicker. His face was relaxed. His body at peace, while his consciousness repaired itself. Where did they go, these coma people? Over what dark landscapes did they travel? Was there any light there at all, or was it a pothole with no light, not even an inkling of ambient light, only what your brain imagines as light?

At seven o'clock I left Olivia with Carlos' parents. I went to my office and sat at my desk. My colleagues came in to see me, to ask after Carlos, even though none of them had liked him, and I answered all of them. At 08.30 I went to see Narciso who made the expert, correct, nearly human sounds. I told him I was opening up an investigation into the disappearance of an ex-*Polícia Judiciária* detective called Lourenço Gonçalves. He didn't respond.

I took a pool car and drove out to Odivelas and sat outside Valentim's apartment block. He surprised me by not keeping me waiting long – another man, perhaps, who wasn't sleeping so well at nights. He banded up his swag of ringlets and I rolled down the window and told him to get in the car.

I cruised into the heavy traffic heading south into town.
'Did you ever meet a guy called Lourenço Gonçalves?' I asked.

He repeated the name to himself and frowned, preparing to lie. I stopped the car in the traffic. Space built up in front of us and noise behind. I gave him the photograph of Gonçalves.

'He was a Security Consultant,' I said, 'which is a perfumed word for Private Investigator. He followed people around. That kind of thing.'

'Why should I know him?'

'Wasn't he the one who told you to put on an interesting little sex show in the Pensão Nuno? You know, something unusual like you, Bruno and an underage blonde . . .' I said. 'Do you remember what happened to her after that, after you made sure she was in the Pensão Nuno having sex with two guys at the same time?'

'She . . . she,' he faltered, as a guy from the car behind came and hammered on my window. 'She went back to school.'

I slammed my foot on the accelarator, floored it, and kept looking at Valentim. I threw his seat belt off. He put his hands out. I slammed on the brakes. His forearms buckled against the dashboard, his head smacked into the windscreen. Blood appeared in a line on his brow. He slumped back into the seat, his fingers feeling along the split skin. I picked up the photograph, pulled his hands away from his face.

'Tell me, Valentim and you're out of here.'

'He offered me money.'

'How much are we talking about?'

'Initially it was a million escudos.'

'Your new computer edit suite.'

He nearly looked ashamed, but that would have drawn on reserves he didn't have.

'Then he told me that I'd probably have to take some heat from your people and . . . and I doubled it.'

'Nice job, Valentim,' I said. 'Tell me your conscience is clear.'

'I thought . . .'

'You thought it was an interest-free gift?' I said. 'You should take a look at the cost of money these days.'

I pulled up and kicked his bony arse out of the car. He cringed over the pavement like a village cur.

I turned round and went back up to the *2° Circular* and took the motorway out to Cascais. I drove to Cabo da Roca, to the last house on mainland Europe. The wind was stronger up there and the house looked sharpened, honed clean in the freezing air.

Felsen was in his enclosed terrace, his head folded down on to his chest like a dead bird. He came to as I sat down.

'Ah,' he said, but he couldn't quite place me.

'Inspector Coelho,' I reminded him, and gave him a few seconds to digest it. 'Who's your lawyer, *Senhor* Felsen?'

'Am I being charged with something?' he asked, confused for a moment. 'I don't know that I have one any more.'

'Did you have a lawyer in prison?'

'I didn't need one. The damage was done. Once you're in . . . it's the devil to get out.'

'And when you got out?'

'Not for some years. Then one came to the house. Or did I go to him? His name was . . .' a shaky finger came out to place the name, but didn't find it.

'Dr Aquilino Oliveira?'

'Yes, that was him. He was my lawyer for . . . maybe ten years. I don't know. He may still be now.'

'Did you tell him your stories?'

'He was a very good listener . . . unusual for a lawyer. They always like to tell you how it is, don't they? With the law and that – how damned complicated it all is and how much you need them.'

'You never mentioned that you knew a political called António Borrego in Caxias prison.'

'A political cleaned out my cell for several months. He asked me about this woman . . . I used to know her name too.'

'Maria Antónia Medinas,' I said. 'The last time we talked you couldn't get her name out of your head. Can you tell me what António Borrego wanted to know about her?'

'He asked if I'd seen her or heard anything about her.'

'Had you?'

'Well, I knew she was dead.'

'How?'

'She'd been murdered . . . if that's what they call it in prison.'

'And did you see who did it?'

'I saw him. I called out to him. Manuel. He was my son, you know, illegitimate son. But he didn't hear me, and the next morning they carried her out,' he said, and he looked as if he might cry, until I realized he was, in fact, disgusted. 'There was so much blood in her skirt, the weight of it . . . it dragged along the ground. It left a brown trail.'

He drifted back into sleep. I sat for a moment looking at

the brilliant clarity, the purity of cold winter sunshine. The visibility was stunning but hard-edged, unforgiving.

I asked Frau Junge about the lawyer. She said he'd looked after a few things for *Senhor* Felsen back in the early eighties, but it wasn't for very long.

'He said it was for ten years.'

'He's an old man, but he still draws on his vanity,' she said.

I'd made the connections, now I was bristling for a fight. The lawyer's Cascais house was empty, closed up for the winter. I called at his Lisbon home but nobody was there either. It was late afternoon when I dropped back in at the hospital. Olivia and Carlos' parents were still sitting almost where I'd left them. There was no news, except that two men had been looking for me.

They found me in the corridor outside the toilets, two men in dark blue raincoats. At a glance you might have thought they were clones – something to do with the way they'd been trained.

'Can we talk?' said one of them. 'Outside would be better.'

'Who are you?'

'We're from the Ministry.'

'Which one's that?'

'Let's go outside.'

The three of us, hands jammed into our coat pockets, sat on an ice-cold bench in the dark courtyard of the hospital with lights all around. Only one of them spoke. The other looked around with the wary eye of a hen that knows what's happened to other hens.

'We've come to tell you to drop your investigation into the disappearance of Lourenço Gonçalves.'

'He used to be a detective with the *Polícia Judiciária*. I have a duty . . .'

'You have a duty, Inspector Coelho,' he said, quietly, agreeing with me that far. 'You have a patriotic duty, which now, is to keep quiet. A result has been achieved and it is the correct one and you must leave it that way.'

'I missed that result,' I said. 'I wasn't aware of anybody winning anything. Did I lose? I feel as if I lost.'

They leaned forward on their elbows and looked at each other across me. The one who didn't speak closed his eyes momentarily.

'We have a scapegoat,' said the talker.

'The Banco de Oceano e Rocha?'

He nodded to see if that was going to be enough.

'There's a police officer in there who might never wake up again,' I said. 'I think his parents might want to know what patriotic duty their son has been involved in.'

'You're the *Inspector Dourado*,' he said, sticking it in. 'You should know what it's about.'

'I'll start then,' I said. 'Nazi gold . . . now you finish.'

He sighed and looked around the dark patch of lawn.

'All the neutral countries during the Second World War,' he said, clasping his hands, 'are being asked to give their pound of flesh. You might have noticed that some Swiss banks recently awarded $1.25 billion to the victims of the Holocaust. The Banco de Oceano e Rocha has an estimated worth of $2.3 billion. We think we now have the potential to be generous.'

'Miguel Rodrigues,' I said, 'there's a guy who ran out of friends.'

The man unclasped his hands and showed me they were empty.

'Those gold bars,' he said, 'with their little swastika stamp on them, next to your sweet face. That wasn't just a publicity stunt for the *Policía Judiciária*. That has saved us a lot of grief. That showed the world that we'd found the pound of flesh and we were prepared to surrender it. You've got to admit, Inspector Coelho, there's some justice in it.'

'In that it's come full circle, through the Nazis who stole it in the first place, through Lehrer, through Felsen, through

Abrantes and right the way round to . . . if not the original owners of the gold, then their families at least,' I said. 'Yes, I can see the justice in that but I'm concerned about the method.'

'Nothing in this world is what it seems,' said the man, touching my shoulder and indicating with a look that, as far as he was concerned, the conversation was over.

'And Lourenço Gonçalves?' I asked, to clear up that loose end for JoJó Silva.

'He's a happy man, Inspector, but he won't be coming back to Portugal.'

'Sold his soul to the devil . . . or shall we call him Dr Aquilino Dias Oliveira?'

'You have to leave Dr Oliveira alone, otherwise it could all go very badly wrong,' he said, severely, meaning it.

'The sacred cow,' I said.

They looked at me with the dead eyes of men who have made things go very badly wrong before.

'I'd like to speak to him.'

'I don't think so.'

'I'm not going to *do* anything to him,' I said. 'I'd just like to speak to him . . . clear a few points up.'

'Have we reached an understanding?'

'We have as long as I can speak to him for ten minutes.'

The silent one got up, took a mobile out of his pocket and walked off. He made two calls, packed up his phone and we left.

They drove me to the lawyer's office in the Chiado in a black Mercedes. We parked and walked down some steps of *calçada* under dry, rustling trees. They buzzed on an unmarked door and we were let in. We walked up to the first floor. They searched me very intrusively and fed me through the door.

I went into a dimly-lit anteroom and on to a corridor. Dr Oliveira was standing at the end of it smiling, immaculately

528

suited. He had his hand out showing me the door of his office, as friendly as if he was my lawyer and I still owed him a big bill.

His office was wood-panelled, with English hunting prints of red-coated men dashing about with great futility and bugling. I sat in a black leather chair which put me at a marginal height disadvantage to him on the other side of his green leather inlaid desk. He leaned back and waited.

'Where is Lourenço Gonçalves by the way?' I asked, just to get started.

'California,' he said. 'He wanted to be somewhere where the sun always shines.'

'I suppose he could have ended up in the foundations of an apartment building around the Expo site. There might have been some propriety in that.'

Dr Oliveira breathed in and closed his eyes as if he was thinking beautiful thoughts to keep the nasty ones away.

'You have some questions, apparently,' he said.

I wrestled with the one question which would give me what I wanted to know, but I couldn't get it out. I was the rummy player who didn't know which cards my opponent was collecting. I came in on a tangent.

'You knew about *Senhor* Felsen from your first job working for Joaquim Abrantes . . . writing him out of the bank's statutes. Did you know why you were doing that?'

'He was a convicted criminal.'

'But did you know why Abrantes had him put away?'

'Not at the time.'

'That only came out when you went back to *Senhor* Felsen?'

'He came to me after he got out of prison. Pedro wouldn't talk to him. He found out that I was the lawyer who'd drawn up the new statutes. He told me his story which I dismissed as fantastic at the time.'

'But you went back to him after . . .'

'Yes,' he cut in hard.

'When did you find out that Manuel Abrantes had raped your wife?'

'*Raped* her?' he said, digging deep into the question.

'Isn't that what happened, *Senhor Doutor*?'

'If he'd raped her, Inspector, she would have told me, wouldn't she? She wouldn't have waited until I looked down on a child I knew instantly was not my own to . . . surely she would have told her husband, Inspector.'

I couldn't tell if there was some madness at play here. Did he actually believe that his wife had consented or was he using the skewed logic of the cuckold to justify his actions?

'Did your wife say she'd been raped?'

'Pah!' he said, and threw his head round to one of the hunting prints, refusing to look at me – not accepting any more questions on that subject.

'What did *Senhor* Felsen know about your . . . scheme?' I asked.

'He was the key,' he said, eyes back on me, riveting. 'I knew a lot from having worked with Joaquim Abrantes but I never knew about the gold. He never spoke about it and Pedro, like a good son, didn't either.'

'So you didn't know about the two remaining bars.'

'Luck . . .' he said.

'He also told you about Maria Antónia Medinas.'

Dr Oliveira chewed on his thumbnail and nodded.

'How did you approach António Borrego?'

'Like we did everybody . . . through Lourenço Gonçalves.'

'When did you decide to use your daughter as bait?'

'*My* daughter?'

'Catarina . . . Oliveira,' I added.

'Gonçalves reported that they were using the same *pensão*. He investigated further and found that Abrantes was always in the adjacent room when she was in the *pensão*. Later on he went into that room and found the mirror. The plan evolved from that situation.'

'Didn't Gonçalves find it difficult to persuade António to kill the girl?'

'I was surprised he killed her. I can only think that something went wrong, that she must have seen his face and he was forced to strangle her. I'm not sure how Gonçalves put the plan to Borrego in the first place, but he told me that once Borrego knew who she was, once he knew the girl's connection to Miguel Rodrigues, then I think Borrego became a difficult man to control. I don't think he was quite balanced. Manuel Abrantes *had* killed his wife and unborn child.'

'Did anyone speak to Borrego afterwards?'

'Gonçalves . . . when he went to pick up the clothes.'

'Didn't he ask Borrego what had happened?'

'Borrego's version of events was that he'd followed them into the Monsanto park. He saw the Mercedes leave the road. He parked up and walked through the trees. He saw the car rocking, heard . . .' he cleared his throat, '. . . heard the girl shouting out. Then Abrantes got out of the car, opened the passenger door, dragged her out and left her on the ground. Borrego waited for the car to leave and . . .'

'And what?' I asked, determined to make him say it, make him say everything.

'And he hit her.'

'With what?'

'He hit her on the head with a hammer, Inspector. You know this. Now let's . . .'

'In the fifteen years that you shared the same house as Catarina you didn't once feel any paternal . . .'

'She was a constant reminder, Inspector,' he said, slowly.

'Of what . . . your disappointment, your . . . ?'

'Let's move along, Inspector. I agreed to ten minutes.'

'If you didn't expect Borrego to kill Catarina, what did you expect of him?'

He played the edge of the table with his fingertips . . . a sonata to clear his mind.

531

'And the Minister of Internal Administration,' I said, 'what did . . . what does he know?'

'He's a politician and a very successful one. Results, like getting elected for instance, are important. How they are achieved . . . not so interesting. He was only concerned with the delivery of Miguel Rodrigues' disgraced head.'

'Yes, I suppose that was an important factor . . . that he was disgraced.'

'We didn't want him to have anywhere to hide.'

We sat in silence while I tried to heave the question over my larynx. Dr Oliveira doodled with his mind.

'You asked about Felsen before,' he said. 'About his involvement. He wasn't involved in any of this . . . business. He was important, of course, because you had to find him. You had to extract his story but he . . . he's a very old man now. His mind's only really up to telling and retelling the story of his life in its many versions.'

'He had the documents though . . . they were important.'

'Yes, I knew that . . . he'd shown them to me.'

'So he was very important to this . . . this intrigue of yours. Very important.'

'Yes,' he said, and looked at me. 'Is there a question here, Inspector?'

'How could you guarantee that I'd find Felsen?' I asked, my palms running with sweat, my heart batting against my ribs.

A frown shot across his brow, faster than a lizard across a hot road.

'You tell me,' he said, his brain rattling through the permutations.

I tried again, a little more direct this time.

'How did Luísa Madrugada make the Felsen connection?'

'Ah!' he said, grasping the matter now. 'Now I see. No, Inspector, she was not involved. Don't worry yourself on that score. Ask her . . . ask her about some interesting notes . . . pointers she found in the books that she was reading at the Biblioteca Nacional, but . . .'

'Was that luck as well? That the investigating officer should have an affair with . . .'

'You don't *have* to believe me. It's no concern of mine,' he said. 'I would have made sure you found Felsen, whether it was in Luísa Madrugada's bed or not. And, Inspector, don't blame her for not telling you about those . . . ah . . . vital clues. I'm sure she loves you – and lovers, especially in the beginning, want to look at their best for each other.'

'Something that you would know about, *Senhor Doutor*,' I said.

'I?'

'A woman always wants to look at her best on her wedding day, Teresa was no exception.'

It shut something down in him. Lights went out in his face, the source of his mild affability dried up and was replaced with that fierceness, that intellectual fierceness I'd seen in his study in Cascais.

'It's easily forgotten, Inspector, that history is not what you read in books. It's a personal thing, and people are vengeful creatures, which is why history will never teach us anything.'

'You got your revenge, I can see that, and you . . . facilitated the revenge of others – António Borrego, Klaus Felsen, even Jorge Raposo had his half-hour . . .'

'. . . and the Jewish people,' he said. 'Don't forget them. They will finally get their property back.'

'If you think that that is any justification for you, *Senhor Doutor* Oliveira, to conduct your own, personal balancing of the vagaries of history by punishing your late wife and murdering her illegitimate daughter, then you must be one of two things – evil or mad. Which are you?'

He leaned forward across his desk, neck dipped, eyes as bright and all-seeing as an eagle's over its territory.

'We are all mad,' he said.

'I only feel it when I'm in your company,' I said, walking to the door.

'We are all mad, Inspector, for the simple reason that we don't know why we exist and this . . .' he waved his hand at the tissue of existence before him, 'this life is how we distract ourselves so that we don't have to think about things too difficult for us to comprehend.'

'There are other ways of distracting yourself, Dr Oliveira.'

'Some of us, perhaps, have more recherché tastes.'

'Yes, I suppose the *frisson* was quite substantial for you – the knowledge that Miguel Rodrigues had sodomized his own daughter before António Borrego cracked her skull open and strangled her.'

He swivelled his chair away from me and faced the window. The leather scoop rocked him.

I closed the door, went down the lighted corridor, down the wooden stairs and out on to the bone-dry *calçada*. The night was piercingly clear with the freshest air Lisbon would ever smell. There was a thin paring of wind-shaved moon and chestnuts were roasting in the square.

Agente Carlos Pinto came out of his coma on Friday 27th November. Two weeks later they inserted a steel plate in the back of his cranium. On a clear day he's sure that he can hear the Bee Gees coming over the Atlantic. I've assured him it's tinnitus. He was lucky to have a thick skull and, I like to think, that his short, dense, unmanageable hair cushioned the blow.

The only thing Carlos couldn't remember was why António Borrego had hit him. I told him that after Felsen had given me his story I'd gone to *A Bandeira Vermelha* and asked António about Maria Antónia Medinas. He'd stalled me. So when, five and a half months later, and after our brittle exchange in the street by the rusted wheel-arch of the white Renault 12, Carlos appeared in the bar on his own to ask about the same woman – the one person‧ who could motivate António to murder Catarina Oliveira – Borrego's paranoia did the rest. He wouldn't have known that Carlos and I had never discussed Maria Antónia Medinas. He wouldn't have known that to us it was just a name that needed some light shed on it. He thought he was finished.

It still hasn't rained. It's still dry and cold. The leaves are still scratching across the *calçada*. *A Bandeira Vermelha* is closed. I've had to find somewhere else to drink my *bicas*, someone else to make my toast.

Olivia still hasn't taught Carlos anything about clothes, he shambles about in that oversized thing, but he's reciprocated in his own way by telling her nothing of murder. He makes her happy in a way that she hasn't been for over a year.

Luísa Madrugada spares me the odd quarter of an hour from her publishing company and I occasionally look up from the book that she's been forcing me to write. Nothing about murder, of course, a children's story.

I've seen the untouchable lawyer too, Dr Oliveira in his Morgan, spanking down the Marginal with a blonde in the passenger seat. He didn't look bothered.

I'm getting out of this house. The landlord offered to sell me an apartment at a good price if I moved out and let him convert this old mansion. I thought it would be a difficult decision to make, but I agreed as soon as he proposed it. We looked at each other astonished.

And I bought a new car. The old one never forgave me for leaving her on the bridge that night. The new car's nothing special but the salesman, highlighting all the extras included, made it sound as if it could go into orbit and dock with *Discovery*. He knew everything, and I questioned him endlessly because it's in my nature, finally I asked him:

'How do they tint the windows so that they're clear in the shade and dark in the sunshine?'

'You know,' he said, without even a pause, holding up a finger. 'That's interesting. It's the only Portuguese element of this car.'

'Is that a selling point?'

'On the glass,' he said, ignoring me, 'they lay a very, very thin layer, less than a micron, a fraction of a micron of the finest Portuguese wolfram.'

I thought about that.

The obscure talent of wolfram.